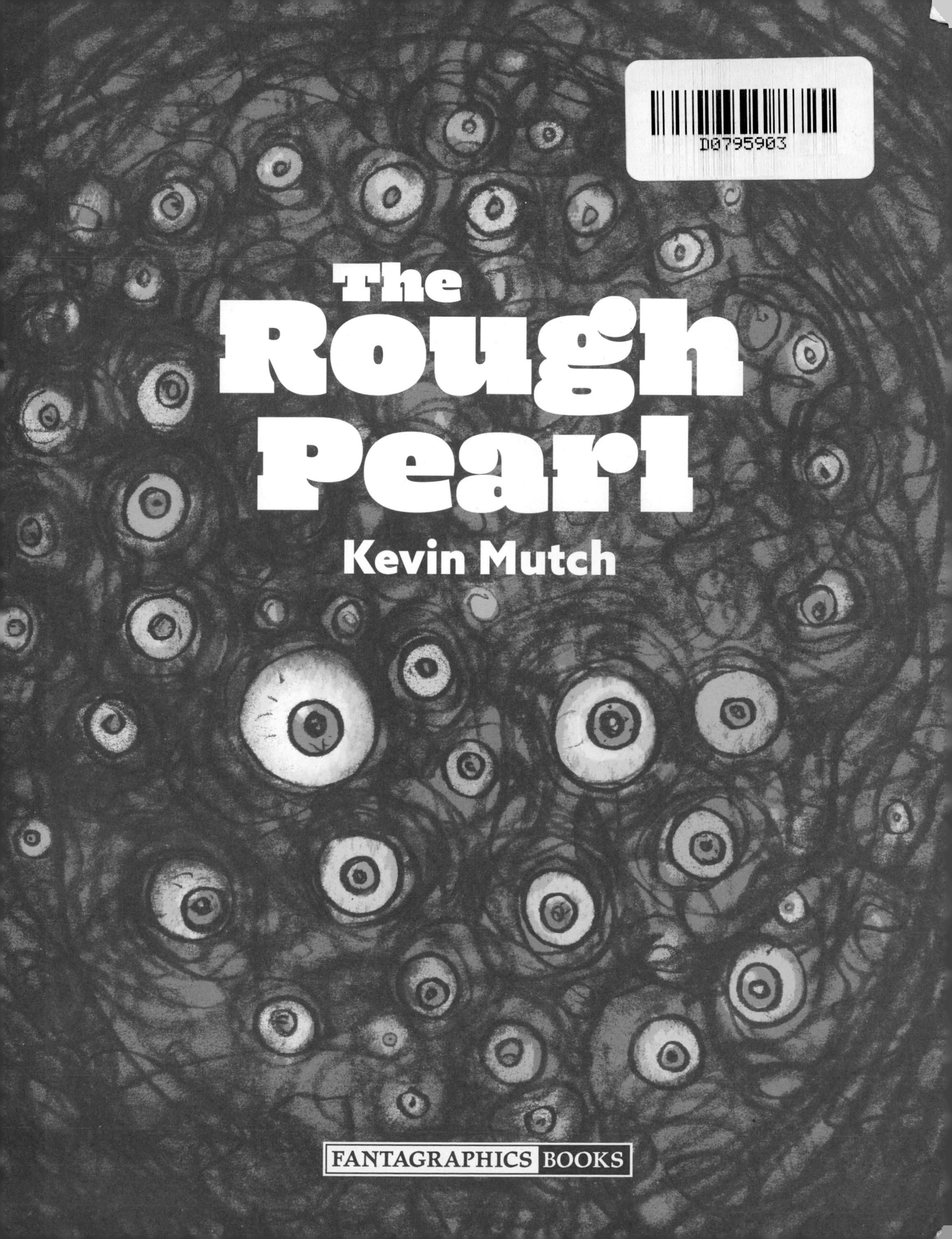
The
Rough
Pearl
Kevin Mutch
FANTAGRAPHICS BOOKS

This book is for the M's in my life: Melissa, Max and Molly.

R.I.P. MES

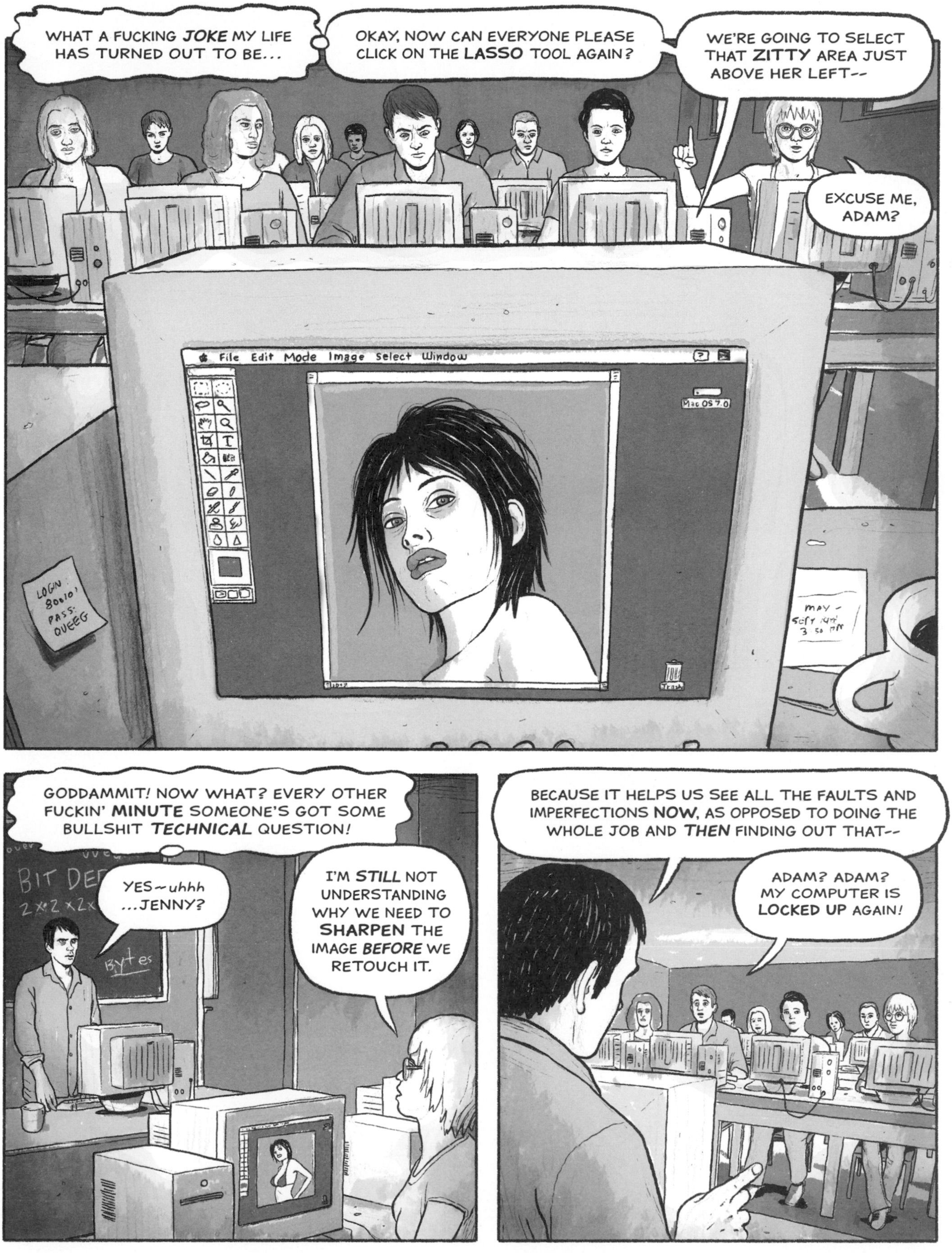
WHAT A FUCKING JOKE MY LIFE HAS TURNED OUT TO BE...
OKAY, NOW CAN EVERYONE PLEASE CLICK ON THE LASSO TOOL AGAIN?
WE'RE GOING TO SELECT THAT ZITTY AREA JUST ABOVE HER LEFT--
EXCUSE ME, ADAM?
File Edit Mode Image Select Window
Mac OS 7.0
Trash
LOGIN: 800101 PASS: QUEEG
GODDAMMIT! NOW WHAT? EVERY OTHER FUCKIN' MINUTE SOMEONE'S GOT SOME BULLSHIT TECHNICAL QUESTION!
YES~uhhh ...JENNY?
Bytes
I'M STILL NOT UNDERSTANDING WHY WE NEED TO SHARPEN THE IMAGE BEFORE WE RETOUCH IT.
BECAUSE IT HELPS US SEE ALL THE FAULTS AND IMPERFECTIONS NOW, AS OPPOSED TO DOING THE WHOLE JOB AND THEN FINDING OUT THAT--
ADAM? ADAM? MY COMPUTER IS LOCKED UP AGAIN!

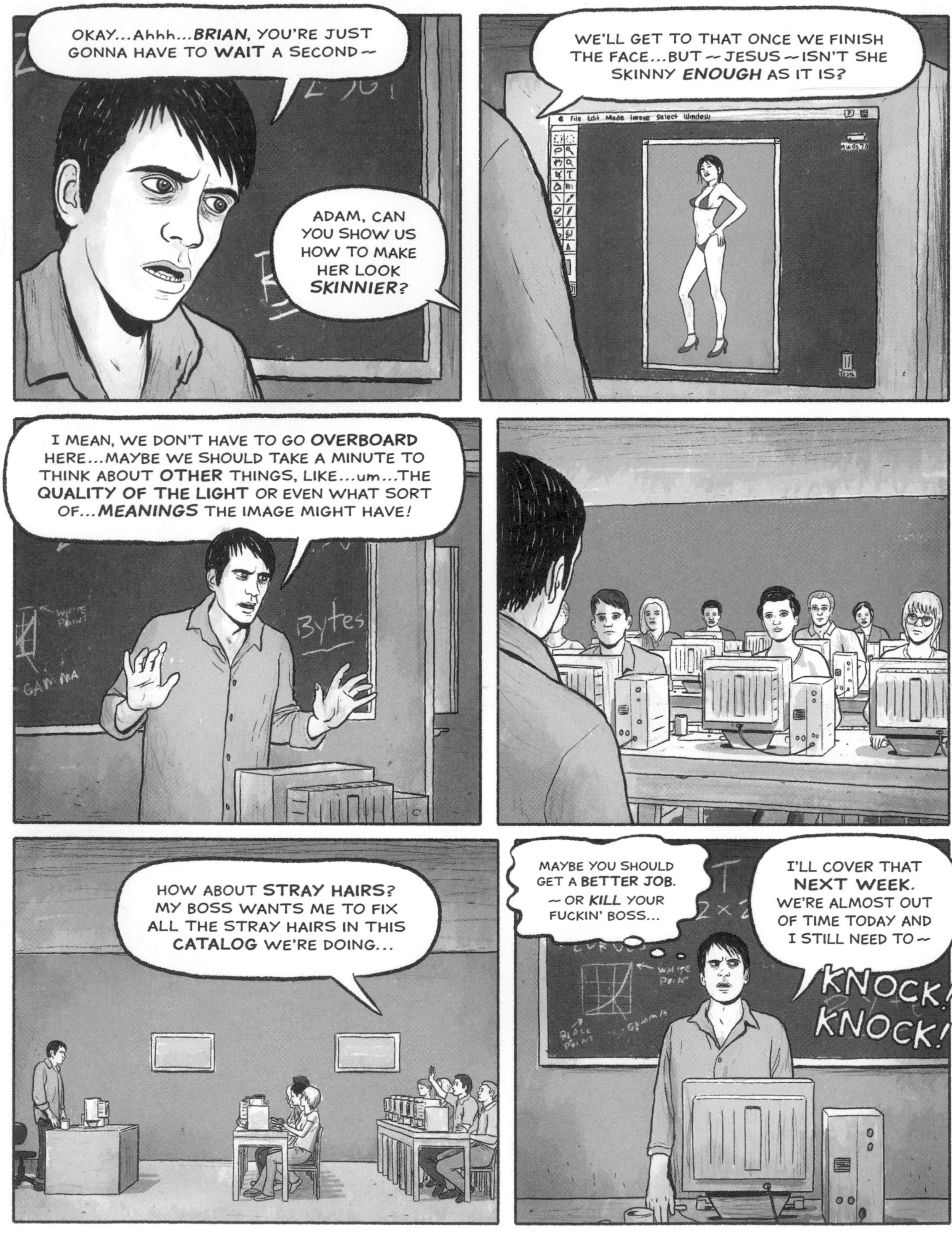
OKAY... Ahhh... BRIAN, YOU'RE JUST GONNA HAVE TO WAIT A SECOND --
ADAM, CAN YOU SHOW US HOW TO MAKE HER LOOK SKINNIER?
WE'LL GET TO THAT ONCE WE FINISH THE FACE... BUT -- JESUS -- ISN'T SHE SKINNY ENOUGH AS IT IS?
File Edit Mode Image Select Window
I MEAN, WE DON'T HAVE TO GO OVERBOARD HERE... MAYBE WE SHOULD TAKE A MINUTE TO THINK ABOUT OTHER THINGS, LIKE... um... THE QUALITY OF THE LIGHT OR EVEN WHAT SORT OF... MEANINGS THE IMAGE MIGHT HAVE!
WHITE POINT
GAMMA
Bytes
HOW ABOUT STRAY HAIRS? MY BOSS WANTS ME TO FIX ALL THE STRAY HAIRS IN THIS CATALOG WE'RE DOING...
MAYBE YOU SHOULD GET A BETTER JOB. -- OR KILL YOUR FUCKIN' BOSS...
I'LL COVER THAT NEXT WEEK. WE'RE ALMOST OUT OF TIME TODAY AND I STILL NEED TO --
WHITE POINT
BLACK POINT
GAMMA
KNOCK! KNOCK!

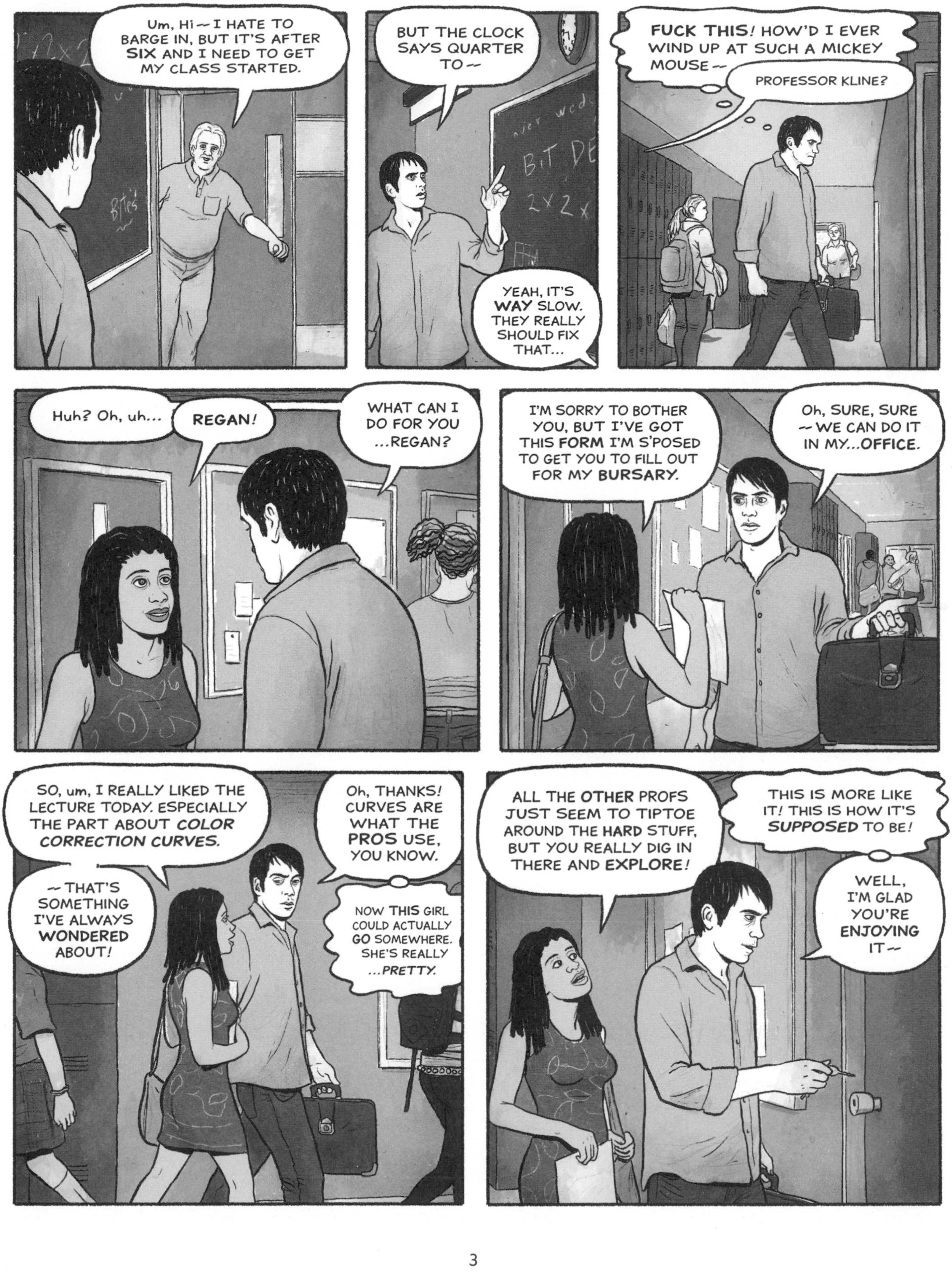
Um, Hi -- I HATE TO BARGE IN, BUT IT'S AFTER SIX AND I NEED TO GET MY CLASS STARTED.
BUT THE CLOCK SAYS QUARTER TO --
YEAH, IT'S WAY SLOW. THEY REALLY SHOULD FIX THAT...
FUCK THIS! HOW'D I EVER WIND UP AT SUCH A MICKEY MOUSE --
PROFESSOR KLINE?
Huh? Oh, uh...
REGAN!
WHAT CAN I DO FOR YOU ...REGAN?
I'M SORRY TO BOTHER YOU, BUT I'VE GOT THIS FORM I'M S'POSED TO GET YOU TO FILL OUT FOR MY BURSARY.
Oh, SURE, SURE -- WE CAN DO IT IN MY...OFFICE.
SO, um, I REALLY LIKED THE LECTURE TODAY. ESPECIALLY THE PART ABOUT COLOR CORRECTION CURVES.
-- THAT'S SOMETHING I'VE ALWAYS WONDERED ABOUT!
Oh, THANKS! CURVES ARE WHAT THE PROS USE, YOU KNOW.
NOW THIS GIRL COULD ACTUALLY GO SOMEWHERE. SHE'S REALLY ...PRETTY.
ALL THE OTHER PROFS JUST SEEM TO TIPTOE AROUND THE HARD STUFF, BUT YOU REALLY DIG IN THERE AND EXPLORE!
THIS IS MORE LIKE IT! THIS IS HOW IT'S SUPPOSED TO BE!
WELL, I'M GLAD YOU'RE ENJOYING IT --

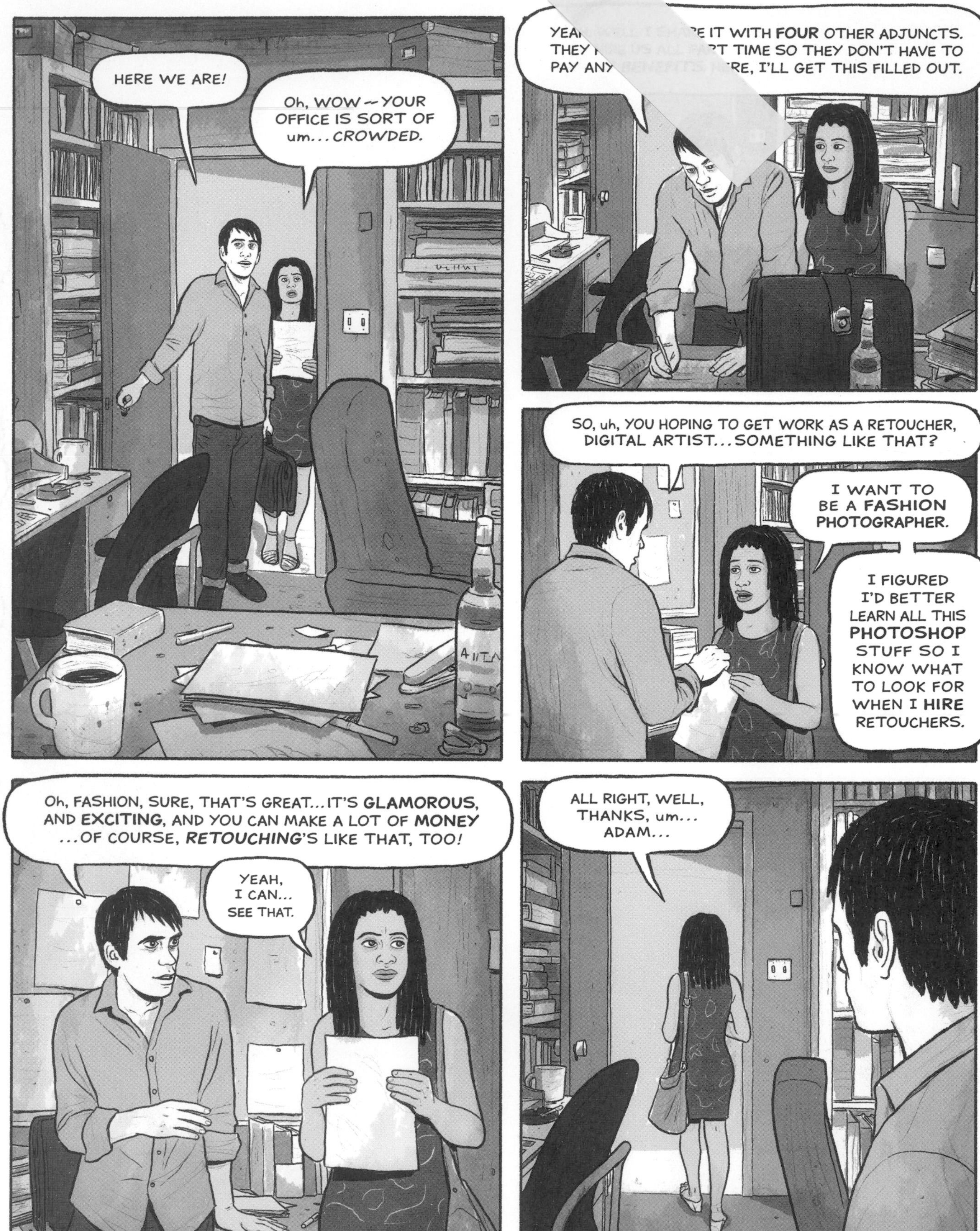
HERE WE ARE!
Oh, WOW—YOUR OFFICE IS SORT OF um... CROWDED.
YEAH, WELL, I SHARE IT WITH FOUR OTHER ADJUNCTS. THEY HIRE US ALL PART TIME SO THEY DON'T HAVE TO PAY ANY BENEFITS. HERE, I'LL GET THIS FILLED OUT.
SO, uh, YOU HOPING TO GET WORK AS A RETOUCHER, DIGITAL ARTIST... SOMETHING LIKE THAT?
I WANT TO BE A FASHION PHOTOGRAPHER.
I FIGURED I'D BETTER LEARN ALL THIS PHOTOSHOP STUFF SO I KNOW WHAT TO LOOK FOR WHEN I HIRE RETOUCHERS.
Oh, FASHION, SURE, THAT'S GREAT... IT'S GLAMOROUS, AND EXCITING, AND YOU CAN MAKE A LOT OF MONEY ...OF COURSE, RETOUCHING'S LIKE THAT, TOO!
YEAH, I CAN... SEE THAT.
ALL RIGHT, WELL, THANKS, um... ADAM...

Hmmph! SO MUCH FOR FOR **IMPRESSING** ALL THE GIRLS WITH MY PRESTIGIOUS *TEACHING JOB.*

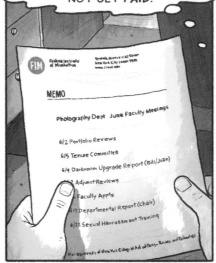

Aw, *CHRIST!* AN' LOOK AT *THIS*— TWENTY MORE **MEETINGS** THEY EXPECT ME TO SHOW UP FOR AND NOT GET *PAID!*

FIM Fashion Institute of Manhattan

Seventh Avenue & 27 Street New York City 10001 9981 www.fimnyc.edu

MEMO _____

Photography Dept June Faculty Meetings

6/2 Portfolio Reviews

6/5 Tenure Committee

6/9 Darkroom Upgrade Report (Bill/Juan)

6/12 Adjunct Reviews

6/16 Faculty Appts

6/17 Departmental Report (chair)

6/22 Sexual Harrassment Training

Pffft! I'M GONNA GO HOME, KNOCK BACK A FEW **BEERS**, AND GET SOMETHING GOIN' IN THE **STUDIO!**

MAYBE IF I SET UP A LITTLE MINIATURE SCENE I COULD GET ANNA TO **POSE** AND COMPOSITE HER INTO ~~

Oh, HEY, **ADAM!** GLAD I **CAUGHT** YOU!

NOW WHAT?

Oh, HI, **BILL**, HOW ARE YA?

GOOD, GOOD! LISTEN, I NEED YOU TO DO ME A **FAVOR!**

THE SEARCH COMMITTEE MEETING GOT BUMPED UP A DAY, SO WE'RE GOING TO NEED YOUR SYLLABUS NOTES **TOMORROW** INSTEAD OF FRIDAY ~~ IT'S *VERY* IMPORTANT.

Oh, *SHIT!*

Uh, SURE, BILL. I GUESS I CAN DO THAT...

PERFECT! JUST DROP IT OFF AT MY **OFFICE.**

SELFISH TENURED OLD **PRICK!** WHY THE **FUCK** DO I LET THESE BASTARDS TAKE **ADVANTAGE** OF ME?

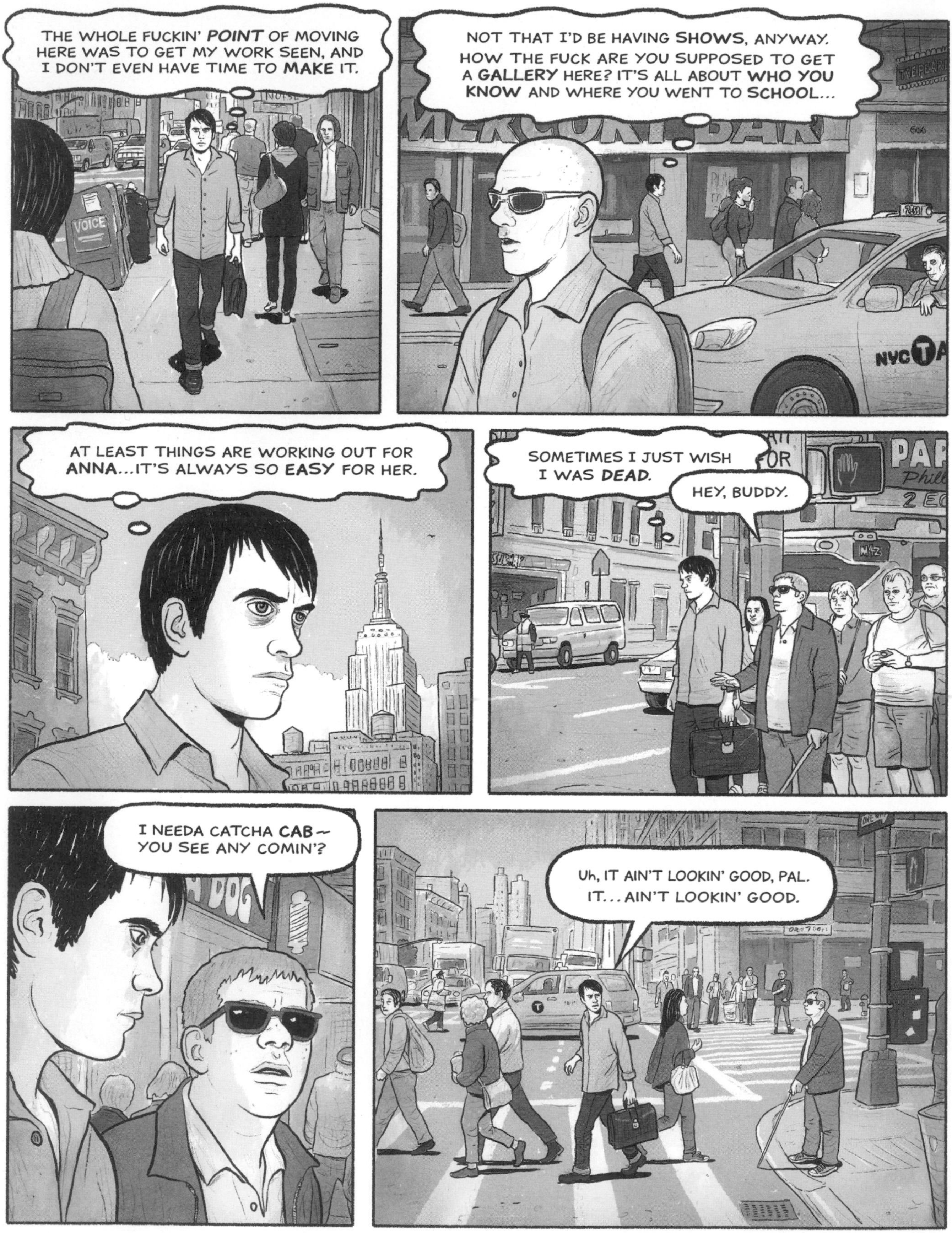
THE WHOLE FUCKIN' POINT OF MOVING HERE WAS TO GET MY WORK SEEN, AND I DON'T EVEN HAVE TIME TO MAKE IT.
VOICE
NOT THAT I'D BE HAVING SHOWS, ANYWAY. HOW THE FUCK ARE YOU SUPPOSED TO GET A GALLERY HERE? IT'S ALL ABOUT WHO YOU KNOW AND WHERE YOU WENT TO SCHOOL...
NYC
AT LEAST THINGS ARE WORKING OUT FOR ANNA...IT'S ALWAYS SO EASY FOR HER.
SOMETIMES I JUST WISH I WAS DEAD.
HEY, BUDDY.
I NEEDA CATCHA CAB— YOU SEE ANY COMIN'?
Uh, IT AIN'T LOOKIN' GOOD, PAL. IT... AIN'T LOOKIN' GOOD.

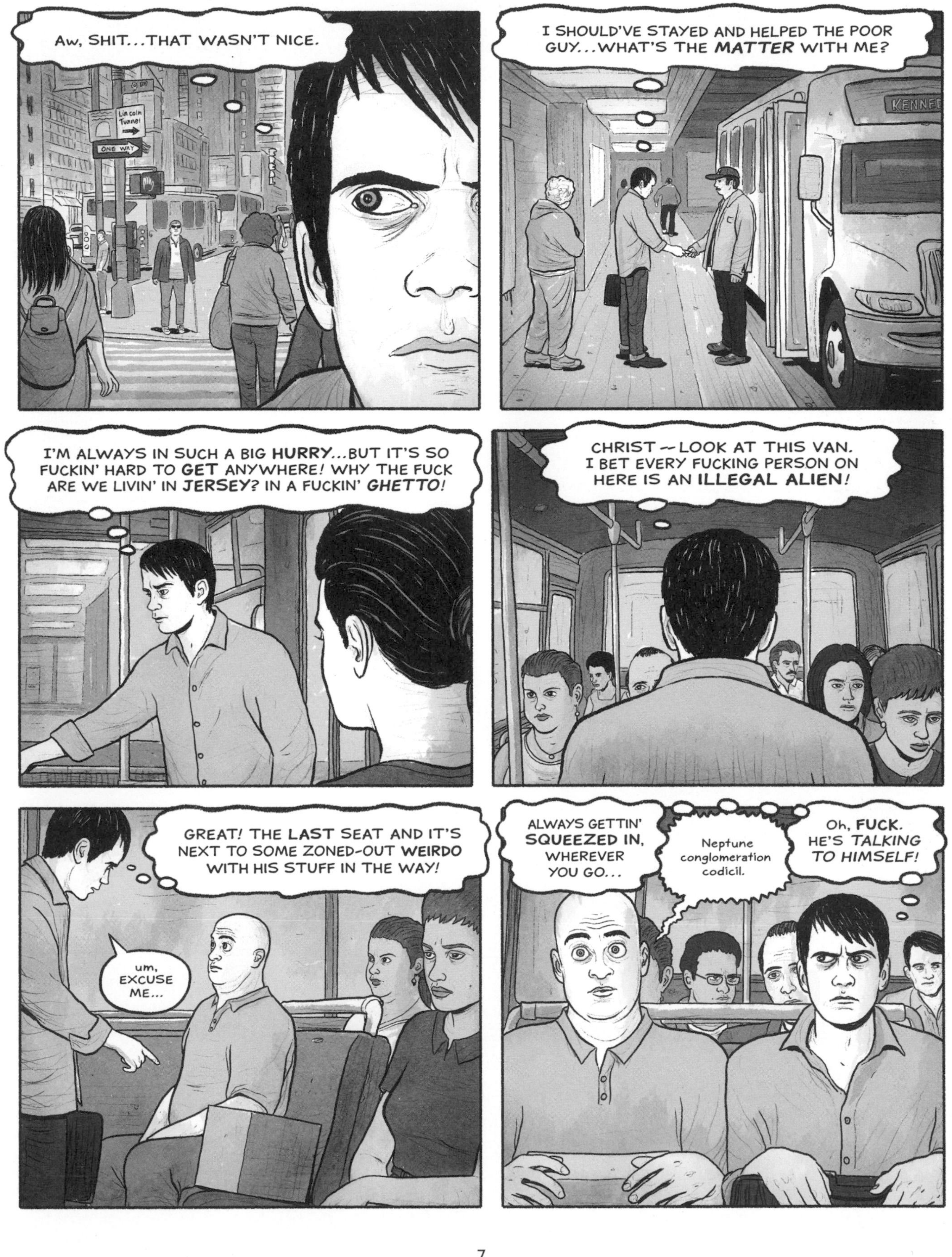
Aw, SHIT... THAT WASN'T NICE.
Lincoln Tunnel
ONE WAY
I SHOULD'VE STAYED AND HELPED THE POOR GUY... WHAT'S THE MATTER WITH ME?
KENNED
I'M ALWAYS IN SUCH A BIG HURRY... BUT IT'S SO FUCKIN' HARD TO GET ANYWHERE! WHY THE FUCK ARE WE LIVIN' IN JERSEY? IN A FUCKIN' GHETTO!
CHRIST -- LOOK AT THIS VAN. I BET EVERY FUCKING PERSON ON HERE IS AN ILLEGAL ALIEN!
GREAT! THE LAST SEAT AND IT'S NEXT TO SOME ZONED-OUT WEIRDO WITH HIS STUFF IN THE WAY!
um, EXCUSE ME...
ALWAYS GETTIN' SQUEEZED IN, WHEREVER YOU GO...
Neptune conglomeration codicil.
Oh, FUCK. HE'S TALKING TO HIMSELF!

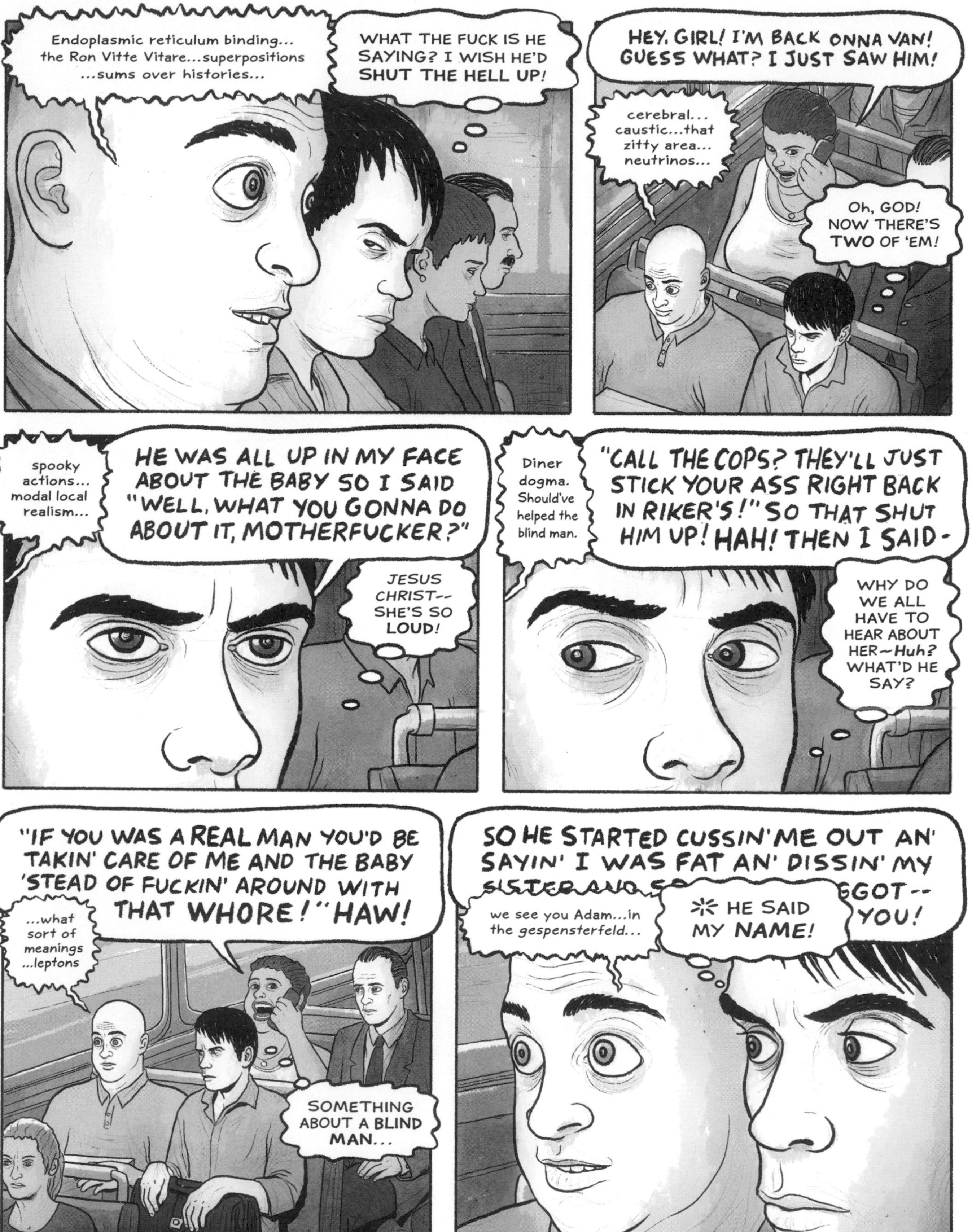

Endoplasmic reticulum binding... the Ron Vitte Vitare...superpositions ...sums over histories...
WHAT THE FUCK IS HE SAYING? I WISH HE'D SHUT THE HELL UP!
HEY, GIRL! I'M BACK ONNA VAN! GUESS WHAT? I JUST SAW HIM!
cerebral... caustic...that zitty area... neutrinos...
Oh, GOD! NOW THERE'S TWO OF 'EM!
spooky actions... modal local realism...
HE WAS ALL UP IN MY FACE ABOUT THE BABY SO I SAID "WELL, WHAT YOU GONNA DO ABOUT IT, MOTHERFUCKER?"
JESUS CHRIST-- SHE'S SO LOUD!
Diner dogma. Should've helped the blind man.
"CALL THE COPS? THEY'LL JUST STICK YOUR ASS RIGHT BACK IN RIKER'S!" SO THAT SHUT HIM UP! HAH! THEN I SAID-
WHY DO WE ALL HAVE TO HEAR ABOUT HER--Huh? WHAT'D HE SAY?
"IF YOU WAS A REAL MAN YOU'D BE TAKIN' CARE OF ME AND THE BABY 'STEAD OF FUCKIN' AROUND WITH THAT WHORE!" HAW!
...what sort of meanings ...leptons
SOMETHING ABOUT A BLIND MAN...
SO HE STARTED CUSSIN' ME OUT AN' SAYIN' I WAS FAT AN' DISSIN' MY ...GGOT-- ...YOU!
we see you Adam...in the gespensterfeld...
HE SAID MY NAME!

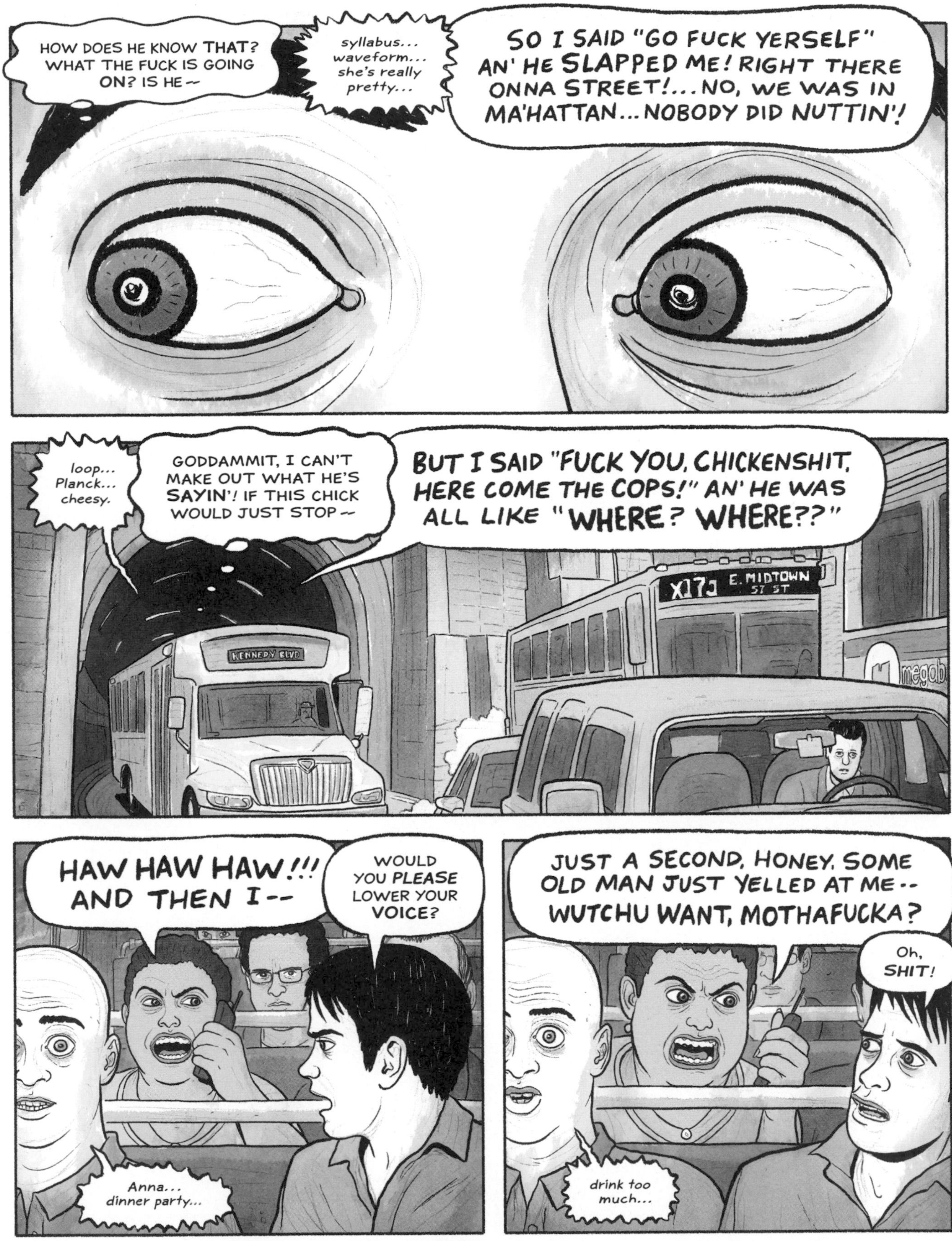
HOW DOES HE KNOW THAT? WHAT THE FUCK IS GOING ON? IS HE--
syllabus... waveform... she's really pretty...
SO I SAID "GO FUCK YERSELF" AN' HE SLAPPED ME! RIGHT THERE ONNA STREET!... NO, WE WAS IN MA'HATTAN... NOBODY DID NUTTIN'!
loop... Planck... cheesy.
GODDAMMIT, I CAN'T MAKE OUT WHAT HE'S SAYIN'! IF THIS CHICK WOULD JUST STOP--
BUT I SAID "FUCK YOU, CHICKENSHIT, HERE COME THE COPS!" AN' HE WAS ALL LIKE "WHERE? WHERE??"
KENNEDY BLVD
X17J E. MIDTOWN 57 ST
HAW HAW HAW!!! AND THEN I--
WOULD YOU PLEASE LOWER YOUR VOICE?
Anna... dinner party...
JUST A SECOND, HONEY. SOME OLD MAN JUST YELLED AT ME-- WUTCHU WANT, MOTHAFUCKA?
Oh, SHIT!
drink too much...

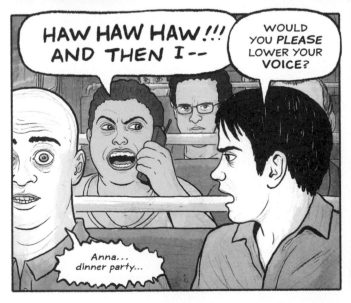

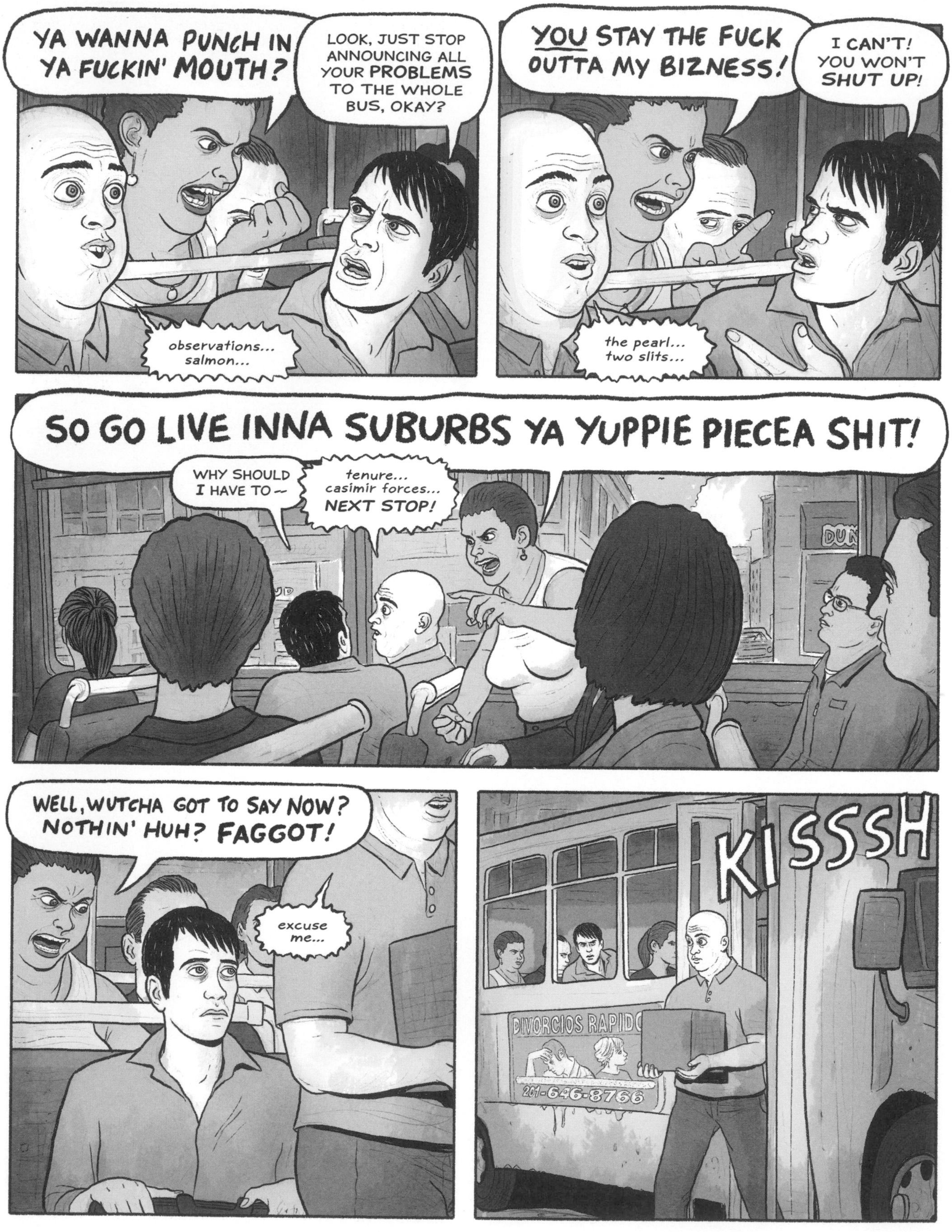
YA WANNA PUNCH IN YA FUCKIN' MOUTH?
LOOK, JUST STOP ANNOUNCING ALL YOUR PROBLEMS TO THE WHOLE BUS, OKAY?
observations... salmon...
YOU STAY THE FUCK OUTTA MY BIZNESS!
I CAN'T! YOU WON'T SHUT UP!
the pearl... two slits...
SO GO LIVE INNA SUBURBS YA YUPPIE PIECEA SHIT!
WHY SHOULD I HAVE TO~
tenure... casimir forces... NEXT STOP!
DUN
WELL, WUTCHA GOT TO SAY NOW? NOTHIN' HUH? FAGGOT!
excuse me...
KISSSH
DIVORCIOS RAPIDO
201-646-8766

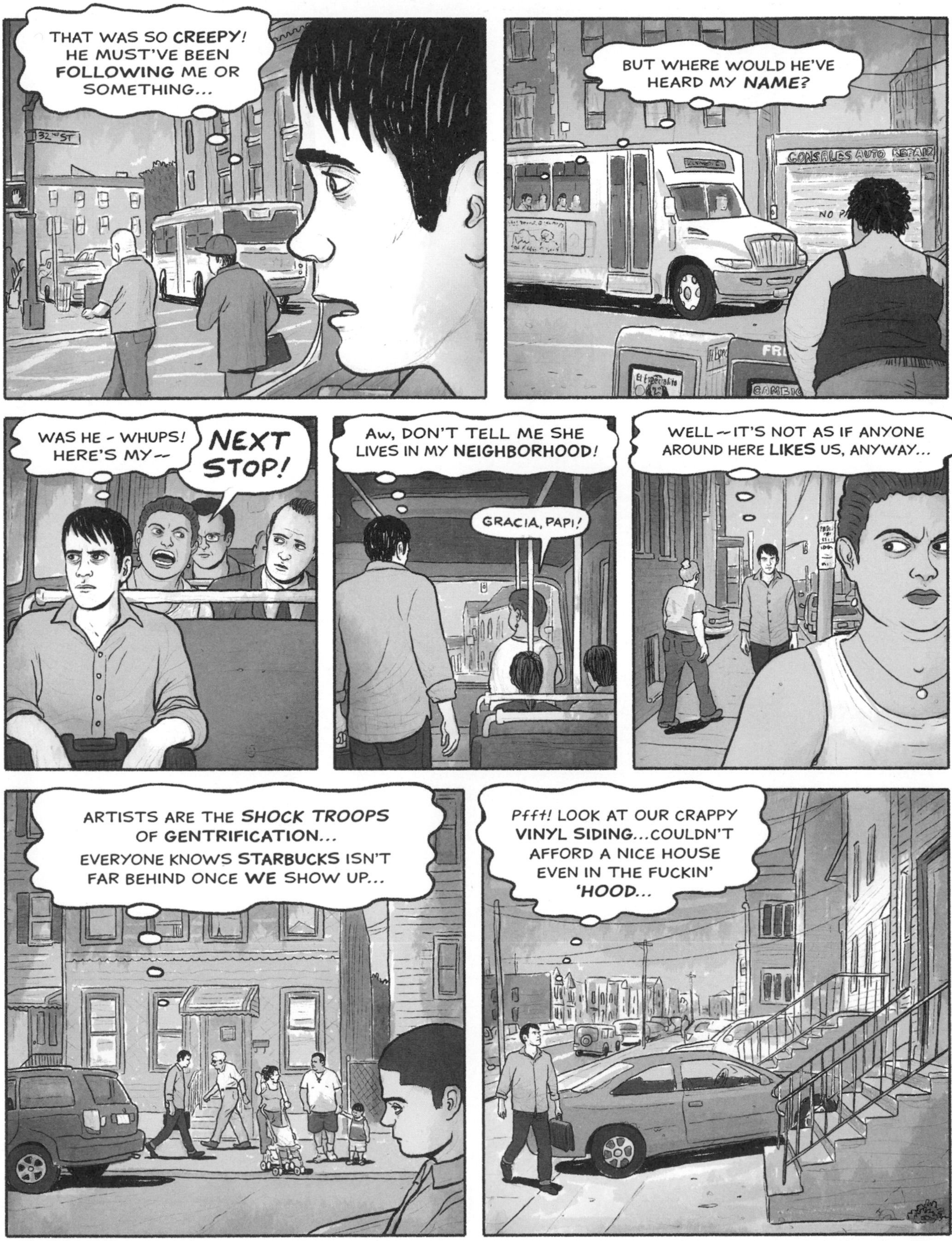

THAT WAS SO CREEPY! HE MUST'VE BEEN FOLLOWING ME OR SOMETHING...
32ND ST
BUT WHERE WOULD HE'VE HEARD MY NAME?
GONSALES AUTO REPAIR
WAS HE - WHUPS! HERE'S MY--
NEXT STOP!
Aw, DON'T TELL ME SHE LIVES IN MY NEIGHBORHOOD!
GRACIA, PAPI!
WELL--IT'S NOT AS IF ANYONE AROUND HERE LIKES US, ANYWAY...
ARTISTS ARE THE SHOCK TROOPS OF GENTRIFICATION... EVERYONE KNOWS STARBUCKS ISN'T FAR BEHIND ONCE WE SHOW UP...
Pfft! LOOK AT OUR CRAPPY VINYL SIDING...COULDN'T AFFORD A NICE HOUSE EVEN IN THE FUCKIN' 'HOOD...

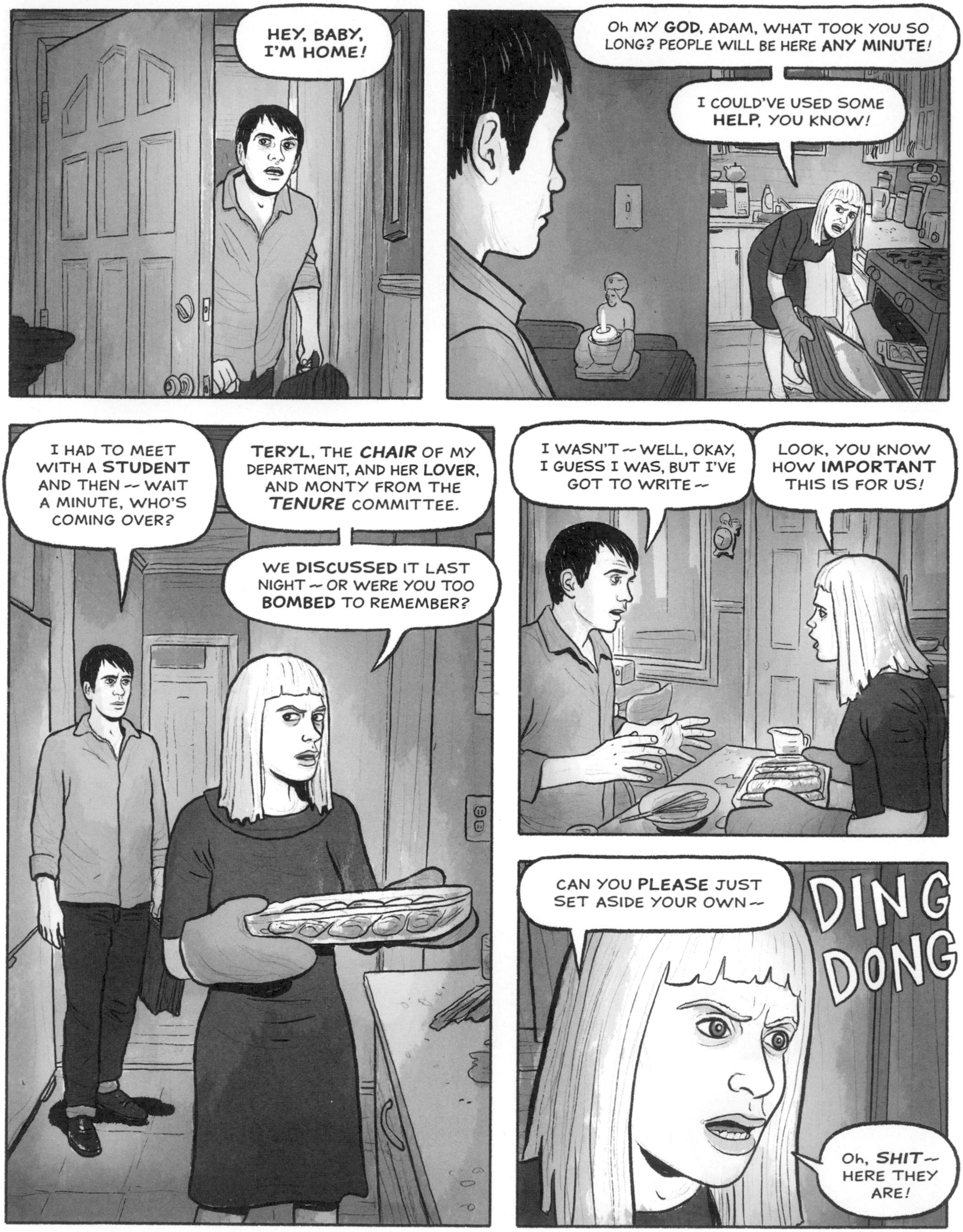
HEY, BABY, I'M HOME!
Oh MY GOD, ADAM, WHAT TOOK YOU SO LONG? PEOPLE WILL BE HERE ANY MINUTE!
I COULD'VE USED SOME HELP, YOU KNOW!
I HAD TO MEET WITH A STUDENT AND THEN -- WAIT A MINUTE, WHO'S COMING OVER?
TERYL, THE CHAIR OF MY DEPARTMENT, AND HER LOVER, AND MONTY FROM THE TENURE COMMITTEE.
WE DISCUSSED IT LAST NIGHT -- OR WERE YOU TOO BOMBED TO REMEMBER?
I WASN'T -- WELL, OKAY, I GUESS I WAS, BUT I'VE GOT TO WRITE --
LOOK, YOU KNOW HOW IMPORTANT THIS IS FOR US!
CAN YOU PLEASE JUST SET ASIDE YOUR OWN --
DING DONG
Oh, SHIT -- HERE THEY ARE!

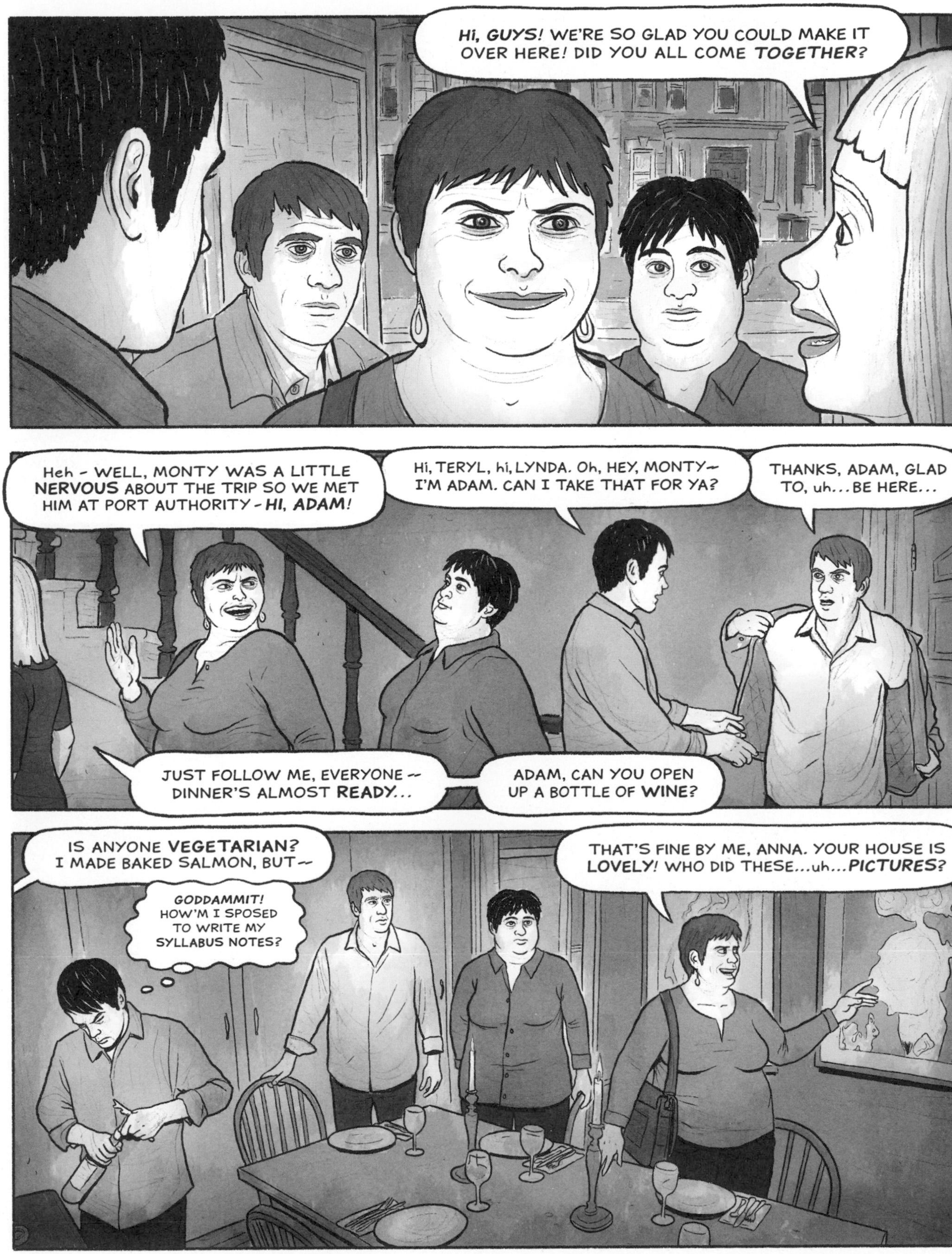

HI, GUYS! WE'RE SO GLAD YOU COULD MAKE IT OVER HERE! DID YOU ALL COME TOGETHER?
Heh - WELL, MONTY WAS A LITTLE NERVOUS ABOUT THE TRIP SO WE MET HIM AT PORT AUTHORITY - HI, ADAM!
Hi, TERYL, hi, LYNDA. Oh, HEY, MONTY -- I'M ADAM. CAN I TAKE THAT FOR YA?
THANKS, ADAM, GLAD TO, uh... BE HERE...
JUST FOLLOW ME, EVERYONE -- DINNER'S ALMOST READY...
ADAM, CAN YOU OPEN UP A BOTTLE OF WINE?
IS ANYONE VEGETARIAN? I MADE BAKED SALMON, BUT --
GODDAMMIT! HOW'M I SPOSED TO WRITE MY SYLLABUS NOTES?
THAT'S FINE BY ME, ANNA. YOUR HOUSE IS LOVELY! WHO DID THESE...uh...PICTURES?

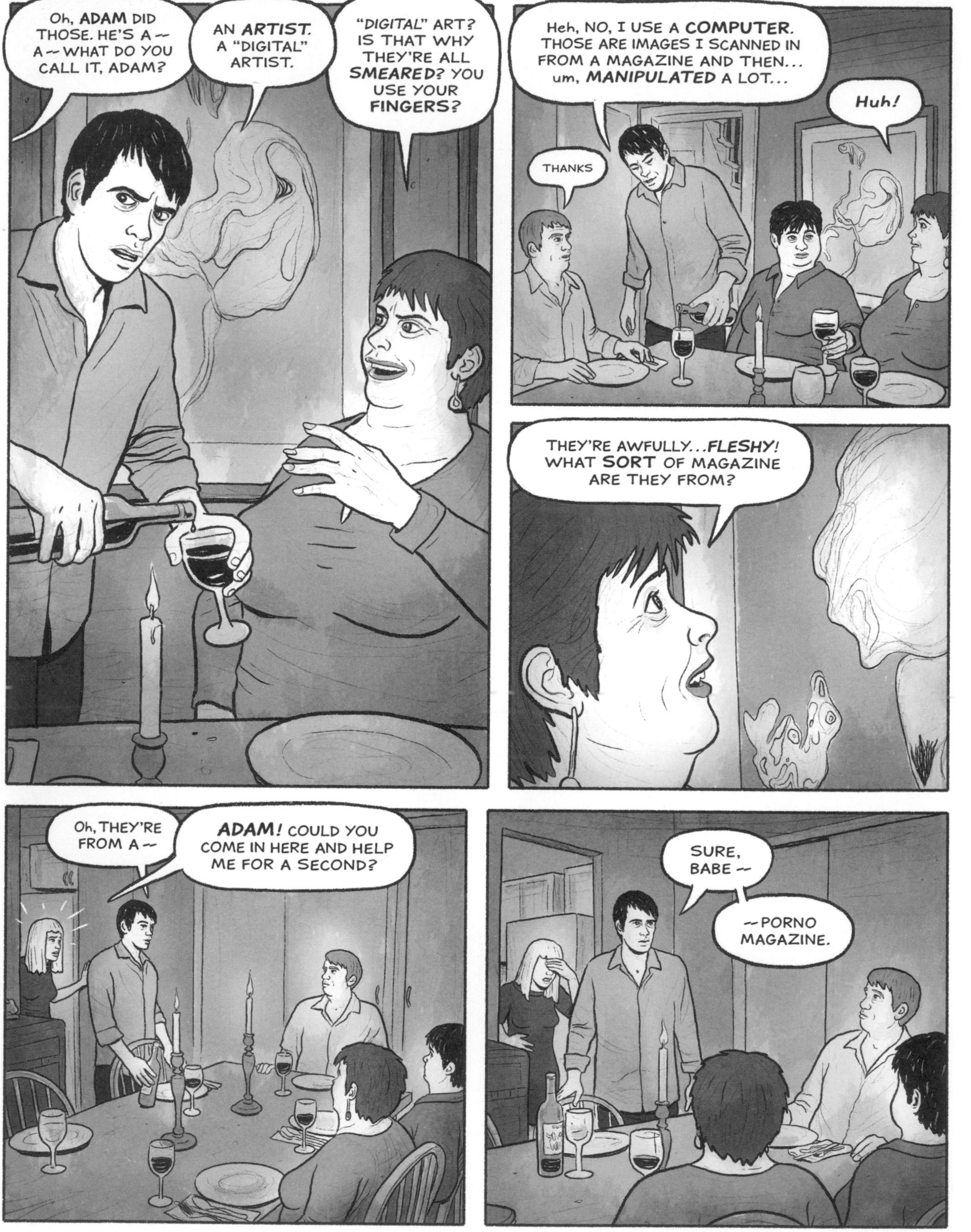
Oh, ADAM DID THOSE. HE'S A -- A -- WHAT DO YOU CALL IT, ADAM?
AN ARTIST. A "DIGITAL" ARTIST.
"DIGITAL" ART? IS THAT WHY THEY'RE ALL SMEARED? YOU USE YOUR FINGERS?
Heh, NO, I USE A COMPUTER. THOSE ARE IMAGES I SCANNED IN FROM A MAGAZINE AND THEN... um, MANIPULATED A LOT...
Huh!
THANKS
THEY'RE AWFULLY...FLESHY! WHAT SORT OF MAGAZINE ARE THEY FROM?
Oh, THEY'RE FROM A --
ADAM! COULD YOU COME IN HERE AND HELP ME FOR A SECOND?
SURE, BABE --
-- PORNO MAGAZINE.

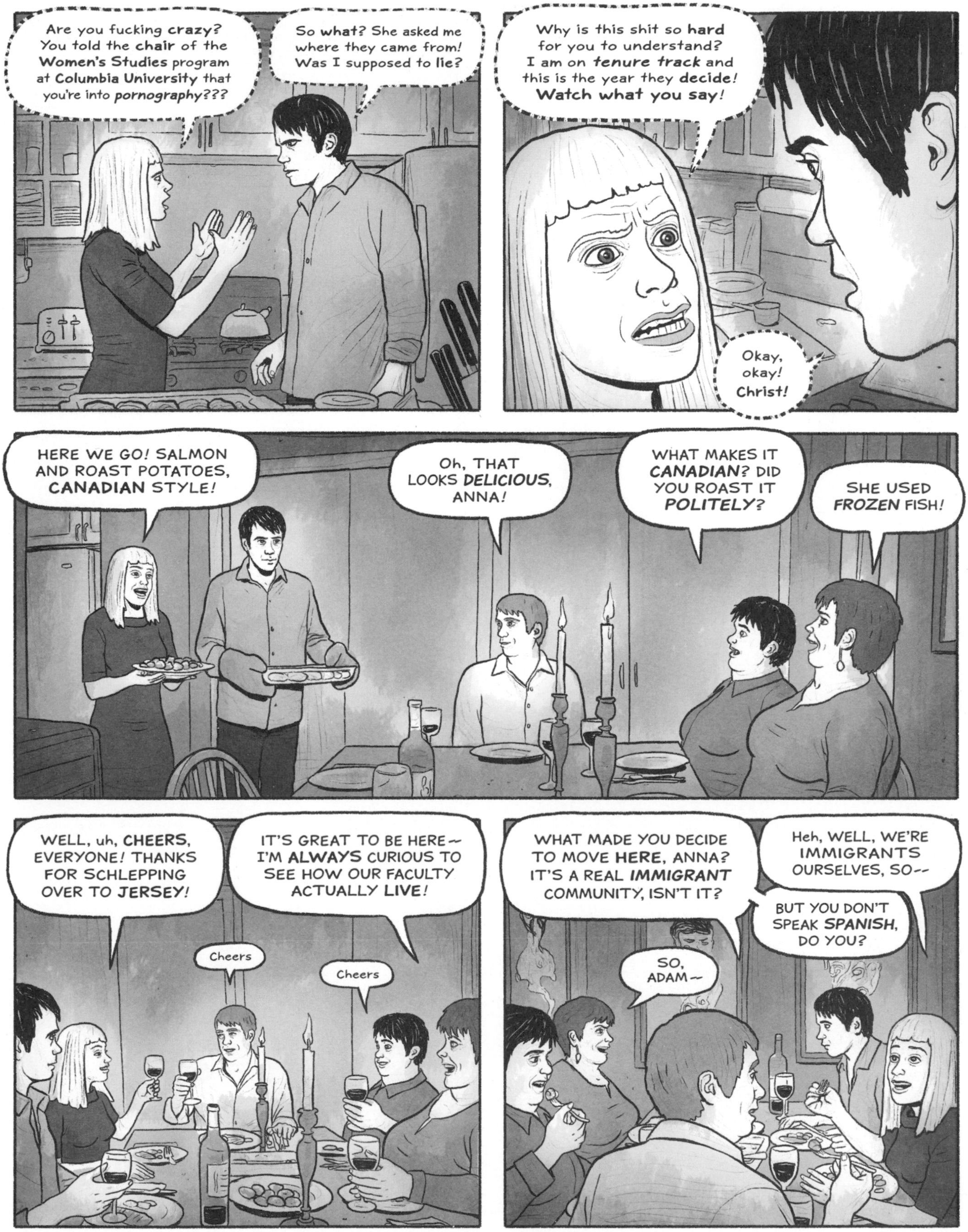
Are you fucking crazy? You told the chair of the Women's Studies program at Columbia University that you're into pornography???
So what? She asked me where they came from! Was I supposed to lie?
Why is this shit so hard for you to understand? I am on tenure track and this is the year they decide! Watch what you say!
Okay, okay! Christ!
HERE WE GO! SALMON AND ROAST POTATOES, CANADIAN STYLE!
Oh, THAT LOOKS DELICIOUS, ANNA!
WHAT MAKES IT CANADIAN? DID YOU ROAST IT POLITELY?
SHE USED FROZEN FISH!
WELL, uh, CHEERS, EVERYONE! THANKS FOR SCHLEPPING OVER TO JERSEY!
IT'S GREAT TO BE HERE– I'M ALWAYS CURIOUS TO SEE HOW OUR FACULTY ACTUALLY LIVE!
Cheers
Cheers
WHAT MADE YOU DECIDE TO MOVE HERE, ANNA? IT'S A REAL IMMIGRANT COMMUNITY, ISN'T IT?
Heh, WELL, WE'RE IMMIGRANTS OURSELVES, SO--
BUT YOU DON'T SPEAK SPANISH, DO YOU?
SO, ADAM–

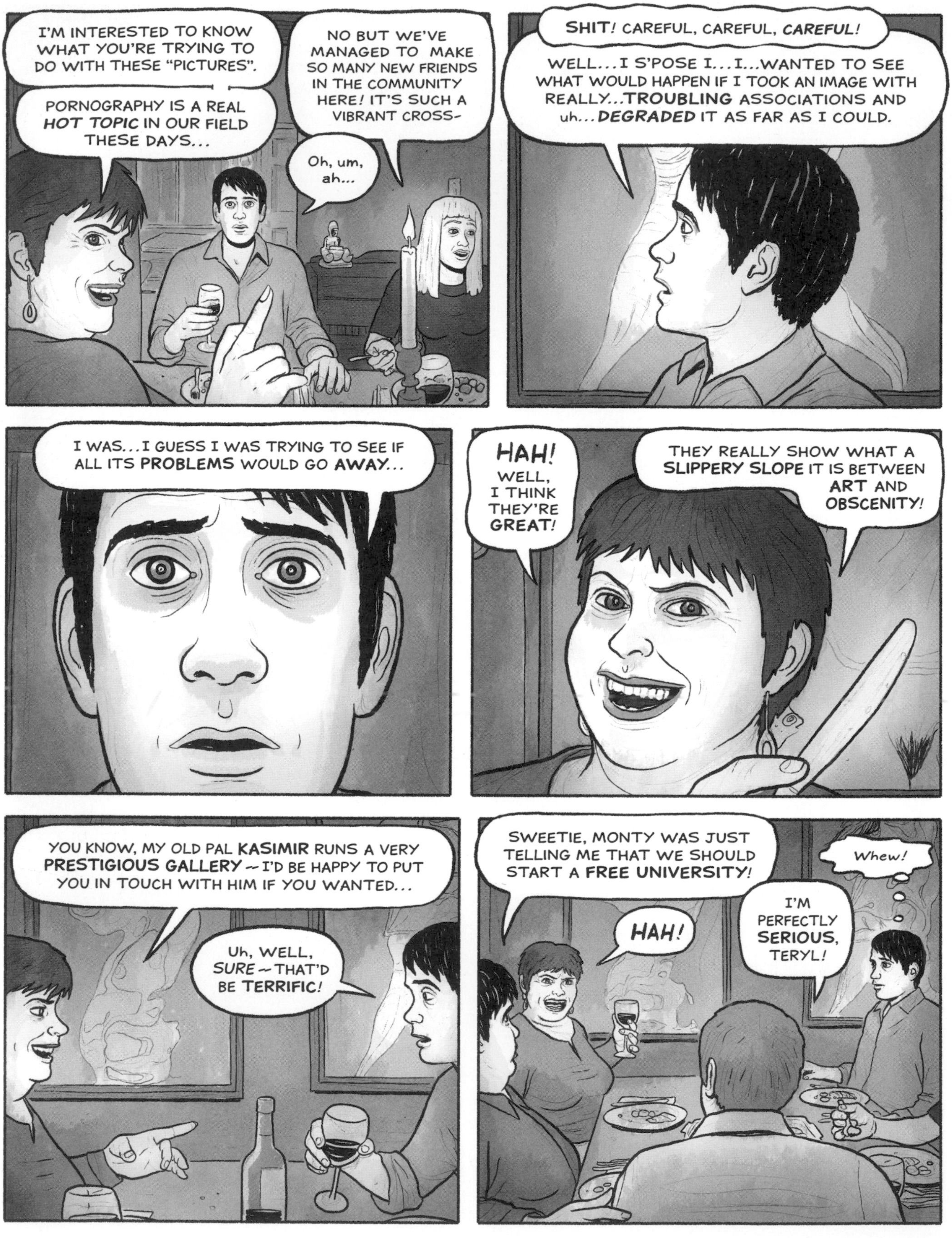
I'M INTERESTED TO KNOW WHAT YOU'RE TRYING TO DO WITH THESE "PICTURES".
PORNOGRAPHY IS A REAL HOT TOPIC IN OUR FIELD THESE DAYS...
NO BUT WE'VE MANAGED TO MAKE SO MANY NEW FRIENDS IN THE COMMUNITY HERE! IT'S SUCH A VIBRANT CROSS-
Oh, um, ah...
SHIT! CAREFUL, CAREFUL, CAREFUL!
WELL...I S'POSE I...I...WANTED TO SEE WHAT WOULD HAPPEN IF I TOOK AN IMAGE WITH REALLY...TROUBLING ASSOCIATIONS AND uh...DEGRADED IT AS FAR AS I COULD.
I WAS...I GUESS I WAS TRYING TO SEE IF ALL ITS PROBLEMS WOULD GO AWAY...
HAH! WELL, I THINK THEY'RE GREAT!
THEY REALLY SHOW WHAT A SLIPPERY SLOPE IT IS BETWEEN ART AND OBSCENITY!
YOU KNOW, MY OLD PAL KASIMIR RUNS A VERY PRESTIGIOUS GALLERY -- I'D BE HAPPY TO PUT YOU IN TOUCH WITH HIM IF YOU WANTED...
Uh, WELL, SURE -- THAT'D BE TERRIFIC!
SWEETIE, MONTY WAS JUST TELLING ME THAT WE SHOULD START A FREE UNIVERSITY!
HAH!
I'M PERFECTLY SERIOUS, TERYL!
Whew!

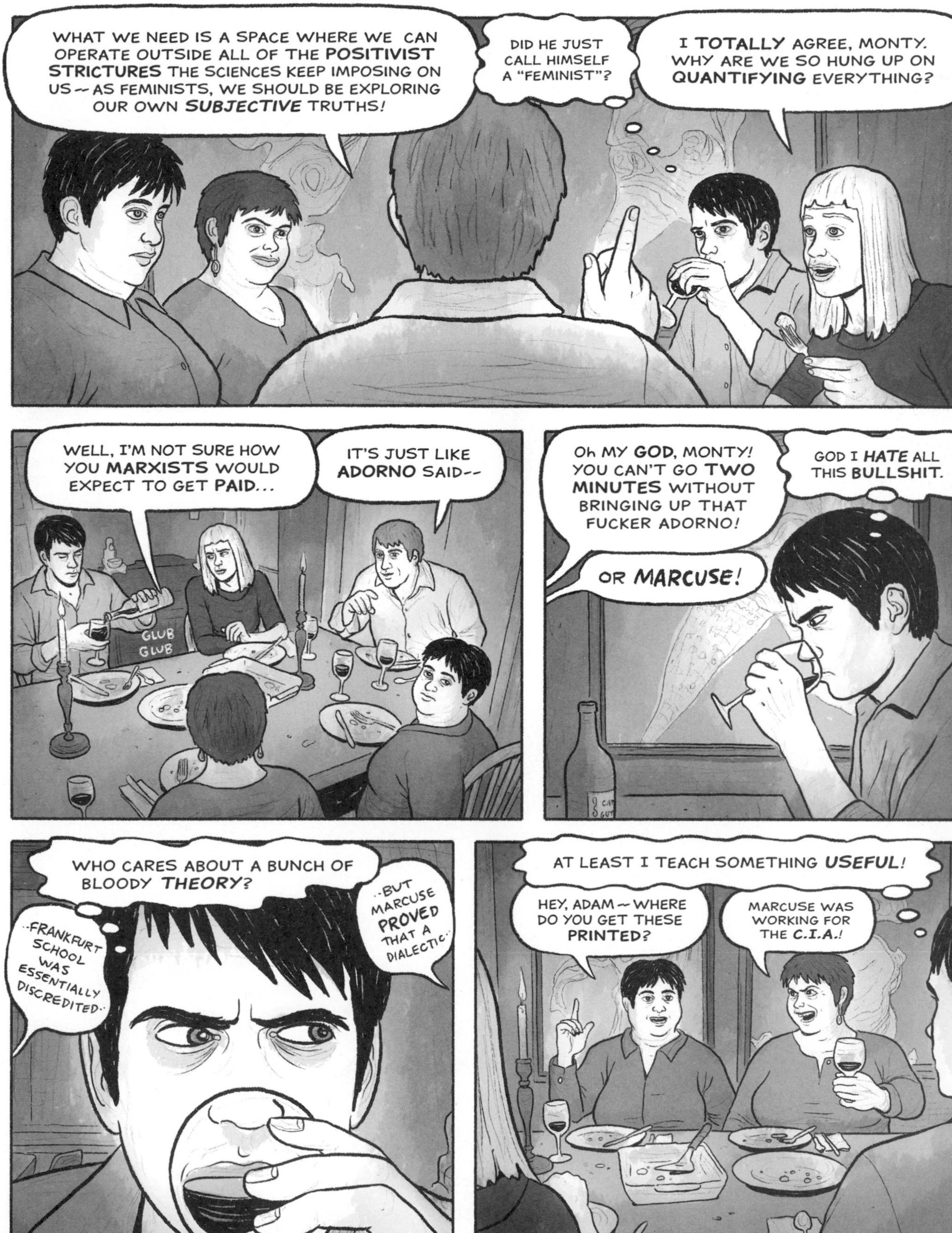
WHAT WE NEED IS A SPACE WHERE WE CAN OPERATE OUTSIDE ALL OF THE POSITIVIST STRICTURES THE SCIENCES KEEP IMPOSING ON US -- AS FEMINISTS, WE SHOULD BE EXPLORING OUR OWN SUBJECTIVE TRUTHS!
DID HE JUST CALL HIMSELF A "FEMINIST"?
I TOTALLY AGREE, MONTY. WHY ARE WE SO HUNG UP ON QUANTIFYING EVERYTHING?
WELL, I'M NOT SURE HOW YOU MARXISTS WOULD EXPECT TO GET PAID...
IT'S JUST LIKE ADORNO SAID--
GLUB GLUB
Oh MY GOD, MONTY! YOU CAN'T GO TWO MINUTES WITHOUT BRINGING UP THAT FUCKER ADORNO!
GOD I HATE ALL THIS BULLSHIT.
OR MARCUSE!
WHO CARES ABOUT A BUNCH OF BLOODY THEORY?
..FRANKFURT SCHOOL WAS ESSENTIALLY DISCREDITED..
..BUT MARCUSE PROVED THAT A DIALECTIC..
AT LEAST I TEACH SOMETHING USEFUL!
HEY, ADAM -- WHERE DO YOU GET THESE PRINTED?
MARCUSE WAS WORKING FOR THE C.I.A.!

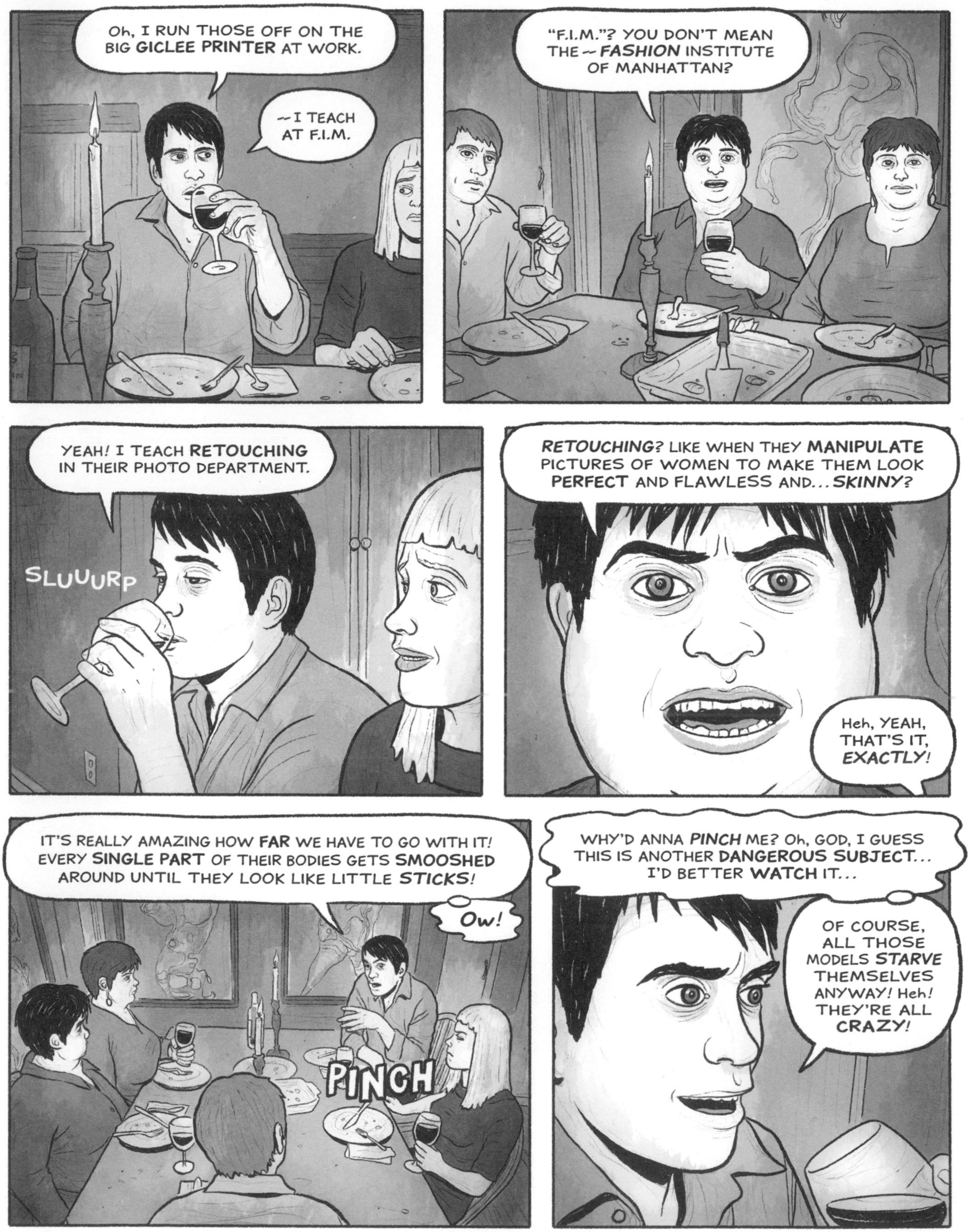

Oh, I RUN THOSE OFF ON THE BIG GICLEE PRINTER AT WORK.
--I TEACH AT F.I.M.
"F.I.M."? YOU DON'T MEAN THE--FASHION INSTITUTE OF MANHATTAN?
YEAH! I TEACH RETOUCHING IN THEIR PHOTO DEPARTMENT.
SLUUURP
RETOUCHING? LIKE WHEN THEY MANIPULATE PICTURES OF WOMEN TO MAKE THEM LOOK PERFECT AND FLAWLESS AND...SKINNY?
Heh, YEAH, THAT'S IT, EXACTLY!
IT'S REALLY AMAZING HOW FAR WE HAVE TO GO WITH IT! EVERY SINGLE PART OF THEIR BODIES GETS SMOOSHED AROUND UNTIL THEY LOOK LIKE LITTLE STICKS!
Ow!
PINCH
WHY'D ANNA PINCH ME? Oh, GOD, I GUESS THIS IS ANOTHER DANGEROUS SUBJECT... I'D BETTER WATCH IT...
OF COURSE, ALL THOSE MODELS STARVE THEMSELVES ANYWAY! Heh! THEY'RE ALL CRAZY!

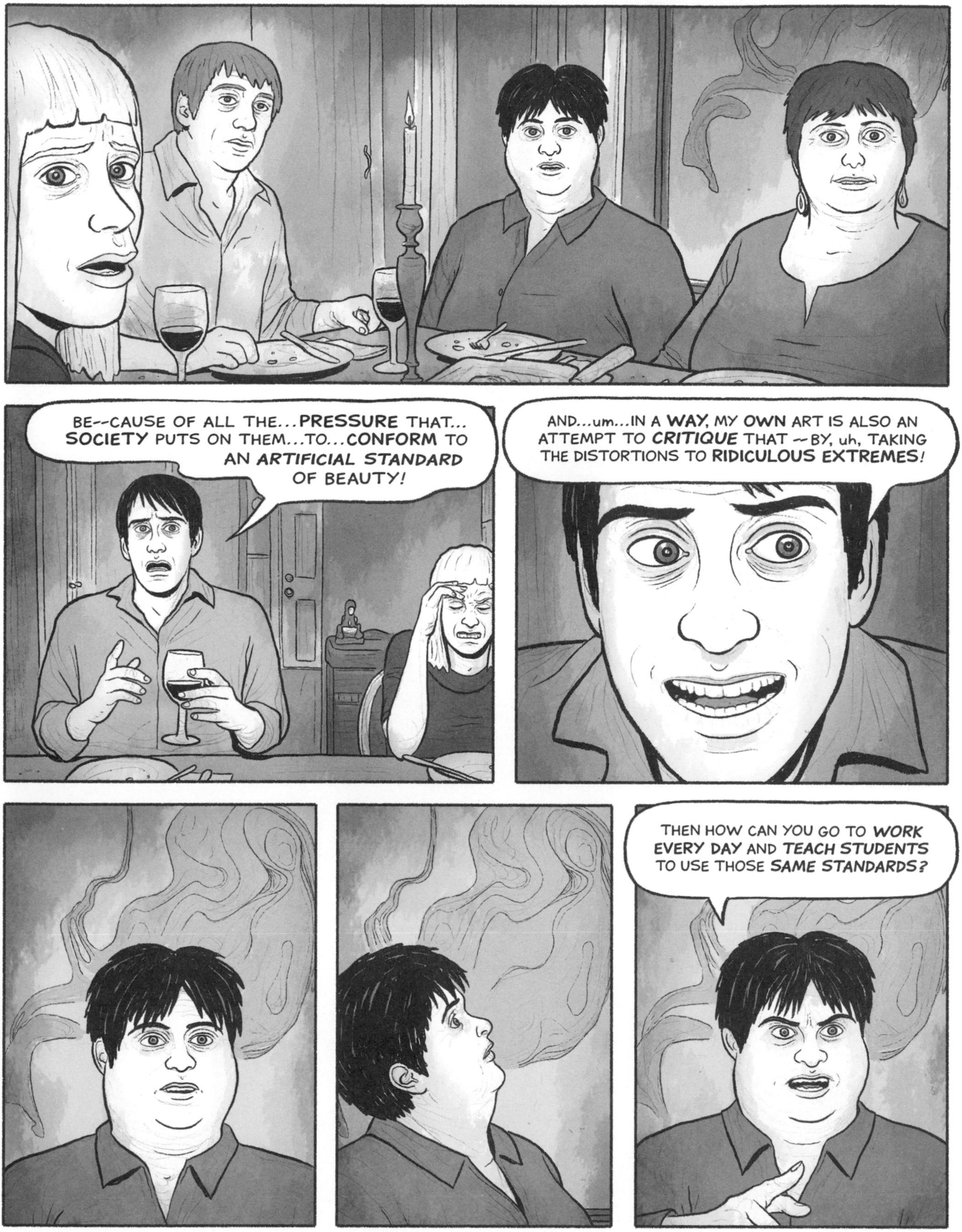

BE--CAUSE OF ALL THE...PRESSURE THAT... SOCIETY PUTS ON THEM...TO...CONFORM TO AN ARTIFICIAL STANDARD OF BEAUTY!
AND...um...IN A WAY, MY OWN ART IS ALSO AN ATTEMPT TO CRITIQUE THAT --BY, uh, TAKING THE DISTORTIONS TO RIDICULOUS EXTREMES!
THEN HOW CAN YOU GO TO WORK EVERY DAY AND TEACH STUDENTS TO USE THOSE SAME STANDARDS?

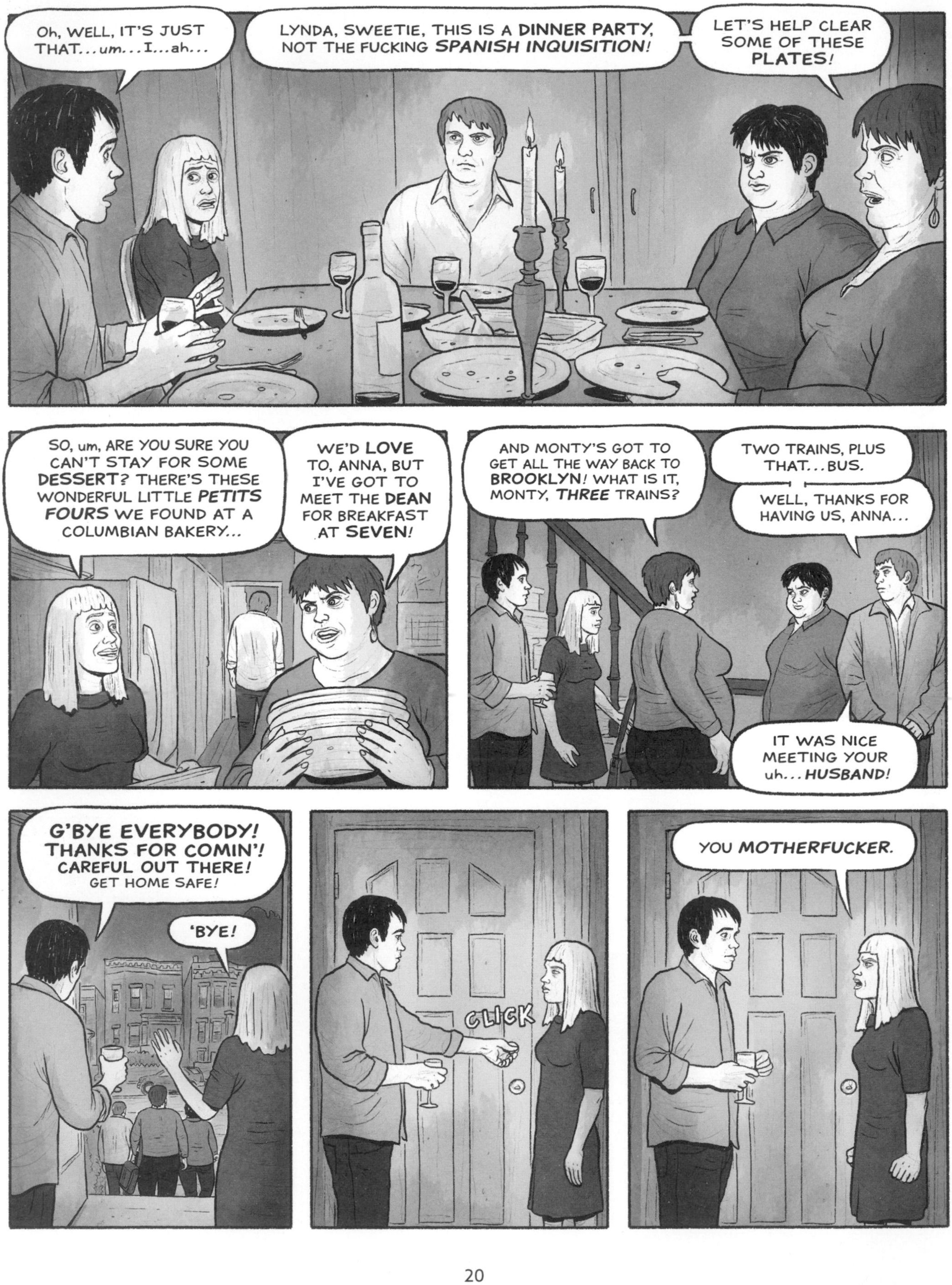
Oh, WELL, IT'S JUST THAT... um... I...ah...
LYNDA, SWEETIE, THIS IS A DINNER PARTY, NOT THE FUCKING SPANISH INQUISITION!
LET'S HELP CLEAR SOME OF THESE PLATES!
SO, um, ARE YOU SURE YOU CAN'T STAY FOR SOME DESSERT? THERE'S THESE WONDERFUL LITTLE PETITS FOURS WE FOUND AT A COLUMBIAN BAKERY...
WE'D LOVE TO, ANNA, BUT I'VE GOT TO MEET THE DEAN FOR BREAKFAST AT SEVEN!
AND MONTY'S GOT TO GET ALL THE WAY BACK TO BROOKLYN! WHAT IS IT, MONTY, THREE TRAINS?
TWO TRAINS, PLUS THAT... BUS.
WELL, THANKS FOR HAVING US, ANNA...
IT WAS NICE MEETING YOUR uh... HUSBAND!
G'BYE EVERYBODY! THANKS FOR COMIN'! CAREFUL OUT THERE! GET HOME SAFE!
'BYE!
CLICK
YOU MOTHERFUCKER.

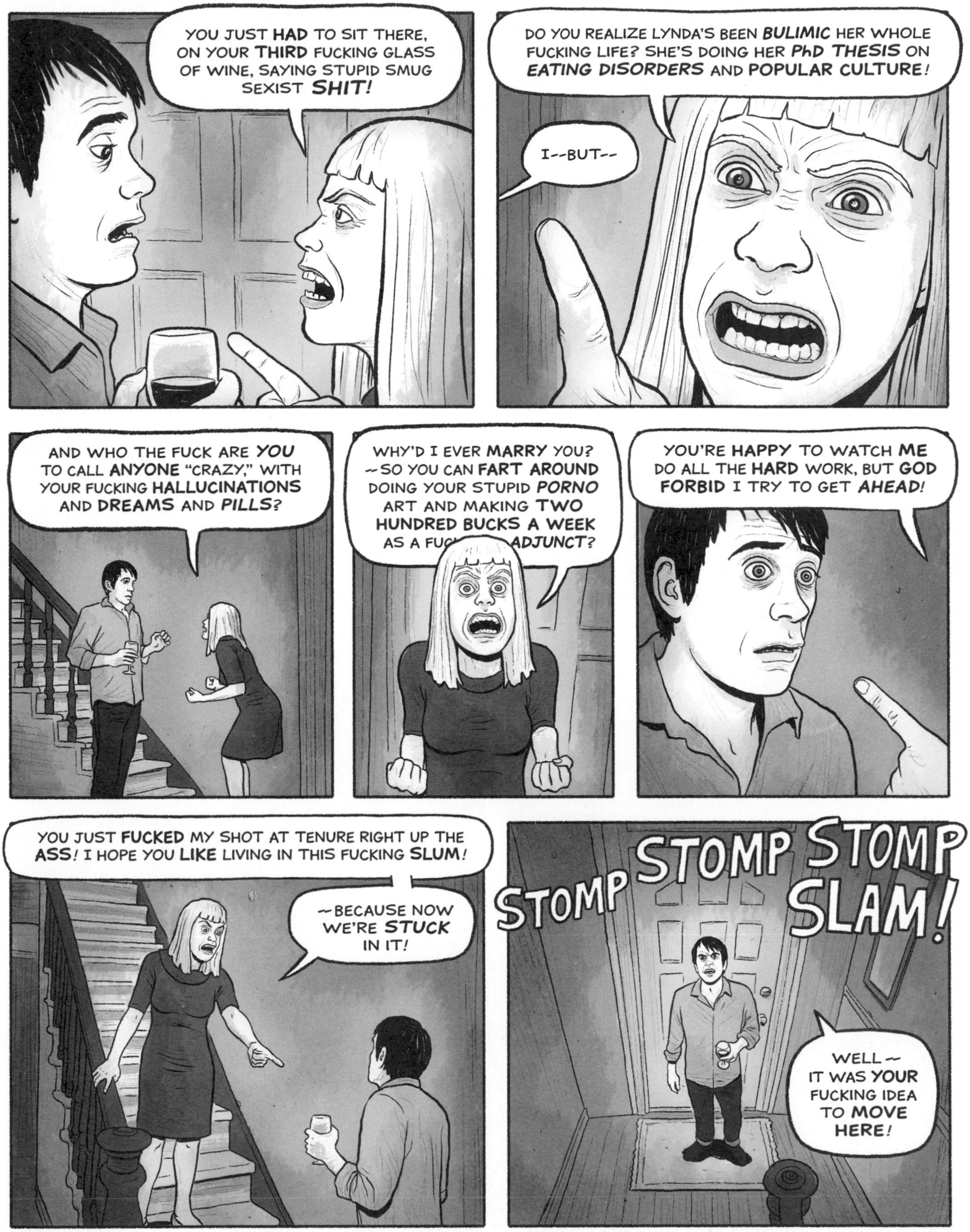
YOU JUST HAD TO SIT THERE, ON YOUR THIRD FUCKING GLASS OF WINE, SAYING STUPID SMUG SEXIST SHIT!
DO YOU REALIZE LYNDA'S BEEN BULIMIC HER WHOLE FUCKING LIFE? SHE'S DOING HER PhD THESIS ON EATING DISORDERS AND POPULAR CULTURE!
I--BUT--
AND WHO THE FUCK ARE YOU TO CALL ANYONE "CRAZY," WITH YOUR FUCKING HALLUCINATIONS AND DREAMS AND PILLS?
WHY'D I EVER MARRY YOU? --SO YOU CAN FART AROUND DOING YOUR STUPID PORNO ART AND MAKING TWO HUNDRED BUCKS A WEEK AS A FUC ADJUNCT?
YOU'RE HAPPY TO WATCH ME DO ALL THE HARD WORK, BUT GOD FORBID I TRY TO GET AHEAD!
YOU JUST FUCKED MY SHOT AT TENURE RIGHT UP THE ASS! I HOPE YOU LIKE LIVING IN THIS FUCKING SLUM!
--BECAUSE NOW WE'RE STUCK IN IT!
STOMP STOMP STOMP
SLAM!
WELL -- IT WAS YOUR FUCKING IDEA TO MOVE HERE!

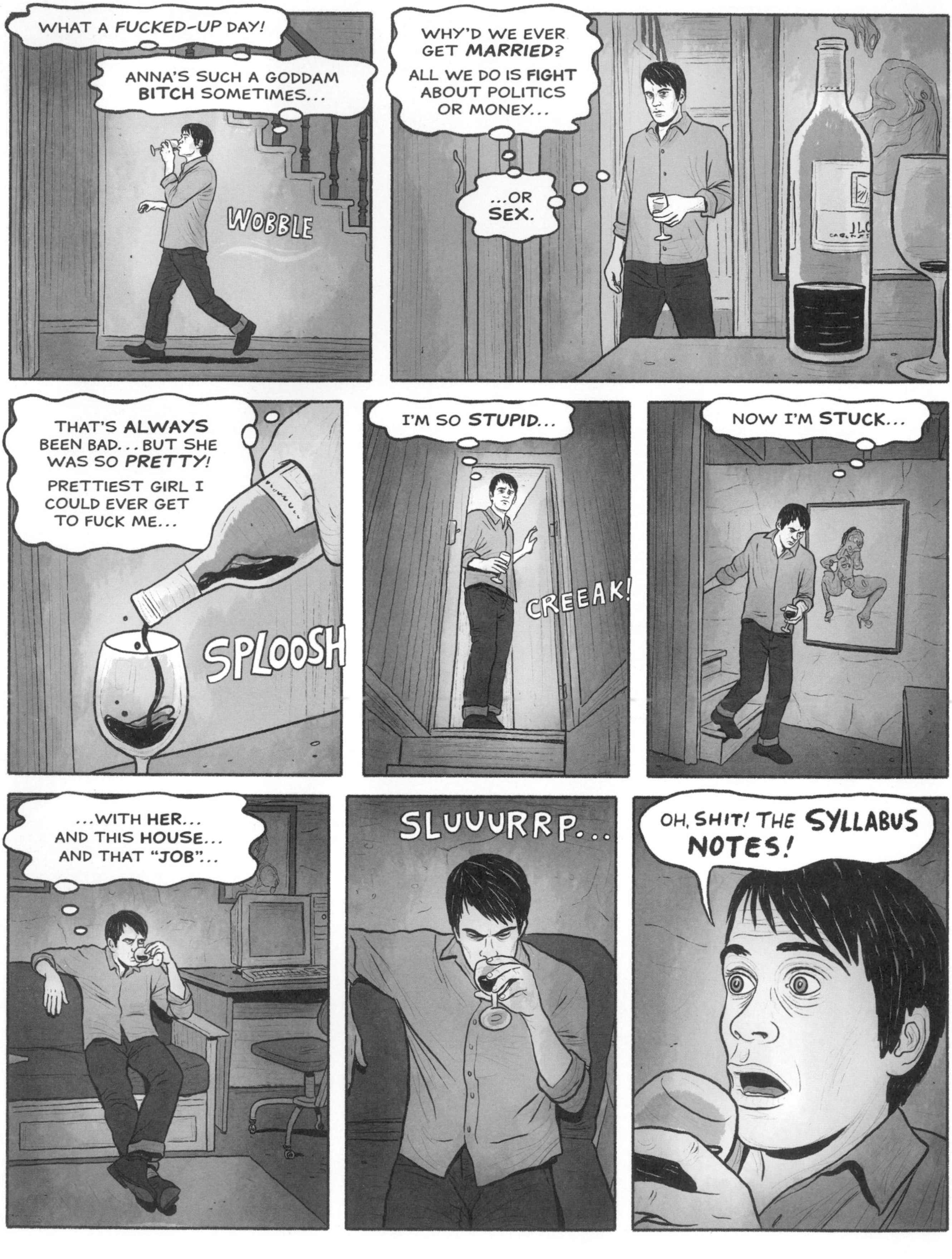
WHAT A FUCKED-UP DAY!
ANNA'S SUCH A GODDAM BITCH SOMETIMES...
WOBBLE
WHY'D WE EVER GET MARRIED?
ALL WE DO IS FIGHT ABOUT POLITICS OR MONEY...
...OR SEX.
THAT'S ALWAYS BEEN BAD... BUT SHE WAS SO PRETTY!
PRETTIEST GIRL I COULD EVER GET TO FUCK ME...
SPLOOSH
I'M SO STUPID...
CREEAK!
NOW I'M STUCK...
...WITH HER... AND THIS HOUSE... AND THAT "JOB"...
SLUUURRP...
OH, SHIT! THE SYLLABUS NOTES!

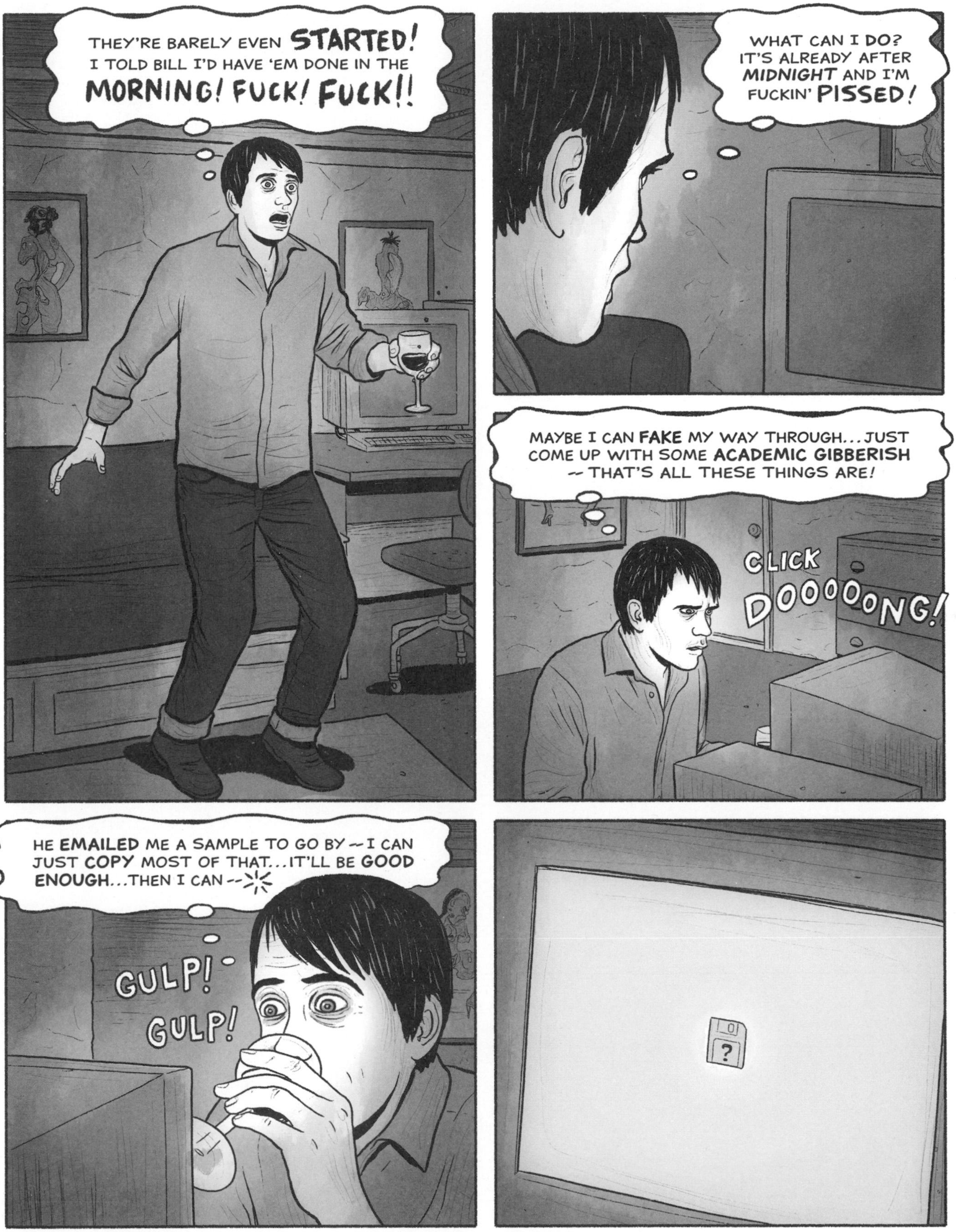
THEY'RE BARELY EVEN STARTED! I TOLD BILL I'D HAVE 'EM DONE IN THE MORNING! FUCK! FUCK!!
WHAT CAN I DO? IT'S ALREADY AFTER MIDNIGHT AND I'M FUCKIN' PISSED!
MAYBE I CAN FAKE MY WAY THROUGH... JUST COME UP WITH SOME ACADEMIC GIBBERISH -- THAT'S ALL THESE THINGS ARE!
CLICK
DOOOOONG!
HE EMAILED ME A SAMPLE TO GO BY -- I CAN JUST COPY MOST OF THAT... IT'LL BE GOOD ENOUGH... THEN I CAN --
GULP!
GULP!
?

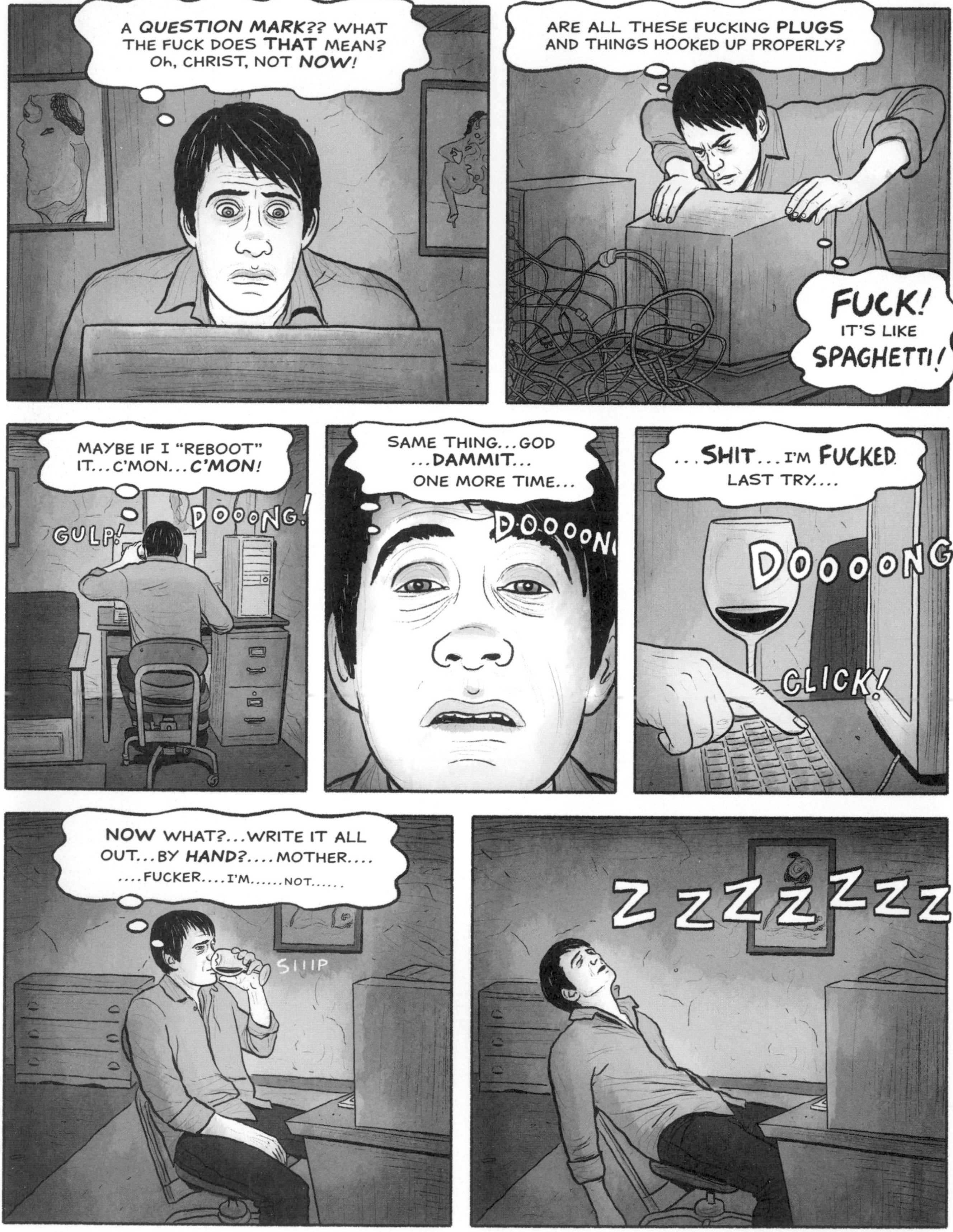
A QUESTION MARK?? WHAT THE FUCK DOES THAT MEAN? Oh, CHRIST, NOT NOW!
ARE ALL THESE FUCKING PLUGS AND THINGS HOOKED UP PROPERLY?
FUCK! IT'S LIKE SPAGHETTI!
MAYBE IF I "REBOOT" IT... C'MON... C'MON!
GULP!
DOOONG!
SAME THING... GOD ...DAMMIT... ONE MORE TIME...
DOOOON
...SHIT... I'M FUCKED. LAST TRY....
DOOOONG
CLICK!
NOW WHAT?... WRITE IT ALL OUT... BY HAND?.... MOTHER.... ....FUCKER.... I'M...... NOT......
SIIIP
Z Z Z Z Z Z Z

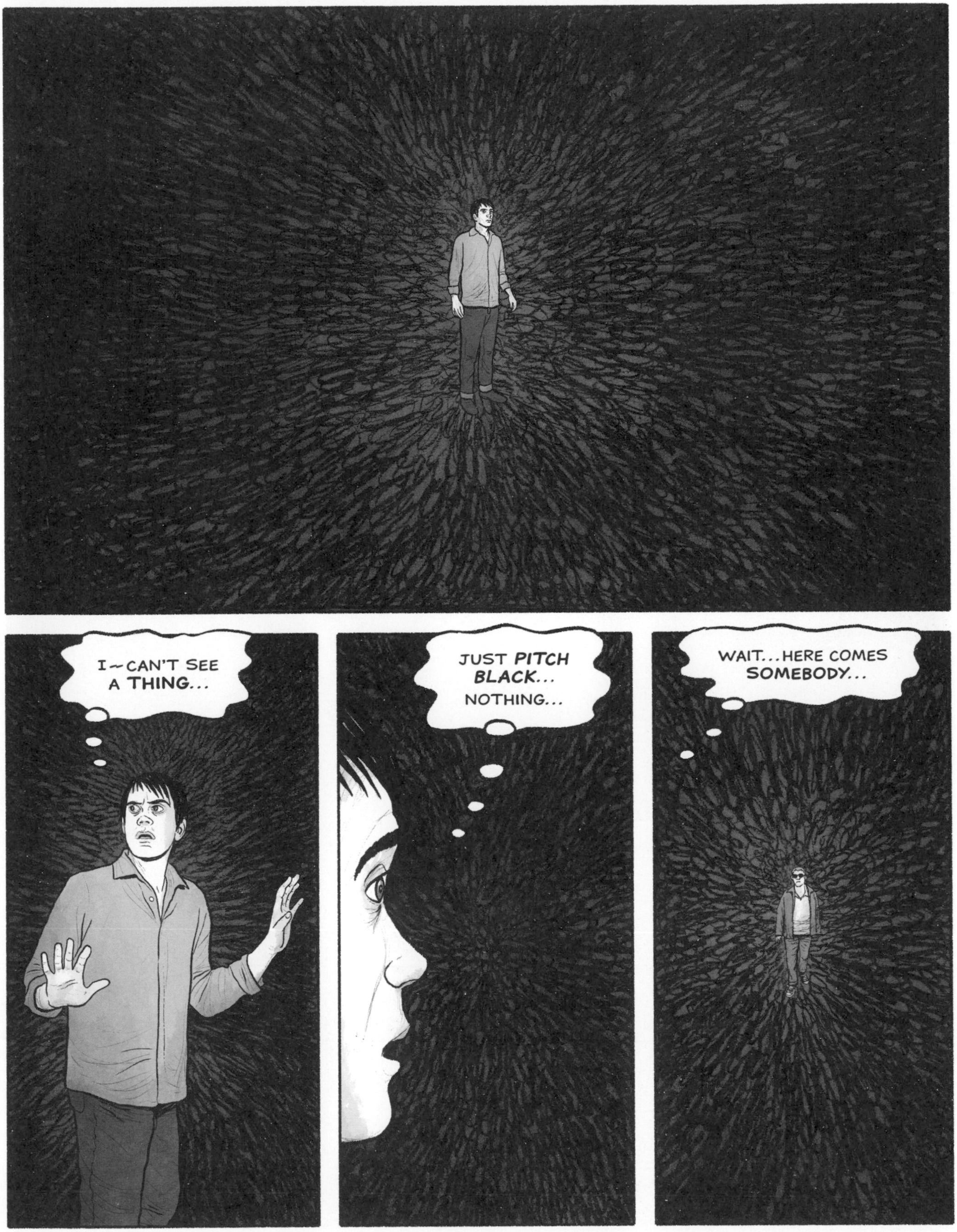
I—CAN'T SEE A THING...
JUST PITCH BLACK... NOTHING...
WAIT... HERE COMES SOMEBODY...

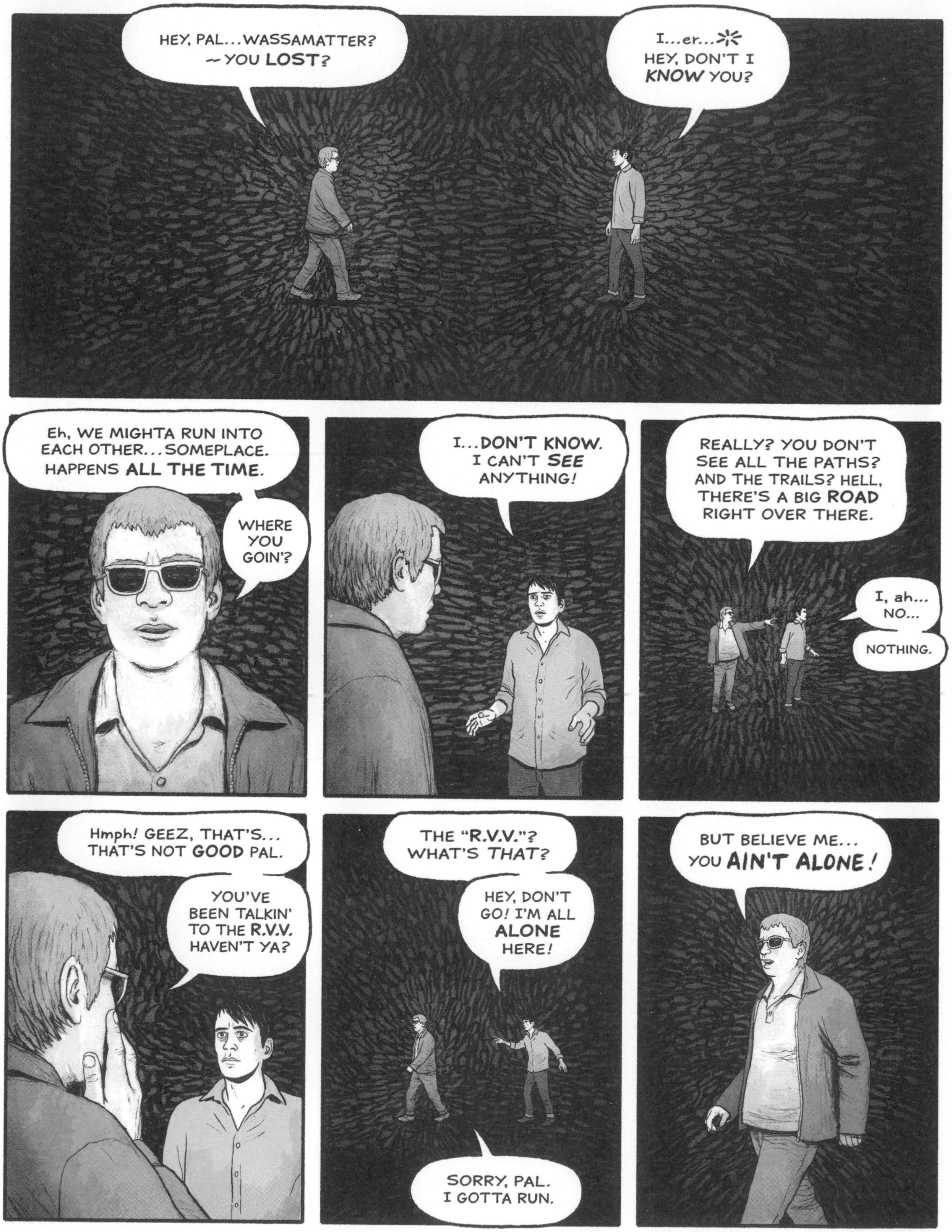
HEY, PAL...WASSAMATTER? ~YOU LOST?
I...er... HEY, DON'T I KNOW YOU?
Eh, WE MIGHTA RUN INTO EACH OTHER...SOMEPLACE. HAPPENS ALL THE TIME.
WHERE YOU GOIN'?
I...DON'T KNOW. I CAN'T SEE ANYTHING!
REALLY? YOU DON'T SEE ALL THE PATHS? AND THE TRAILS? HELL, THERE'S A BIG ROAD RIGHT OVER THERE.
I, ah... NO...
NOTHING.
Hmph! GEEZ, THAT'S... THAT'S NOT GOOD PAL.
YOU'VE BEEN TALKIN' TO THE R.V.V. HAVEN'T YA?
THE "R.V.V."? WHAT'S THAT?
HEY, DON'T GO! I'M ALL ALONE HERE!
SORRY, PAL. I GOTTA RUN.
BUT BELIEVE ME... YOU AIN'T ALONE!

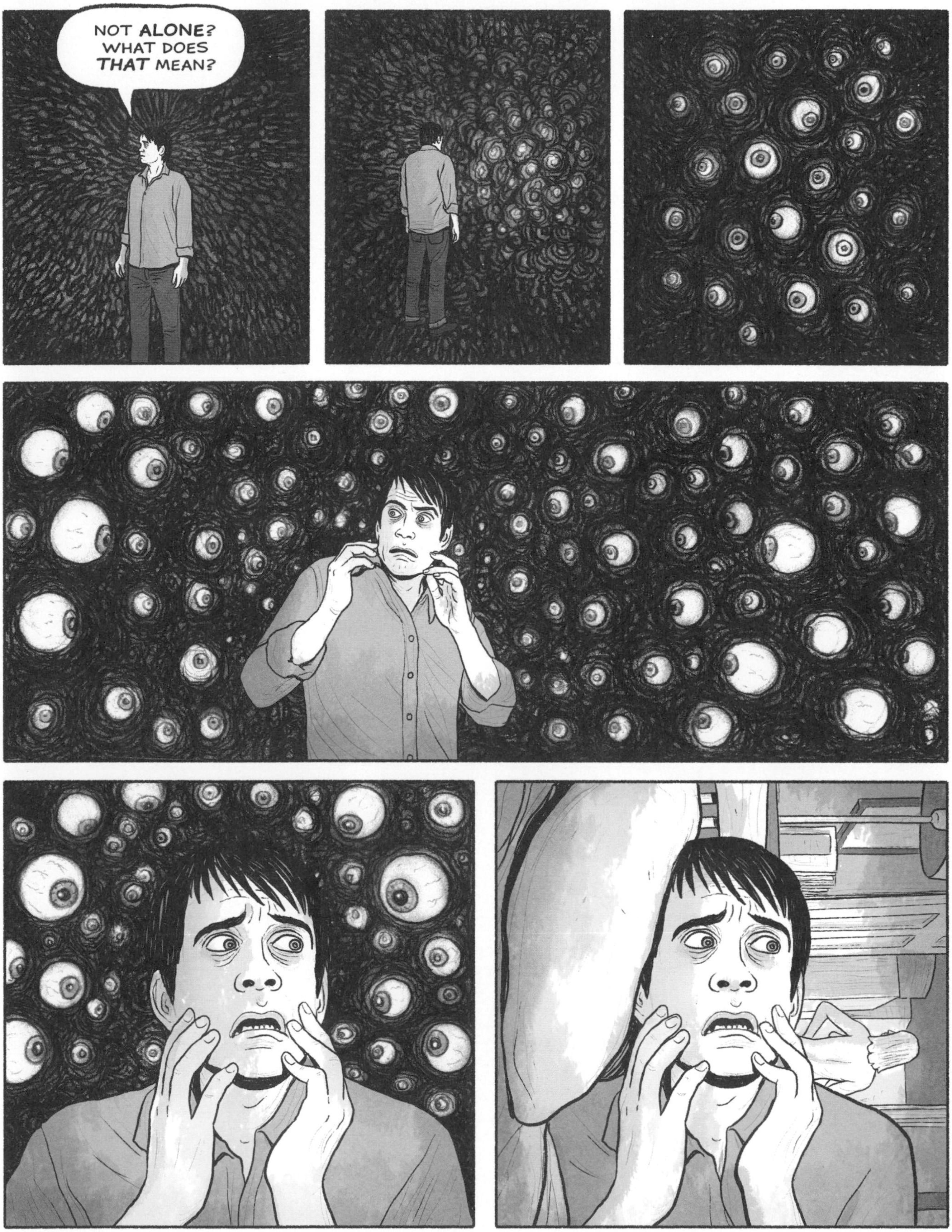
NOT ALONE? WHAT DOES THAT MEAN?

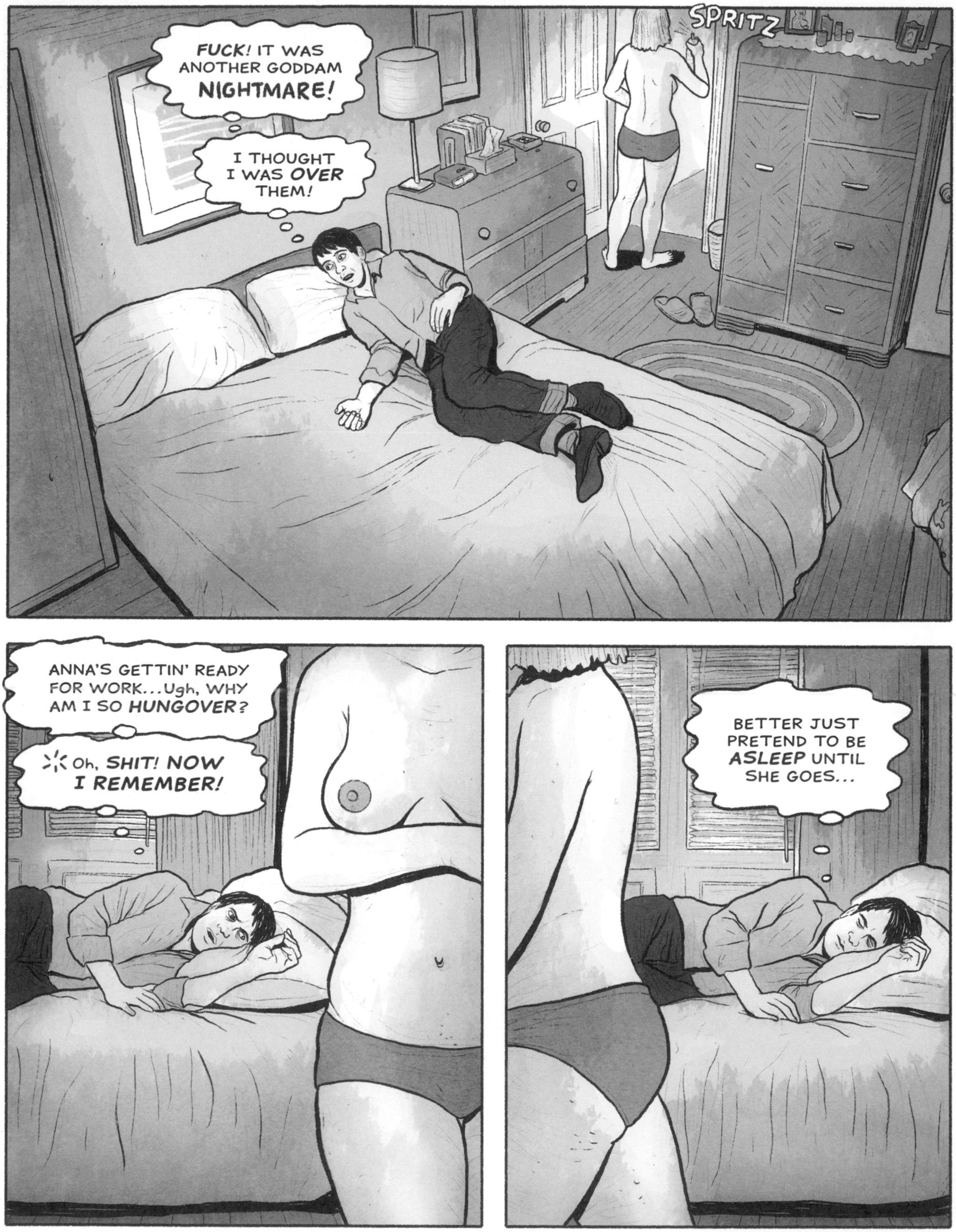
SPRITZ
FUCK! IT WAS ANOTHER GODDAM NIGHTMARE!
I THOUGHT I WAS OVER THEM!
ANNA'S GETTIN' READY FOR WORK... Ugh, WHY AM I SO HUNGOVER?
Oh, SHIT! NOW I REMEMBER!
BETTER JUST PRETEND TO BE ASLEEP UNTIL SHE GOES...

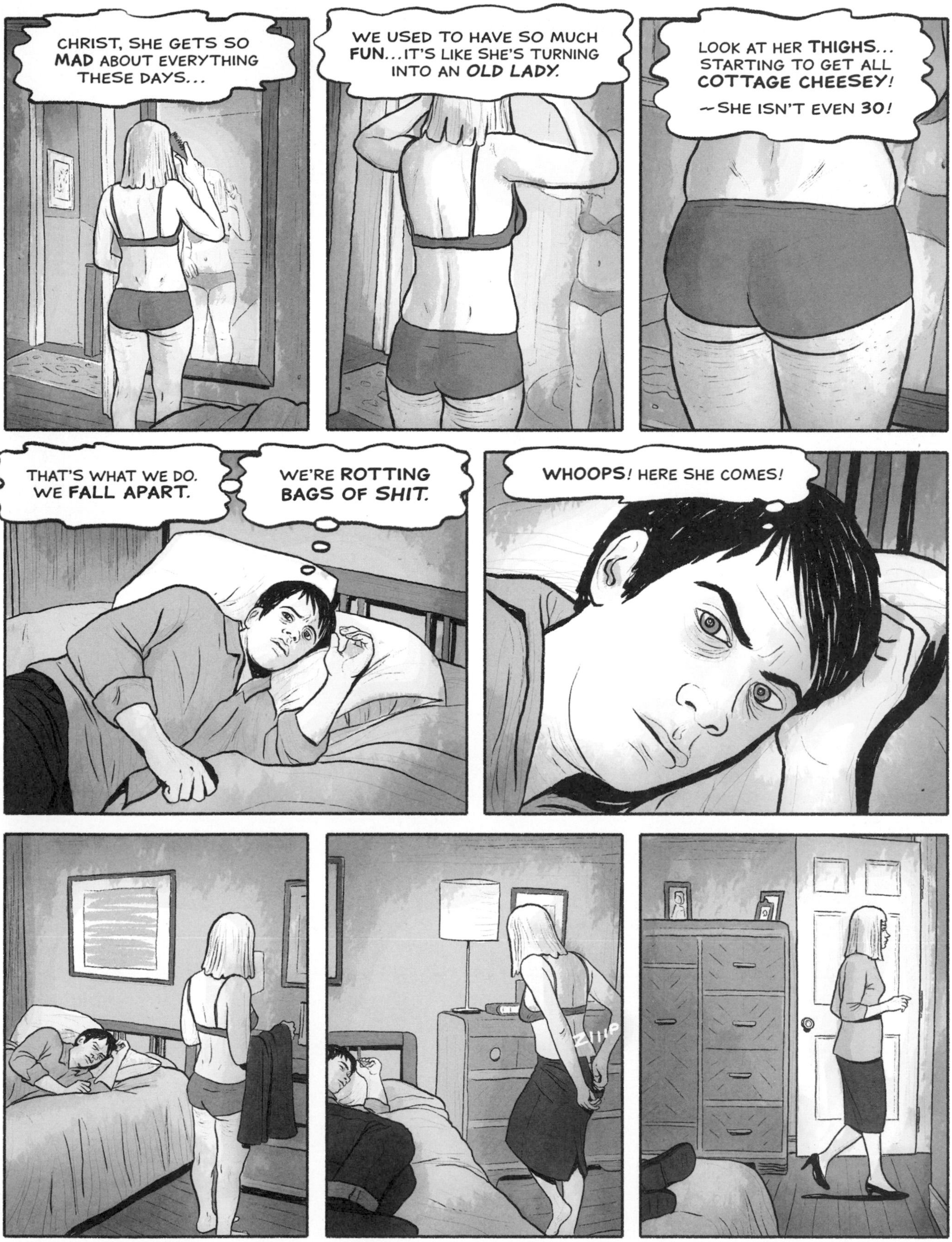
CHRIST, SHE GETS SO MAD ABOUT EVERYTHING THESE DAYS...
WE USED TO HAVE SO MUCH FUN...IT'S LIKE SHE'S TURNING INTO AN OLD LADY.
LOOK AT HER THIGHS... STARTING TO GET ALL COTTAGE CHEESEY!
~SHE ISN'T EVEN 30!
THAT'S WHAT WE DO. WE FALL APART.
WE'RE ROTTING BAGS OF SHIT.
WHOOPS! HERE SHE COMES!
ZIIIP

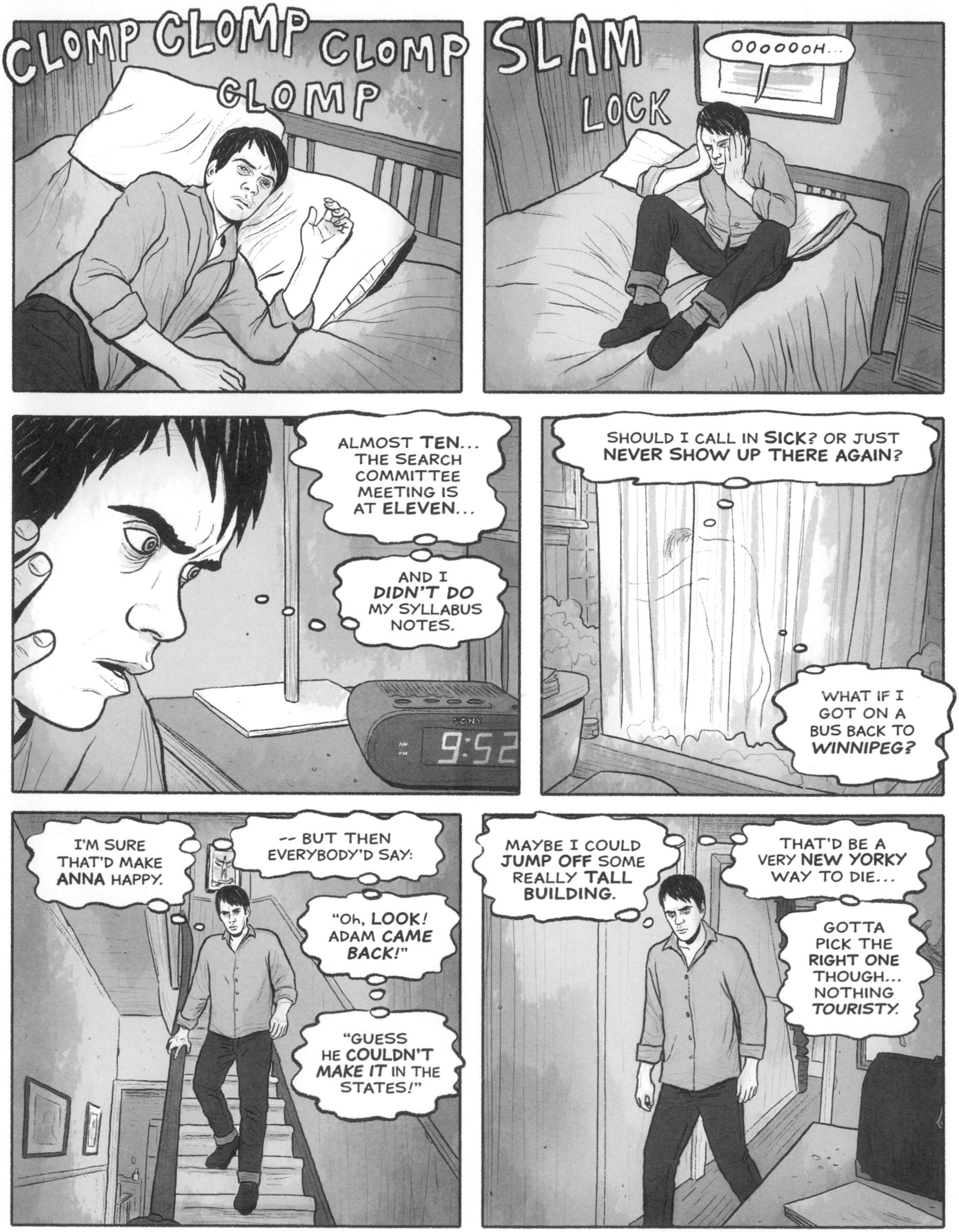
CLOMP CLOMP CLOMP
CLOMP
SLAM
LOCK
OOOOOOH...
ALMOST TEN... THE SEARCH COMMITTEE MEETING IS AT ELEVEN...
AND I DIDN'T DO MY SYLLABUS NOTES.
SONY
9:52
SHOULD I CALL IN SICK? OR JUST NEVER SHOW UP THERE AGAIN?
WHAT IF I GOT ON A BUS BACK TO WINNIPEG?
I'M SURE THAT'D MAKE ANNA HAPPY.
-- BUT THEN EVERYBODY'D SAY:
"Oh, LOOK! ADAM CAME BACK!"
"GUESS HE COULDN'T MAKE IT IN THE STATES!"
MAYBE I COULD JUMP OFF SOME REALLY TALL BUILDING.
THAT'D BE A VERY NEW YORKY WAY TO DIE...
GOTTA PICK THE RIGHT ONE THOUGH... NOTHING TOURISTY.

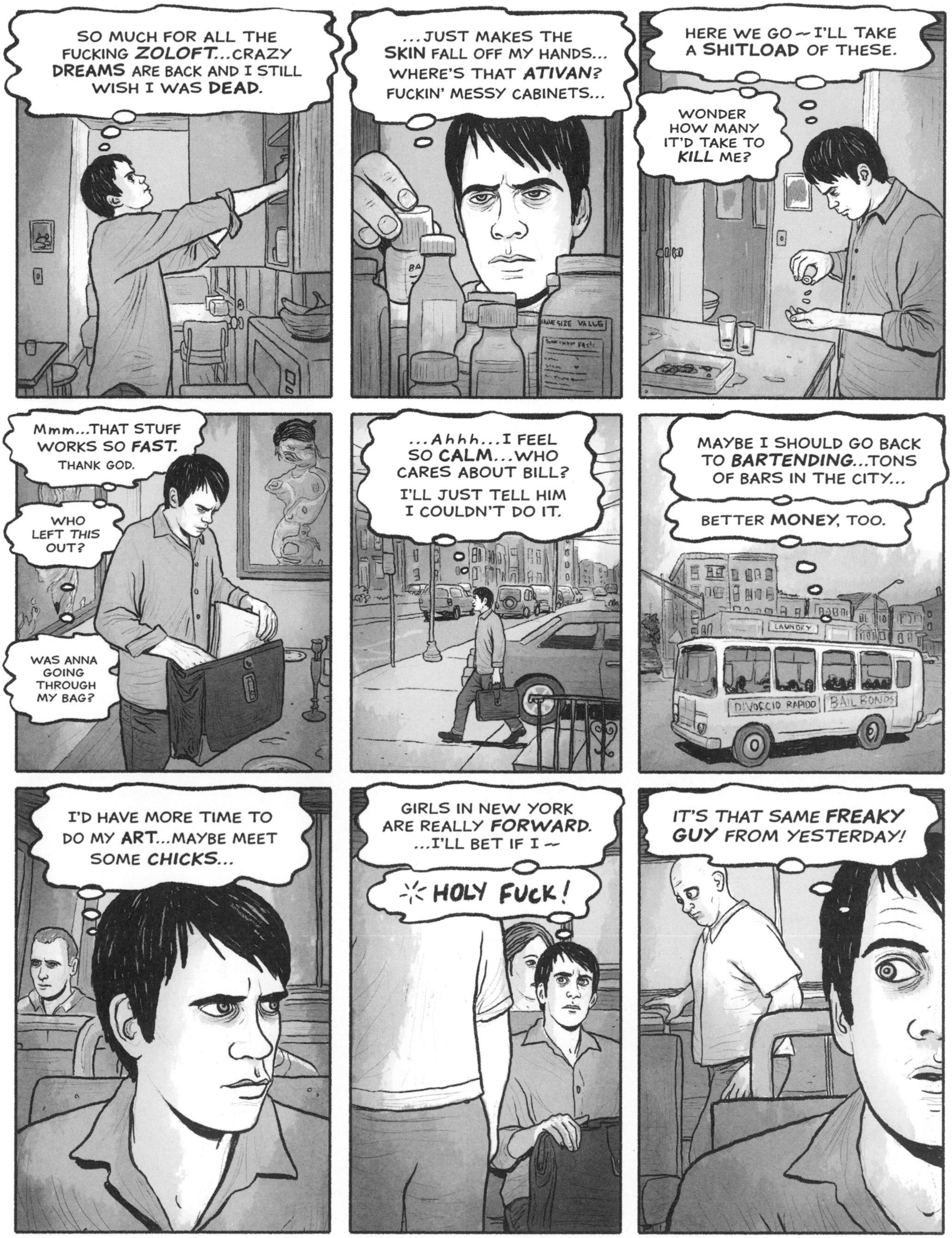
SO MUCH FOR ALL THE FUCKING ZOLOFT...CRAZY DREAMS ARE BACK AND I STILL WISH I WAS DEAD.
...JUST MAKES THE SKIN FALL OFF MY HANDS... WHERE'S THAT ATIVAN? FUCKIN' MESSY CABINETS...
HERE WE GO~I'LL TAKE A SHITLOAD OF THESE.
WONDER HOW MANY IT'D TAKE TO KILL ME?
Mmm...THAT STUFF WORKS SO FAST. THANK GOD.
WHO LEFT THIS OUT?
WAS ANNA GOING THROUGH MY BAG?
...Ahhh...I FEEL SO CALM...WHO CARES ABOUT BILL?
I'LL JUST TELL HIM I COULDN'T DO IT.
MAYBE I SHOULD GO BACK TO BARTENDING...TONS OF BARS IN THE CITY...
BETTER MONEY, TOO.
LAUNDRY
DIVORCIO RAPIDO
BAIL BONDS
I'D HAVE MORE TIME TO DO MY ART...MAYBE MEET SOME CHICKS...
GIRLS IN NEW YORK ARE REALLY FORWARD. ...I'LL BET IF I~
HOLY FUCK!
IT'S THAT SAME FREAKY GUY FROM YESTERDAY!

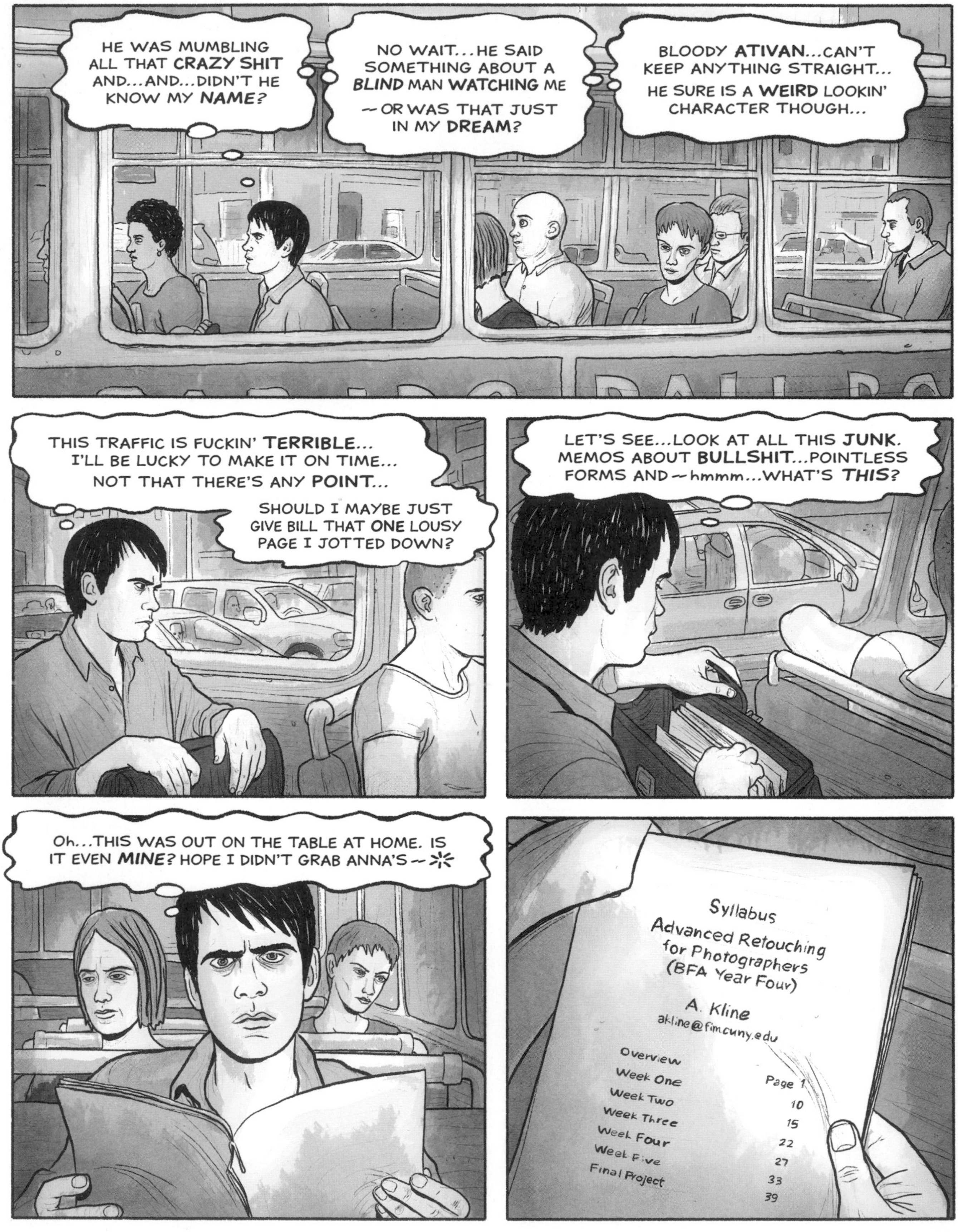
HE WAS MUMBLING ALL THAT CRAZY SHIT AND...AND...DIDN'T HE KNOW MY NAME?
NO WAIT...HE SAID SOMETHING ABOUT A BLIND MAN WATCHING ME —OR WAS THAT JUST IN MY DREAM?
BLOODY ATIVAN...CAN'T KEEP ANYTHING STRAIGHT... HE SURE IS A WEIRD LOOKIN' CHARACTER THOUGH...
THIS TRAFFIC IS FUCKIN' TERRIBLE... I'LL BE LUCKY TO MAKE IT ON TIME... NOT THAT THERE'S ANY POINT...
SHOULD I MAYBE JUST GIVE BILL THAT ONE LOUSY PAGE I JOTTED DOWN?
LET'S SEE...LOOK AT ALL THIS JUNK. MEMOS ABOUT BULLSHIT...POINTLESS FORMS AND —hmmm...WHAT'S THIS?
Oh...THIS WAS OUT ON THE TABLE AT HOME. IS IT EVEN MINE? HOPE I DIDN'T GRAB ANNA'S —
Syllabus
Advanced Retouching for Photographers (BFA Year Four)
A. Kline
akline@fimcuny.edu
Overview
Week One Page 1
Week Two 10
Week Three 15
Week Four 22
Week Five 27
Final Project 33
39

JESUS CHRIST! THIS IS THE WHOLE SYLLABUS! THERE'S FORTY-FIVE FUCKIN' PAGES HERE!

WHEN DID I...I...I DIDN'T WRITE THIS! THIS TOOK SOMEONE A WEEK! WHAT THE FUCK IS GOING ON???

IT~IT SURE SOUNDS LIKE SOMETHING I'D SAY ...IT'S EXACTLY HOW I DO ALL THIS STUFF ...RIGHT DOWN TO THE LITTLE DETAILS!

bigger hair" or

15. Turn the Color Correction Curve Lay make sure the correction still seems perfe after some time spent working on an imag

16. Avoid using the Dodge and Burn tools. darkened, select them with the Lasso Tool s on how defined the area to be corrected is). remove, or soften the area affected by the C Brush, Lasso and Fill or the Gaussian Blur that you can always re-open th each Layer so

THIS IS ~ IT'S LIKE BACK IN CANADA, WHEN I KEPT SEEING THINGS ~ ALL THAT AWFUL SCARY SHIT!

Oh, GOD ~ PLEASE DON'T LET THAT HAPPEN AGAIN!

✳ ~WHAT IF I START SEEIN' Z~

PORT AUTHORITY! ÚLTIMA PARADA!

KISSHH!

OKAY, OKAY, SETTLE DOWN! THIS IS ACTUALLY GOOD...I'LL JUST GIVE THE SYLLABUS TO BILL. PROBLEM SOLVED!

IT'S NOT A NIGHTMARE! IT'S MORE LIKE A DREAM COME TRUE!

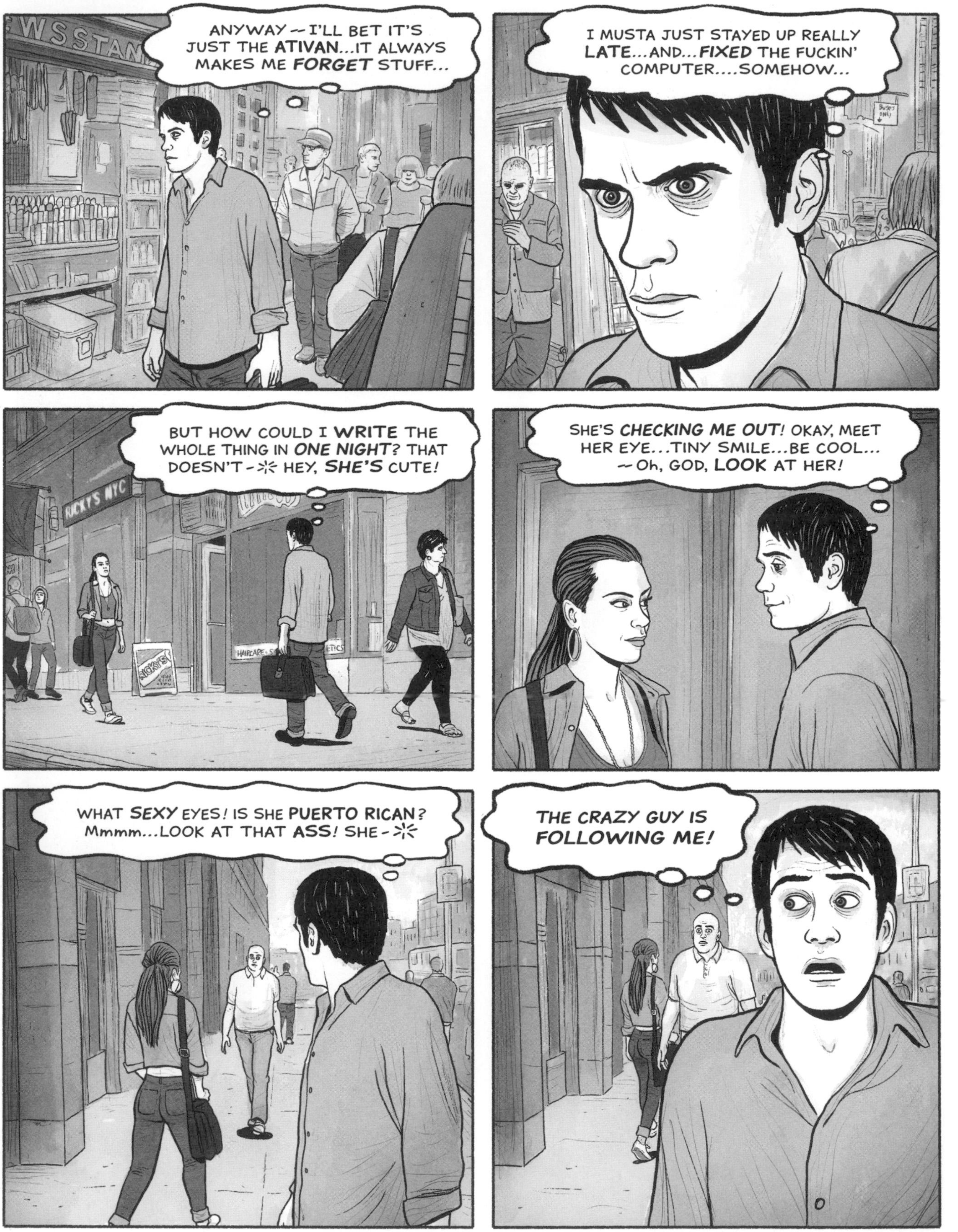
ANYWAY -- I'LL BET IT'S JUST THE ATIVAN...IT ALWAYS MAKES ME FORGET STUFF...
I MUSTA JUST STAYED UP REALLY LATE...AND...FIXED THE FUCKIN' COMPUTER....SOMEHOW...
BUT HOW COULD I WRITE THE WHOLE THING IN ONE NIGHT? THAT DOESN'T - HEY, SHE'S CUTE!
SHE'S CHECKING ME OUT! OKAY, MEET HER EYE...TINY SMILE...BE COOL... -- Oh, GOD, LOOK AT HER!
WHAT SEXY EYES! IS SHE PUERTO RICAN? Mmmm...LOOK AT THAT ASS! SHE -
THE CRAZY GUY IS FOLLOWING ME!

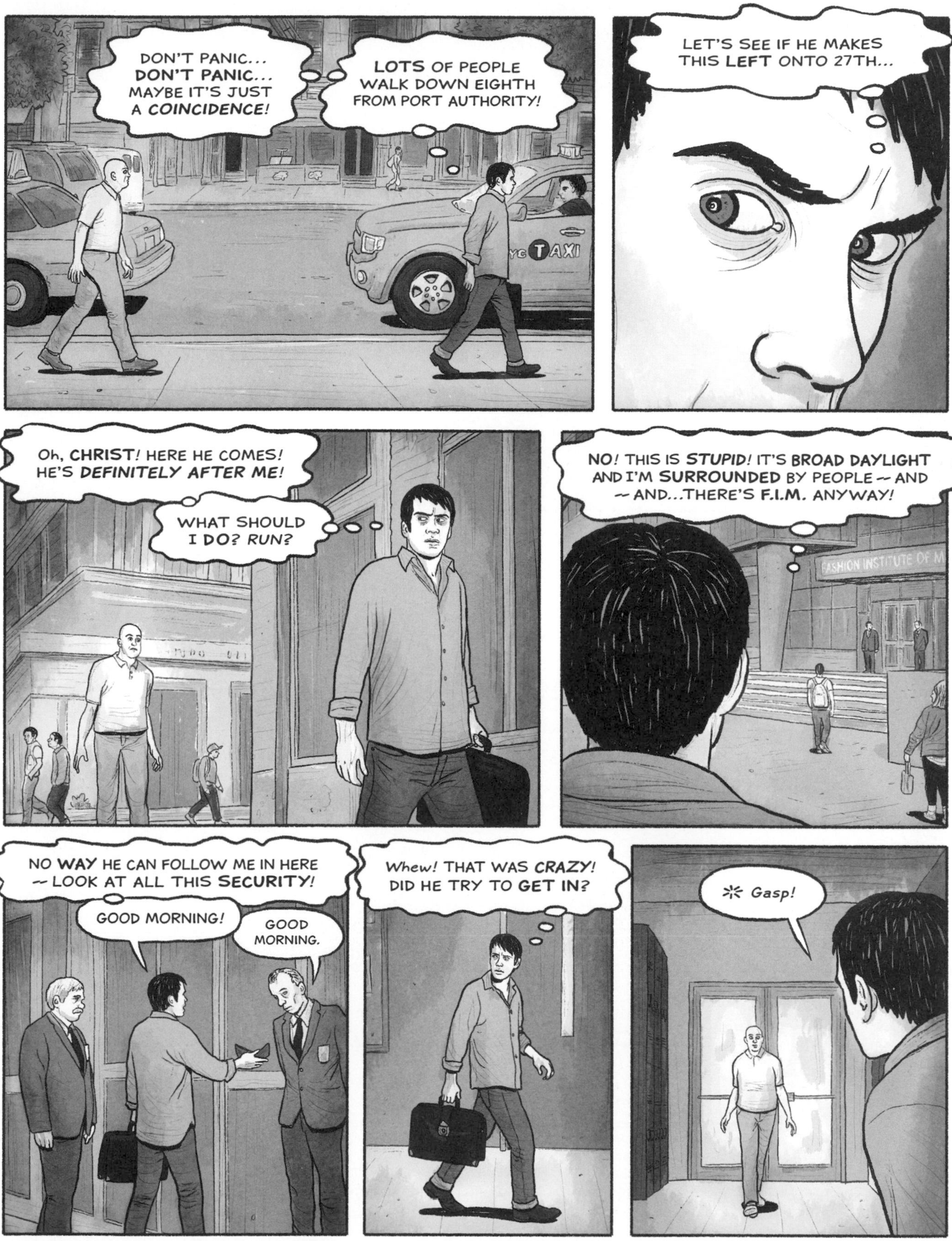

DON'T PANIC... DON'T PANIC... MAYBE IT'S JUST A COINCIDENCE!
LOTS OF PEOPLE WALK DOWN EIGHTH FROM PORT AUTHORITY!
LET'S SEE IF HE MAKES THIS LEFT ONTO 27TH...
Oh, CHRIST! HERE HE COMES! HE'S DEFINITELY AFTER ME!
WHAT SHOULD I DO? RUN?
NO! THIS IS STUPID! IT'S BROAD DAYLIGHT AND I'M SURROUNDED BY PEOPLE -- AND -- AND...THERE'S F.I.M. ANYWAY!
FASHION INSTITUTE OF M
NO WAY HE CAN FOLLOW ME IN HERE -- LOOK AT ALL THIS SECURITY!
GOOD MORNING!
GOOD MORNING.
Whew! THAT WAS CRAZY! DID HE TRY TO GET IN?
Gasp!

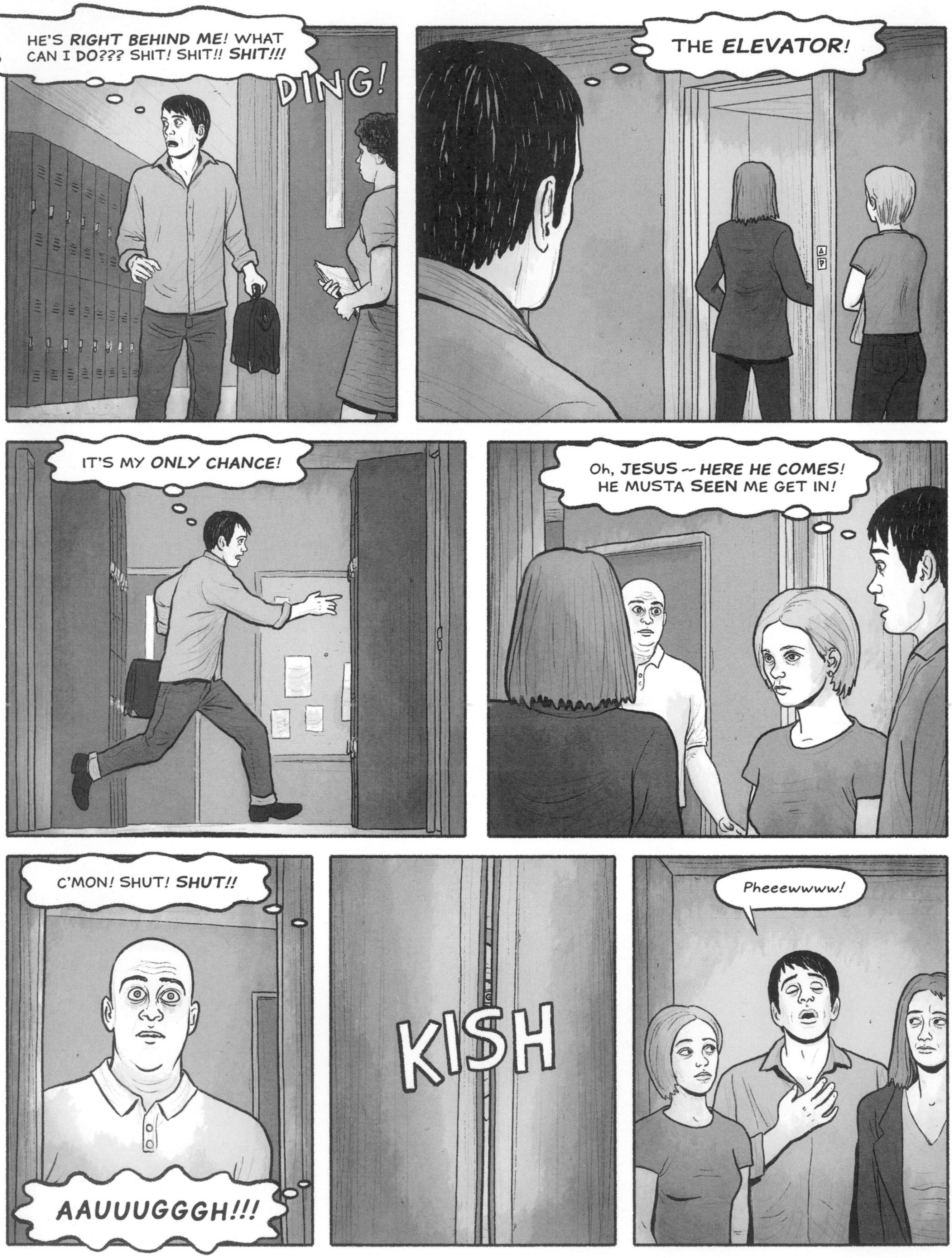
HE'S RIGHT BEHIND ME! WHAT CAN I DO??? SHIT! SHIT!! SHIT!!!
DING!
THE ELEVATOR!
IT'S MY ONLY CHANCE!
Oh, JESUS -- HERE HE COMES! HE MUSTA SEEN ME GET IN!
C'MON! SHUT! SHUT!!
AAUUUGGGH!!!
KISH
Pheeewwww!

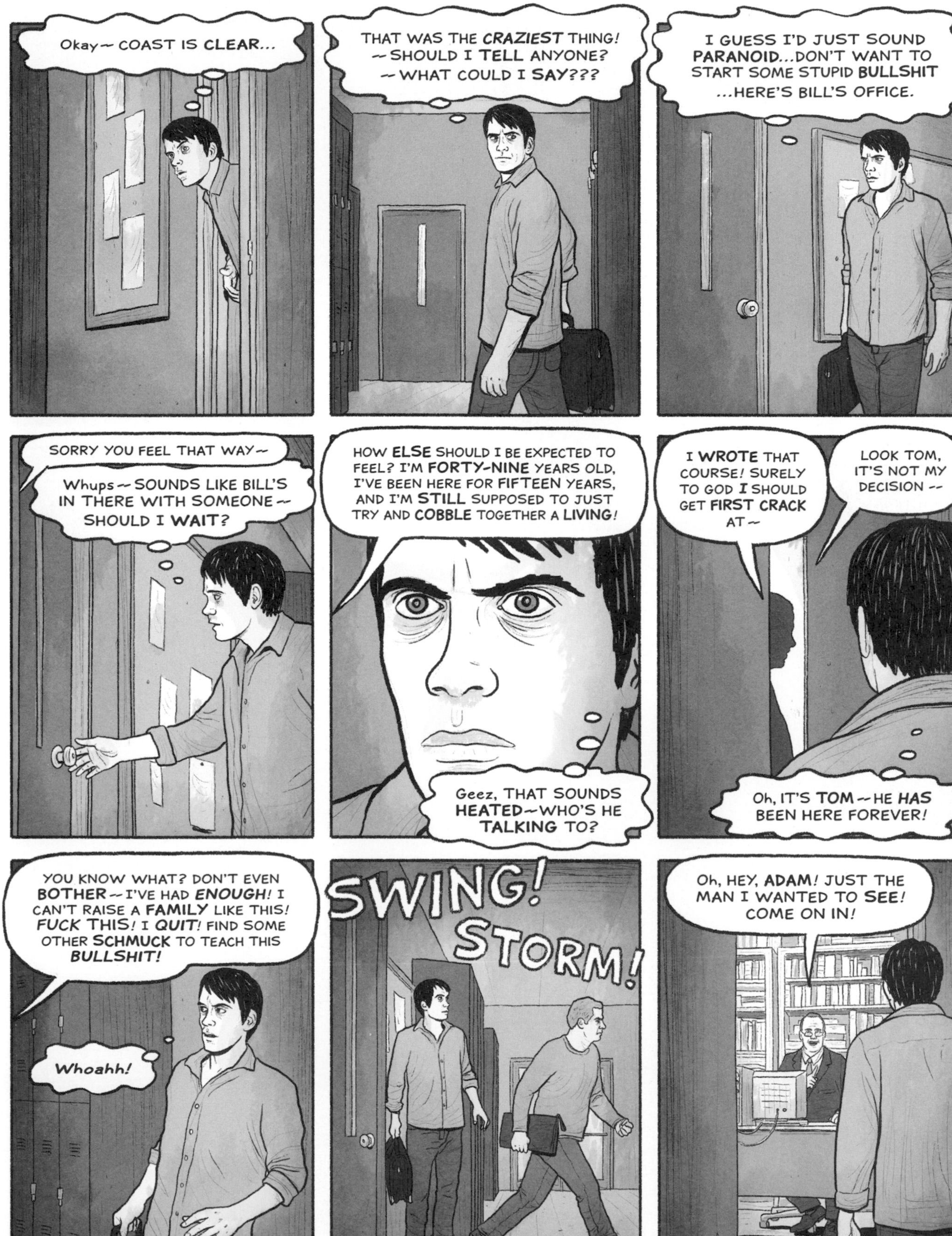
Okay-- COAST IS CLEAR...
THAT WAS THE CRAZIEST THING! --SHOULD I TELL ANYONE? --WHAT COULD I SAY???
I GUESS I'D JUST SOUND PARANOID...DON'T WANT TO START SOME STUPID BULLSHIT ...HERE'S BILL'S OFFICE.
SORRY YOU FEEL THAT WAY--
Whups--SOUNDS LIKE BILL'S IN THERE WITH SOMEONE-- SHOULD I WAIT?
HOW ELSE SHOULD I BE EXPECTED TO FEEL? I'M FORTY-NINE YEARS OLD, I'VE BEEN HERE FOR FIFTEEN YEARS, AND I'M STILL SUPPOSED TO JUST TRY AND COBBLE TOGETHER A LIVING!
Geez, THAT SOUNDS HEATED--WHO'S HE TALKING TO?
I WROTE THAT COURSE! SURELY TO GOD I SHOULD GET FIRST CRACK AT--
LOOK TOM, IT'S NOT MY DECISION --
Oh, IT'S TOM--HE HAS BEEN HERE FOREVER!
YOU KNOW WHAT? DON'T EVEN BOTHER--I'VE HAD ENOUGH! I CAN'T RAISE A FAMILY LIKE THIS! FUCK THIS! I QUIT! FIND SOME OTHER SCHMUCK TO TEACH THIS BULLSHIT!
Whoahh!
SWING!
STORM!
Oh, HEY, ADAM! JUST THE MAN I WANTED TO SEE! COME ON IN!

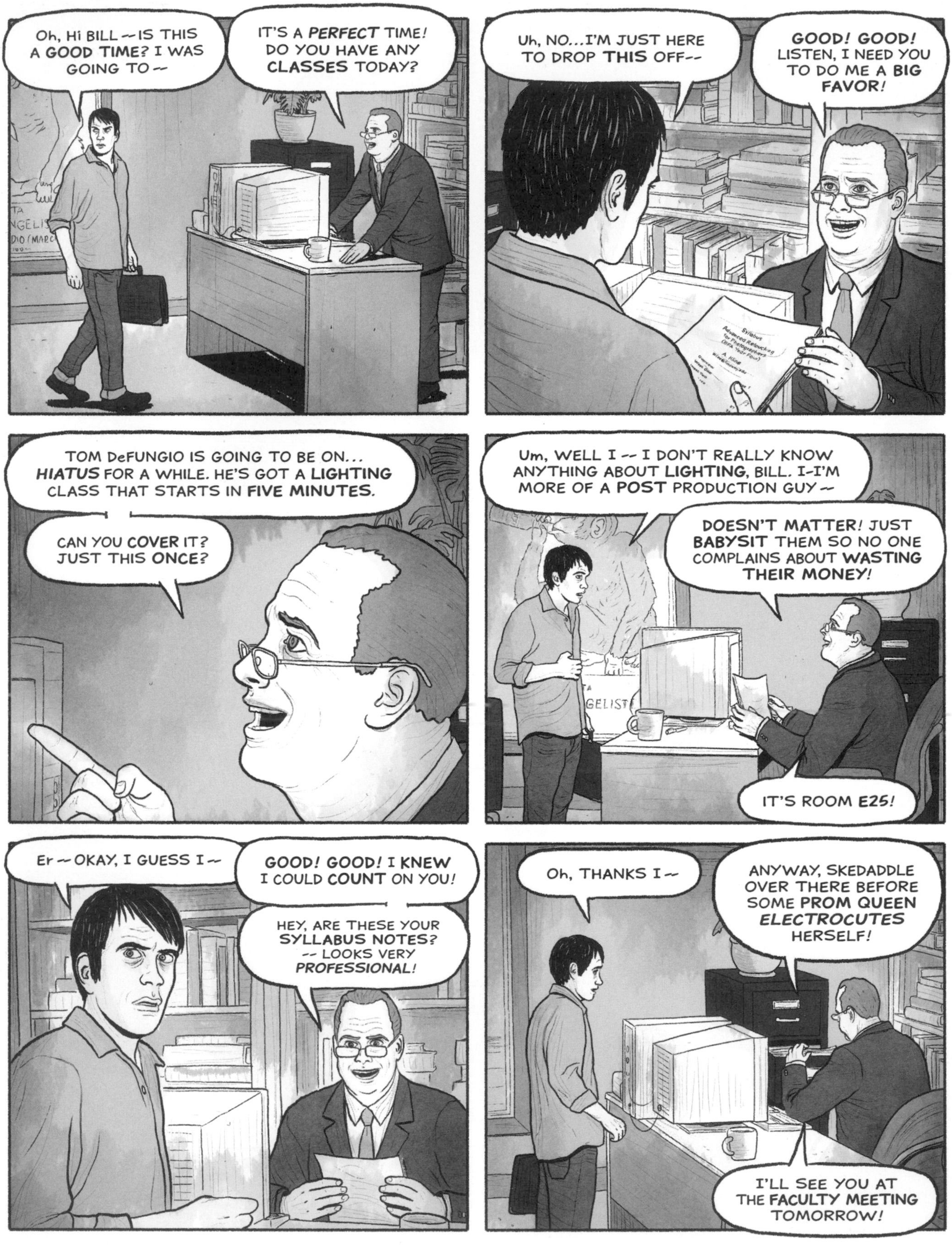
Oh, Hi BILL -- IS THIS A GOOD TIME? I WAS GOING TO --
IT'S A PERFECT TIME! DO YOU HAVE ANY CLASSES TODAY?
Uh, NO... I'M JUST HERE TO DROP THIS OFF--
GOOD! GOOD! LISTEN, I NEED YOU TO DO ME A BIG FAVOR!
TOM DeFUNGIO IS GOING TO BE ON... HIATUS FOR A WHILE. HE'S GOT A LIGHTING CLASS THAT STARTS IN FIVE MINUTES.
CAN YOU COVER IT? JUST THIS ONCE?
Um, WELL I -- I DON'T REALLY KNOW ANYTHING ABOUT LIGHTING, BILL. I-I'M MORE OF A POST PRODUCTION GUY --
DOESN'T MATTER! JUST BABYSIT THEM SO NO ONE COMPLAINS ABOUT WASTING THEIR MONEY!
IT'S ROOM E25!
Er -- OKAY, I GUESS I --
GOOD! GOOD! I KNEW I COULD COUNT ON YOU!
HEY, ARE THESE YOUR SYLLABUS NOTES? -- LOOKS VERY PROFESSIONAL!
Oh, THANKS I --
ANYWAY, SKEDADDLE OVER THERE BEFORE SOME PROM QUEEN ELECTROCUTES HERSELF!
I'LL SEE YOU AT THE FACULTY MEETING TOMORROW!

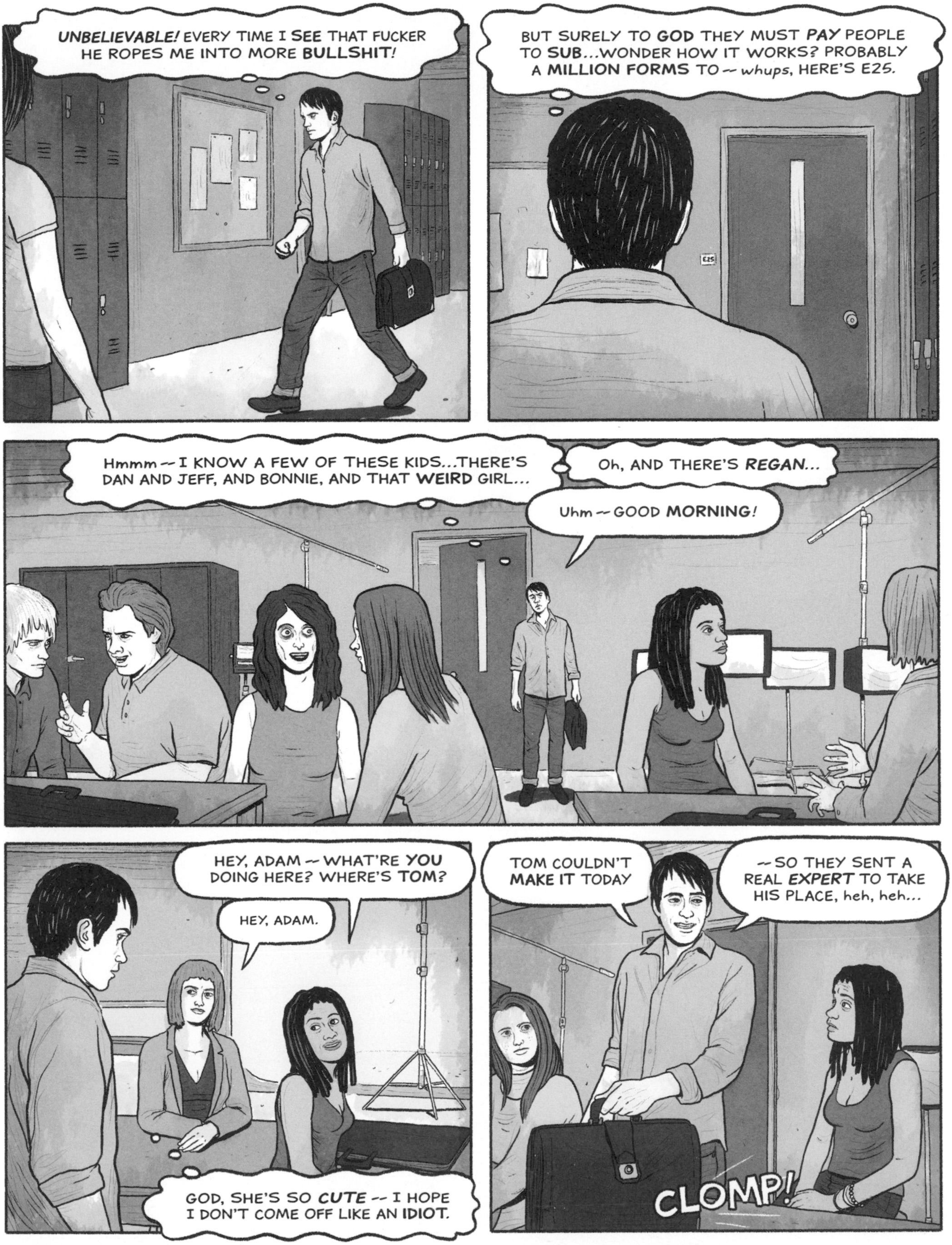
UNBELIEVABLE! EVERY TIME I SEE THAT FUCKER HE ROPES ME INTO MORE BULLSHIT!
BUT SURELY TO GOD THEY MUST PAY PEOPLE TO SUB...WONDER HOW IT WORKS? PROBABLY A MILLION FORMS TO -- whups, HERE'S E25.
E25
Hmmm -- I KNOW A FEW OF THESE KIDS...THERE'S DAN AND JEFF, AND BONNIE, AND THAT WEIRD GIRL...
Oh, AND THERE'S REGAN...
Uhm -- GOOD MORNING!
HEY, ADAM -- WHAT'RE YOU DOING HERE? WHERE'S TOM?
HEY, ADAM.
GOD, SHE'S SO CUTE -- I HOPE I DON'T COME OFF LIKE AN IDIOT.
TOM COULDN'T MAKE IT TODAY
-- SO THEY SENT A REAL EXPERT TO TAKE HIS PLACE, heh, heh...
CLOMP!

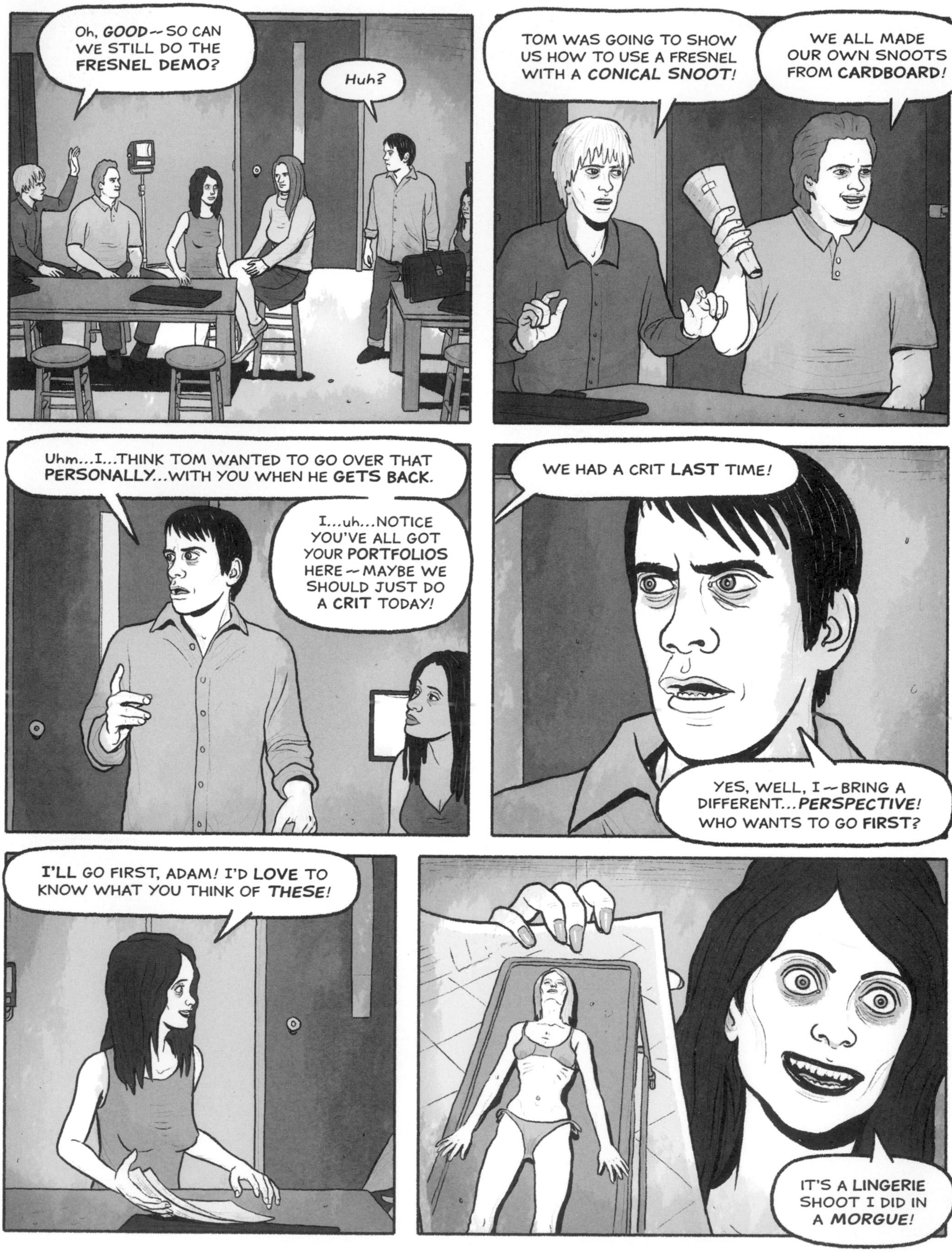
Oh, GOOD-- SO CAN WE STILL DO THE FRESNEL DEMO?
Huh?
TOM WAS GOING TO SHOW US HOW TO USE A FRESNEL WITH A CONICAL SNOOT!
WE ALL MADE OUR OWN SNOOTS FROM CARDBOARD!
Uhm...I...THINK TOM WANTED TO GO OVER THAT PERSONALLY...WITH YOU WHEN HE GETS BACK.
I...uh...NOTICE YOU'VE ALL GOT YOUR PORTFOLIOS HERE-- MAYBE WE SHOULD JUST DO A CRIT TODAY!
WE HAD A CRIT LAST TIME!
YES, WELL, I-- BRING A DIFFERENT...PERSPECTIVE! WHO WANTS TO GO FIRST?
I'LL GO FIRST, ADAM! I'D LOVE TO KNOW WHAT YOU THINK OF THESE!
IT'S A LINGERIE SHOOT I DID IN A MORGUE!

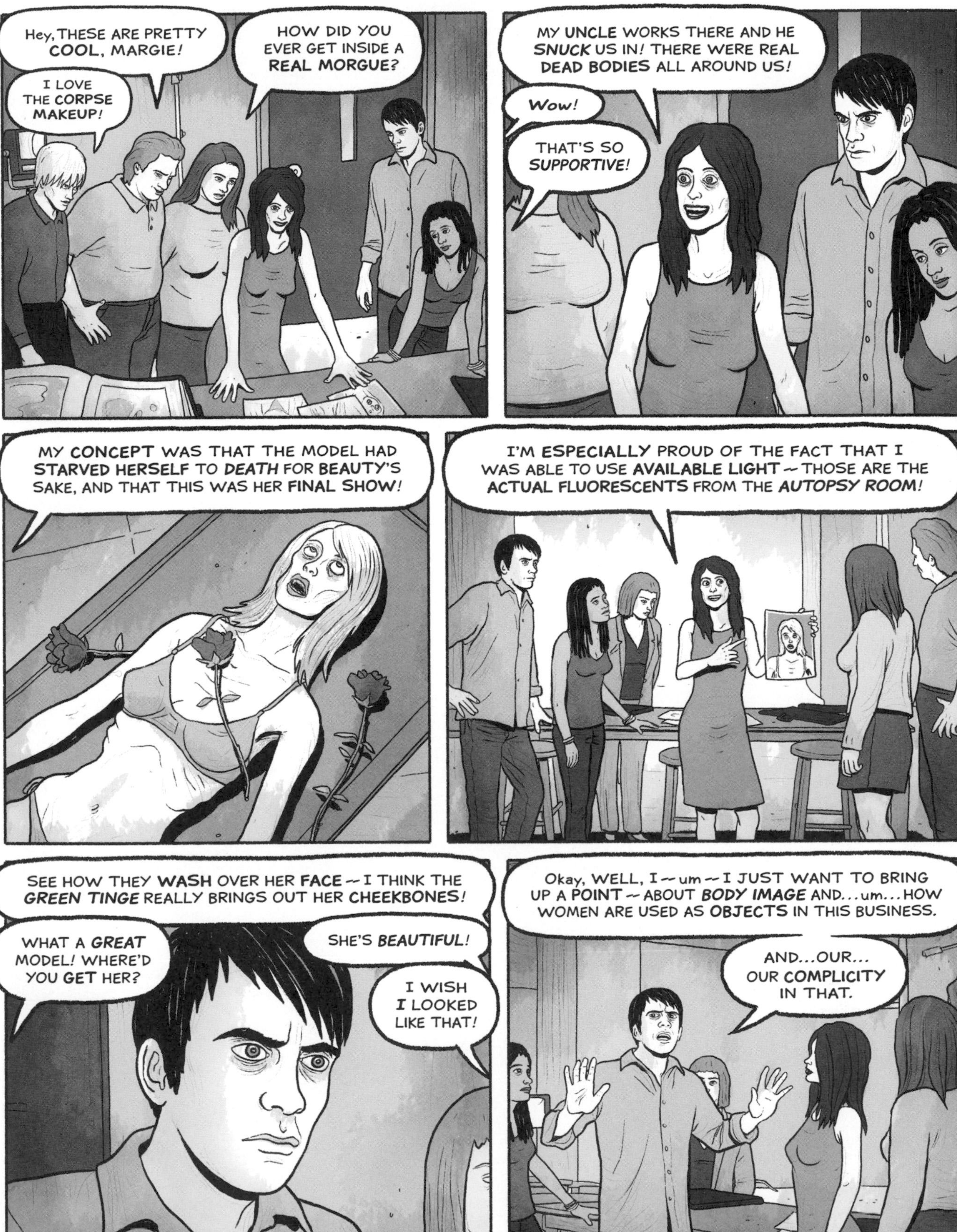
Hey, THESE ARE PRETTY COOL, MARGIE!
I LOVE THE CORPSE MAKEUP!
HOW DID YOU EVER GET INSIDE A REAL MORGUE?
MY UNCLE WORKS THERE AND HE SNUCK US IN! THERE WERE REAL DEAD BODIES ALL AROUND US!
Wow!
THAT'S SO SUPPORTIVE!
MY CONCEPT WAS THAT THE MODEL HAD STARVED HERSELF TO DEATH FOR BEAUTY'S SAKE, AND THAT THIS WAS HER FINAL SHOW!
I'M ESPECIALLY PROUD OF THE FACT THAT I WAS ABLE TO USE AVAILABLE LIGHT -- THOSE ARE THE ACTUAL FLUORESCENTS FROM THE AUTOPSY ROOM!
SEE HOW THEY WASH OVER HER FACE -- I THINK THE GREEN TINGE REALLY BRINGS OUT HER CHEEKBONES!
WHAT A GREAT MODEL! WHERE'D YOU GET HER?
SHE'S BEAUTIFUL!
I WISH I LOOKED LIKE THAT!
Okay, WELL, I -- um -- I JUST WANT TO BRING UP A POINT -- ABOUT BODY IMAGE AND... um... HOW WOMEN ARE USED AS OBJECTS IN THIS BUSINESS.
AND... OUR... OUR COMPLICITY IN THAT.

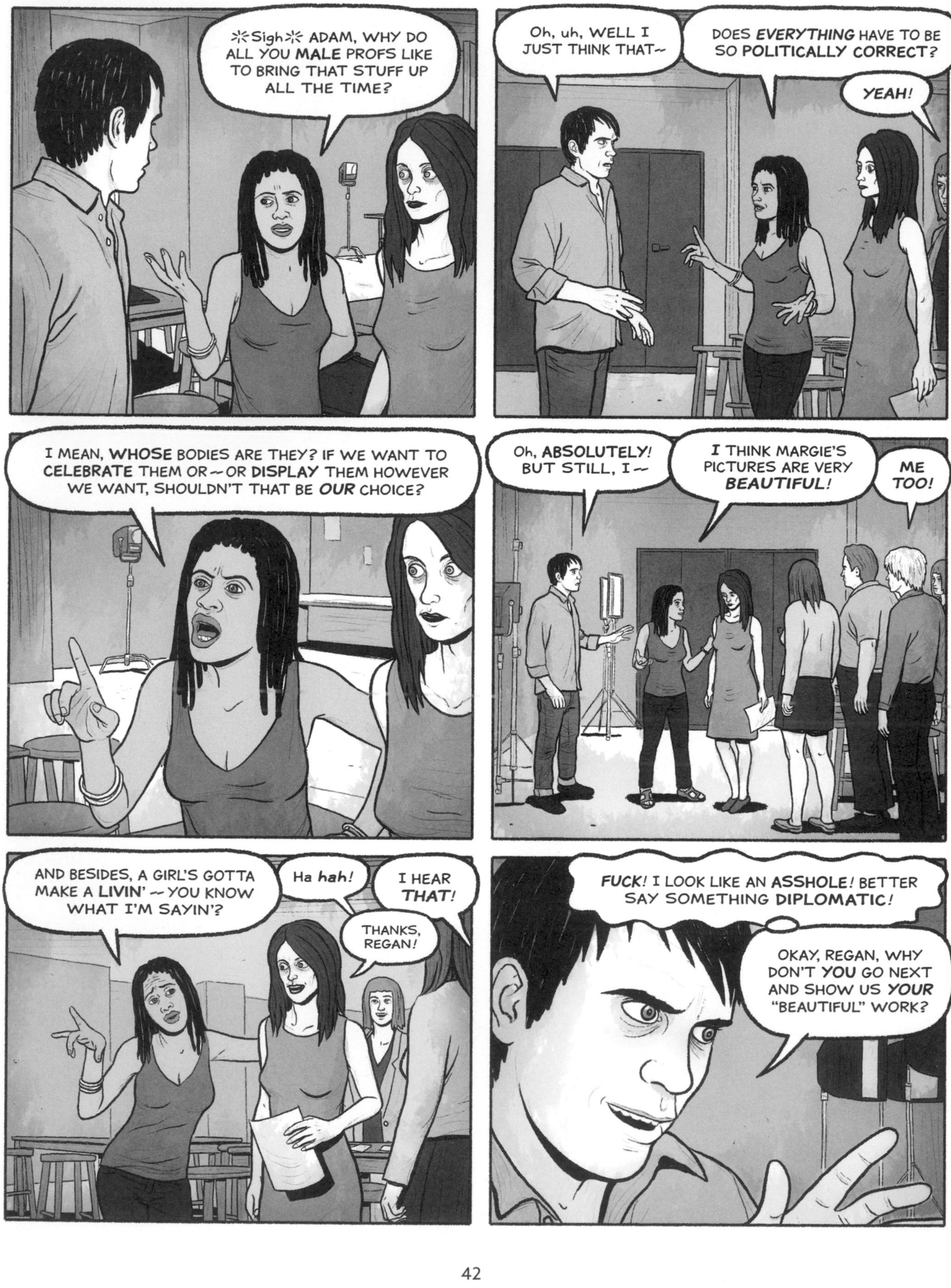
✳Sigh✳ ADAM, WHY DO ALL YOU MALE PROFS LIKE TO BRING THAT STUFF UP ALL THE TIME?
Oh, uh, WELL I JUST THINK THAT--
DOES EVERYTHING HAVE TO BE SO POLITICALLY CORRECT?
YEAH!
I MEAN, WHOSE BODIES ARE THEY? IF WE WANT TO CELEBRATE THEM OR--OR DISPLAY THEM HOWEVER WE WANT, SHOULDN'T THAT BE OUR CHOICE?
Oh, ABSOLUTELY! BUT STILL, I--
I THINK MARGIE'S PICTURES ARE VERY BEAUTIFUL!
ME TOO!
AND BESIDES, A GIRL'S GOTTA MAKE A LIVIN'--YOU KNOW WHAT I'M SAYIN'?
Ha hah!
I HEAR THAT!
THANKS, REGAN!
FUCK! I LOOK LIKE AN ASSHOLE! BETTER SAY SOMETHING DIPLOMATIC!
OKAY, REGAN, WHY DON'T YOU GO NEXT AND SHOW US YOUR "BEAUTIFUL" WORK?

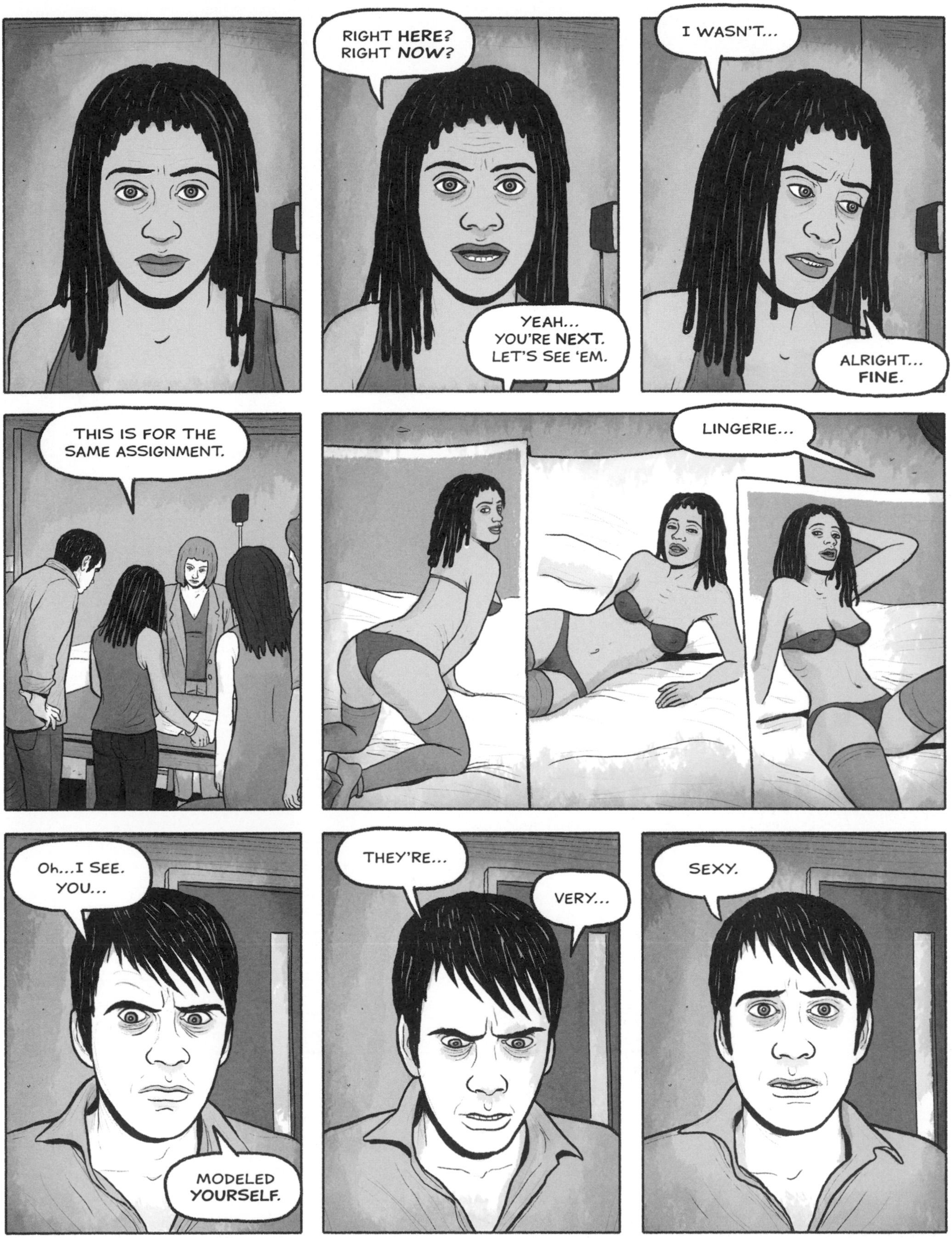
RIGHT HERE? RIGHT NOW?
YEAH... YOU'RE NEXT. LET'S SEE 'EM.
I WASN'T...
ALRIGHT... FINE.
THIS IS FOR THE SAME ASSIGNMENT.
LINGERIE...
Oh...I SEE. YOU...
MODELED YOURSELF.
THEY'RE...
VERY...
SEXY.

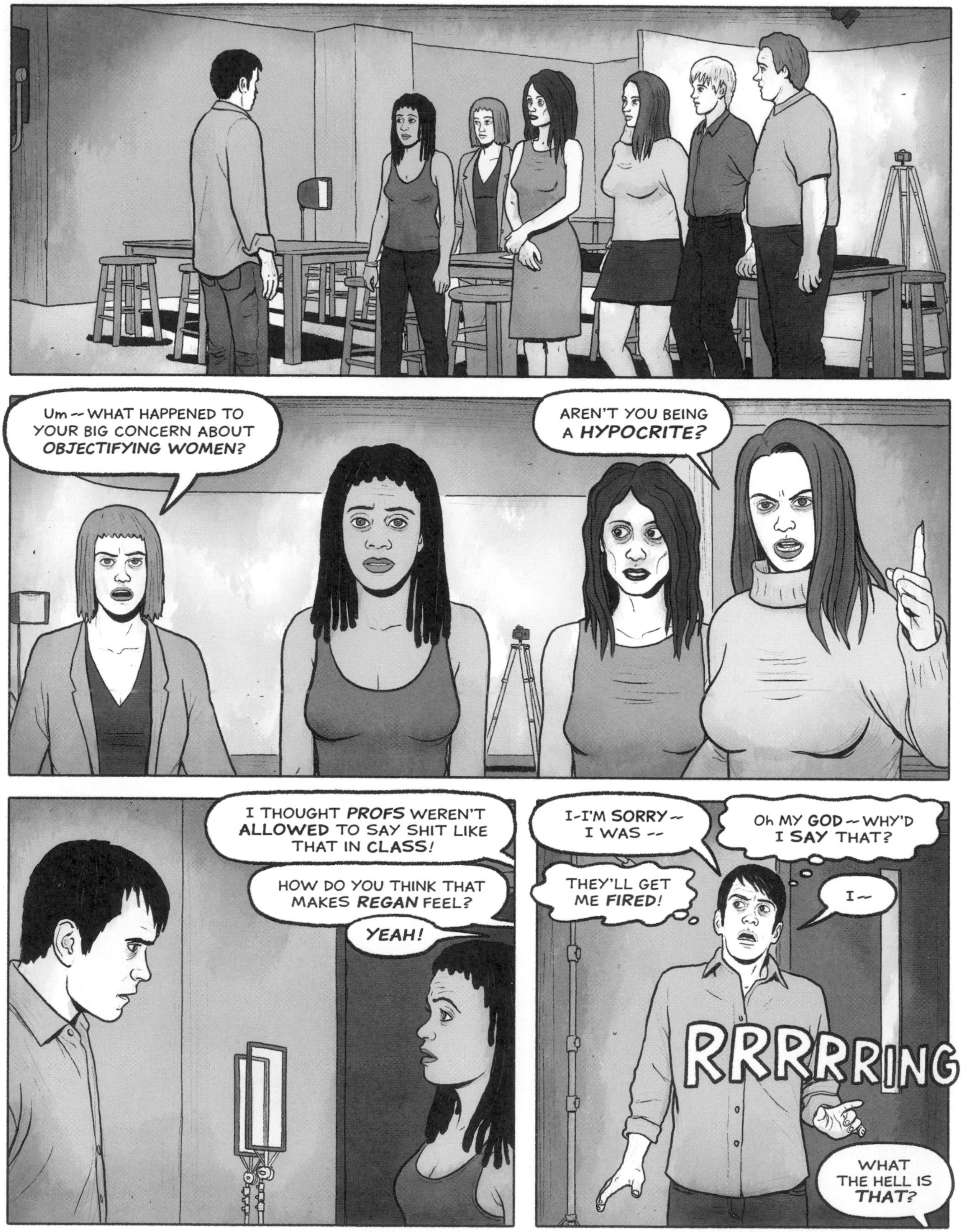
Um -- WHAT HAPPENED TO YOUR BIG CONCERN ABOUT OBJECTIFYING WOMEN?
AREN'T YOU BEING A HYPOCRITE?
I THOUGHT PROFS WEREN'T ALLOWED TO SAY SHIT LIKE THAT IN CLASS!
HOW DO YOU THINK THAT MAKES REGAN FEEL?
YEAH!
I-I'M SORRY -- I WAS --
Oh MY GOD -- WHY'D I SAY THAT?
THEY'LL GET ME FIRED!
I --
RRRRRING
WHAT THE HELL IS THAT?

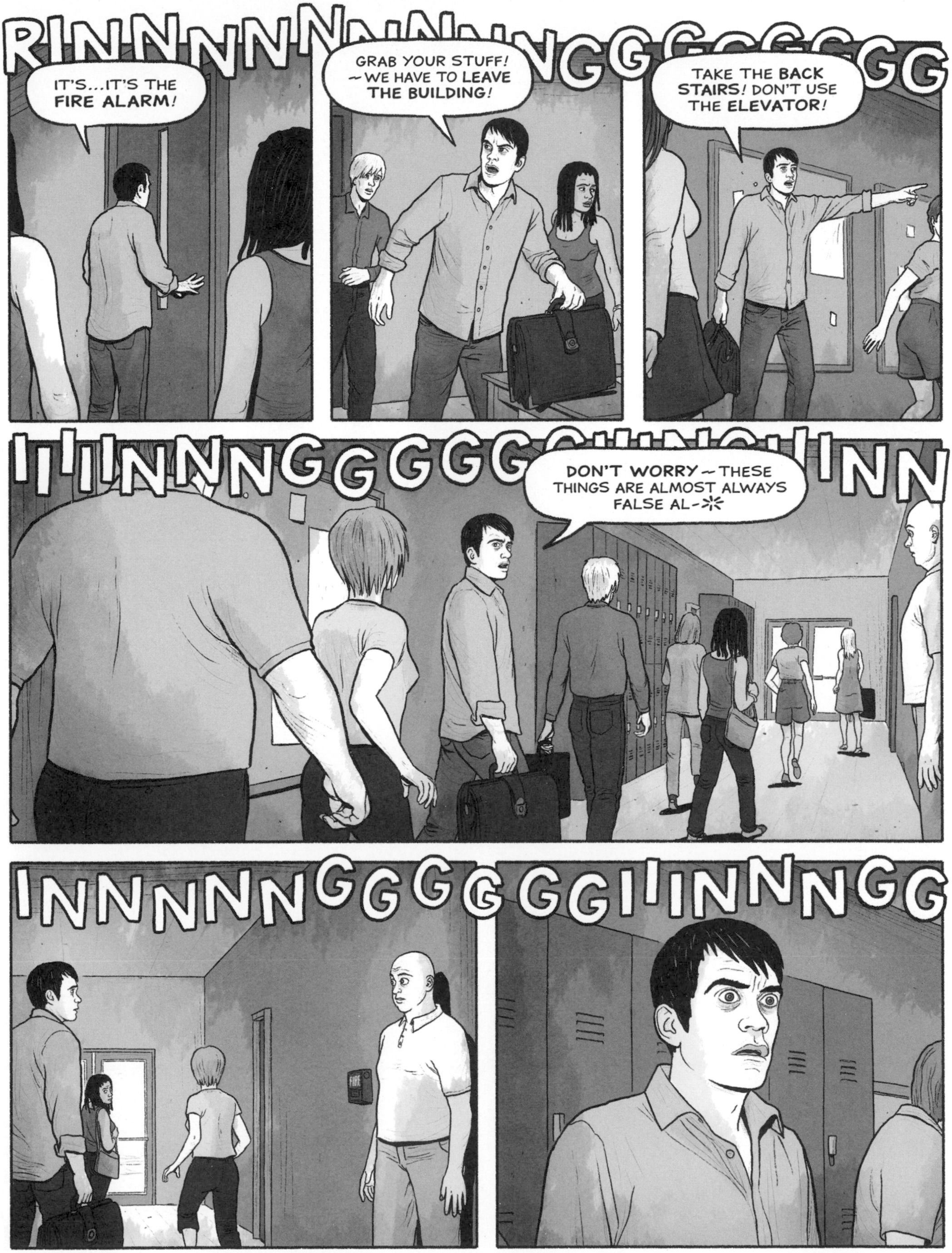
RINNNNNNNNNNGGGGGGGG
IT'S...IT'S THE FIRE ALARM!
GRAB YOUR STUFF! ~WE HAVE TO LEAVE THE BUILDING!
TAKE THE BACK STAIRS! DON'T USE THE ELEVATOR!
IIINNNNGGGG
DON'T WORRY~THESE THINGS ARE ALMOST ALWAYS FALSE AL-
IINN
INNNNNGGGGGGIINNNGG
FIRE

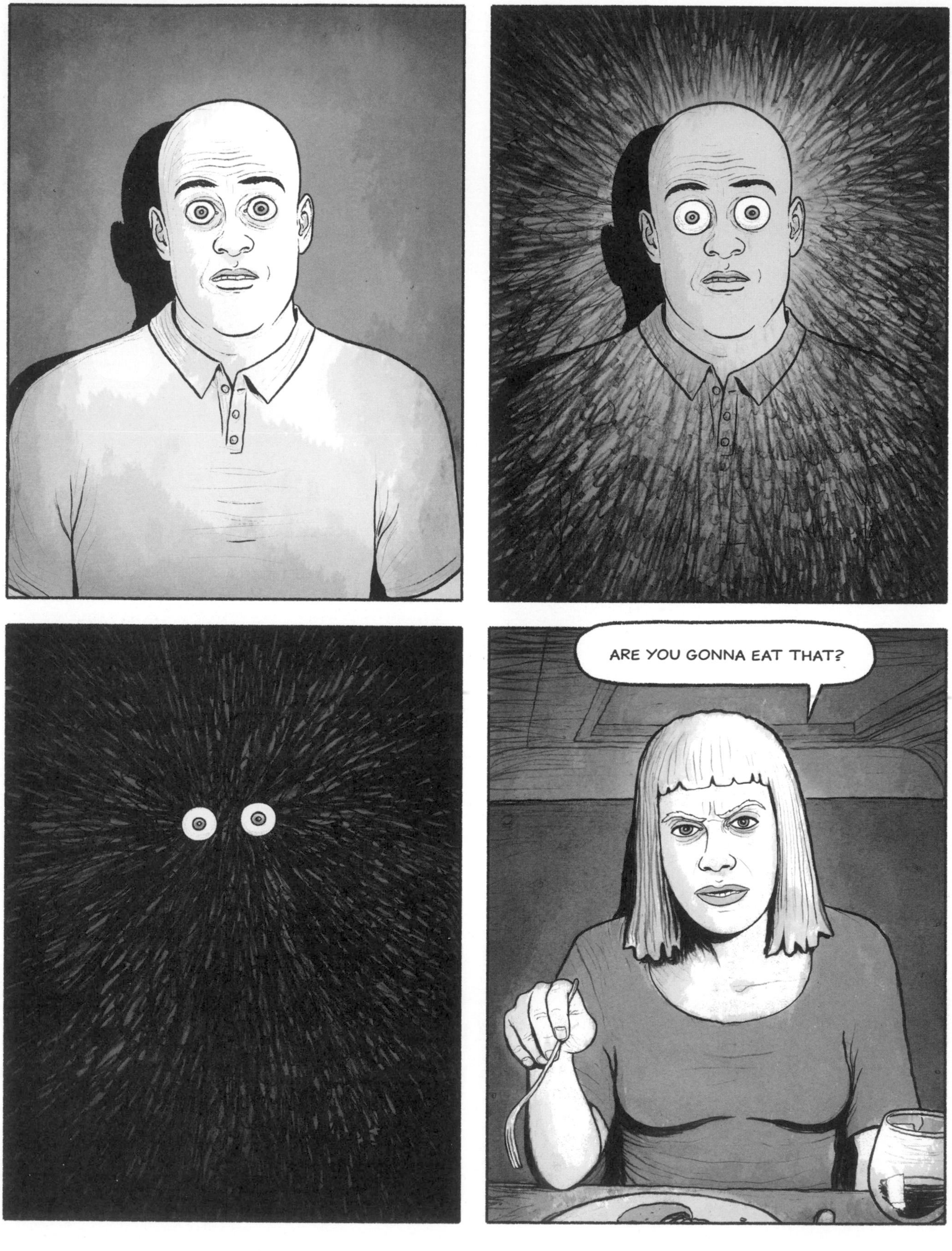
ARE YOU GONNA EAT THAT?

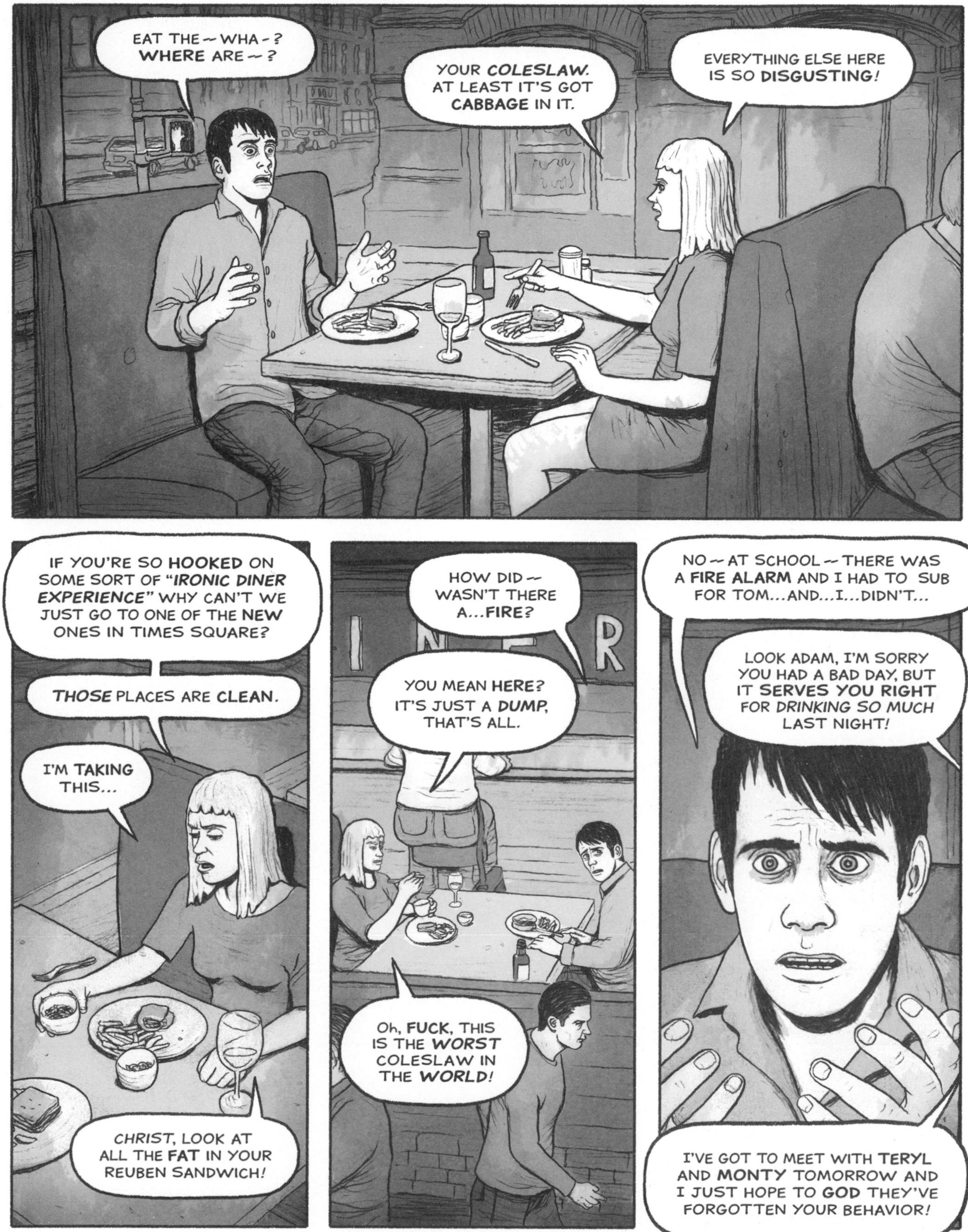

EAT THE -- WHA - ? WHERE ARE -- ?
YOUR COLESLAW. AT LEAST IT'S GOT CABBAGE IN IT.
EVERYTHING ELSE HERE IS SO DISGUSTING!
IF YOU'RE SO HOOKED ON SOME SORT OF "IRONIC DINER EXPERIENCE" WHY CAN'T WE JUST GO TO ONE OF THE NEW ONES IN TIMES SQUARE?
THOSE PLACES ARE CLEAN.
I'M TAKING THIS...
CHRIST, LOOK AT ALL THE FAT IN YOUR REUBEN SANDWICH!
HOW DID -- WASN'T THERE A...FIRE?
YOU MEAN HERE? IT'S JUST A DUMP, THAT'S ALL.
Oh, FUCK, THIS IS THE WORST COLESLAW IN THE WORLD!
NO -- AT SCHOOL -- THERE WAS A FIRE ALARM AND I HAD TO SUB FOR TOM...AND...I...DIDN'T...
LOOK ADAM, I'M SORRY YOU HAD A BAD DAY, BUT IT SERVES YOU RIGHT FOR DRINKING SO MUCH LAST NIGHT!
I'VE GOT TO MEET WITH TERYL AND MONTY TOMORROW AND I JUST HOPE TO GOD THEY'VE FORGOTTEN YOUR BEHAVIOR!

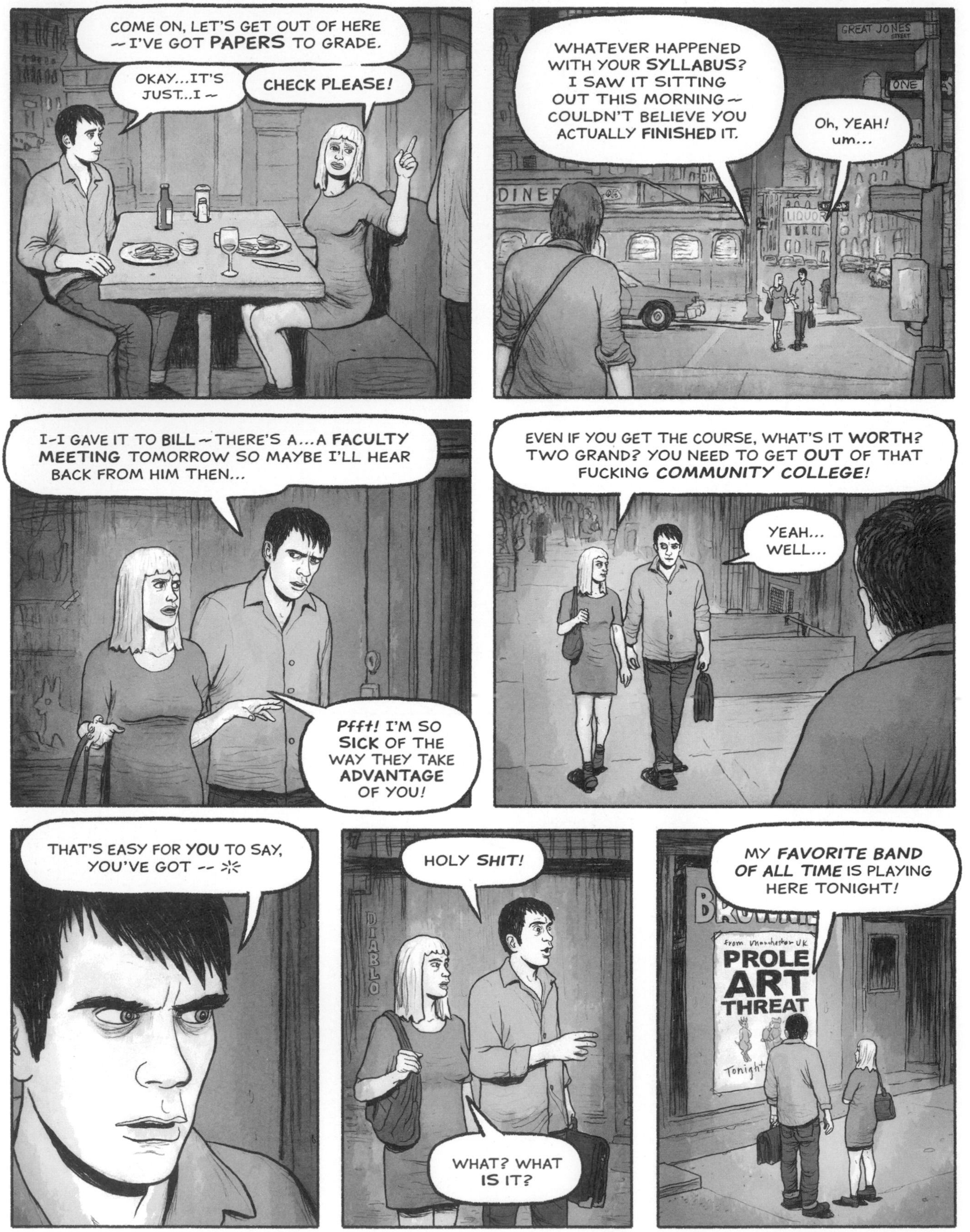
COME ON, LET'S GET OUT OF HERE — I'VE GOT PAPERS TO GRADE.
OKAY...IT'S JUST...I —
CHECK PLEASE!
GREAT JONES STREET
ONE
WHATEVER HAPPENED WITH YOUR SYLLABUS? I SAW IT SITTING OUT THIS MORNING — COULDN'T BELIEVE YOU ACTUALLY FINISHED IT.
Oh, YEAH! um...
DINER
LIQUOR
I-I GAVE IT TO BILL — THERE'S A...A FACULTY MEETING TOMORROW SO MAYBE I'LL HEAR BACK FROM HIM THEN...
Pfft! I'M SO SICK OF THE WAY THEY TAKE ADVANTAGE OF YOU!
EVEN IF YOU GET THE COURSE, WHAT'S IT WORTH? TWO GRAND? YOU NEED TO GET OUT OF THAT FUCKING COMMUNITY COLLEGE!
YEAH... WELL...
THAT'S EASY FOR YOU TO SAY, YOU'VE GOT --
HOLY SHIT!
DIABLO
WHAT? WHAT IS IT?
MY FAVORITE BAND OF ALL TIME IS PLAYING HERE TONIGHT!
from Manchester UK
PROLE ART THREAT
Tonight

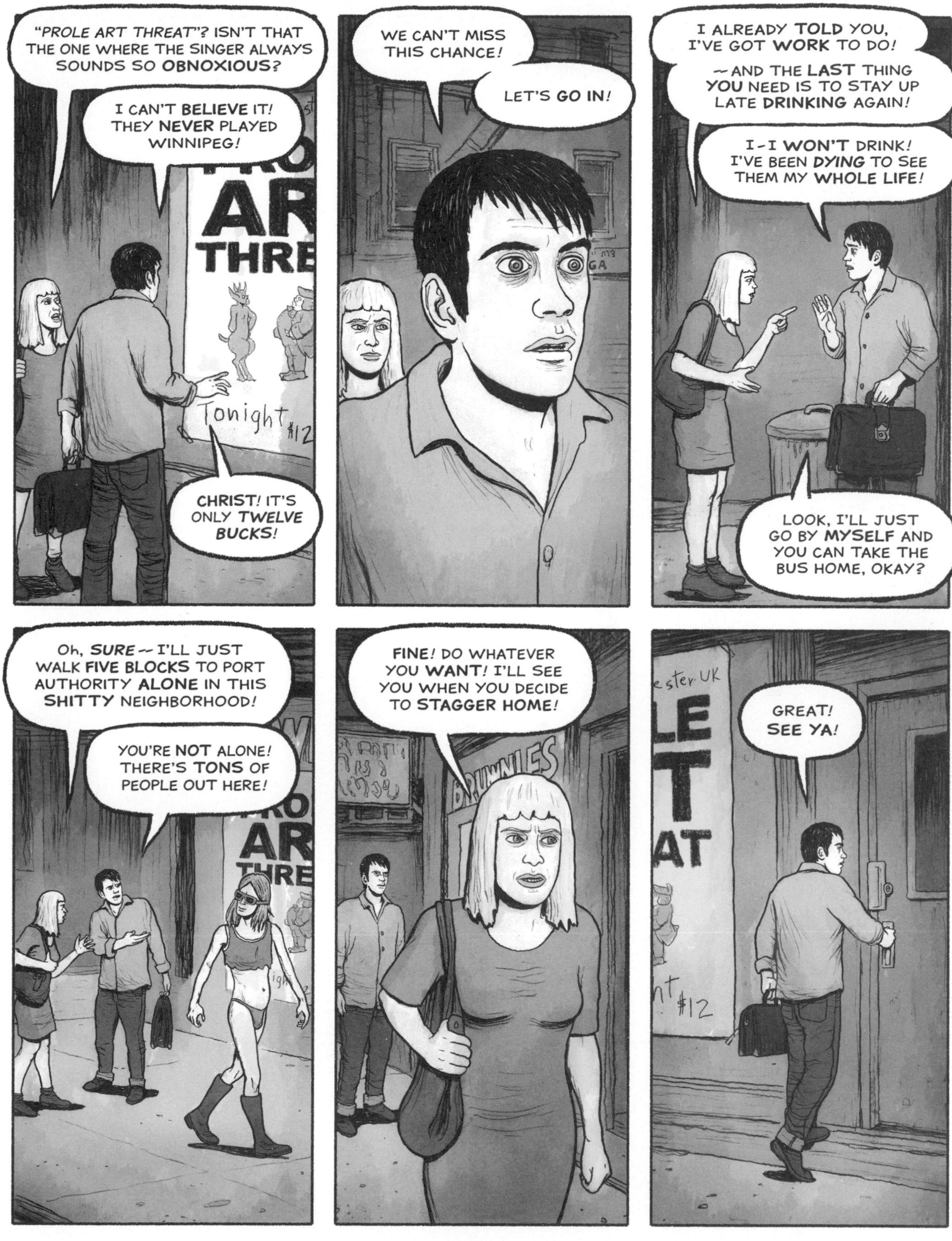
"PROLE ART THREAT"? ISN'T THAT THE ONE WHERE THE SINGER ALWAYS SOUNDS SO OBNOXIOUS?
I CAN'T BELIEVE IT! THEY NEVER PLAYED WINNIPEG!
ART THRE
Tonight $12
CHRIST! IT'S ONLY TWELVE BUCKS!
WE CAN'T MISS THIS CHANCE!
LET'S GO IN!
I ALREADY TOLD YOU, I'VE GOT WORK TO DO!
--AND THE LAST THING YOU NEED IS TO STAY UP LATE DRINKING AGAIN!
I-I WON'T DRINK! I'VE BEEN DYING TO SEE THEM MY WHOLE LIFE!
LOOK, I'LL JUST GO BY MYSELF AND YOU CAN TAKE THE BUS HOME, OKAY?
Oh, SURE-- I'LL JUST WALK FIVE BLOCKS TO PORT AUTHORITY ALONE IN THIS SHITTY NEIGHBORHOOD!
YOU'RE NOT ALONE! THERE'S TONS OF PEOPLE OUT HERE!
FINE! DO WHATEVER YOU WANT! I'LL SEE YOU WHEN YOU DECIDE TO STAGGER HOME!
GREAT! SEE YA!

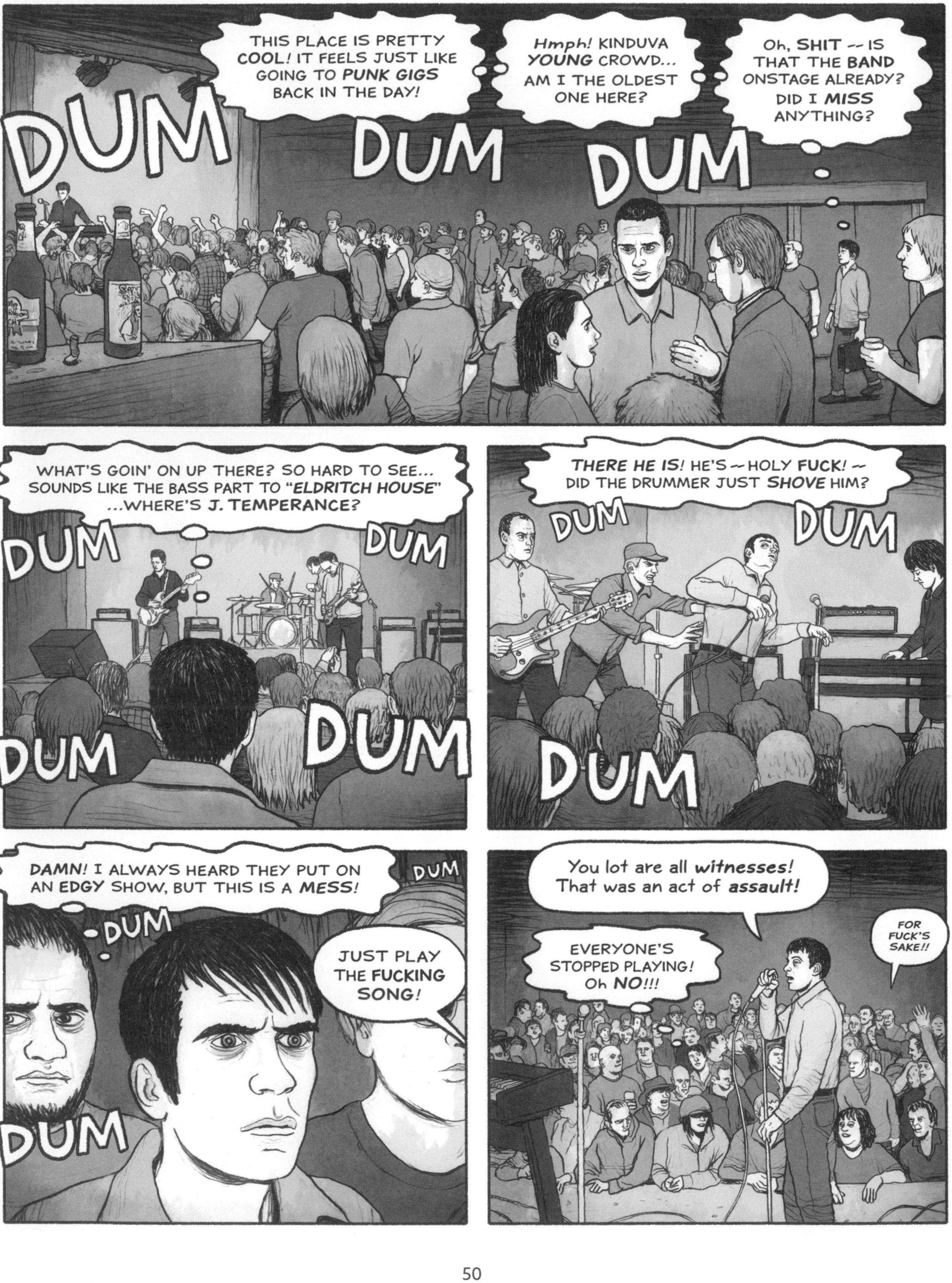
THIS PLACE IS PRETTY COOL! IT FEELS JUST LIKE GOING TO PUNK GIGS BACK IN THE DAY!
Hmph! KINDUVA YOUNG CROWD... AM I THE OLDEST ONE HERE?
Oh, SHIT -- IS THAT THE BAND ONSTAGE ALREADY? DID I MISS ANYTHING?
DUM
DUM
DUM
WHAT'S GOIN' ON UP THERE? SO HARD TO SEE... SOUNDS LIKE THE BASS PART TO "ELDRITCH HOUSE" ...WHERE'S J. TEMPERANCE?
DUM
DUM
DUM
DUM
THERE HE IS! HE'S -- HOLY FUCK! -- DID THE DRUMMER JUST SHOVE HIM?
DUM
DUM
DUM
DAMN! I ALWAYS HEARD THEY PUT ON AN EDGY SHOW, BUT THIS IS A MESS!
DUM
DUM
JUST PLAY THE FUCKING SONG!
DUM
You lot are all witnesses! That was an act of assault!
EVERYONE'S STOPPED PLAYING! Oh NO!!!
FOR FUCK'S SAKE!!

But when a Bengali bus driver tried to bite me, these brave boys were nowhere to be found!
FUCK OFF!
WE QUIT!
You better look at me!
Oh MY FUCKING GOD! THEY'RE LEAVING???
SPOKEN WORD!
I DIDN'T GET TO SEE A SINGLE SONG!
Art is the only true reality...I read that in the New York Times yesterday.
Hah! A CAPELLA!
THIS IS BULLSHIT!
FUCK THIS!
DRUNK ASSHOLE!
You better look!
GET THE BAND BACK ONSTAGE!
FUCKIN' PLAY!
WELL, THAT'S THE STORY OF MY GODDAM LIFE...
I had a dream!
SHUT THE FUCK UP!
FUCK THIS SHIT!
ALWAYS IN THE RIGHT PLACE AT THE WRONG TIME.
In the ghost field!
HEY, ADAM!
FUCK YOU!
Huh?

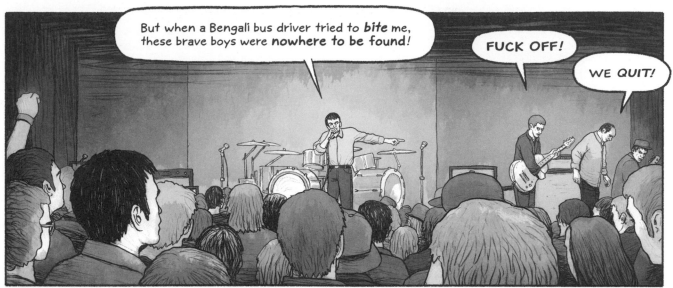

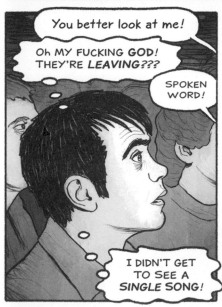

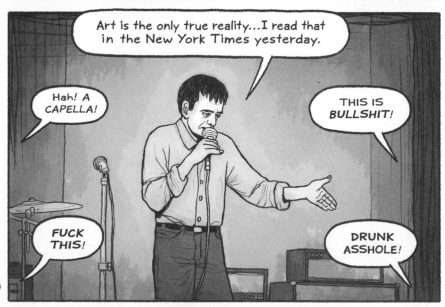

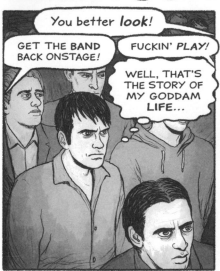

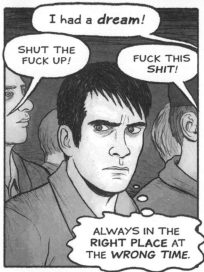

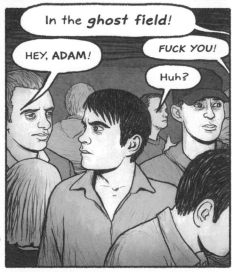

ADAM! ~ PROFESSOR KLINE! OVER HERE!

It was all just fantastic lies...

WHO'S ~

HOLY SHIT! IT'S THOSE KIDS FROM SCHOOL, WHAT'S THEIR NAMES?...uh...

DARYL AND JEFF! Um, HOW'S IT GOING?

WOW, WHAT'RE YOU DOIN' HERE?

ARE YOU INTO THIS STUFF?

PUNKS NOT DEAD

Oh, WELL, SURE, I'VE BEEN LISTENING ~

WASN'T THAT AN AWESOME GIG?

THEY PLAYED EVERY SONG I WANTED TO HEAR!

AND THE FIGHT AT THE END WAS CLASSIC!

GEEZ, I'M SURPRISED YOU MADE IT HERE, THOUGH ~ AFTER TODAY!

Huh? WHADDA YOU MEAN?

WELL, AFTER YOU...PASSED OUT!

THAT WAS FUCKED UP!

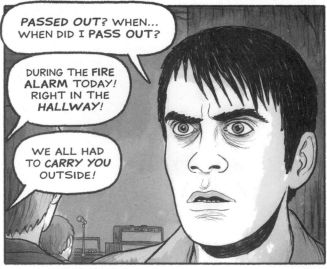

PASSED OUT? WHEN... WHEN DID I PASS OUT?

DURING THE FIRE ALARM TODAY! RIGHT IN THE HALLWAY!

WE ALL HAD TO CARRY YOU OUTSIDE!

DUDE ~ YOU SERIOUSLY DON'T REMEMBER?

MAYBE YOU SHOULD GO SEE A DOCTOR!

YEAH! CHRIST, IF REGAN HADN'T CAUGHT YOU YOU WOULDA FALLEN DOWN THE STAIRS!

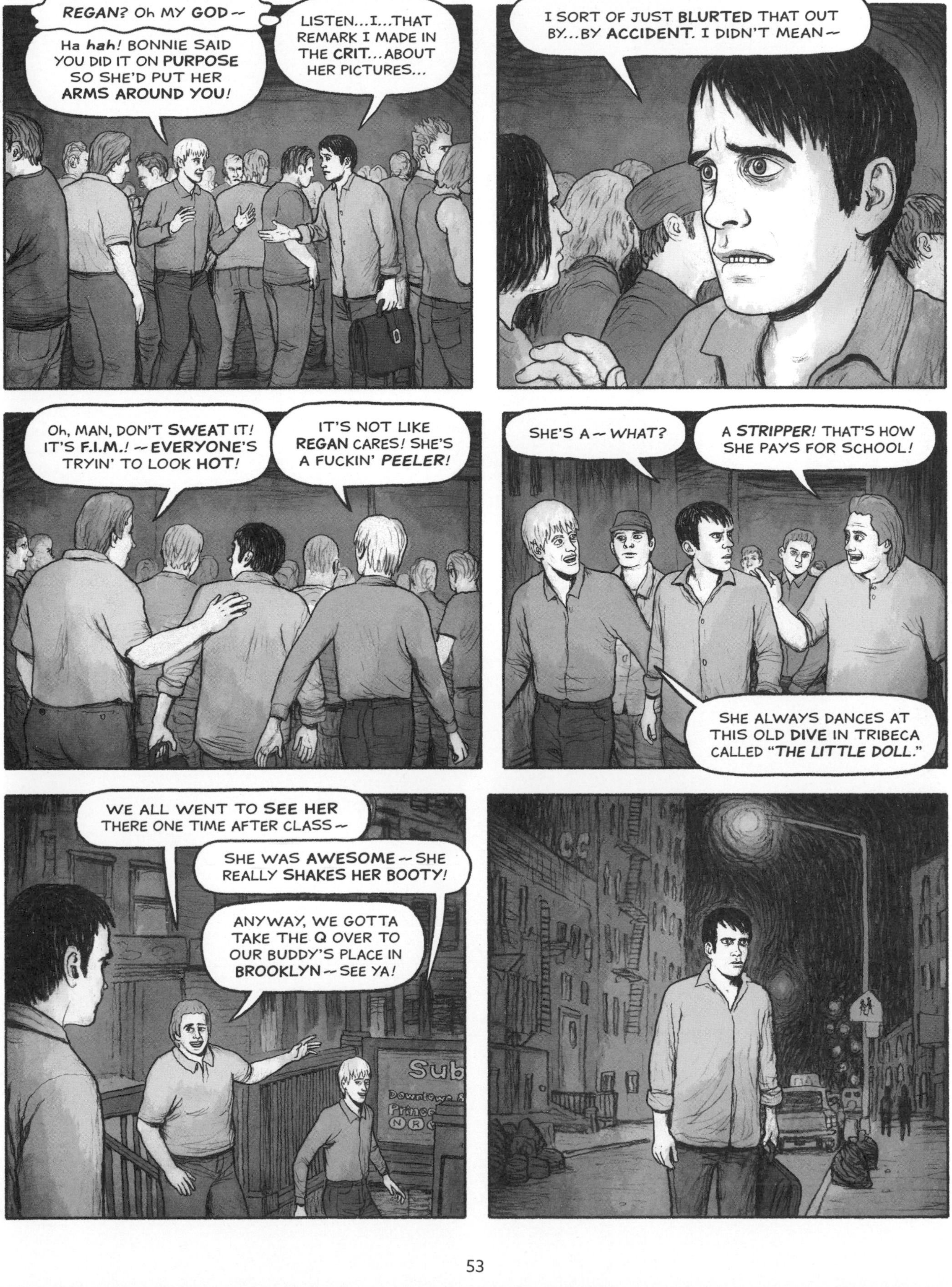
REGAN? Oh MY GOD--
Ha hah! BONNIE SAID YOU DID IT ON PURPOSE SO SHE'D PUT HER ARMS AROUND YOU!
LISTEN...I...THAT REMARK I MADE IN THE CRIT...ABOUT HER PICTURES...
I SORT OF JUST BLURTED THAT OUT BY...BY ACCIDENT. I DIDN'T MEAN--
Oh, MAN, DON'T SWEAT IT! IT'S F.I.M.! --EVERYONE'S TRYIN' TO LOOK HOT!
IT'S NOT LIKE REGAN CARES! SHE'S A FUCKIN' PEELER!
SHE'S A--WHAT?
A STRIPPER! THAT'S HOW SHE PAYS FOR SCHOOL!
SHE ALWAYS DANCES AT THIS OLD DIVE IN TRIBECA CALLED "THE LITTLE DOLL."
WE ALL WENT TO SEE HER THERE ONE TIME AFTER CLASS--
SHE WAS AWESOME--SHE REALLY SHAKES HER BOOTY!
ANYWAY, WE GOTTA TAKE THE Q OVER TO OUR BUDDY'S PLACE IN BROOKLYN--SEE YA!
Sub

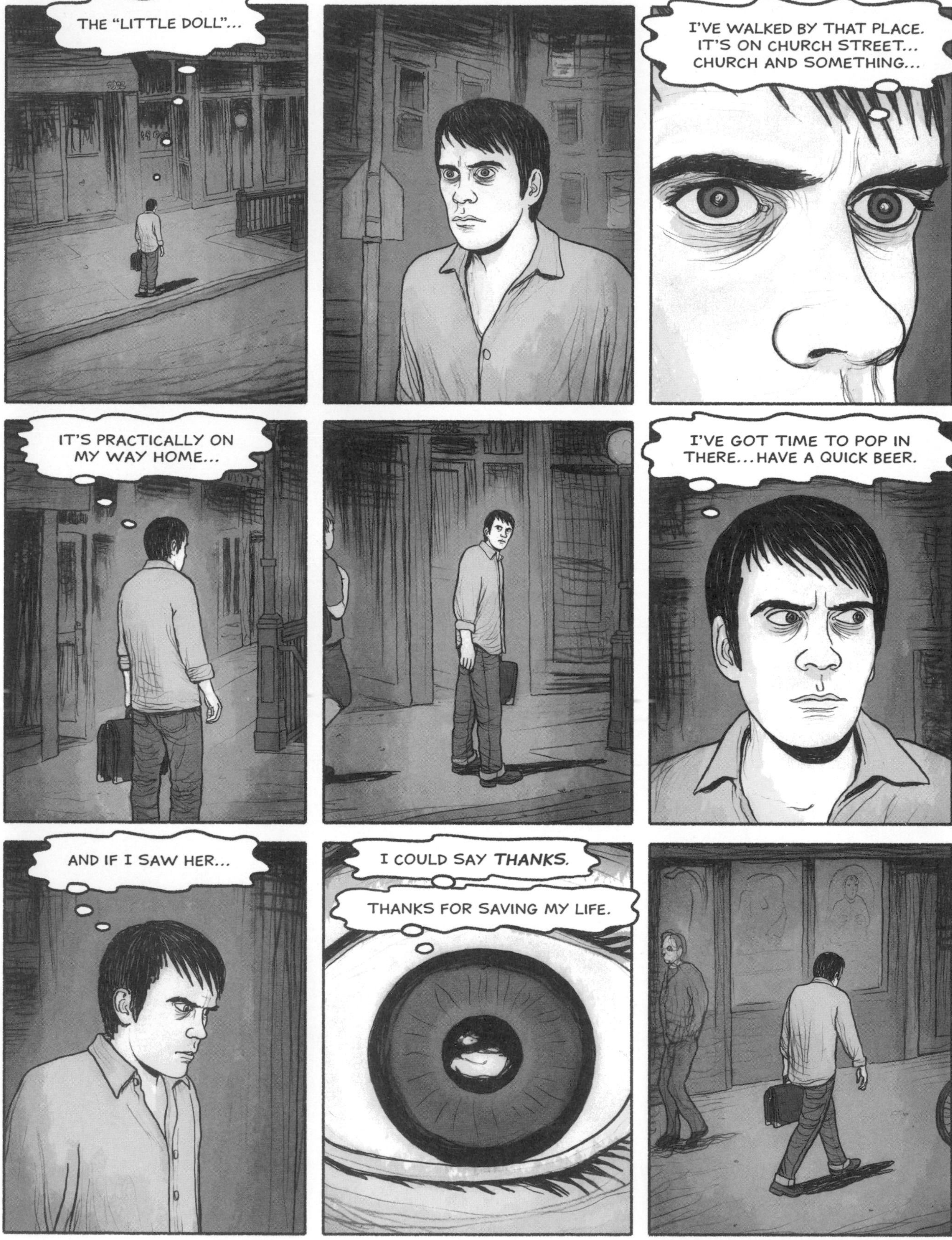
THE "LITTLE DOLL"...
I'VE WALKED BY THAT PLACE. IT'S ON CHURCH STREET... CHURCH AND SOMETHING...
IT'S PRACTICALLY ON MY WAY HOME...
I'VE GOT TIME TO POP IN THERE... HAVE A QUICK BEER.
AND IF I SAW HER...
I COULD SAY **THANKS.**
THANKS FOR SAVING MY LIFE.

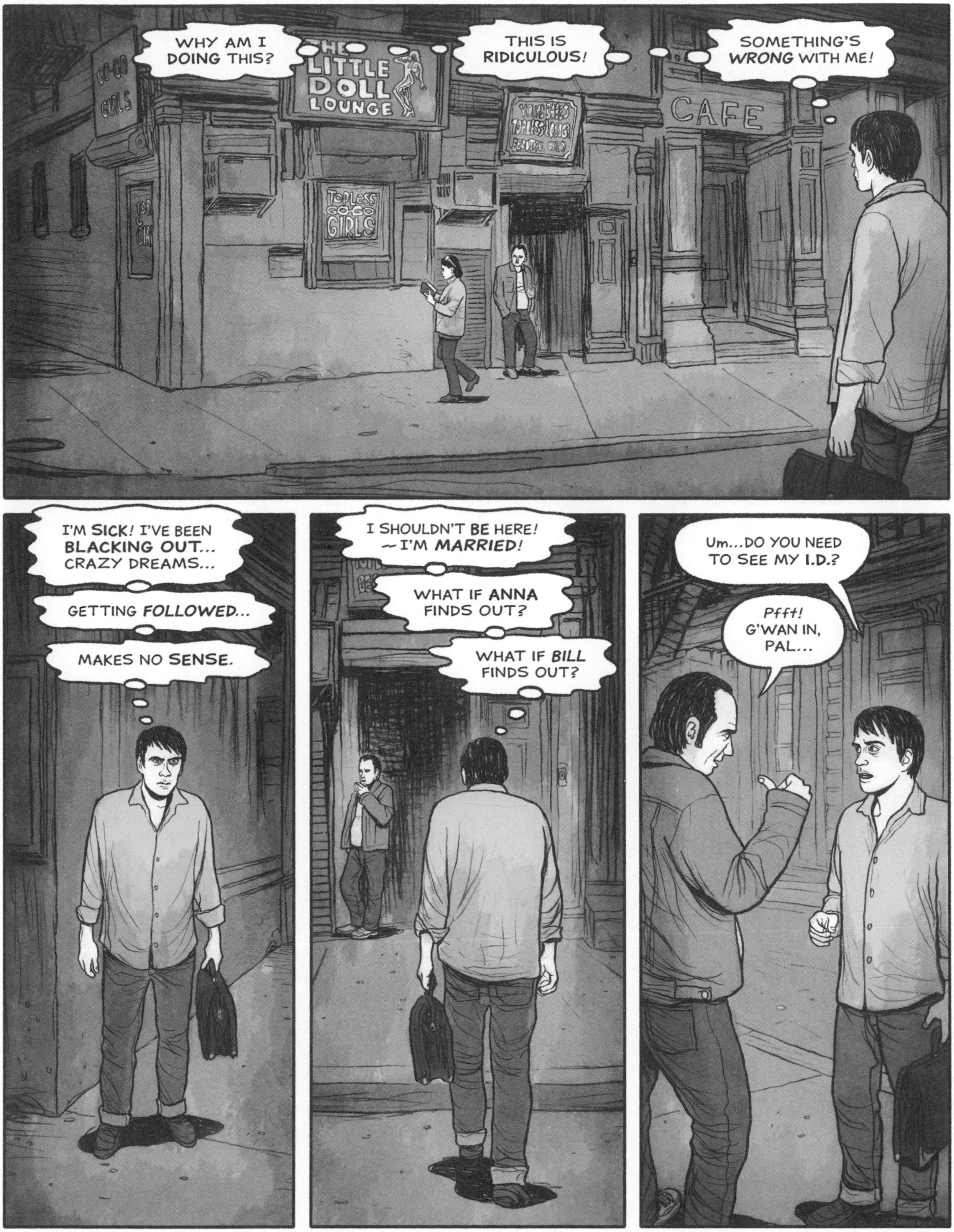
WHY AM I DOING THIS?
THE LITTLE DOLL LOUNGE
THIS IS RIDICULOUS!
SOMETHING'S WRONG WITH ME!
GO-GO GIRLS
CAFE
TOPLESS GO-GO GIRLS
I'M SICK! I'VE BEEN BLACKING OUT... CRAZY DREAMS...
GETTING FOLLOWED...
MAKES NO SENSE.
I SHOULDN'T BE HERE! —I'M MARRIED!
WHAT IF ANNA FINDS OUT?
WHAT IF BILL FINDS OUT?
Um...DO YOU NEED TO SEE MY I.D.?
Pfft! G'WAN IN, PAL...

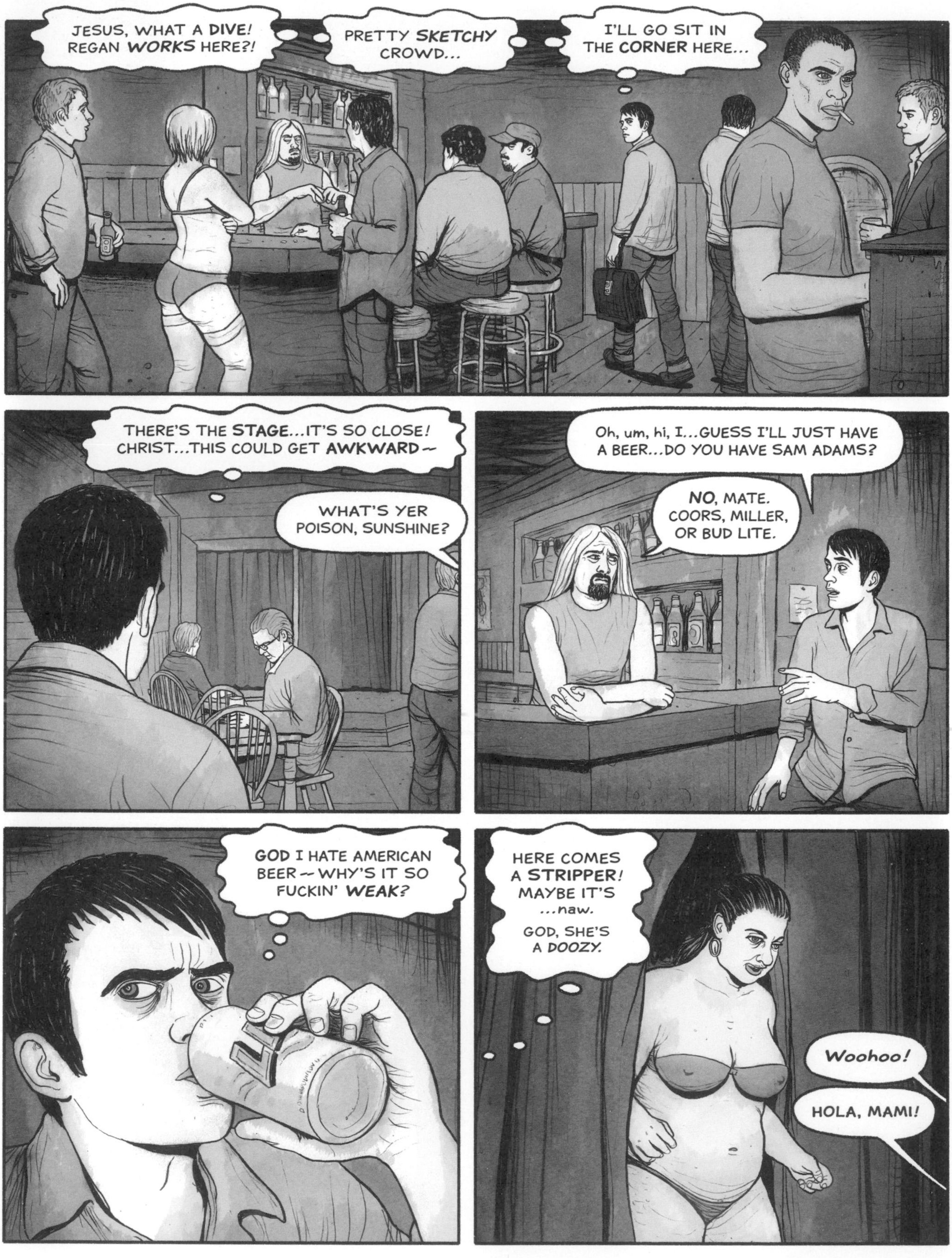
JESUS, WHAT A DIVE! REGAN WORKS HERE?!
PRETTY SKETCHY CROWD...
I'LL GO SIT IN THE CORNER HERE...
THERE'S THE STAGE...IT'S SO CLOSE! CHRIST...THIS COULD GET AWKWARD--
WHAT'S YER POISON, SUNSHINE?
Oh, um, hi, I...GUESS I'LL JUST HAVE A BEER...DO YOU HAVE SAM ADAMS?
NO, MATE. COORS, MILLER, OR BUD LITE.
GOD I HATE AMERICAN BEER--WHY'S IT SO FUCKIN' WEAK?
HERE COMES A STRIPPER! MAYBE IT'S ...naw.
GOD, SHE'S A DOOZY.
Woohoo!
HOLA, MAMI!

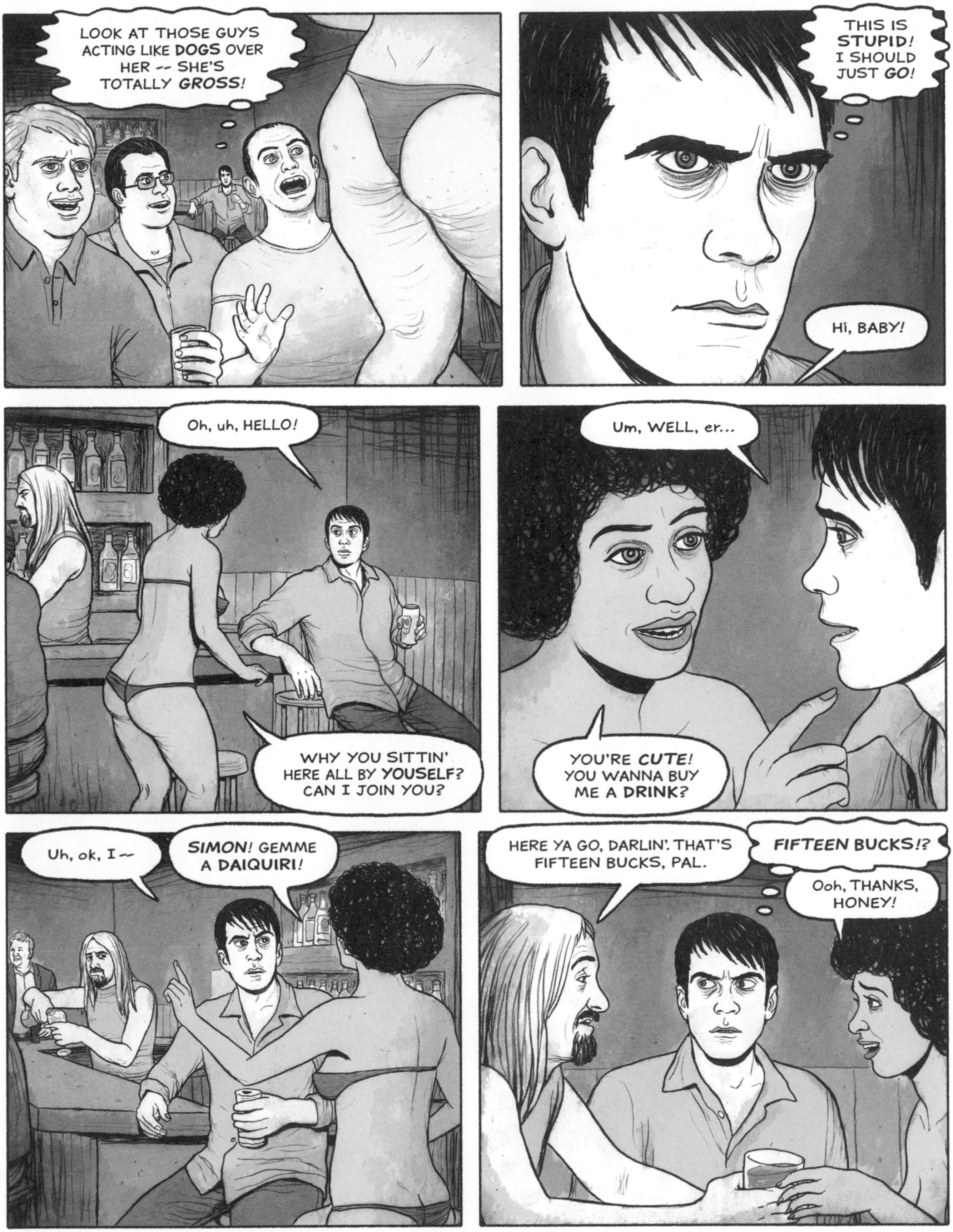
LOOK AT THOSE GUYS ACTING LIKE DOGS OVER HER -- SHE'S TOTALLY GROSS!
THIS IS STUPID! I SHOULD JUST GO!
Hi, BABY!
Oh, uh, HELLO!
WHY YOU SITTIN' HERE ALL BY YOUSELF? CAN I JOIN YOU?
Um, WELL, er...
YOU'RE CUTE! YOU WANNA BUY ME A DRINK?
Uh, ok, I --
SIMON! GEMME A DAIQUIRI!
HERE YA GO, DARLIN'. THAT'S FIFTEEN BUCKS, PAL.
FIFTEEN BUCKS!?
Ooh, THANKS, HONEY!

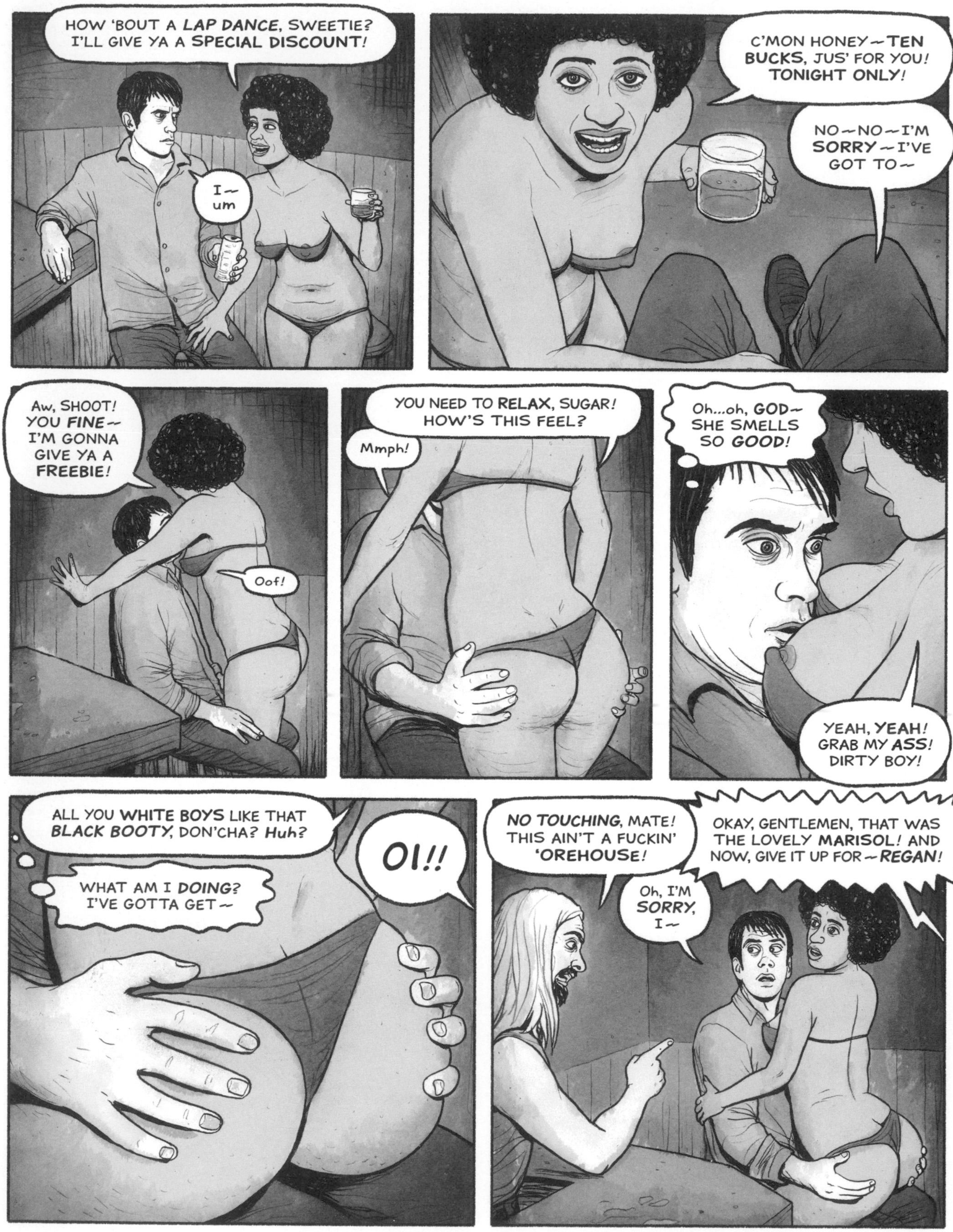

HOW 'BOUT A LAP DANCE, SWEETIE? I'LL GIVE YA A SPECIAL DISCOUNT!
I— um
C'MON HONEY—TEN BUCKS, JUS' FOR YOU! TONIGHT ONLY!
NO—NO—I'M SORRY—I'VE GOT TO—
Aw, SHOOT! YOU FINE—I'M GONNA GIVE YA A FREEBIE!
Oof!
YOU NEED TO RELAX, SUGAR! HOW'S THIS FEEL?
Mmph!
Oh...oh, GOD—SHE SMELLS SO GOOD!
YEAH, YEAH! GRAB MY ASS! DIRTY BOY!
ALL YOU WHITE BOYS LIKE THAT BLACK BOOTY, DON'CHA? Huh?
WHAT AM I DOING? I'VE GOTTA GET—
OI!!
NO TOUCHING, MATE! THIS AIN'T A FUCKIN' 'OREHOUSE!
Oh, I'M SORRY, I—
OKAY, GENTLEMEN, THAT WAS THE LOVELY MARISOL! AND NOW, GIVE IT UP FOR—REGAN!

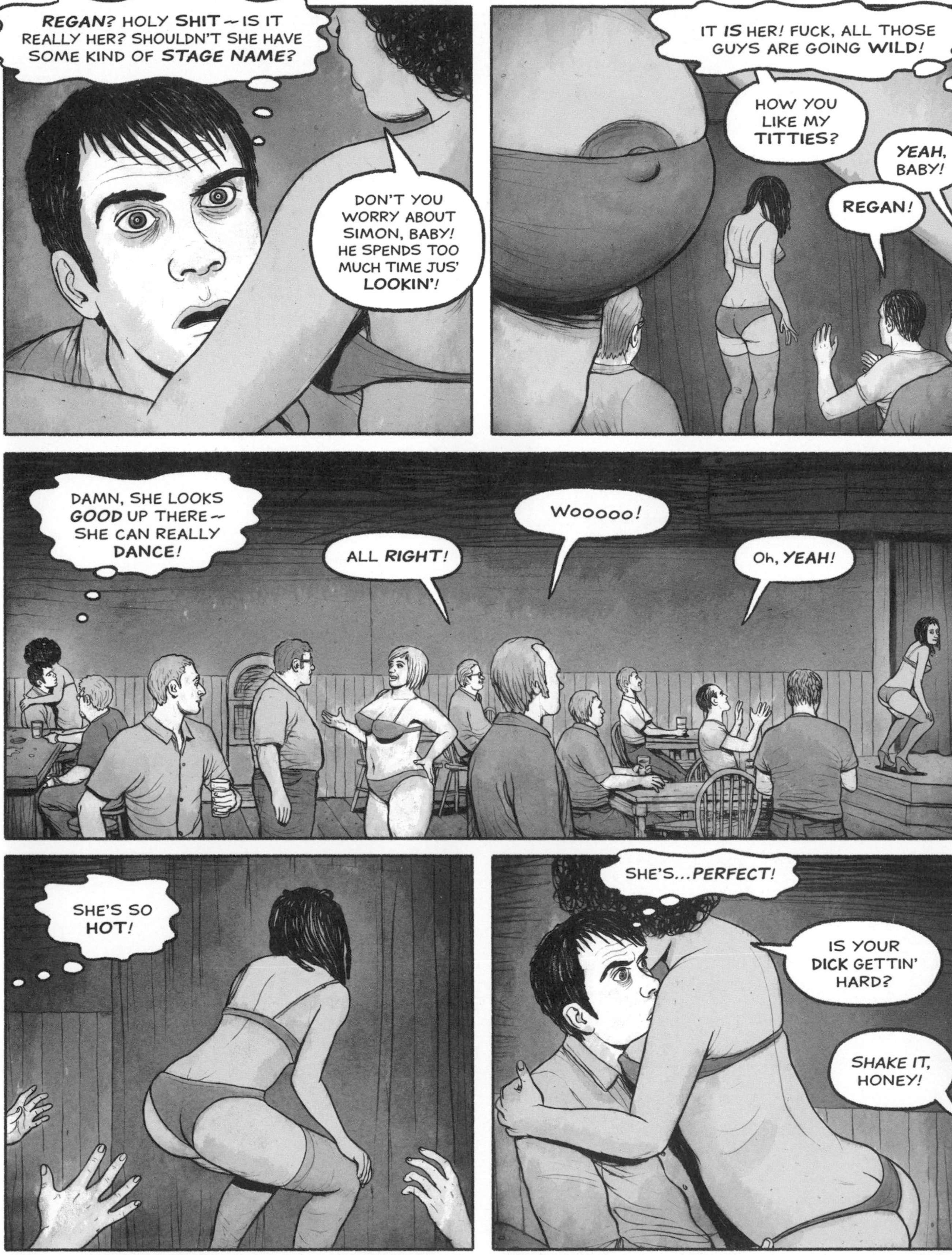
REGAN? HOLY SHIT ~ IS IT REALLY HER? SHOULDN'T SHE HAVE SOME KIND OF STAGE NAME?
DON'T YOU WORRY ABOUT SIMON, BABY! HE SPENDS TOO MUCH TIME JUS' LOOKIN'!
IT IS HER! FUCK, ALL THOSE GUYS ARE GOING WILD!
HOW YOU LIKE MY TITTIES?
YEAH, BABY!
REGAN!
DAMN, SHE LOOKS GOOD UP THERE ~ SHE CAN REALLY DANCE!
ALL RIGHT!
Wooooo!
Oh, YEAH!
SHE'S SO HOT!
SHE'S...PERFECT!
IS YOUR DICK GETTIN' HARD?
SHAKE IT, HONEY!

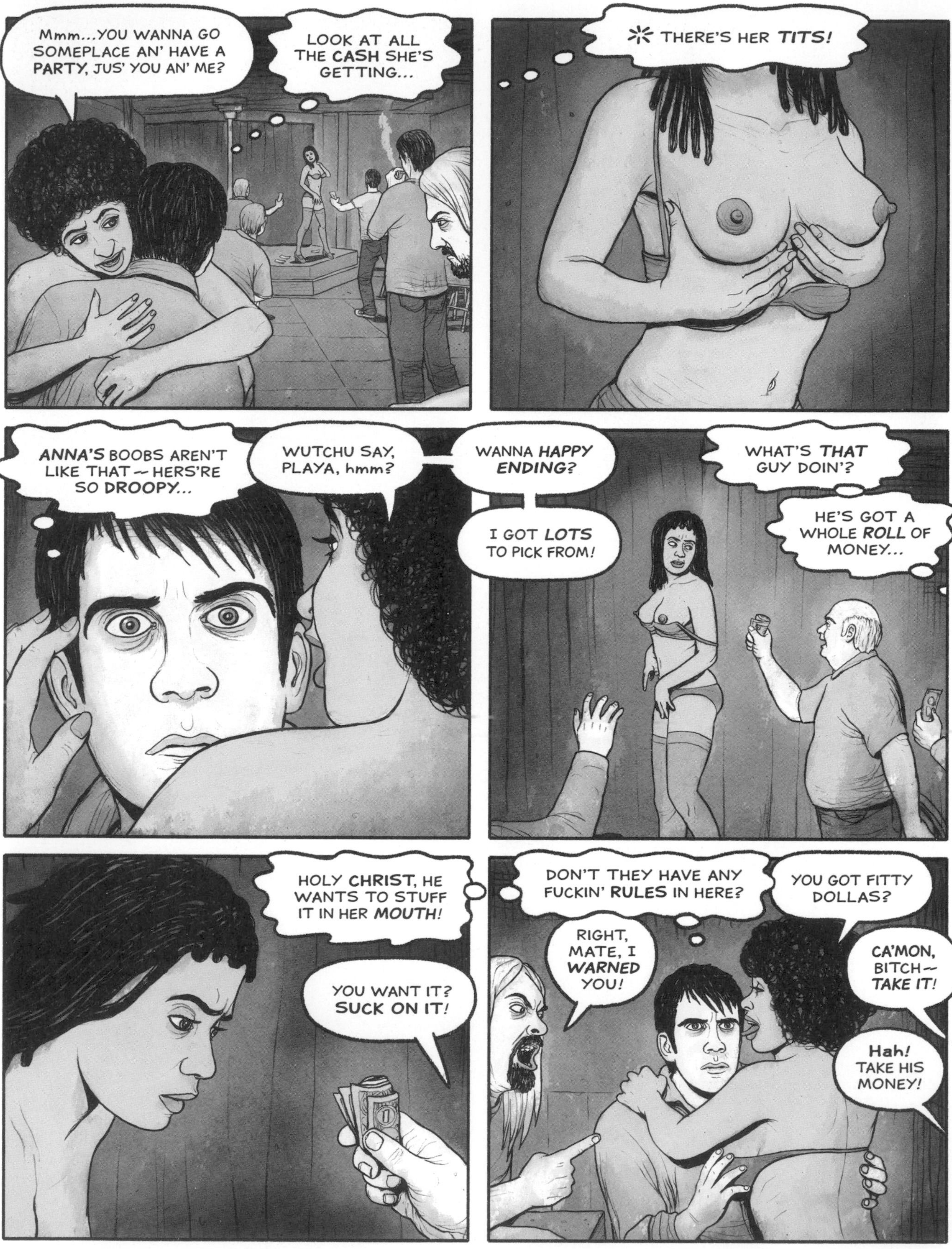
Mmm...YOU WANNA GO SOMEPLACE AN' HAVE A PARTY, JUS' YOU AN' ME?
LOOK AT ALL THE CASH SHE'S GETTING...
THERE'S HER TITS!
ANNA'S BOOBS AREN'T LIKE THAT—HERS'RE SO DROOPY...
WUTCHU SAY, PLAYA, hmm?
WANNA HAPPY ENDING?
I GOT LOTS TO PICK FROM!
WHAT'S THAT GUY DOIN'?
HE'S GOT A WHOLE ROLL OF MONEY...
HOLY CHRIST, HE WANTS TO STUFF IT IN HER MOUTH!
YOU WANT IT? SUCK ON IT!
DON'T THEY HAVE ANY FUCKIN' RULES IN HERE?
YOU GOT FITTY DOLLAS?
RIGHT, MATE, I WARNED YOU!
CA'MON, BITCH—TAKE IT!
Hah! TAKE HIS MONEY!

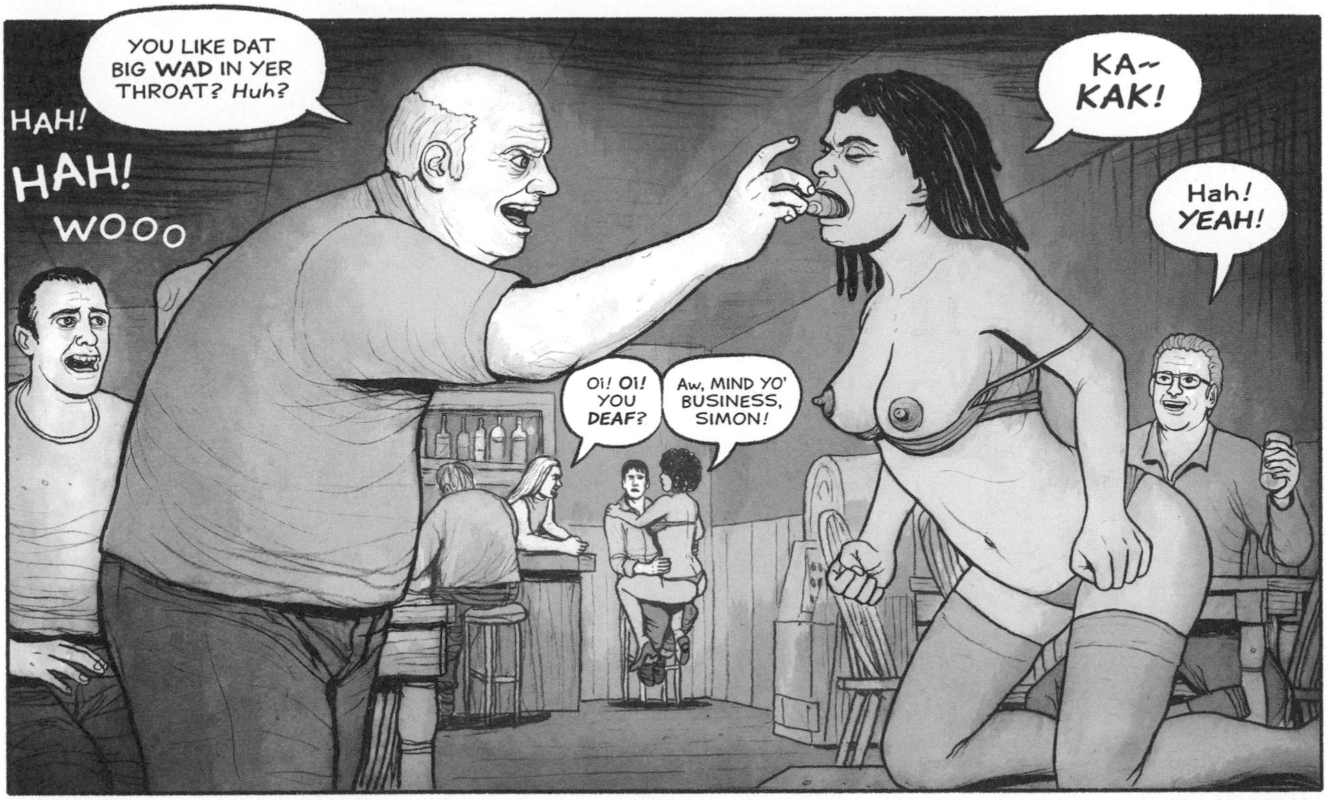
YOU LIKE DAT BIG WAD IN YER THROAT? Huh?
HAH!
HAH!
WOOO
KA-KAK!
Hah! YEAH!
Oi! Oi! YOU DEAF?
Aw, MIND YO' BUSINESS, SIMON!

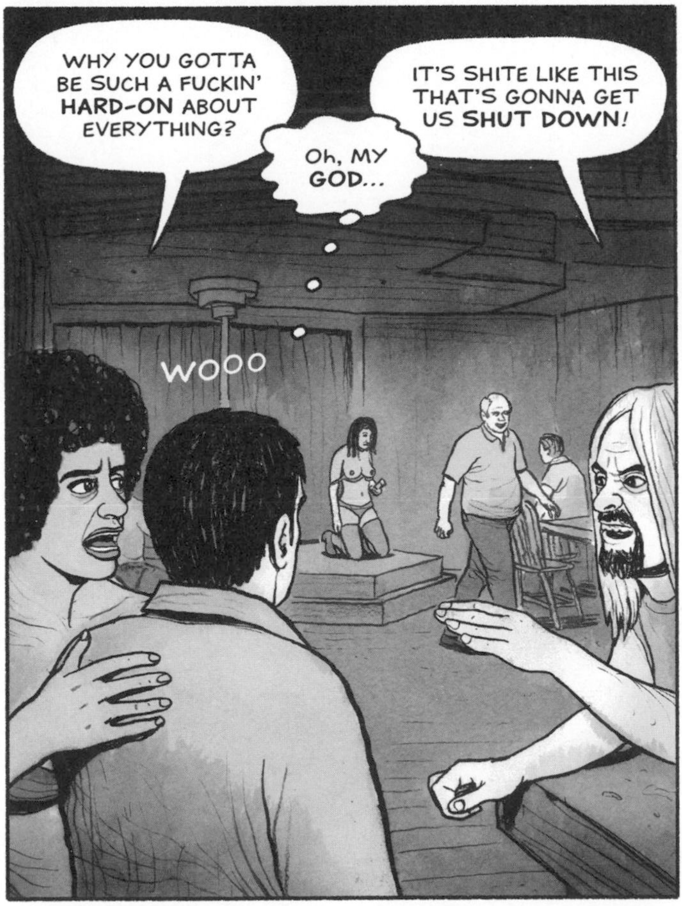
WHY YOU GOTTA BE SUCH A FUCKIN' HARD-ON ABOUT EVERYTHING?
IT'S SHITE LIKE THIS THAT'S GONNA GET US SHUT DOWN!
Oh, MY GOD...
WOOO

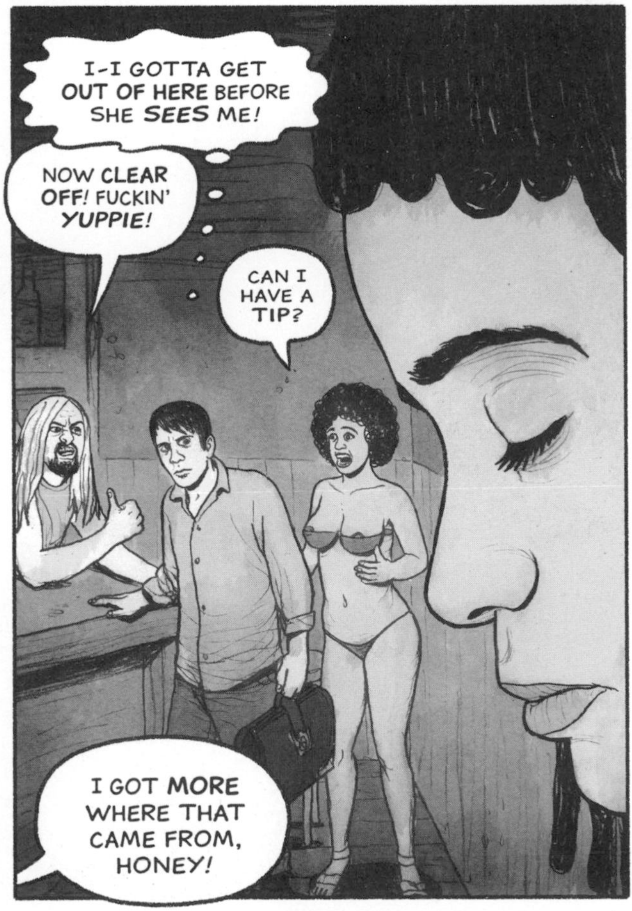
I-I GOTTA GET OUT OF HERE BEFORE SHE SEES ME!
NOW CLEAR OFF! FUCKIN' YUPPIE!
CAN I HAVE A TIP?
I GOT MORE WHERE THAT CAME FROM, HONEY!

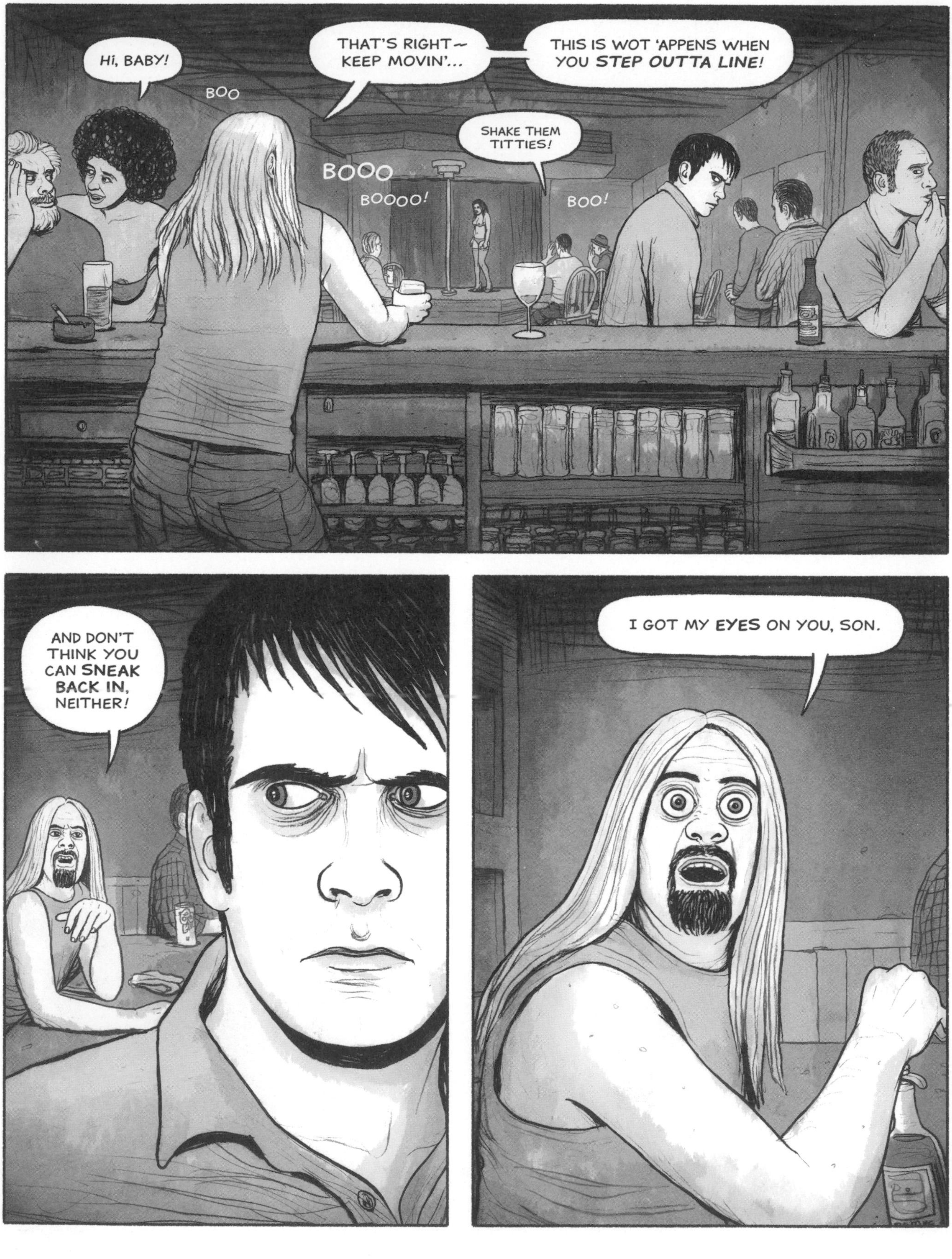
Hi, BABY!
BOO
THAT'S RIGHT— KEEP MOVIN'...
THIS IS WOT 'APPENS WHEN YOU STEP OUTTA LINE!
SHAKE THEM TITTIES!
BOOO
BOOOO!
BOO!
AND DON'T THINK YOU CAN SNEAK BACK IN, NEITHER!
I GOT MY EYES ON YOU, SON.

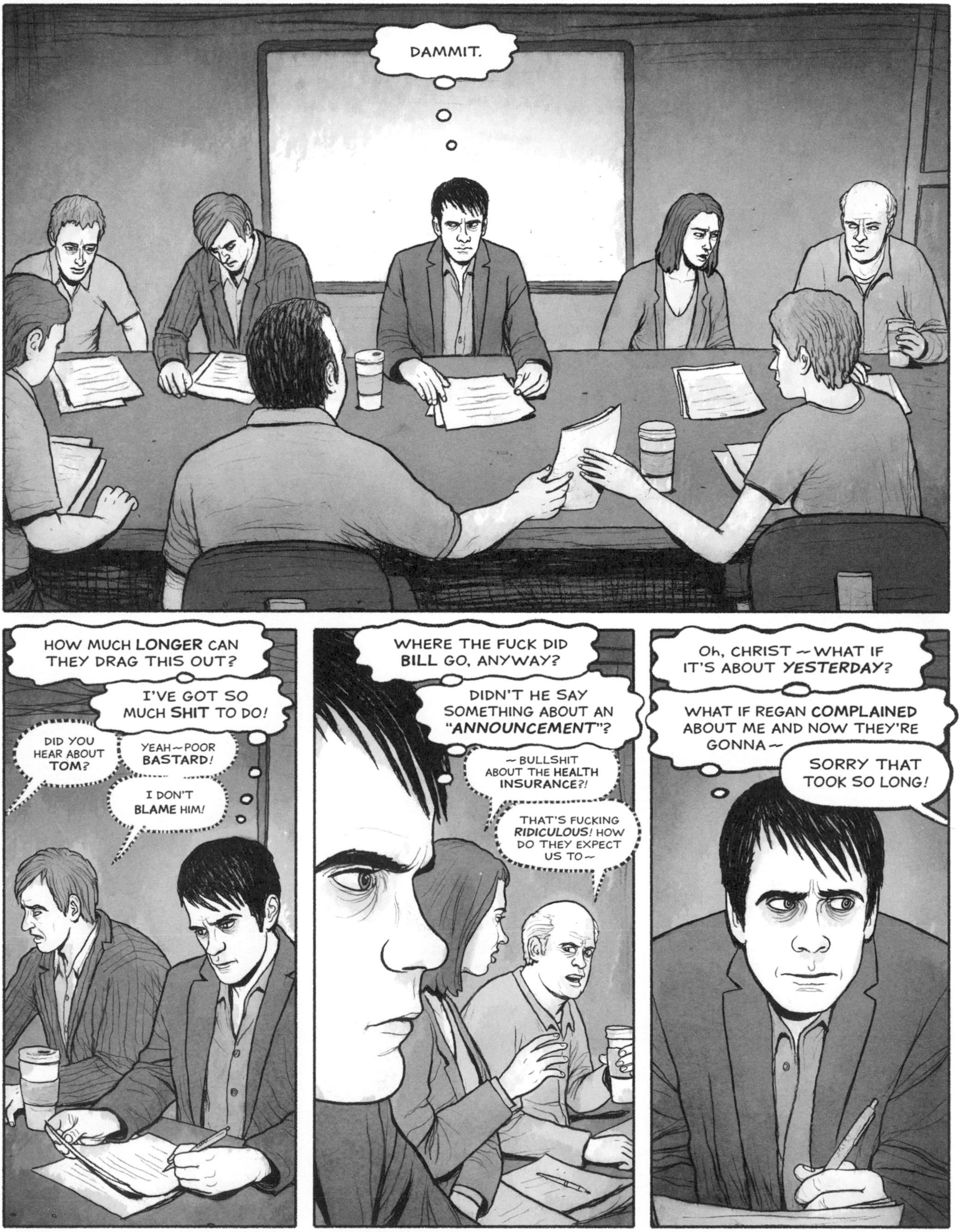
DAMMIT.
HOW MUCH **LONGER** CAN THEY DRAG THIS OUT?
I'VE GOT SO MUCH **SHIT** TO DO!
DID YOU HEAR ABOUT **TOM**?
YEAH ~ POOR **BASTARD**!
I DON'T **BLAME** HIM!
WHERE THE FUCK DID **BILL** GO, ANYWAY?
DIDN'T HE SAY SOMETHING ABOUT AN "***ANNOUNCEMENT***"?
~ BULLSHIT ABOUT THE **HEALTH INSURANCE**?!
THAT'S FUCKING ***RIDICULOUS***! HOW DO THEY EXPECT US TO ~
Oh, CHRIST ~ WHAT IF IT'S ABOUT ***YESTERDAY***?
WHAT IF REGAN **COMPLAINED** ABOUT ME AND NOW THEY'RE GONNA ~
SORRY THAT TOOK SO LONG!

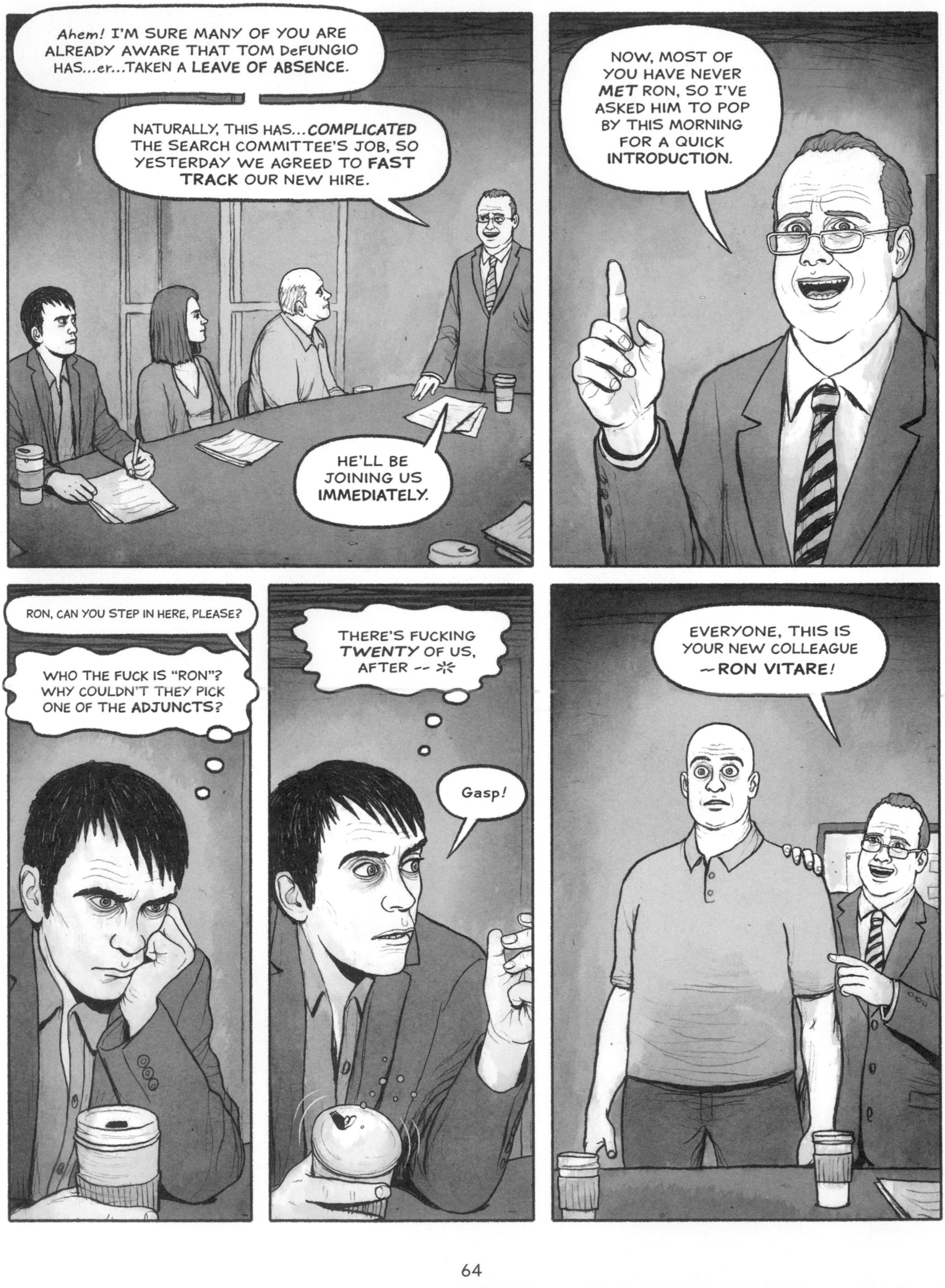

Ahem! I'M SURE MANY OF YOU ARE ALREADY AWARE THAT TOM DeFUNGIO HAS...er...TAKEN A LEAVE OF ABSENCE.
NATURALLY, THIS HAS...COMPLICATED THE SEARCH COMMITTEE'S JOB, SO YESTERDAY WE AGREED TO FAST TRACK OUR NEW HIRE.
HE'LL BE JOINING US IMMEDIATELY.
NOW, MOST OF YOU HAVE NEVER MET RON, SO I'VE ASKED HIM TO POP BY THIS MORNING FOR A QUICK INTRODUCTION.
RON, CAN YOU STEP IN HERE, PLEASE?
WHO THE FUCK IS "RON"? WHY COULDN'T THEY PICK ONE OF THE ADJUNCTS?
THERE'S FUCKING TWENTY OF US, AFTER -- *
Gasp!
EVERYONE, THIS IS YOUR NEW COLLEAGUE --RON VITARE!

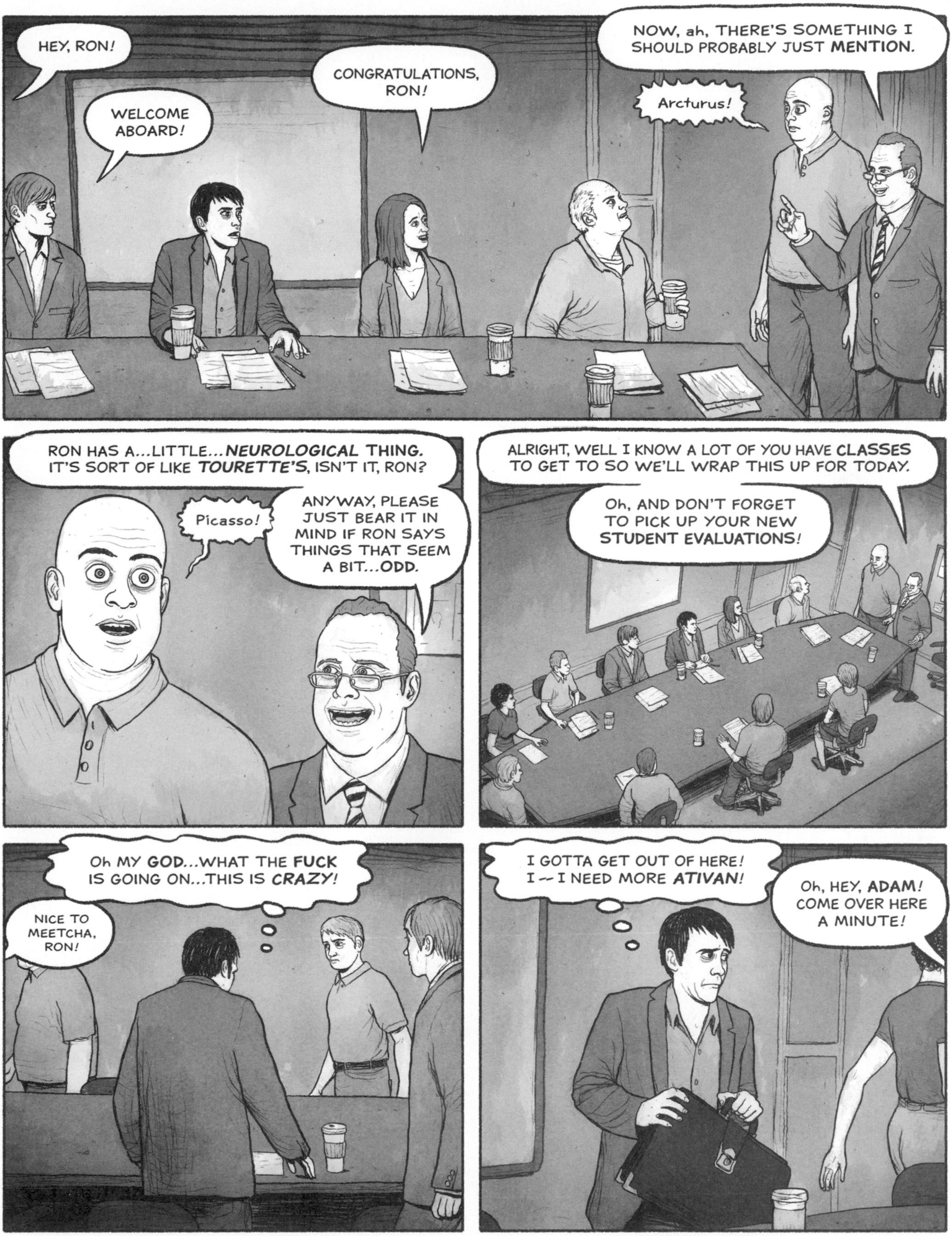
HEY, RON!
WELCOME ABOARD!
CONGRATULATIONS, RON!
Arcturus!
NOW, ah, THERE'S SOMETHING I SHOULD PROBABLY JUST MENTION.
RON HAS A...LITTLE...NEUROLOGICAL THING. IT'S SORT OF LIKE TOURETTE'S, ISN'T IT, RON?
Picasso!
ANYWAY, PLEASE JUST BEAR IT IN MIND IF RON SAYS THINGS THAT SEEM A BIT...ODD.
ALRIGHT, WELL I KNOW A LOT OF YOU HAVE CLASSES TO GET TO SO WE'LL WRAP THIS UP FOR TODAY.
Oh, AND DON'T FORGET TO PICK UP YOUR NEW STUDENT EVALUATIONS!
Oh MY GOD...WHAT THE FUCK IS GOING ON...THIS IS CRAZY!
NICE TO MEETCHA, RON!
I GOTTA GET OUT OF HERE! I -- I NEED MORE ATIVAN!
Oh, HEY, ADAM! COME OVER HERE A MINUTE!

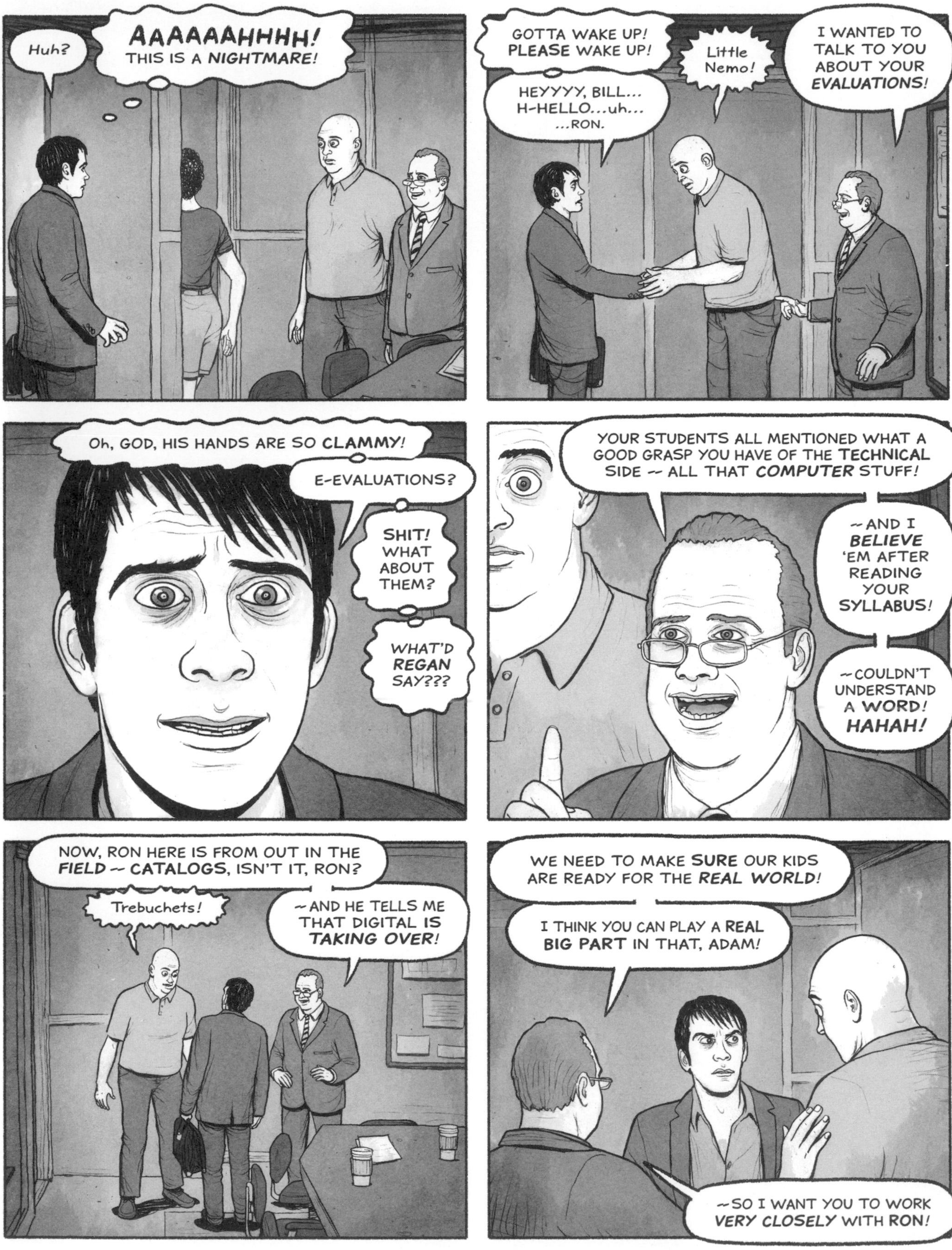

Huh?
AAAAAAHHHH! THIS IS A NIGHTMARE!
GOTTA WAKE UP! PLEASE WAKE UP!
HEYYYY, BILL... H-HELLO...uh... ...RON.
Little Nemo!
I WANTED TO TALK TO YOU ABOUT YOUR EVALUATIONS!
Oh, GOD, HIS HANDS ARE SO CLAMMY!
E-EVALUATIONS?
SHIT! WHAT ABOUT THEM?
WHAT'D REGAN SAY???
YOUR STUDENTS ALL MENTIONED WHAT A GOOD GRASP YOU HAVE OF THE TECHNICAL SIDE -- ALL THAT COMPUTER STUFF!
--AND I BELIEVE 'EM AFTER READING YOUR SYLLABUS!
--COULDN'T UNDERSTAND A WORD! HAHAH!
NOW, RON HERE IS FROM OUT IN THE FIELD -- CATALOGS, ISN'T IT, RON?
Trebuchets!
--AND HE TELLS ME THAT DIGITAL IS TAKING OVER!
WE NEED TO MAKE SURE OUR KIDS ARE READY FOR THE REAL WORLD!
I THINK YOU CAN PLAY A REAL BIG PART IN THAT, ADAM!
--SO I WANT YOU TO WORK VERY CLOSELY WITH RON!

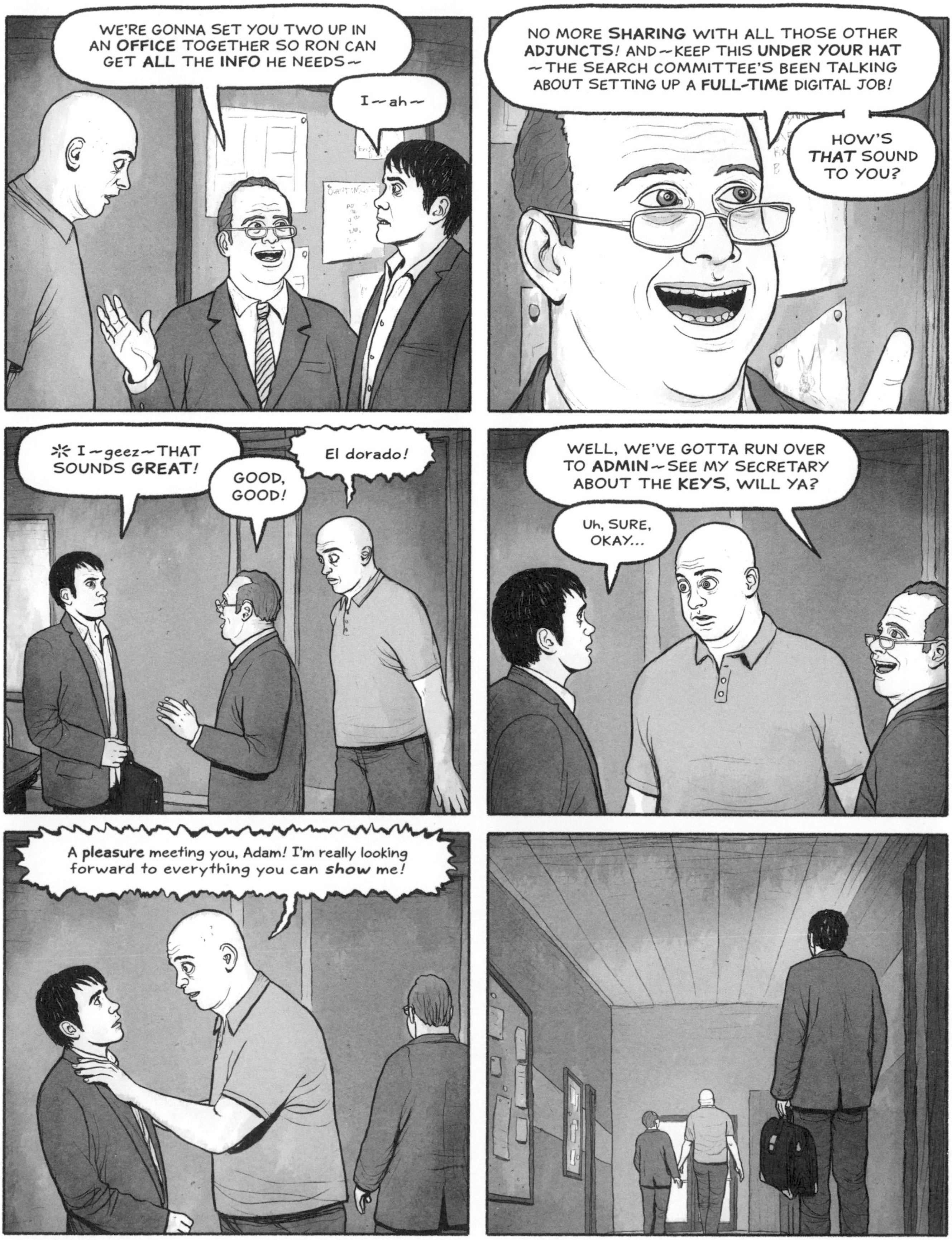
WE'RE GONNA SET YOU TWO UP IN AN OFFICE TOGETHER SO RON CAN GET ALL THE INFO HE NEEDS~
I~ah~
NO MORE SHARING WITH ALL THOSE OTHER ADJUNCTS! AND~KEEP THIS UNDER YOUR HAT ~THE SEARCH COMMITTEE'S BEEN TALKING ABOUT SETTING UP A FULL-TIME DIGITAL JOB!
HOW'S THAT SOUND TO YOU?
I~geez~THAT SOUNDS GREAT!
GOOD, GOOD!
El dorado!
WELL, WE'VE GOTTA RUN OVER TO ADMIN~SEE MY SECRETARY ABOUT THE KEYS, WILL YA?
Uh, SURE, OKAY...
A pleasure meeting you, Adam! I'm really looking forward to everything you can show me!

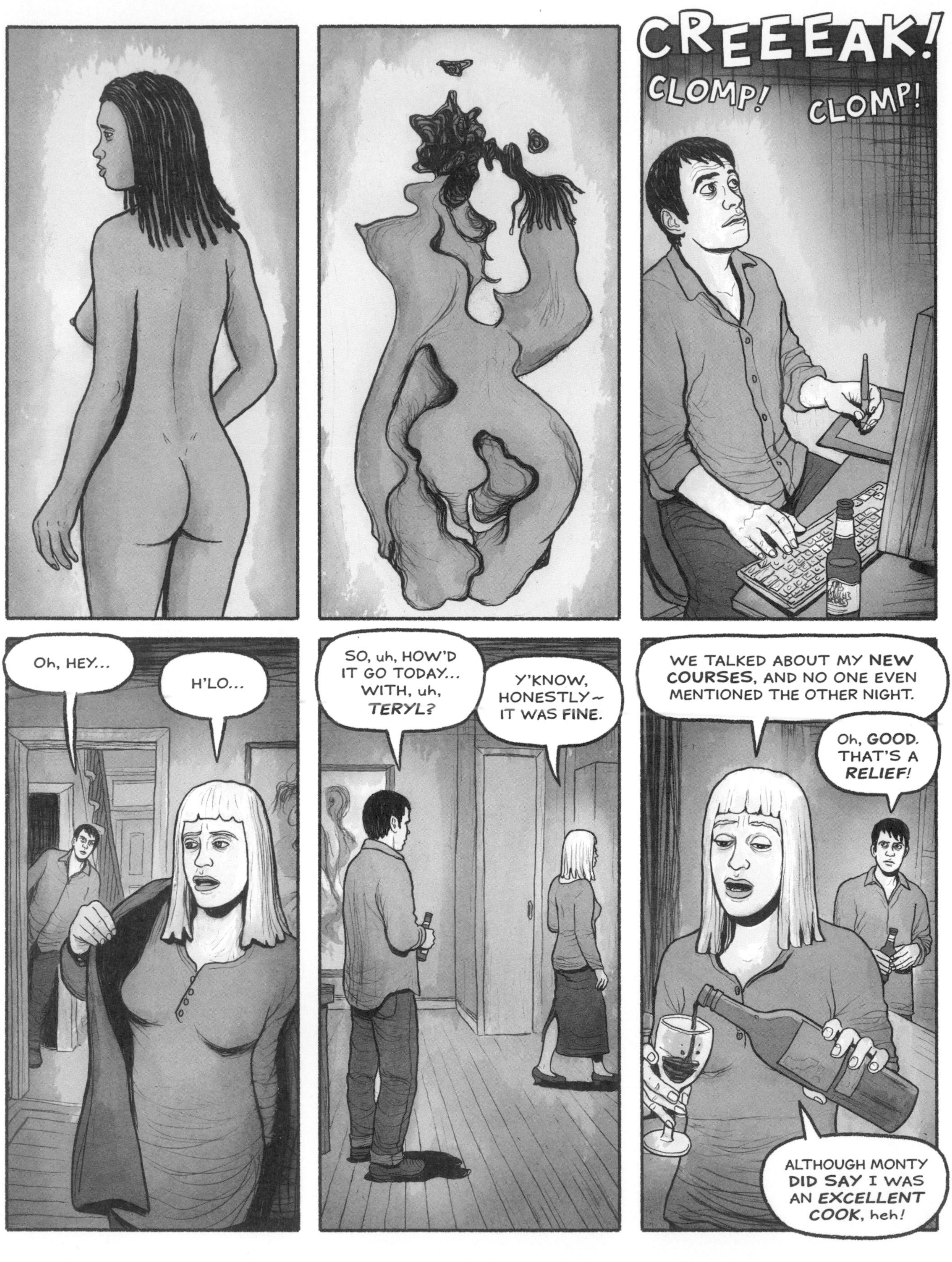
CREEEAK!
CLOMP! CLOMP!
Oh, HEY...
H'LO...
SO, uh, HOW'D IT GO TODAY... WITH, uh, TERYL?
Y'KNOW, HONESTLY~ IT WAS FINE.
WE TALKED ABOUT MY NEW COURSES, AND NO ONE EVEN MENTIONED THE OTHER NIGHT.
Oh, GOOD. THAT'S A RELIEF!
ALTHOUGH MONTY DID SAY I WAS AN EXCELLENT COOK, heh!

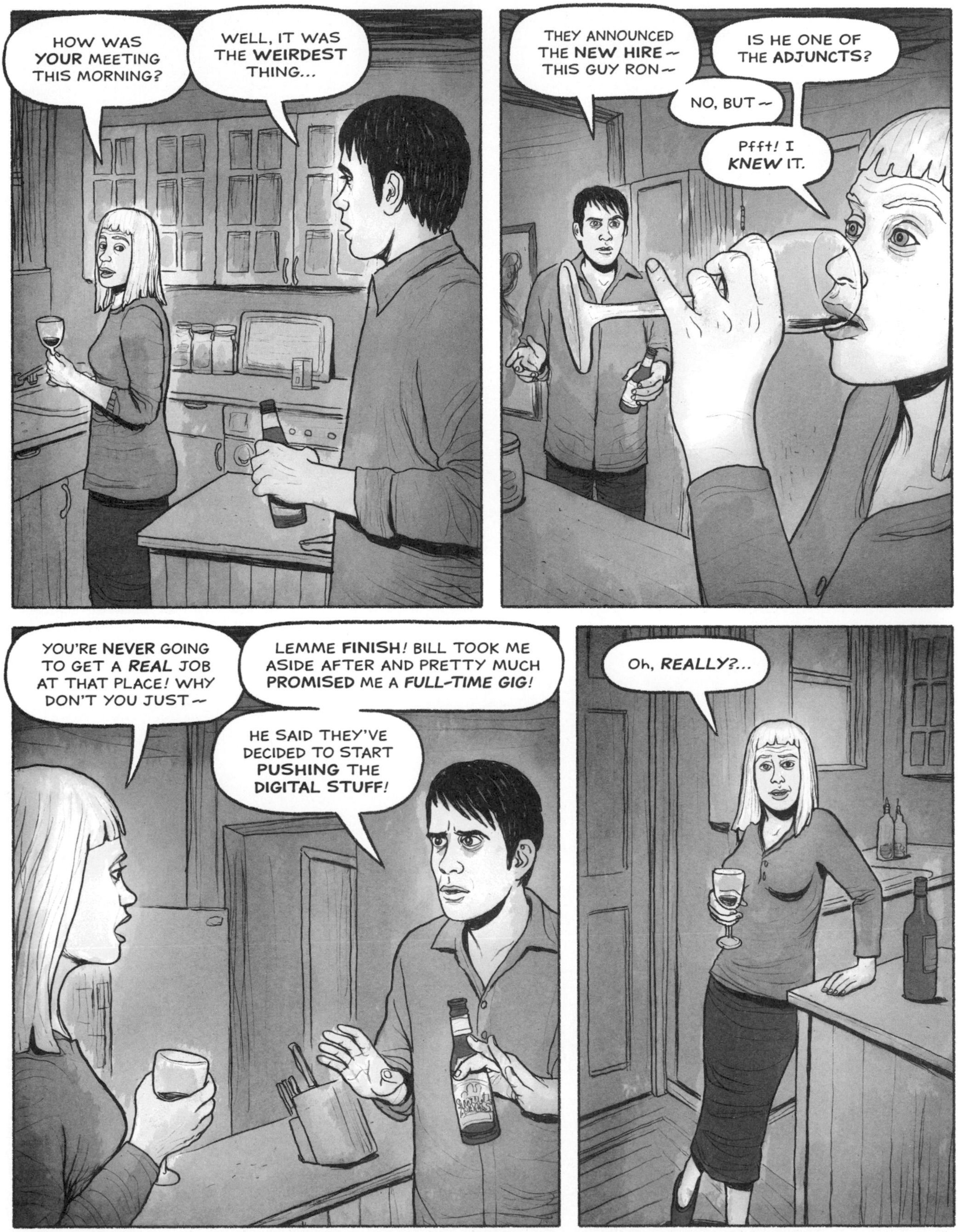
HOW WAS YOUR MEETING THIS MORNING?
WELL, IT WAS THE WEIRDEST THING...
THEY ANNOUNCED THE NEW HIRE– THIS GUY RON–
IS HE ONE OF THE ADJUNCTS?
NO, BUT–
Pfft! I KNEW IT.
YOU'RE NEVER GOING TO GET A REAL JOB AT THAT PLACE! WHY DON'T YOU JUST–
LEMME FINISH! BILL TOOK ME ASIDE AFTER AND PRETTY MUCH PROMISED ME A FULL-TIME GIG!
HE SAID THEY'VE DECIDED TO START PUSHING THE DIGITAL STUFF!
Oh, REALLY?...

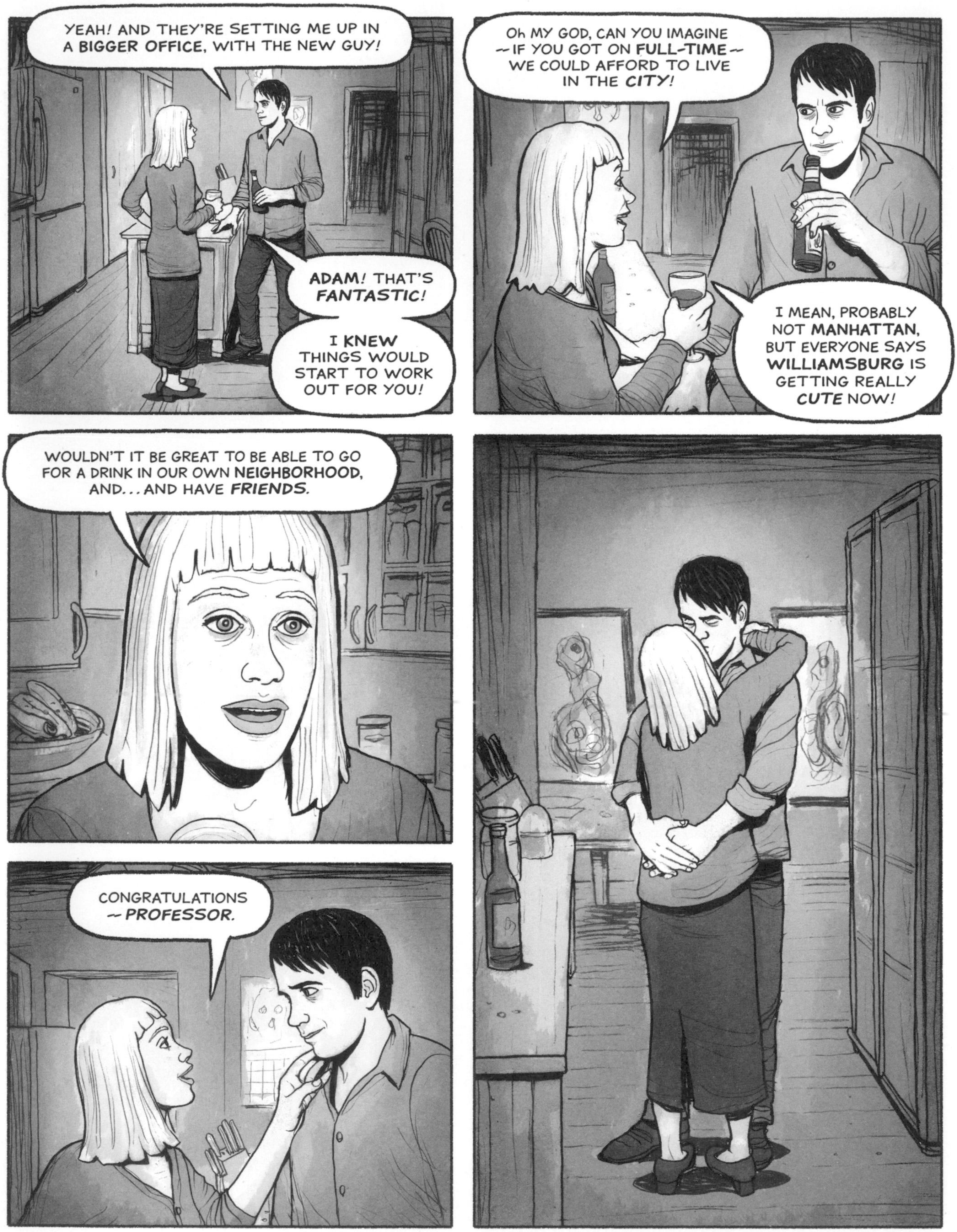
YEAH! AND THEY'RE SETTING ME UP IN A BIGGER OFFICE, WITH THE NEW GUY!
ADAM! THAT'S FANTASTIC!
I KNEW THINGS WOULD START TO WORK OUT FOR YOU!
Oh MY GOD, CAN YOU IMAGINE --IF YOU GOT ON FULL-TIME-- WE COULD AFFORD TO LIVE IN THE CITY!
I MEAN, PROBABLY NOT MANHATTAN, BUT EVERYONE SAYS WILLIAMSBURG IS GETTING REALLY CUTE NOW!
WOULDN'T IT BE GREAT TO BE ABLE TO GO FOR A DRINK IN OUR OWN NEIGHBORHOOD, AND... AND HAVE FRIENDS.
CONGRATULATIONS --PROFESSOR.

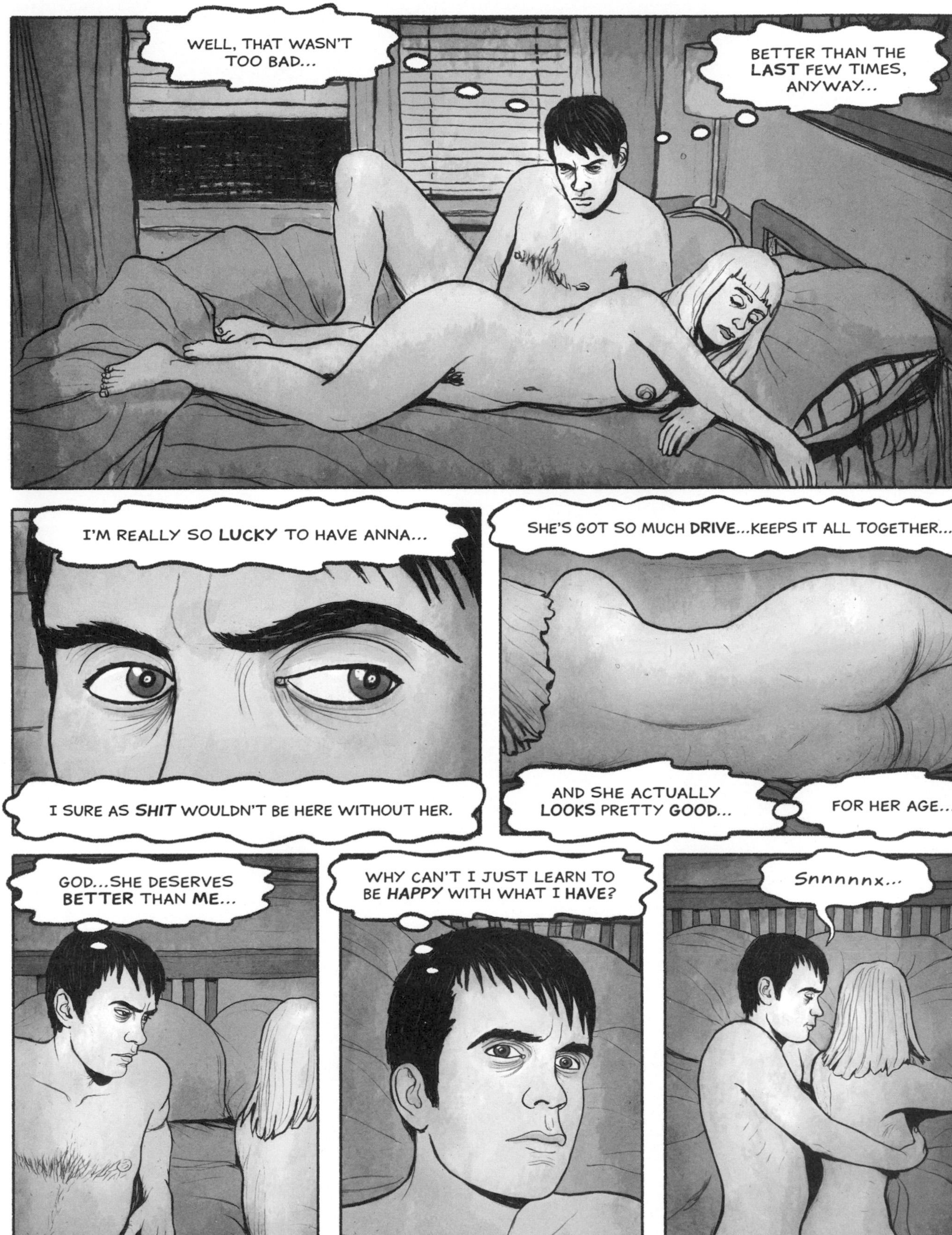
WELL, THAT WASN'T TOO BAD...
BETTER THAN THE LAST FEW TIMES, ANYWAY...
I'M REALLY SO LUCKY TO HAVE ANNA...
I SURE AS SHIT WOULDN'T BE HERE WITHOUT HER.
SHE'S GOT SO MUCH DRIVE...KEEPS IT ALL TOGETHER...
AND SHE ACTUALLY LOOKS PRETTY GOOD...
FOR HER AGE...
GOD...SHE DESERVES BETTER THAN ME...
WHY CAN'T I JUST LEARN TO BE HAPPY WITH WHAT I HAVE?
Snnnnnx...

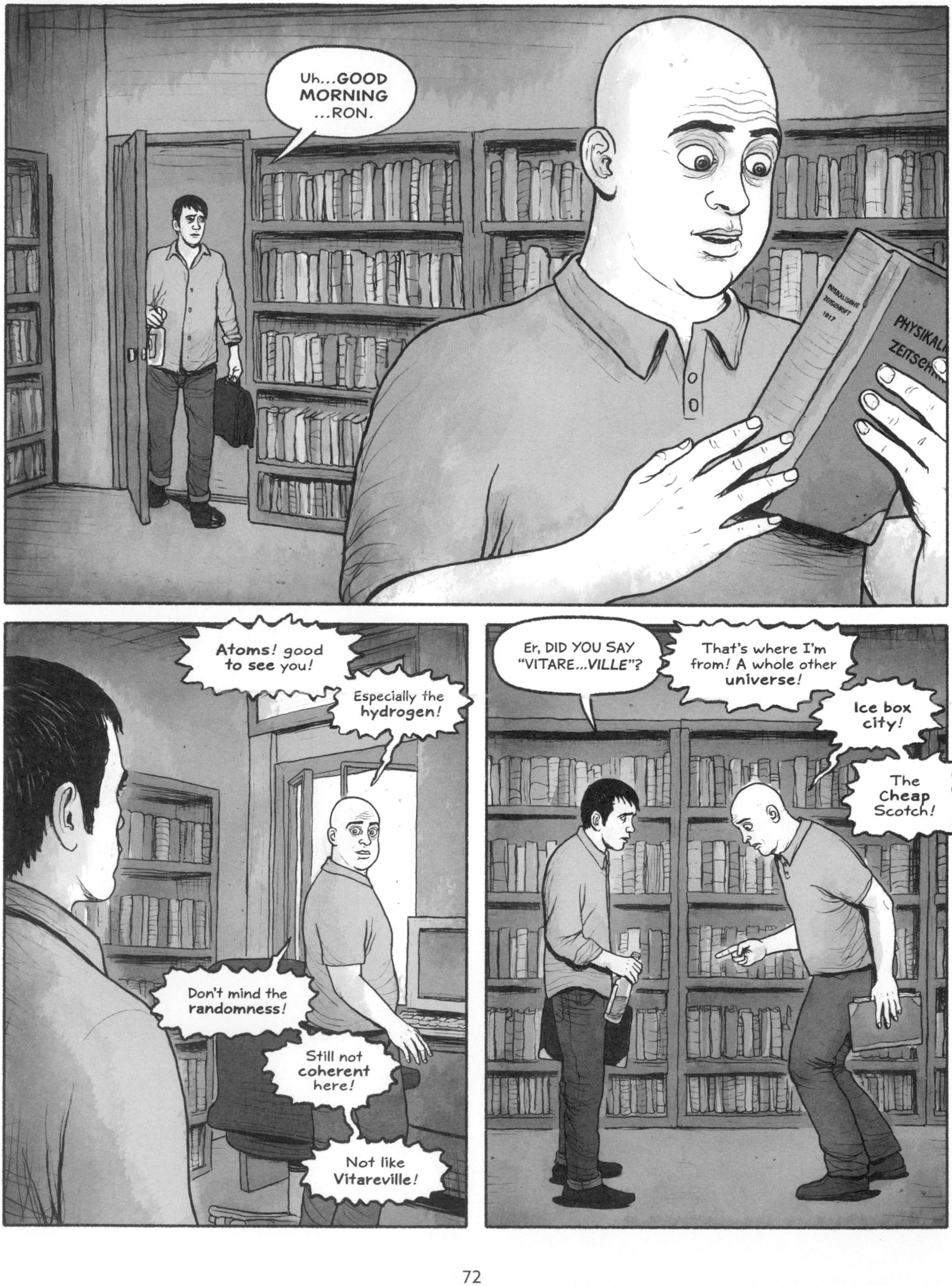
Uh...GOOD MORNING ...RON.
PHYSIKALISCHE ZEITSCHRIFT 1917
PHYSIKALI ZEITSCH
Atoms! good to see you!
Especially the hydrogen!
Don't mind the randomness!
Still not coherent here!
Not like Vitareville!
Er, DID YOU SAY "VITARE...VILLE"?
That's where I'm from! A whole other universe!
Ice box city!
The Cheap Scotch!

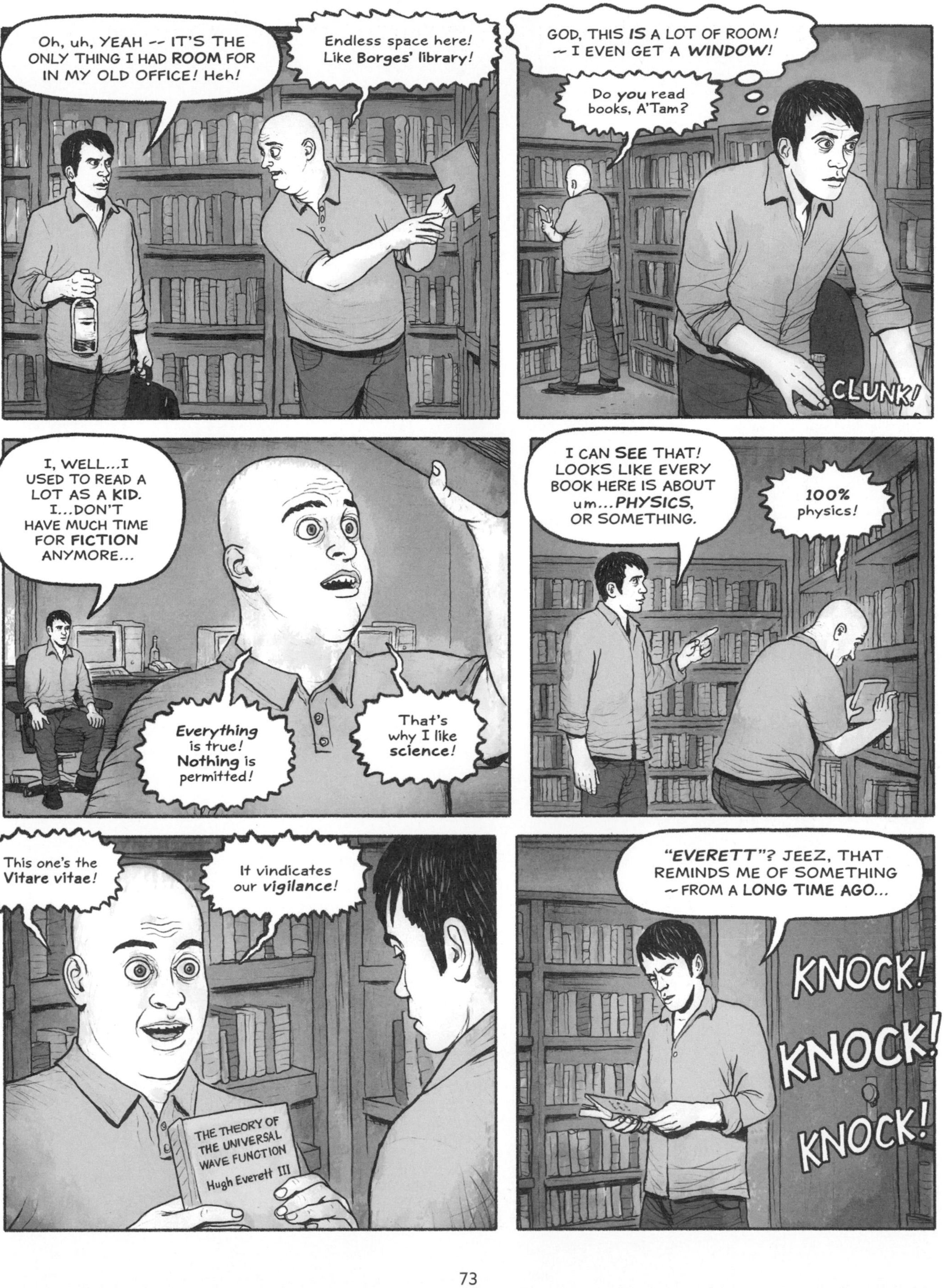

Oh, uh, YEAH -- IT'S THE ONLY THING I HAD ROOM FOR IN MY OLD OFFICE! Heh!
Endless space here! Like Borges' library!
GOD, THIS IS A LOT OF ROOM! — I EVEN GET A WINDOW!
Do you read books, A'Tam?
CLUNK!
I, WELL...I USED TO READ A LOT AS A KID. I...DON'T HAVE MUCH TIME FOR FICTION ANYMORE...
Everything is true! Nothing is permitted!
That's why I like science!
I CAN SEE THAT! LOOKS LIKE EVERY BOOK HERE IS ABOUT um...PHYSICS, OR SOMETHING.
100% physics!
This one's the Vitare vitae!
It vindicates our vigilance!
THE THEORY OF THE UNIVERSAL WAVE FUNCTION
Hugh Everett III
"EVERETT"? JEEZ, THAT REMINDS ME OF SOMETHING — FROM A LONG TIME AGO...
KNOCK!
KNOCK!
KNOCK!

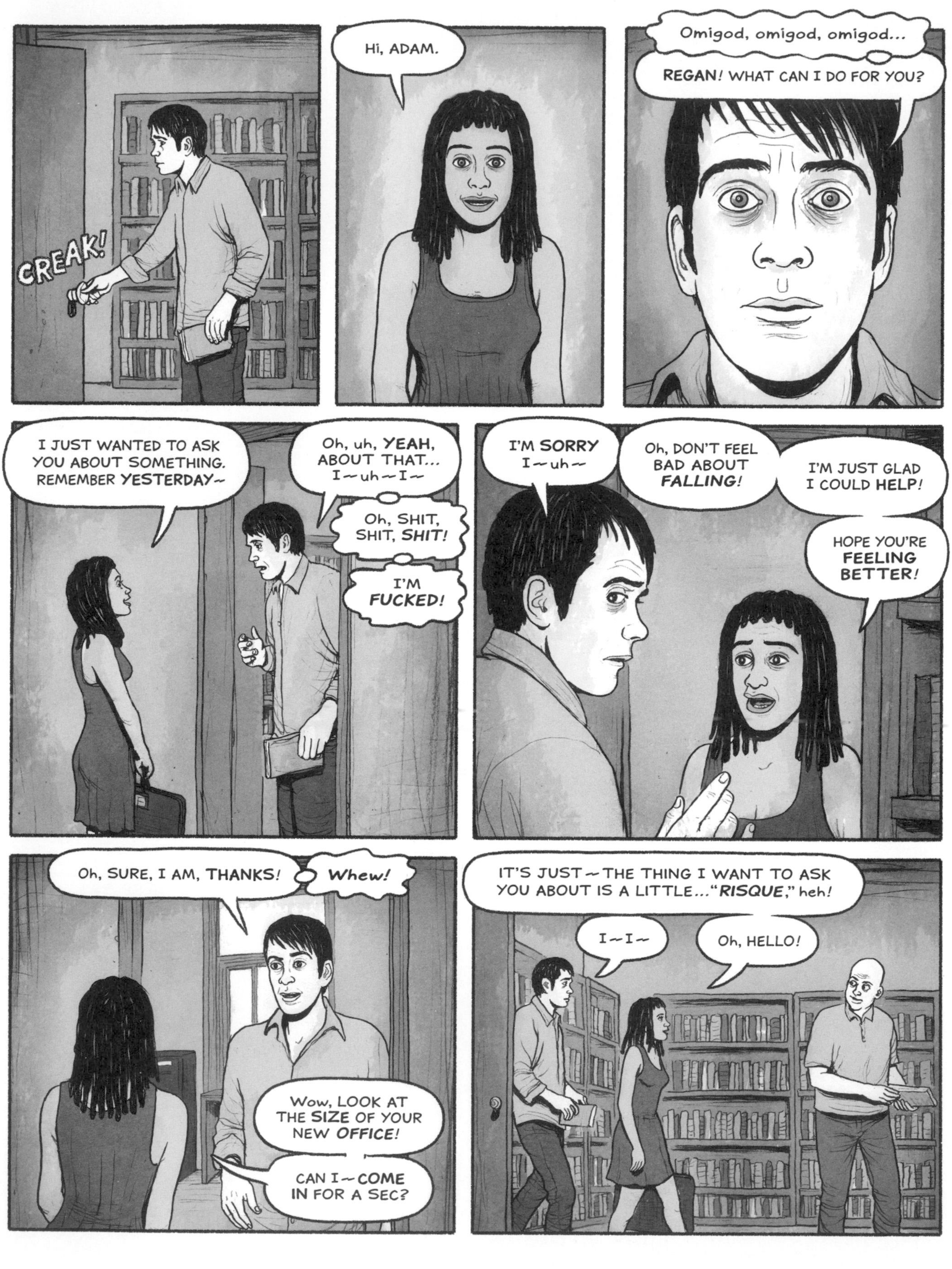
CREAK!
Hi, ADAM.
Omigod, omigod, omigod...
REGAN! WHAT CAN I DO FOR YOU?
I JUST WANTED TO ASK YOU ABOUT SOMETHING. REMEMBER YESTERDAY--
Oh, uh, YEAH, ABOUT THAT... I--uh--I--
Oh, SHIT, SHIT, SHIT!
I'M FUCKED!
I'M SORRY I--uh--
Oh, DON'T FEEL BAD ABOUT FALLING!
I'M JUST GLAD I COULD HELP!
HOPE YOU'RE FEELING BETTER!
Oh, SURE, I AM, THANKS!
Whew!
Wow, LOOK AT THE SIZE OF YOUR NEW OFFICE!
CAN I--COME IN FOR A SEC?
IT'S JUST--THE THING I WANT TO ASK YOU ABOUT IS A LITTLE..."RISQUE," heh!
I--I--
Oh, HELLO!

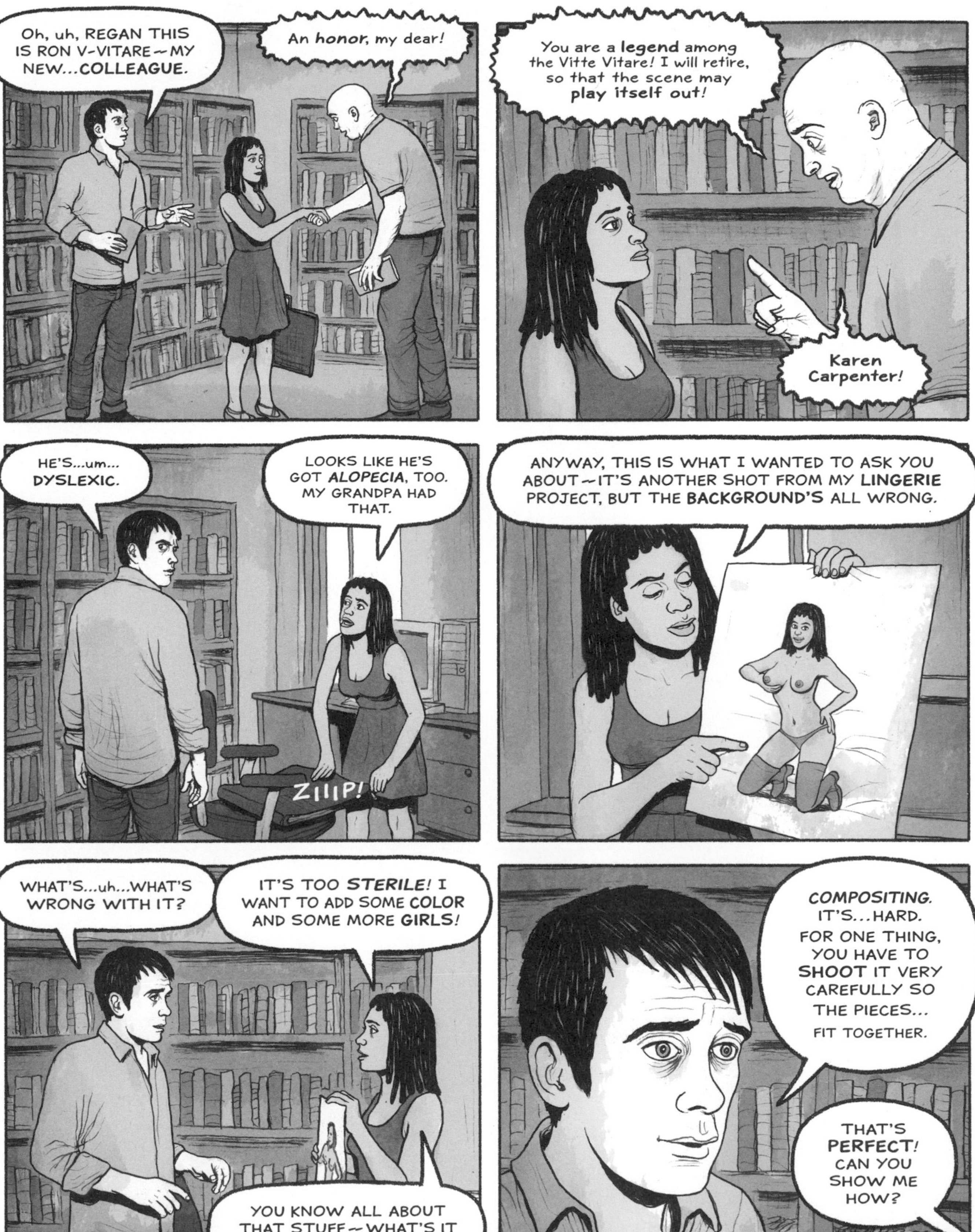
Oh, uh, REGAN THIS IS RON V-VITARE—MY NEW...COLLEAGUE.
An honor, my dear!
You are a legend among the Vitte Vitare! I will retire, so that the scene may play itself out!
Karen Carpenter!
HE'S...um... DYSLEXIC.
LOOKS LIKE HE'S GOT ALOPECIA, TOO. MY GRANDPA HAD THAT.
ZIIIP!
ANYWAY, THIS IS WHAT I WANTED TO ASK YOU ABOUT—IT'S ANOTHER SHOT FROM MY LINGERIE PROJECT, BUT THE BACKGROUND'S ALL WRONG.
WHAT'S...uh...WHAT'S WRONG WITH IT?
IT'S TOO STERILE! I WANT TO ADD SOME COLOR AND SOME MORE GIRLS!
YOU KNOW ALL ABOUT THAT STUFF—WHAT'S IT CALLED? "COMPOSING"?
COMPOSITING. IT'S...HARD. FOR ONE THING, YOU HAVE TO SHOOT IT VERY CAREFULLY SO THE PIECES... FIT TOGETHER.
THAT'S PERFECT! CAN YOU SHOW ME HOW?

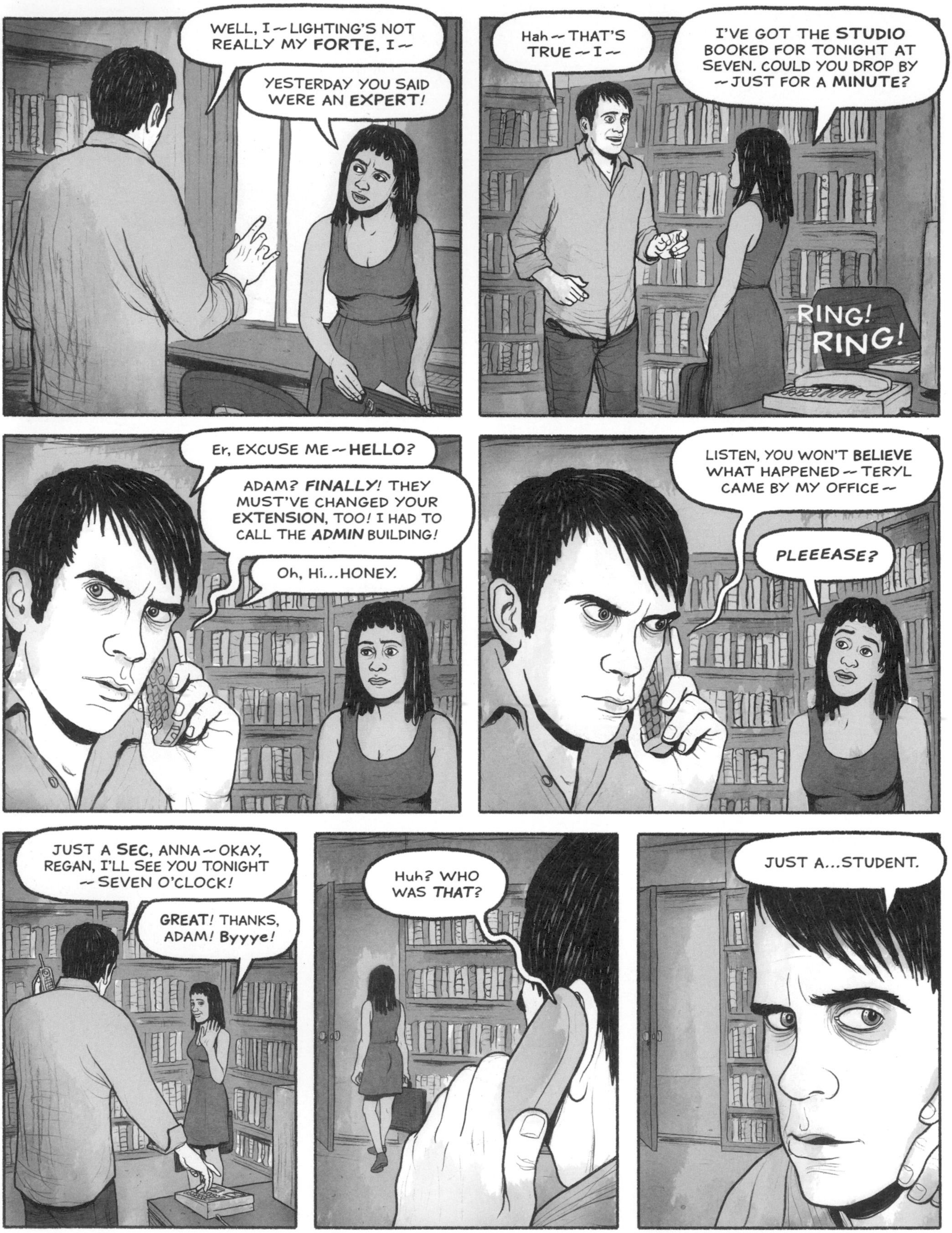
WELL, I -- LIGHTING'S NOT REALLY MY FORTE, I --
YESTERDAY YOU SAID WERE AN EXPERT!
Hah -- THAT'S TRUE -- I --
I'VE GOT THE STUDIO BOOKED FOR TONIGHT AT SEVEN. COULD YOU DROP BY -- JUST FOR A MINUTE?
RING! RING!
Er, EXCUSE ME -- HELLO?
ADAM? FINALLY! THEY MUST'VE CHANGED YOUR EXTENSION, TOO! I HAD TO CALL THE ADMIN BUILDING!
Oh, Hi... HONEY.
LISTEN, YOU WON'T BELIEVE WHAT HAPPENED -- TERYL CAME BY MY OFFICE --
PLEEEASE?
JUST A SEC, ANNA -- OKAY, REGAN, I'LL SEE YOU TONIGHT -- SEVEN O'CLOCK!
GREAT! THANKS, ADAM! Byyye!
Huh? WHO WAS THAT?
JUST A... STUDENT.

Hmph ~ ALRIGHT, **LISTEN** ~ TERYL CAME BY MY OFFICE WITH HER FRIEND *KASIMIR* AND THEY SAW YOUR **PRINT** NEXT TO ~

WHO'S *CASIMIR?*

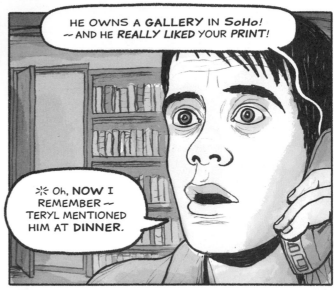

HE OWNS A **GALLERY** IN *SoHo!* ~ AND HE *REALLY LIKED* YOUR *PRINT!*

☀ Oh, **NOW I REMEMBER** ~ TERYL MENTIONED HIM AT **DINNER.**

OKAY, SO THE THING IS ~ HE'S GOING TO BE IN *JERSEY CITY* TOMORROW, AND I SUGGESTED HE COULD STOP BY TO **MEET** YOU ~ AND SEE YOUR **WORK!**

WHAT?! *REALLY?*

HE'S COMING BY AT **9 AM** ~ SO MAKE SURE YOU'RE **READY!**

ALRIGHT? I GOTTA RUN!

I ~ YEAH ~ SURE, BABE ~ THAT'S *GREAT!*

OK, *LOVE YOU,* 'BYE!

LOVE YOU TOO! 'BYE!

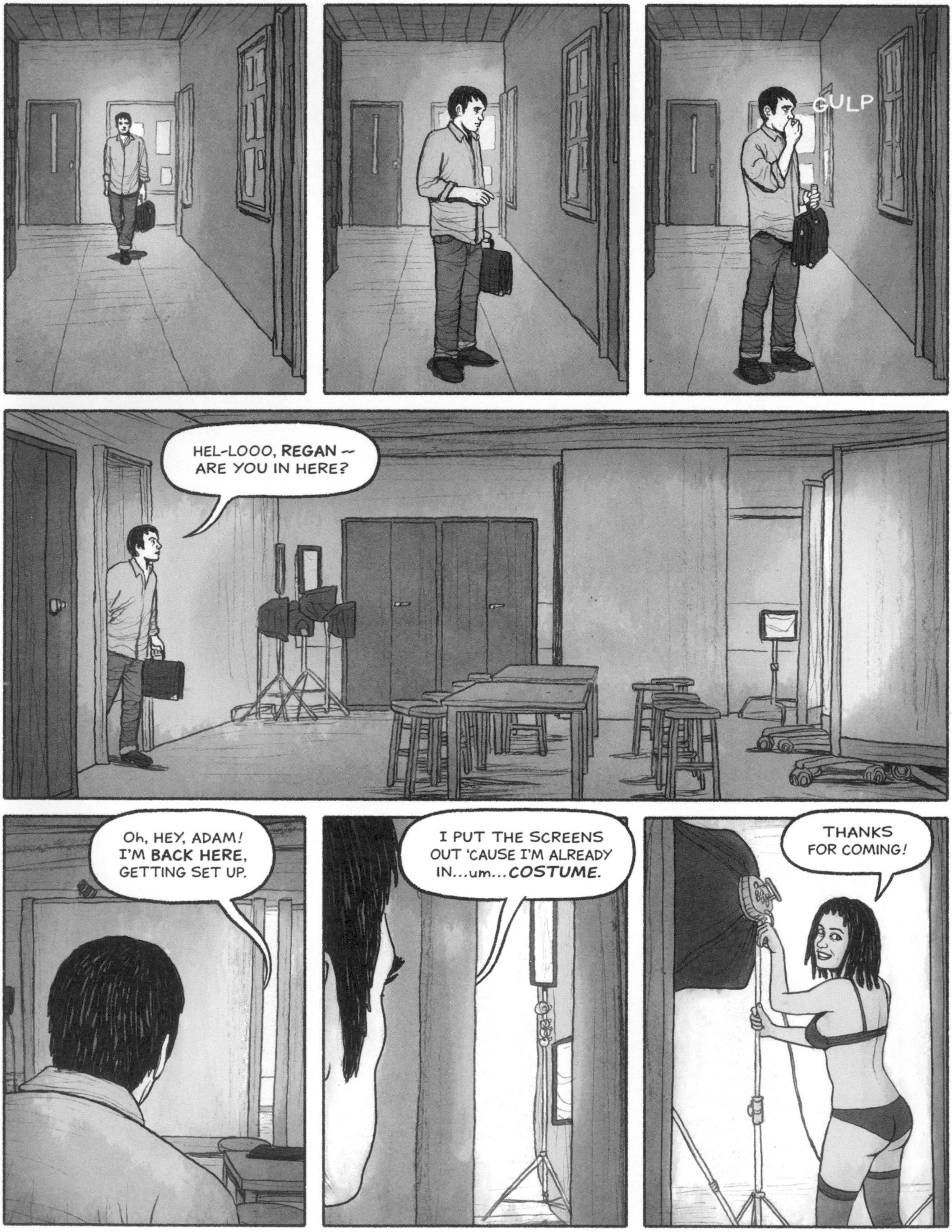
GULP
HEL-LOOO, REGAN -- ARE YOU IN HERE?
Oh, HEY, ADAM! I'M BACK HERE, GETTING SET UP.
I PUT THE SCREENS OUT 'CAUSE I'M ALREADY IN...um...COSTUME.
THANKS FOR COMING!

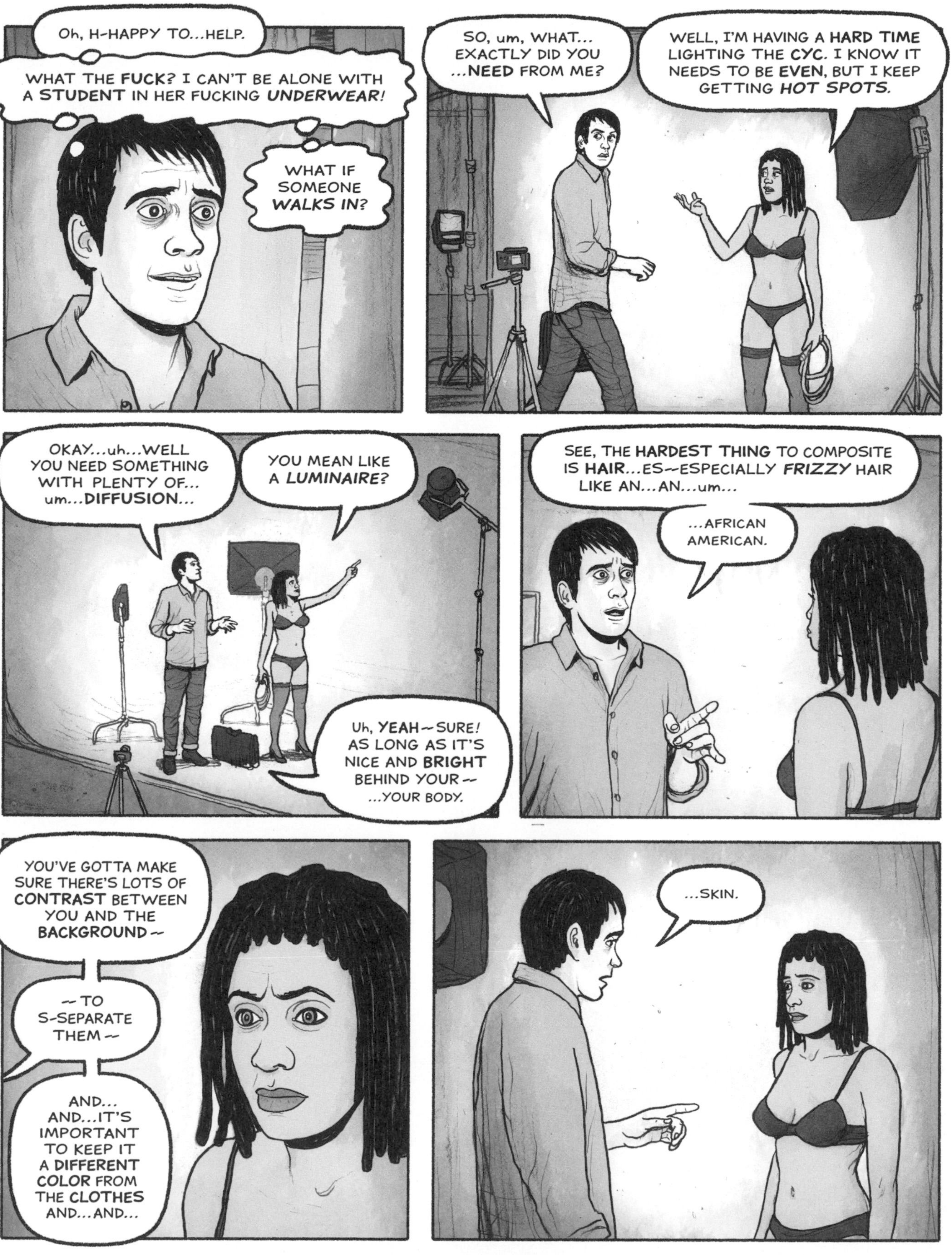
Oh, H-HAPPY TO...HELP.
WHAT THE **FUCK**? I CAN'T BE ALONE WITH A **STUDENT** IN HER FUCKING ***UNDERWEAR***!
WHAT IF SOMEONE ***WALKS IN***?
SO, um, WHAT... EXACTLY DID YOU ...**NEED** FROM ME?
WELL, I'M HAVING A **HARD TIME** LIGHTING THE **CYC**. I KNOW IT NEEDS TO BE **EVEN**, BUT I KEEP GETTING ***HOT SPOTS***.
OKAY...uh...WELL YOU NEED SOMETHING WITH PLENTY OF... um...**DIFFUSION**...
YOU MEAN LIKE A ***LUMINAIRE***?
Uh, **YEAH**--SURE! AS LONG AS IT'S NICE AND **BRIGHT** BEHIND YOUR-- ...YOUR BODY.
SEE, THE **HARDEST THING** TO COMPOSITE IS **HAIR**...ES--ESPECIALLY ***FRIZZY*** HAIR LIKE AN...AN...um...
...AFRICAN AMERICAN.
YOU'VE GOTTA MAKE SURE THERE'S LOTS OF **CONTRAST** BETWEEN YOU AND THE **BACKGROUND**--
--TO S-SEPARATE THEM--
AND... AND...IT'S IMPORTANT TO KEEP IT A **DIFFERENT COLOR** FROM THE **CLOTHES** AND...AND...
...SKIN.

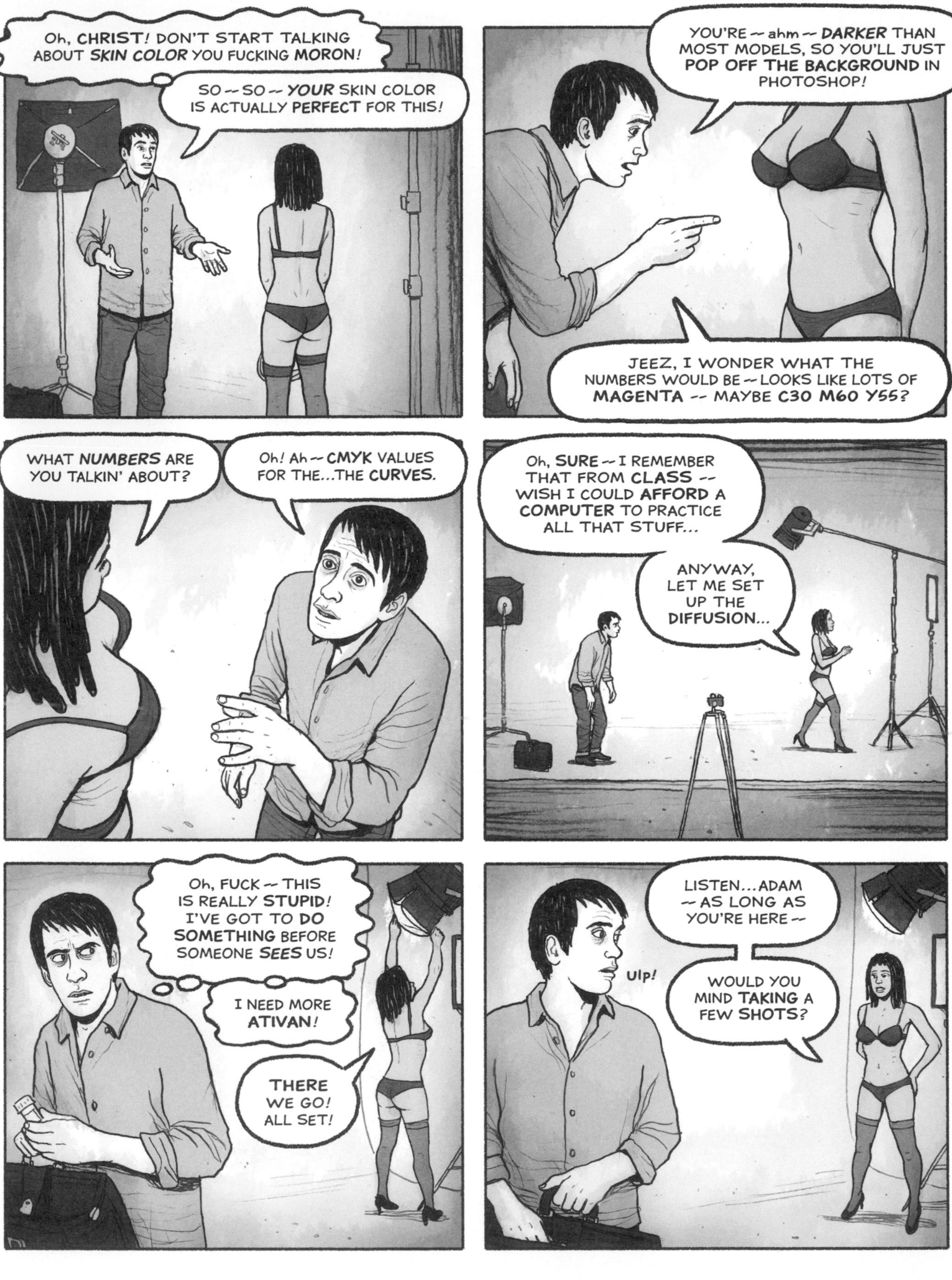
Oh, CHRIST! DON'T START TALKING ABOUT SKIN COLOR YOU FUCKING MORON!
SO -- SO -- YOUR SKIN COLOR IS ACTUALLY PERFECT FOR THIS!
YOU'RE -- ahm -- DARKER THAN MOST MODELS, SO YOU'LL JUST POP OFF THE BACKGROUND IN PHOTOSHOP!
JEEZ, I WONDER WHAT THE NUMBERS WOULD BE -- LOOKS LIKE LOTS OF MAGENTA -- MAYBE C30 M60 Y55?
WHAT NUMBERS ARE YOU TALKIN' ABOUT?
Oh! Ah -- CMYK VALUES FOR THE... THE CURVES.
Oh, SURE -- I REMEMBER THAT FROM CLASS -- WISH I COULD AFFORD A COMPUTER TO PRACTICE ALL THAT STUFF...
ANYWAY, LET ME SET UP THE DIFFUSION...
Oh, FUCK -- THIS IS REALLY STUPID! I'VE GOT TO DO SOMETHING BEFORE SOMEONE SEES US!
I NEED MORE ATIVAN!
THERE WE GO! ALL SET!
LISTEN... ADAM -- AS LONG AS YOU'RE HERE --
Ulp!
WOULD YOU MIND TAKING A FEW SHOTS?

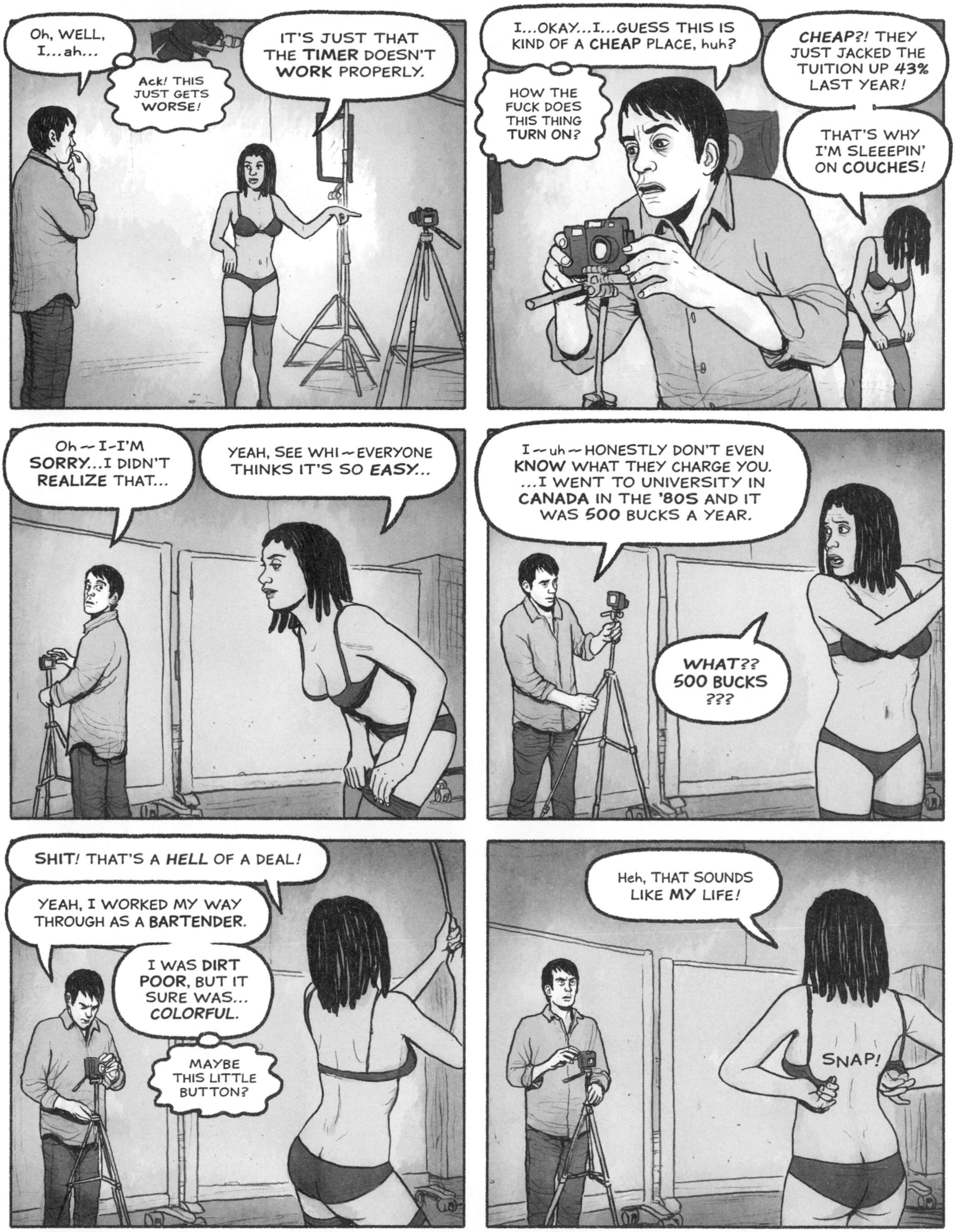

Oh, WELL, I...ah...
Ack! THIS JUST GETS WORSE!
IT'S JUST THAT THE TIMER DOESN'T WORK PROPERLY.
I...OKAY...I...GUESS THIS IS KIND OF A CHEAP PLACE, huh?
HOW THE FUCK DOES THIS THING TURN ON?
CHEAP?! THEY JUST JACKED THE TUITION UP 43% LAST YEAR!
THAT'S WHY I'M SLEEPIN' ON COUCHES!
Oh — I-I'M SORRY...I DIDN'T REALIZE THAT...
YEAH, SEE WHI — EVERYONE THINKS IT'S SO EASY...
I — uh — HONESTLY DON'T EVEN KNOW WHAT THEY CHARGE YOU. ...I WENT TO UNIVERSITY IN CANADA IN THE '80S AND IT WAS 500 BUCKS A YEAR.
WHAT?? 500 BUCKS ???
SHIT! THAT'S A HELL OF A DEAL!
YEAH, I WORKED MY WAY THROUGH AS A BARTENDER.
I WAS DIRT POOR, BUT IT SURE WAS... COLORFUL.
MAYBE THIS LITTLE BUTTON?
Heh, THAT SOUNDS LIKE MY LIFE!
SNAP!

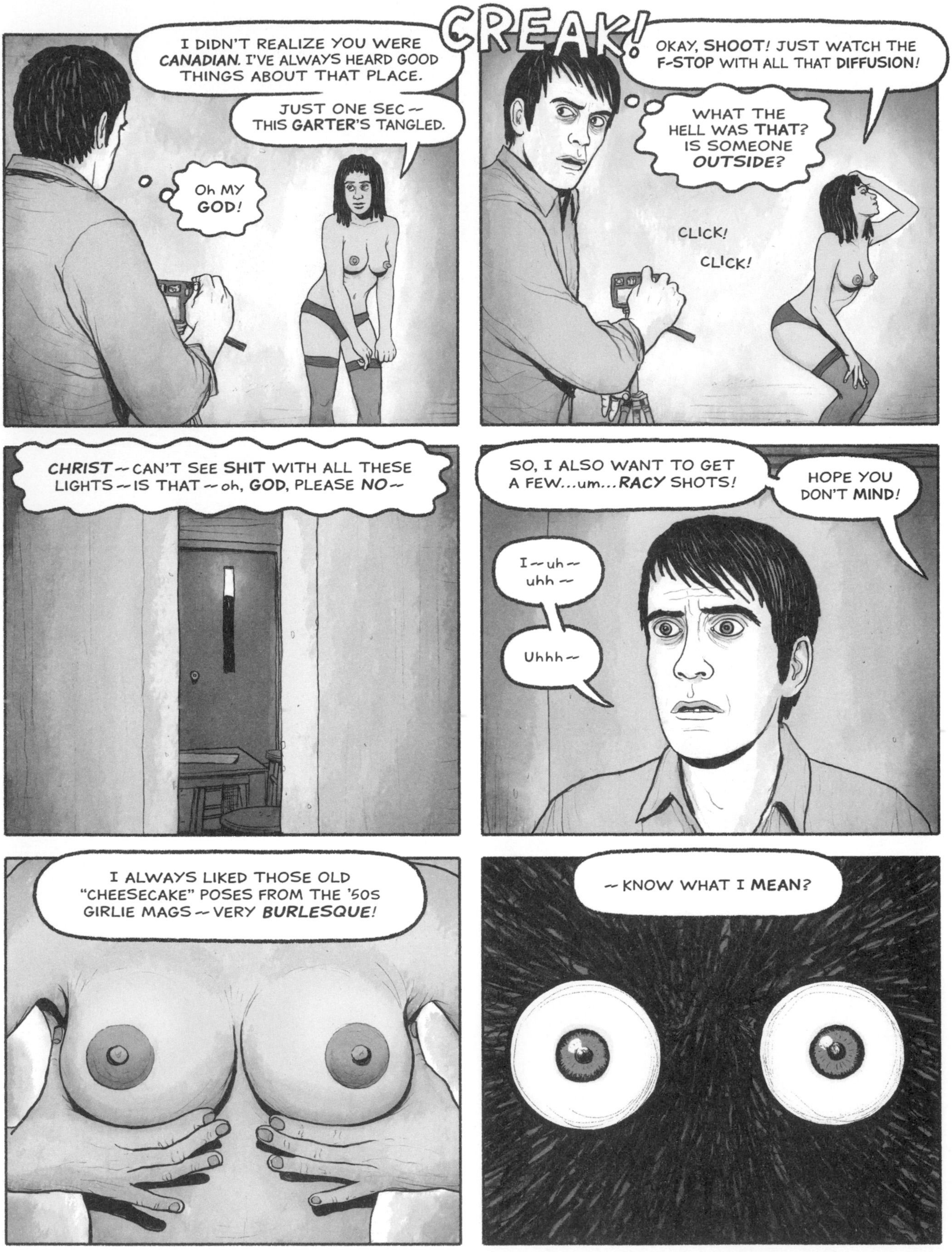

CREAK!
I DIDN'T REALIZE YOU WERE CANADIAN. I'VE ALWAYS HEARD GOOD THINGS ABOUT THAT PLACE.
JUST ONE SEC-- THIS GARTER'S TANGLED.
Oh MY GOD!
OKAY, SHOOT! JUST WATCH THE F-STOP WITH ALL THAT DIFFUSION!
WHAT THE HELL WAS THAT? IS SOMEONE OUTSIDE?
CLICK!
CLICK!
CHRIST-- CAN'T SEE SHIT WITH ALL THESE LIGHTS-- IS THAT-- oh, GOD, PLEASE NO--
SO, I ALSO WANT TO GET A FEW...um...RACY SHOTS!
HOPE YOU DON'T MIND!
I-- uh-- uhh--
Uhhh--
I ALWAYS LIKED THOSE OLD "CHEESECAKE" POSES FROM THE '50S GIRLIE MAGS-- VERY BURLESQUE!
--KNOW WHAT I MEAN?

Oh, HEY, PAL! YOU OKAY?
YER JUST ah...STANDIN' THERE.
I...
I'M SICK, I GUESS...
SORRY TO HEAR THAT, BUDDY.
LISTEN, IT'S NONE OF MY BUSINESS, BUT I COULDN'T HELP NOTICIN' YOUR PATH.
MY...uh... PATH?
YEAH, SEE? IT'S GOIN' IN ONE STRAIGHT LINE...
TH' WHOLE WAY.
I...DON'T SEE IT.
Uh-oh! I BET THE R.V.V. PUT YOU IN QUARANTINE!

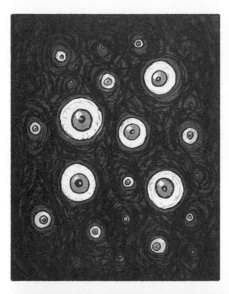

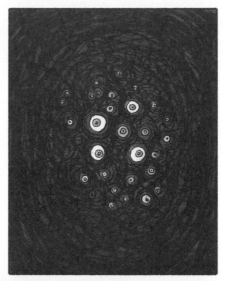

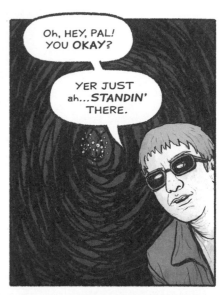

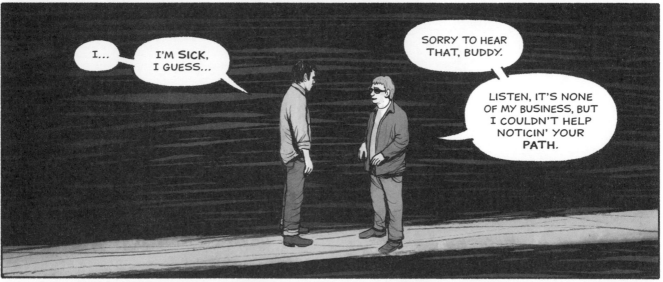

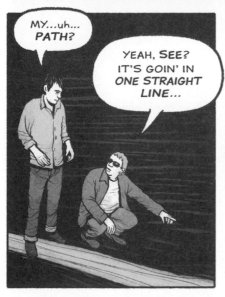

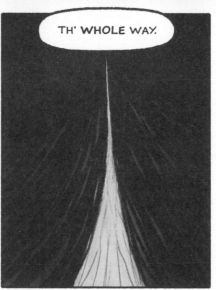

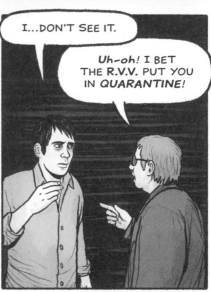

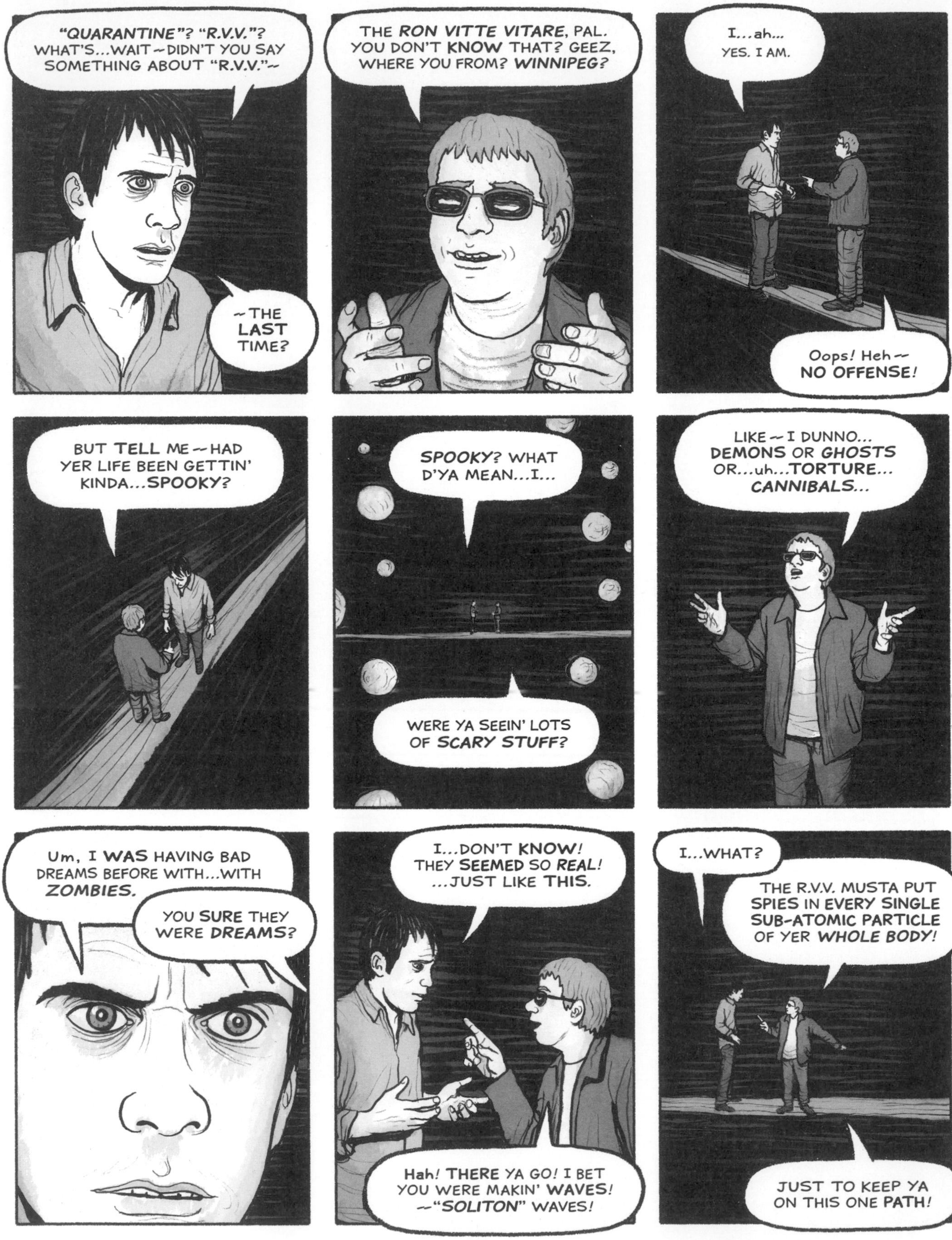
"QUARANTINE"? "R.V.V."? WHAT'S...WAIT–DIDN'T YOU SAY SOMETHING ABOUT "R.V.V."–
–THE LAST TIME?
THE RON VITTE VITARE, PAL. YOU DON'T KNOW THAT? GEEZ, WHERE YOU FROM? WINNIPEG?
I...ah... YES. I AM.
Oops! Heh– NO OFFENSE!
BUT TELL ME–HAD YER LIFE BEEN GETTIN' KINDA...SPOOKY?
SPOOKY? WHAT D'YA MEAN...I...
WERE YA SEEIN' LOTS OF SCARY STUFF?
LIKE–I DUNNO... DEMONS OR GHOSTS OR...uh...TORTURE... CANNIBALS...
Um, I WAS HAVING BAD DREAMS BEFORE WITH...WITH ZOMBIES.
YOU SURE THEY WERE DREAMS?
I...DON'T KNOW! THEY SEEMED SO REAL! ...JUST LIKE THIS.
Hah! THERE YA GO! I BET YOU WERE MAKIN' WAVES! –"SOLITON" WAVES!
I...WHAT?
THE R.V.V. MUSTA PUT SPIES IN EVERY SINGLE SUB-ATOMIC PARTICLE OF YER WHOLE BODY!
JUST TO KEEP YA ON THIS ONE PATH!

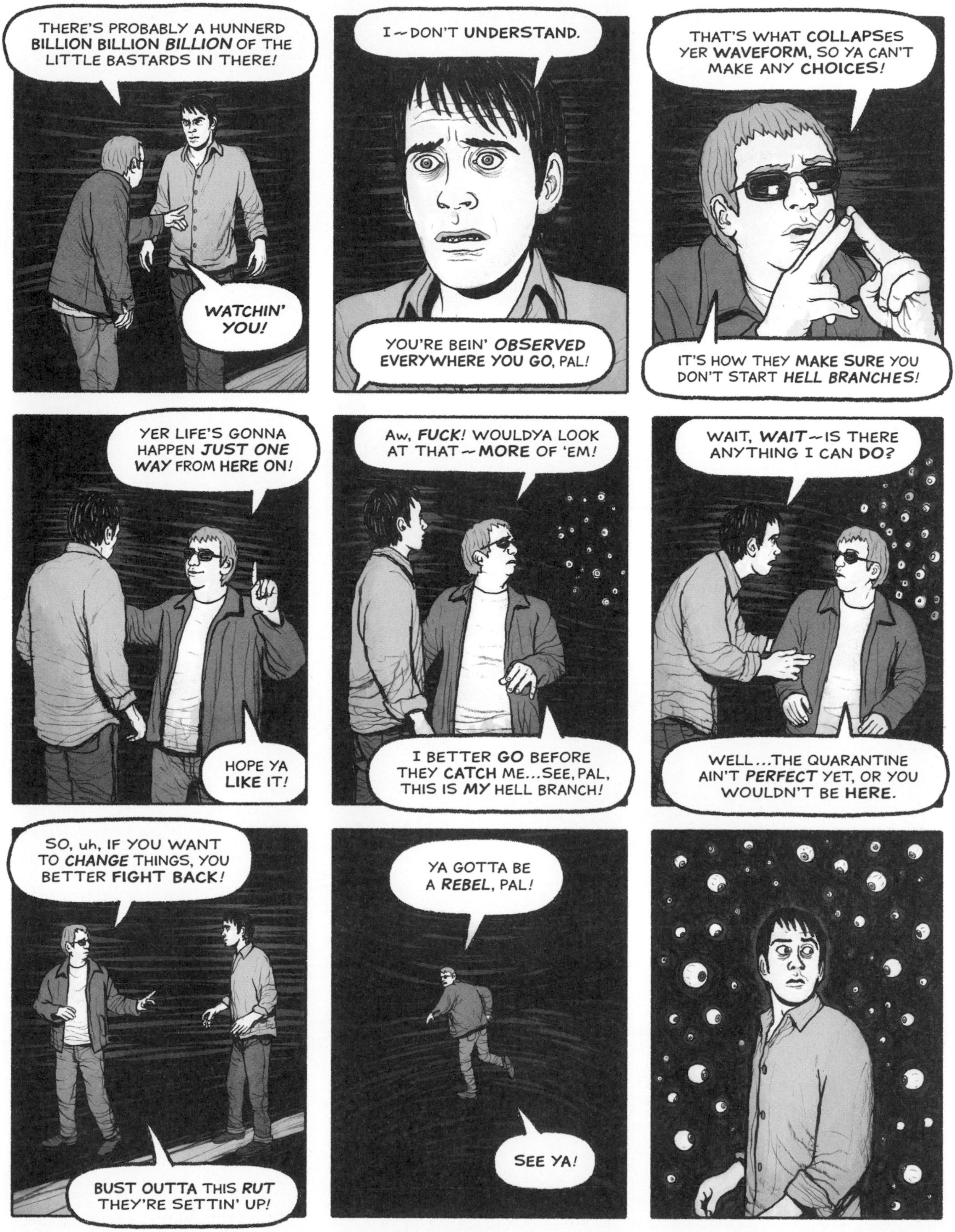
THERE'S PROBABLY A HUNNERD BILLION BILLION BILLION OF THE LITTLE BASTARDS IN THERE!
WATCHIN' YOU!
I--DON'T UNDERSTAND.
YOU'RE BEIN' OBSERVED EVERYWHERE YOU GO, PAL!
THAT'S WHAT COLLAPSEs YER WAVEFORM, SO YA CAN'T MAKE ANY CHOICES!
IT'S HOW THEY MAKE SURE YOU DON'T START HELL BRANCHES!
YER LIFE'S GONNA HAPPEN JUST ONE WAY FROM HERE ON!
HOPE YA LIKE IT!
Aw, FUCK! WOULDYA LOOK AT THAT--MORE OF 'EM!
I BETTER GO BEFORE THEY CATCH ME...SEE, PAL, THIS IS MY HELL BRANCH!
WAIT, WAIT--IS THERE ANYTHING I CAN DO?
WELL...THE QUARANTINE AIN'T PERFECT YET, OR YOU WOULDN'T BE HERE.
SO, uh, IF YOU WANT TO CHANGE THINGS, YOU BETTER FIGHT BACK!
BUST OUTTA THIS RUT THEY'RE SETTIN' UP!
YA GOTTA BE A REBEL, PAL!
SEE YA!

 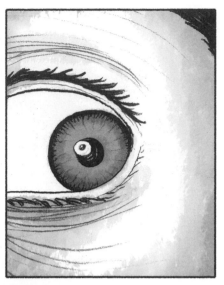 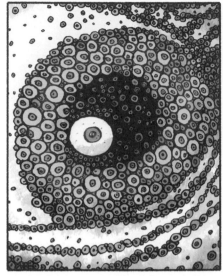

DING DONG DING DONG

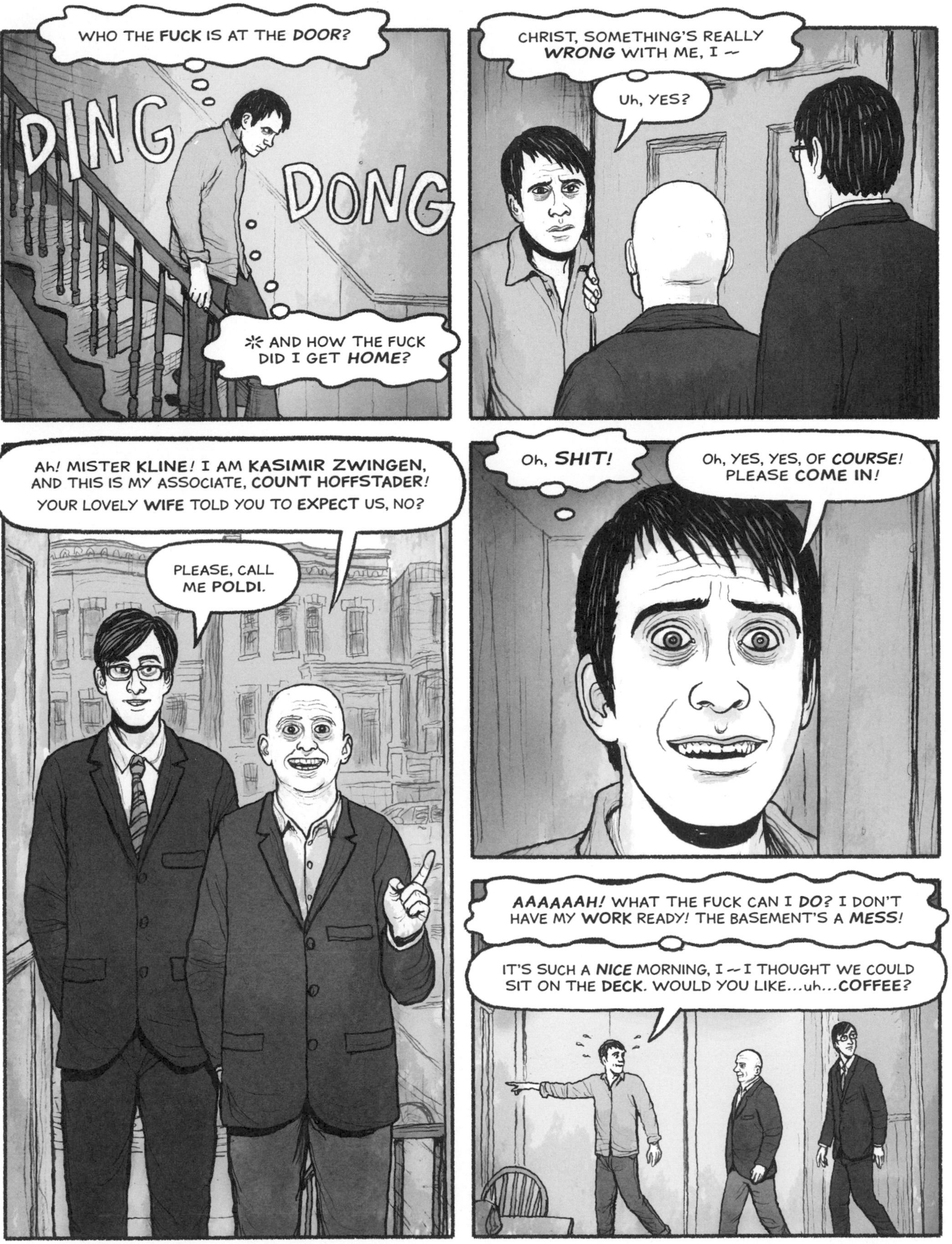
WHO THE FUCK IS AT THE DOOR?
DING
DONG
AND HOW THE FUCK DID I GET HOME?
CHRIST, SOMETHING'S REALLY WRONG WITH ME, I --
Uh, YES?
Ah! MISTER KLINE! I AM KASIMIR ZWINGEN, AND THIS IS MY ASSOCIATE, COUNT HOFFSTADER! YOUR LOVELY WIFE TOLD YOU TO EXPECT US, NO?
PLEASE, CALL ME POLDI.
Oh, SHIT!
Oh, YES, YES, OF COURSE! PLEASE COME IN!
AAAAAAH! WHAT THE FUCK CAN I DO? I DON'T HAVE MY WORK READY! THE BASEMENT'S A MESS!
IT'S SUCH A NICE MORNING, I -- I THOUGHT WE COULD SIT ON THE DECK. WOULD YOU LIKE...uh...COFFEE?

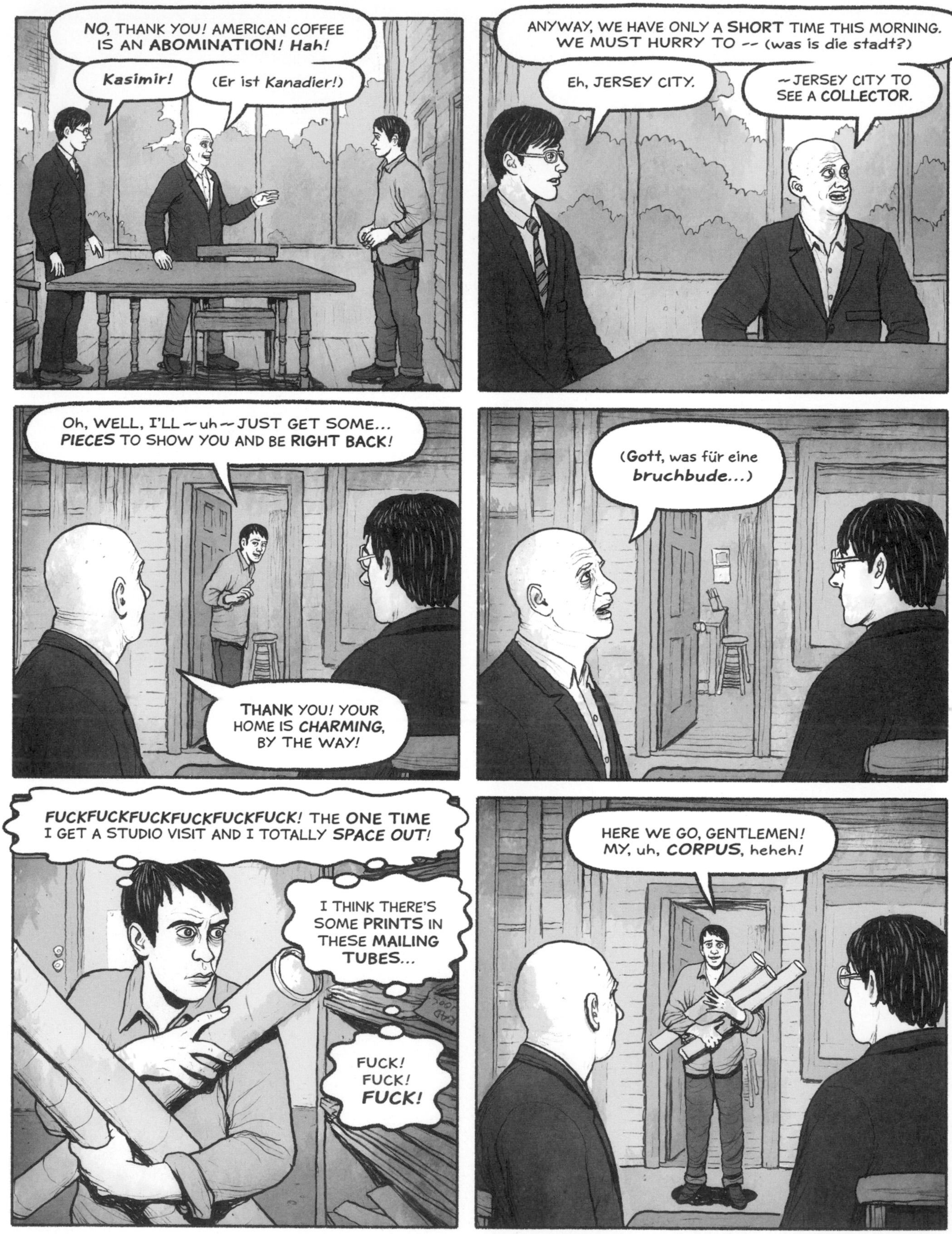
NO, THANK YOU! AMERICAN COFFEE IS AN ABOMINATION! Hah!
Kasimir!
(Er ist Kanadier!)
ANYWAY, WE HAVE ONLY A SHORT TIME THIS MORNING. WE MUST HURRY TO -- (was is die stadt?)
Eh, JERSEY CITY.
~JERSEY CITY TO SEE A COLLECTOR.
Oh, WELL, I'LL~uh~JUST GET SOME... PIECES TO SHOW YOU AND BE RIGHT BACK!
THANK YOU! YOUR HOME IS CHARMING, BY THE WAY!
(Gott, was für eine bruchbude...)
FUCKFUCKFUCKFUCKFUCKFUCK! THE ONE TIME I GET A STUDIO VISIT AND I TOTALLY SPACE OUT!
I THINK THERE'S SOME PRINTS IN THESE MAILING TUBES...
FUCK! FUCK! FUCK!
HERE WE GO, GENTLEMEN! MY, uh, CORPUS, heheh!

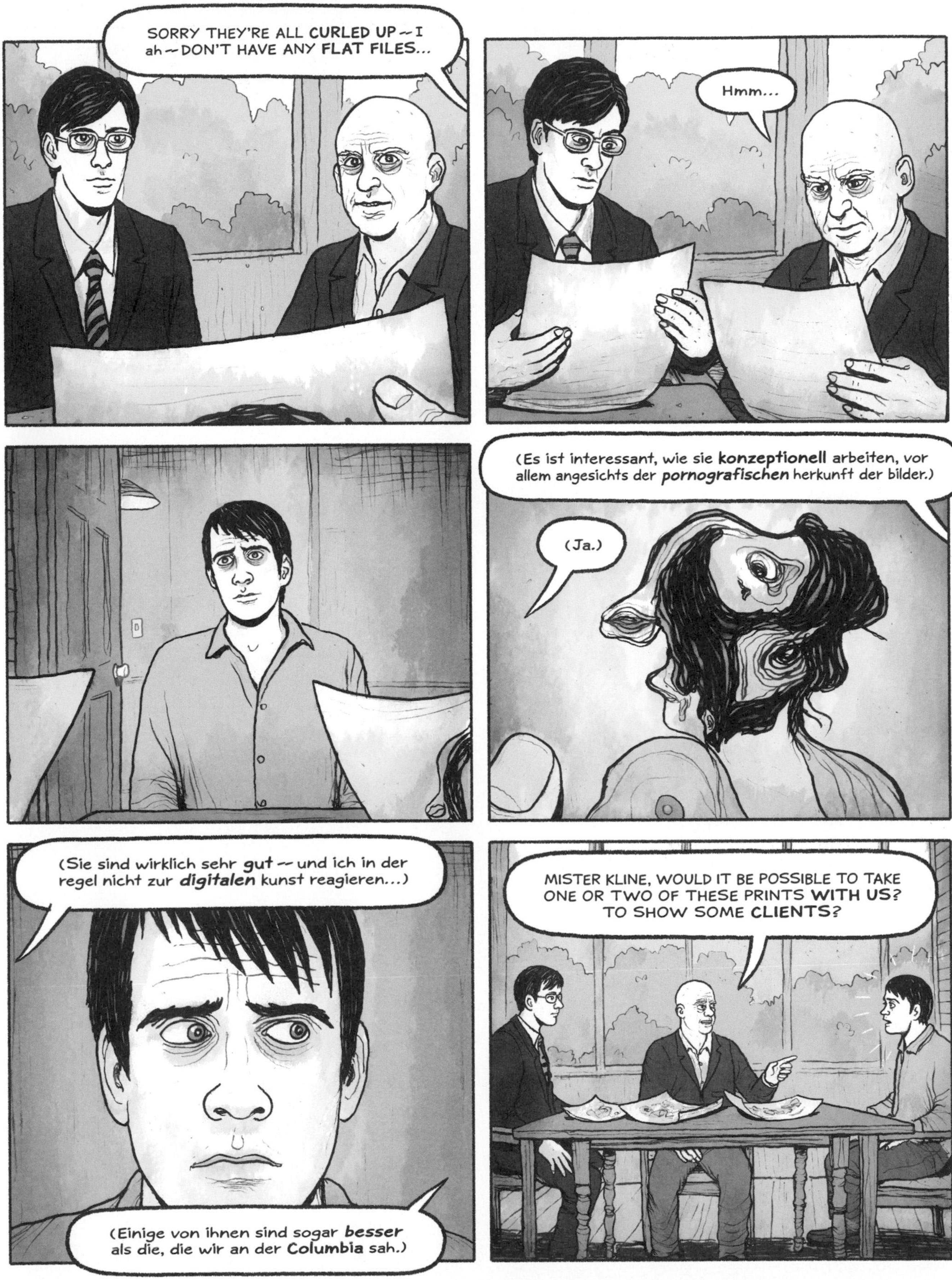
SORRY THEY'RE ALL CURLED UP -- I ah -- DON'T HAVE ANY FLAT FILES...
Hmm...
(Es ist interessant, wie sie konzeptionell arbeiten, vor allem angesichts der pornografischen herkunft der bilder.)
(Ja.)
(Sie sind wirklich sehr gut -- und ich in der regel nicht zur digitalen kunst reagieren...)
(Einige von ihnen sind sogar besser als die, die wir an der Columbia sah.)
MISTER KLINE, WOULD IT BE POSSIBLE TO TAKE ONE OR TWO OF THESE PRINTS WITH US? TO SHOW SOME CLIENTS?

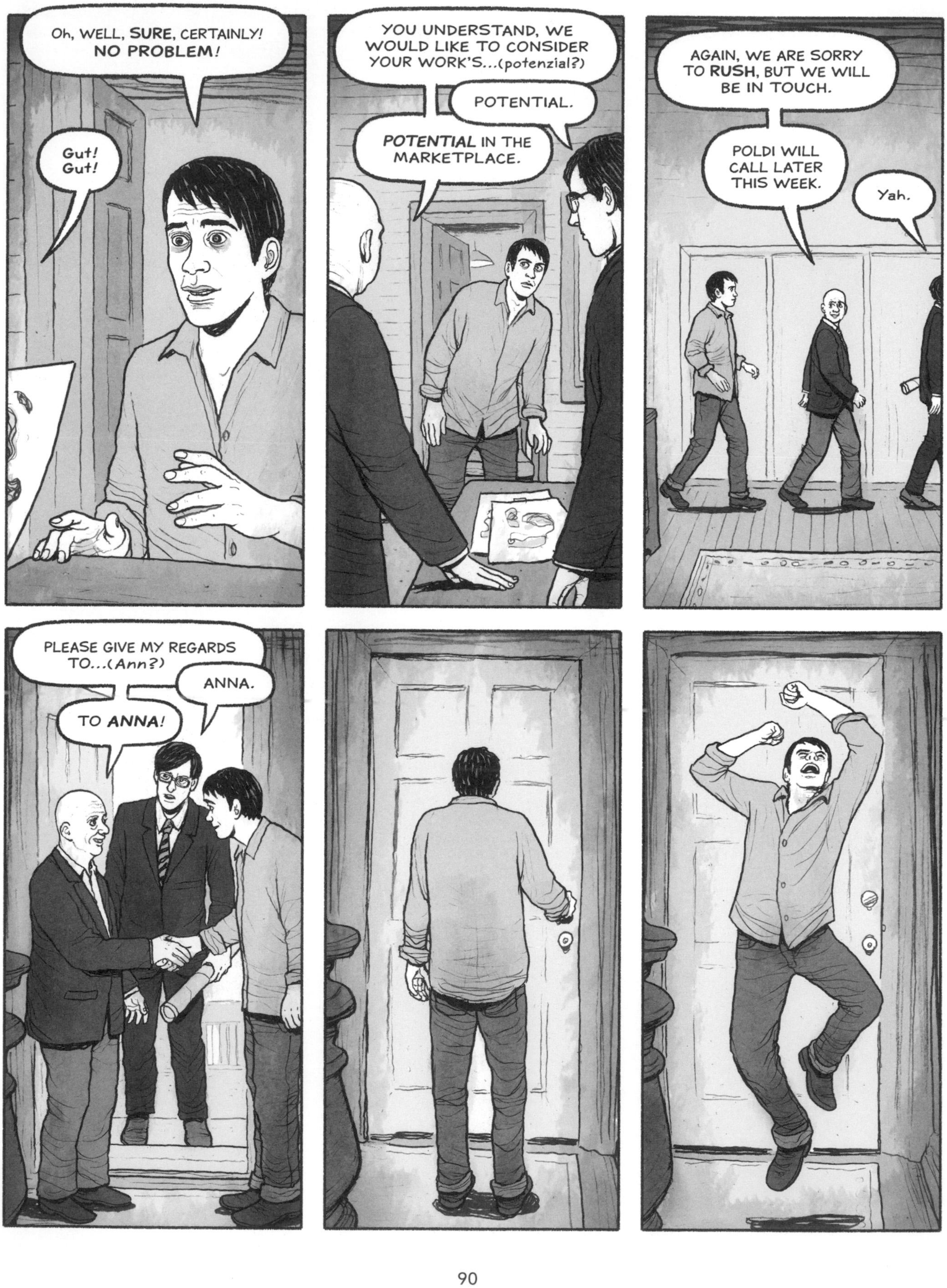
Oh, WELL, SURE, CERTAINLY! NO PROBLEM!
Gut! Gut!
YOU UNDERSTAND, WE WOULD LIKE TO CONSIDER YOUR WORK'S...(potenzial?)
POTENTIAL.
POTENTIAL IN THE MARKETPLACE.
AGAIN, WE ARE SORRY TO RUSH, BUT WE WILL BE IN TOUCH.
POLDI WILL CALL LATER THIS WEEK.
Yah.
PLEASE GIVE MY REGARDS TO...(Ann?)
ANNA.
TO ANNA!

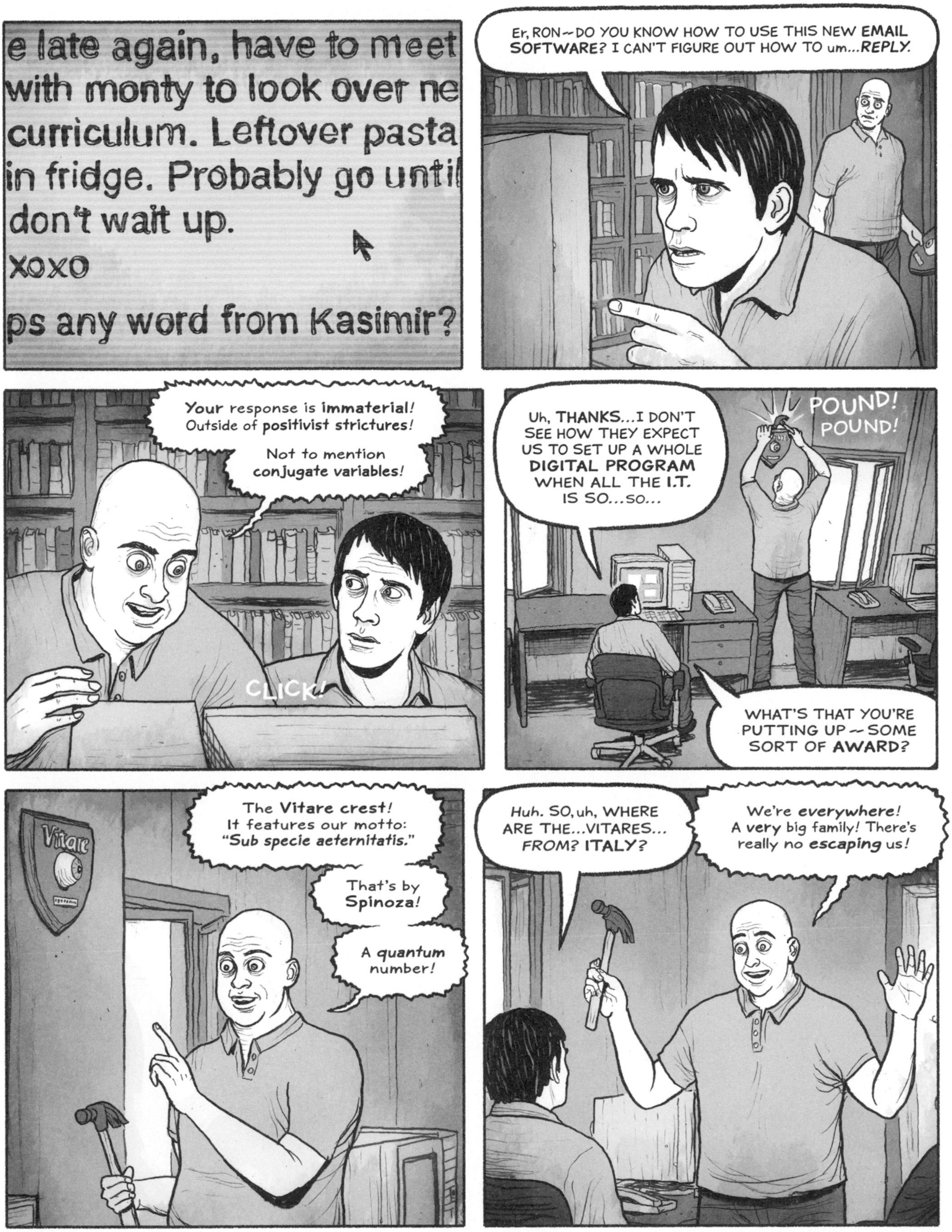
e late again, have to meet
with monty to look over ne
curriculum. Leftover pasta
in fridge. Probably go until
don't wait up.
xoxo
ps any word from Kasimir?
Er, RON--DO YOU KNOW HOW TO USE THIS NEW EMAIL SOFTWARE? I CAN'T FIGURE OUT HOW TO um...REPLY.
Your response is immaterial! Outside of positivist strictures!
Not to mention conjugate variables!
CLICK!
Uh, THANKS...I DON'T SEE HOW THEY EXPECT US TO SET UP A WHOLE DIGITAL PROGRAM WHEN ALL THE I.T. IS SO...so...
POUND! POUND!
WHAT'S THAT YOU'RE PUTTING UP--SOME SORT OF AWARD?
Vitare
The Vitare crest! It features our motto: "Sub specie aeternitatis."
That's by Spinoza!
A quantum number!
Huh. SO, uh, WHERE ARE THE...VITARES... FROM? ITALY?
We're everywhere! A very big family! There's really no escaping us!

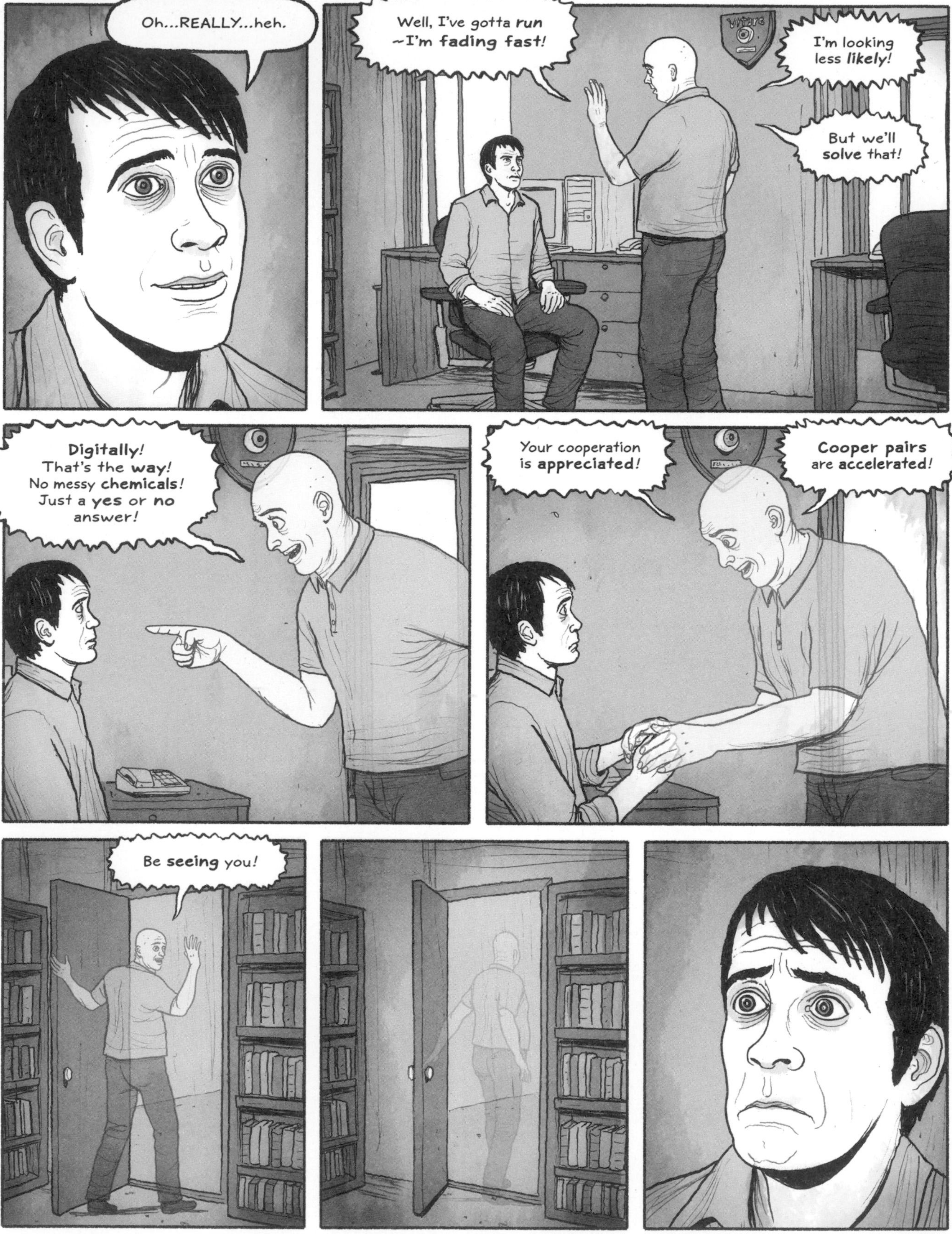
Oh...REALLY...heh.
Well, I've gotta run ~I'm fading fast!
I'm looking less likely!
But we'll solve that!
Digitally! That's the way! No messy chemicals! Just a yes or no answer!
Your cooperation is appreciated!
Cooper pairs are accelerated!
Be seeing you!

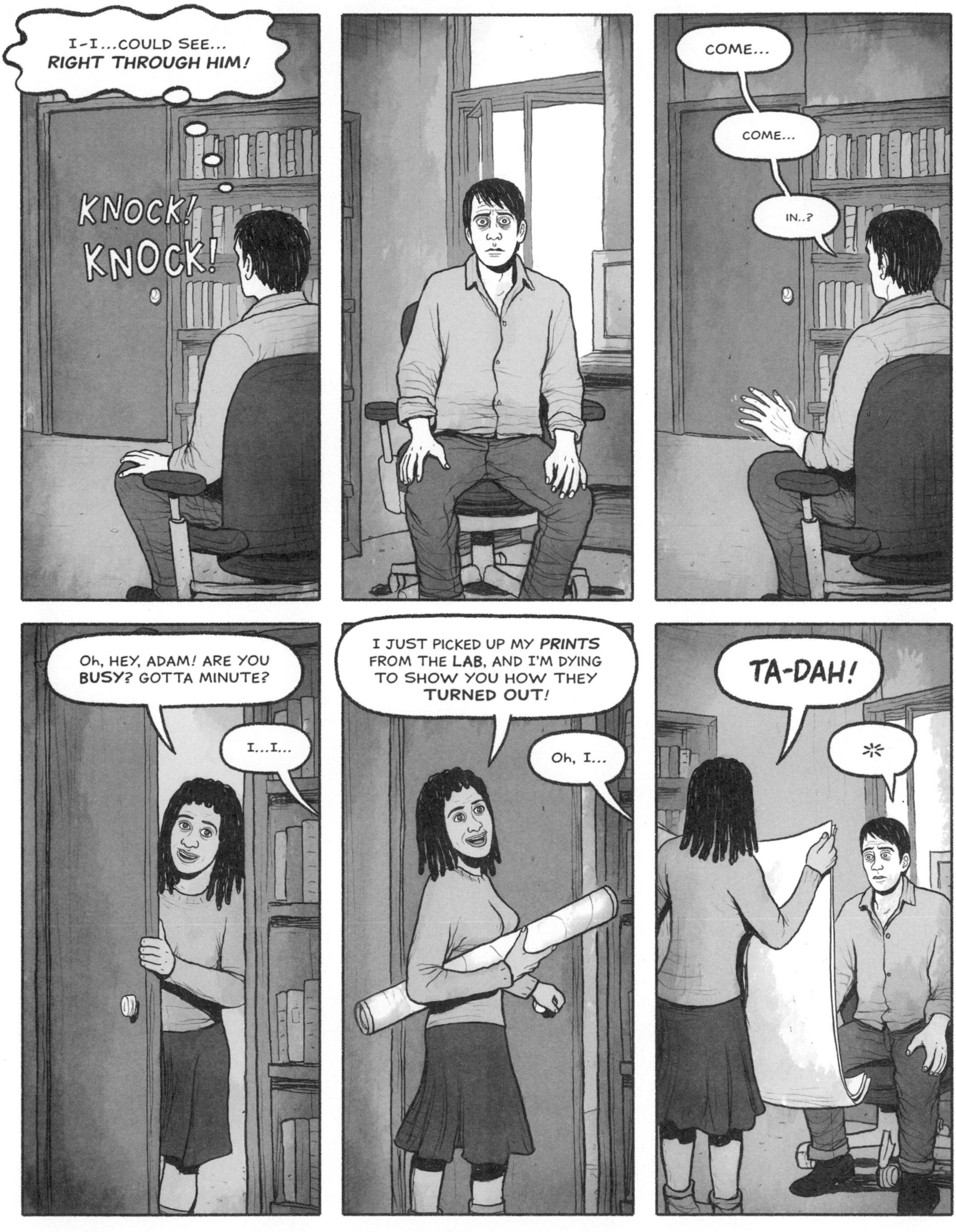
I-I...COULD SEE... RIGHT THROUGH HIM!
KNOCK! KNOCK!
COME...
COME...
IN..?
Oh, HEY, ADAM! ARE YOU BUSY? GOTTA MINUTE?
I...I...
I JUST PICKED UP MY PRINTS FROM THE LAB, AND I'M DYING TO SHOW YOU HOW THEY TURNED OUT!
Oh, I...
TA-DAH!
*

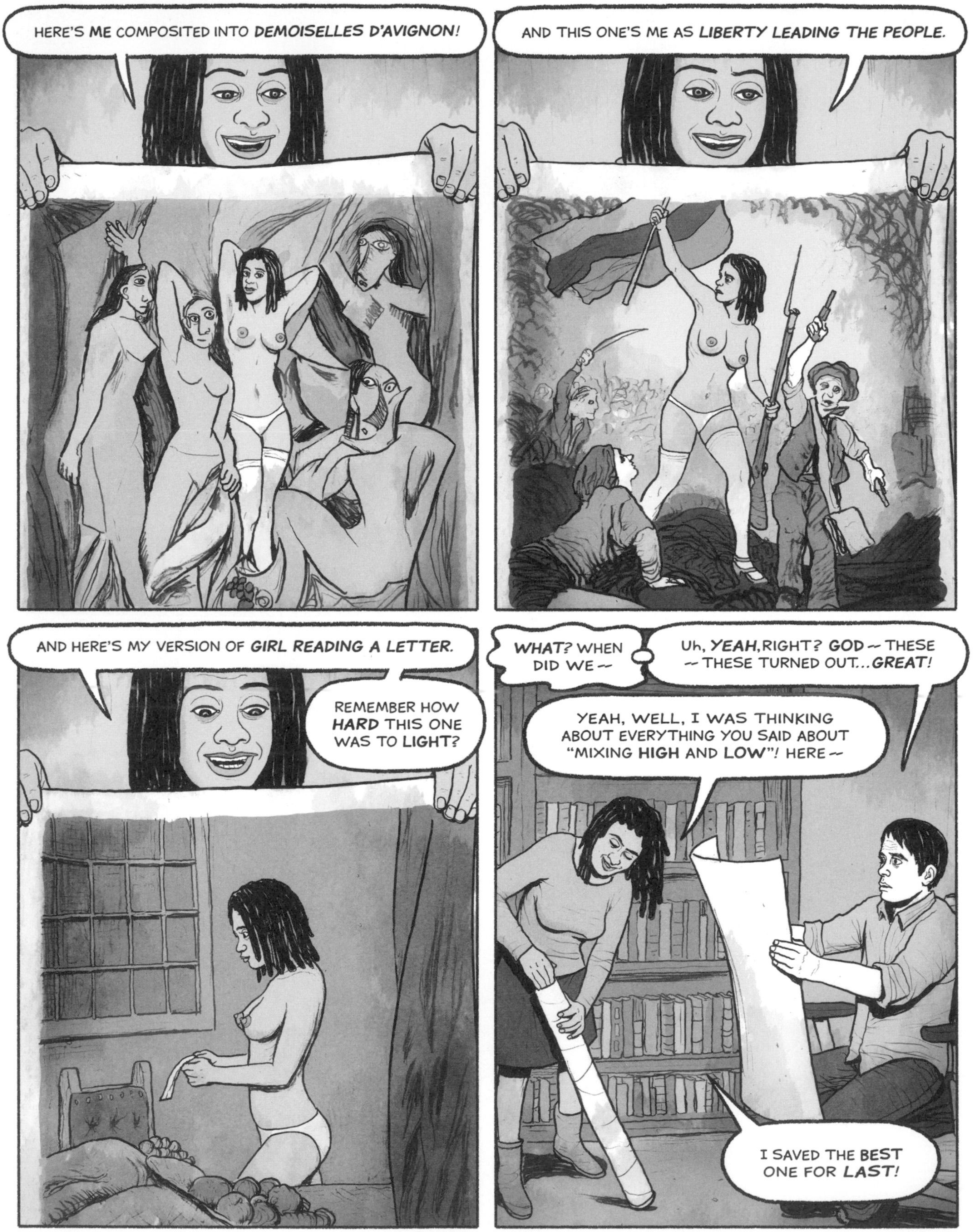
HERE'S ME COMPOSITED INTO DEMOISELLES D'AVIGNON!
AND THIS ONE'S ME AS LIBERTY LEADING THE PEOPLE.
AND HERE'S MY VERSION OF GIRL READING A LETTER.
REMEMBER HOW HARD THIS ONE WAS TO LIGHT?
WHAT? WHEN DID WE--
Uh, YEAH, RIGHT? GOD-- THESE --THESE TURNED OUT...GREAT!
YEAH, WELL, I WAS THINKING ABOUT EVERYTHING YOU SAID ABOUT "MIXING HIGH AND LOW"! HERE--
I SAVED THE BEST ONE FOR LAST!

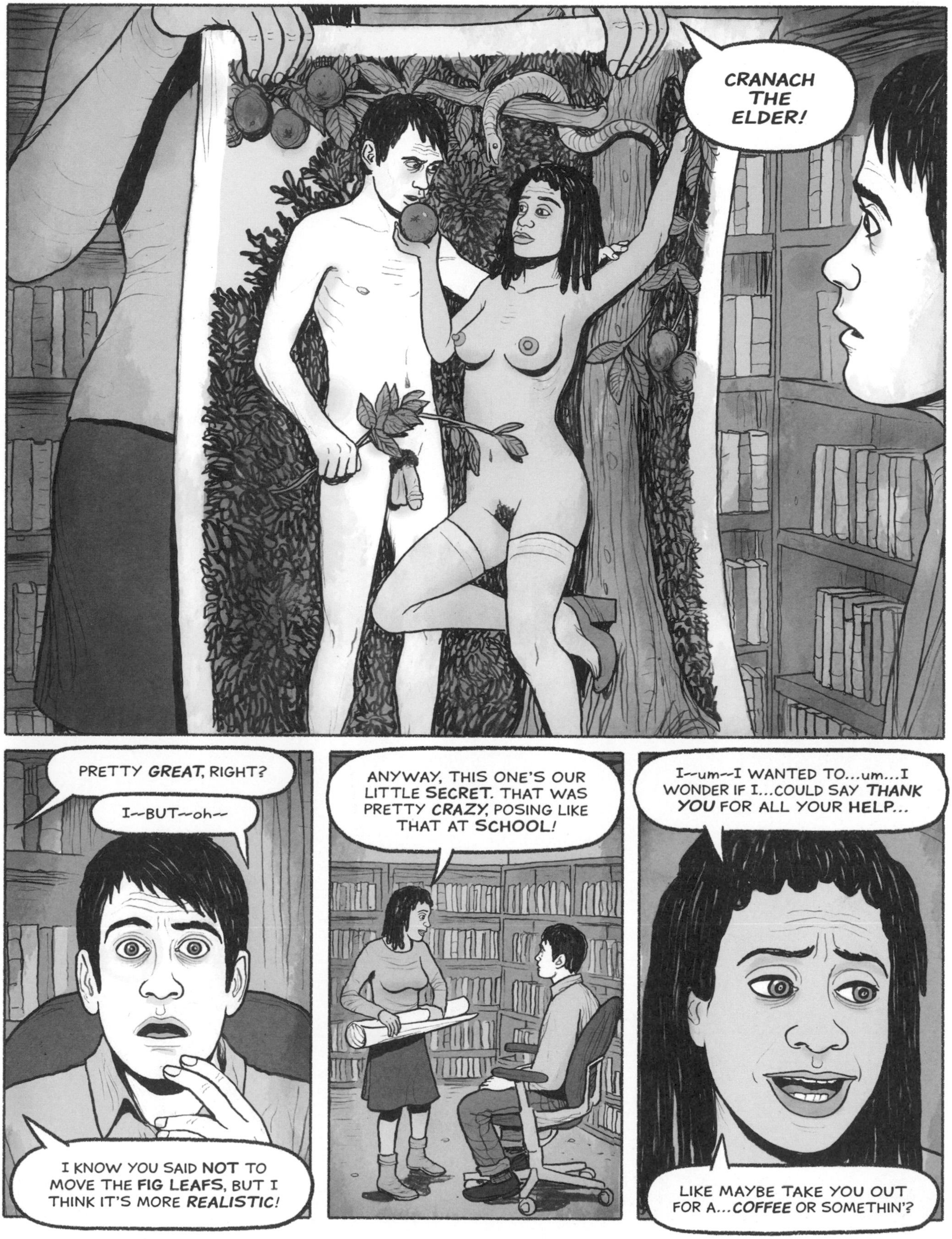
CRANACH THE ELDER!
PRETTY GREAT, RIGHT?
I--BUT--oh--
I KNOW YOU SAID NOT TO MOVE THE FIG LEAFS, BUT I THINK IT'S MORE REALISTIC!
ANYWAY, THIS ONE'S OUR LITTLE SECRET. THAT WAS PRETTY CRAZY, POSING LIKE THAT AT SCHOOL!
I--um--I WANTED TO...um...I WONDER IF I...COULD SAY THANK YOU FOR ALL YOUR HELP...
LIKE MAYBE TAKE YOU OUT FOR A...COFFEE OR SOMETHIN'?

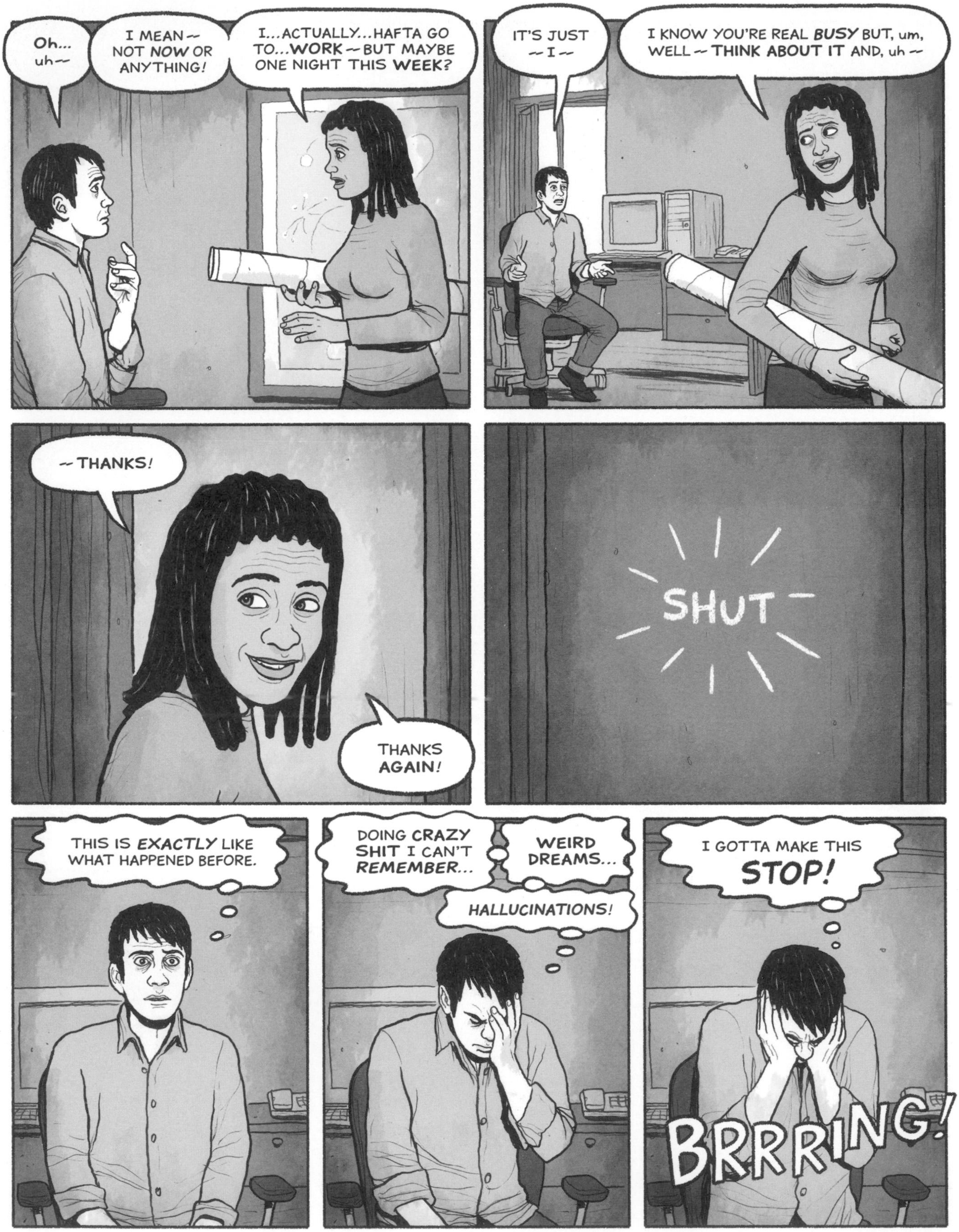
Oh... uh--
I MEAN-- NOT NOW OR ANYTHING!
I...ACTUALLY...HAFTA GO TO...WORK--BUT MAYBE ONE NIGHT THIS WEEK?
IT'S JUST --I--
I KNOW YOU'RE REAL BUSY BUT, um, WELL--THINK ABOUT IT AND, uh--
--THANKS!
THANKS AGAIN!
SHUT
THIS IS EXACTLY LIKE WHAT HAPPENED BEFORE.
DOING CRAZY SHIT I CAN'T REMEMBER...
WEIRD DREAMS...
HALLUCINATIONS!
I GOTTA MAKE THIS STOP!
BRRRING!

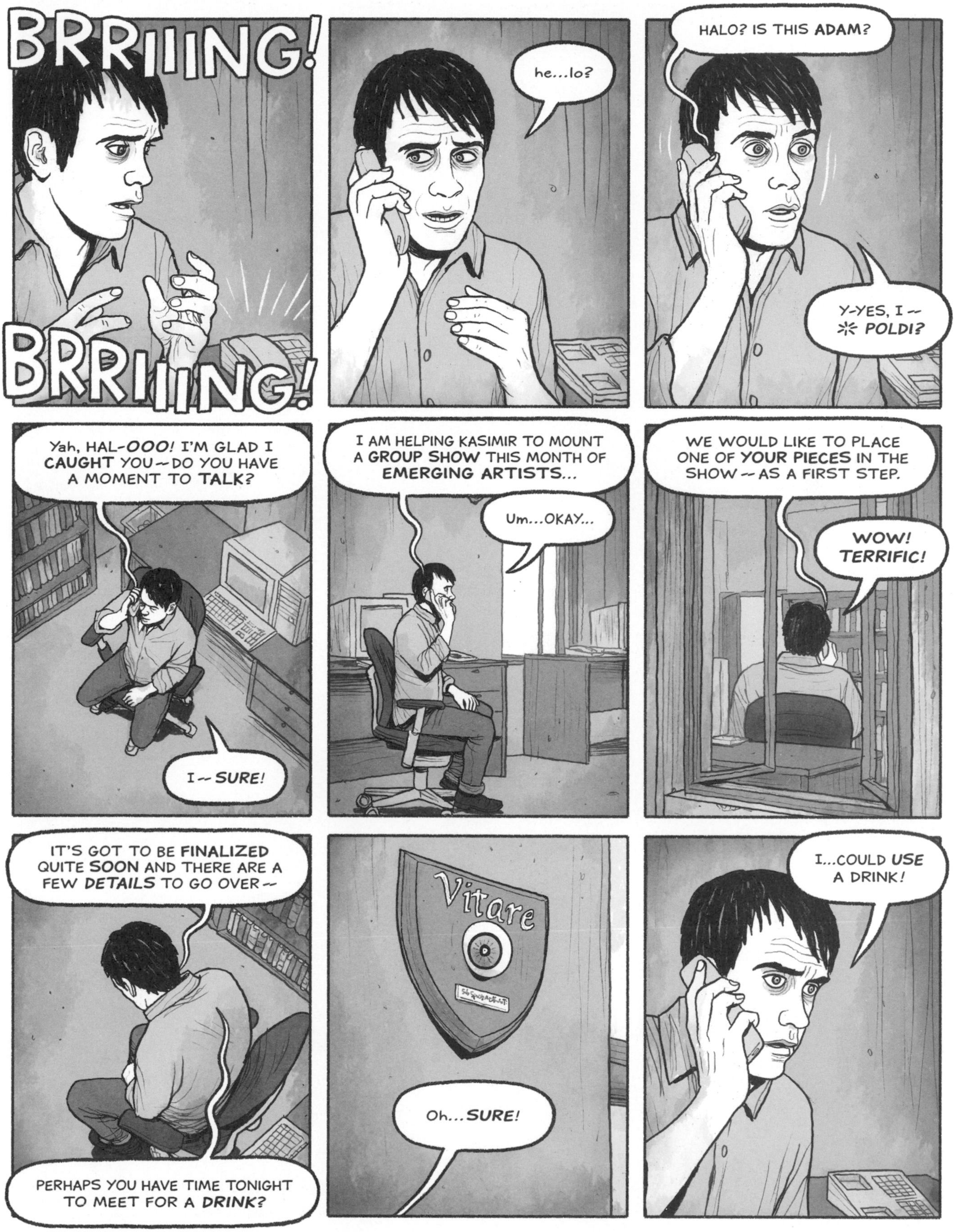
BRRIIING!
BRRIIING!
he...lo?
HALO? IS THIS ADAM?
Y-YES, I -- POLDI?
Yah, HAL-OOO! I'M GLAD I CAUGHT YOU -- DO YOU HAVE A MOMENT TO TALK?
I -- SURE!
I AM HELPING KASIMIR TO MOUNT A GROUP SHOW THIS MONTH OF EMERGING ARTISTS...
Um...OKAY...
WE WOULD LIKE TO PLACE ONE OF YOUR PIECES IN THE SHOW -- AS A FIRST STEP.
WOW! TERRIFIC!
IT'S GOT TO BE FINALIZED QUITE SOON AND THERE ARE A FEW DETAILS TO GO OVER --
PERHAPS YOU HAVE TIME TONIGHT TO MEET FOR A DRINK?
Vitare
Oh...SURE!
I...COULD USE A DRINK!

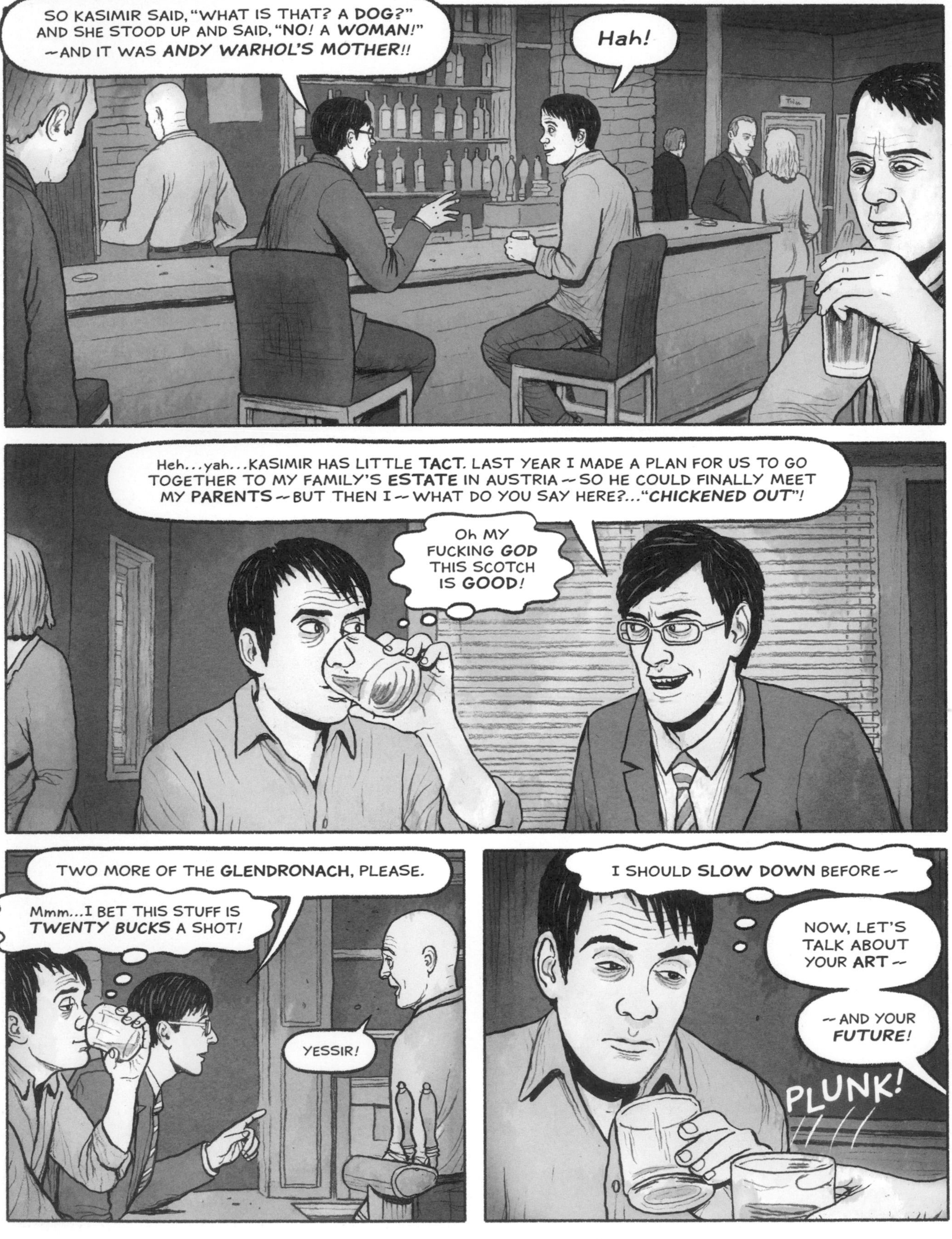
SO KASIMIR SAID, "WHAT IS THAT? A DOG?" AND SHE STOOD UP AND SAID, "NO! A WOMAN!" --AND IT WAS ANDY WARHOL'S MOTHER!!
Hah!
Heh...yah...KASIMIR HAS LITTLE TACT. LAST YEAR I MADE A PLAN FOR US TO GO TOGETHER TO MY FAMILY'S ESTATE IN AUSTRIA -- SO HE COULD FINALLY MEET MY PARENTS -- BUT THEN I -- WHAT DO YOU SAY HERE?..."CHICKENED OUT"!
Oh MY FUCKING GOD THIS SCOTCH IS GOOD!
TWO MORE OF THE GLENDRONACH, PLEASE.
Mmm...I BET THIS STUFF IS TWENTY BUCKS A SHOT!
YESSIR!
I SHOULD SLOW DOWN BEFORE --
NOW, LET'S TALK ABOUT YOUR ART --
-- AND YOUR FUTURE!
PLUNK!

KASIMIR AND MYSELF BOTH AGREE THAT THIS IS **INTERESTING** WORK AND VERY...*OF THE MOMENT.*

BUT ~ FOR CONTEXT ~ YOU SHOULD UNDERSTAND THAT KASIMIR IS A BIT **OLDER.** HE WORRIES A LITTLE ABOUT HOW **DIGITAL** WORK WILL FARE IN THE **MARKET.**

NEVERTHELESS, I HAVE ADVISED HIM THAT THIS IS A GOOD OPPORTUNITY TO...*EXPLORE.* YOU SEE MY **MEANING?**

Uh, SURE...

CHRIST, THAT BARTENDER COULD BE **RON'S BROTHER!** SAME **BULGY EYES, BALD** AS AN EGG...WEIRD **STARES...**

SO FOR NOW LET US SAY THAT I WILL REPRESENT YOU TO KASIMIR, AND YOU AND I CAN WORK TOGETHER ON A STRATEGY TO

I FEEL LIKE THIS *HAPPENED BEFORE* ...SOMEWHERE **ELSE**...I ~

SO IS THAT ~ **ATTRACTIVE** TO YOU?

Oh, uh, *YES!* ABSOLUTELY!

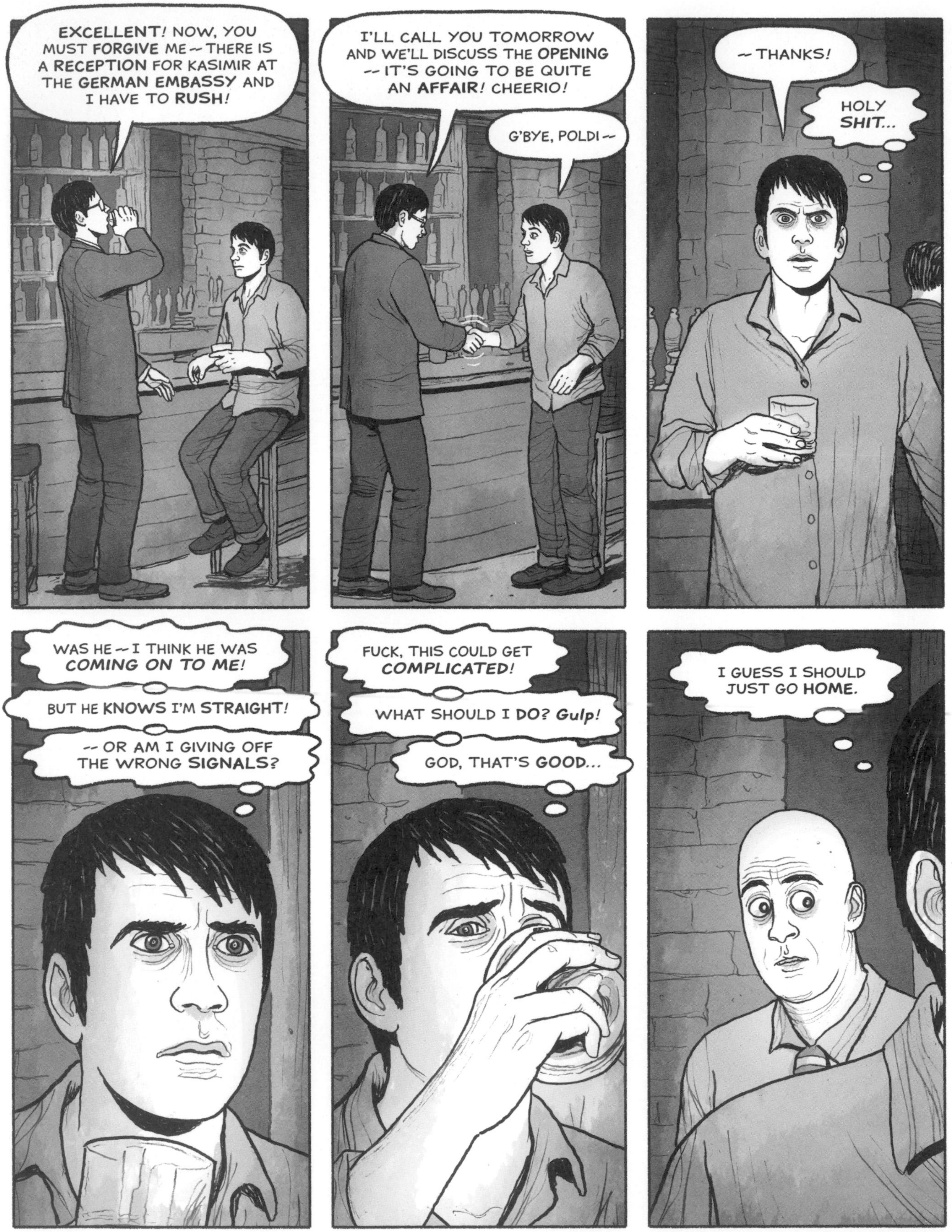
EXCELLENT! NOW, YOU MUST FORGIVE ME -- THERE IS A RECEPTION FOR KASIMIR AT THE GERMAN EMBASSY AND I HAVE TO RUSH!
I'LL CALL YOU TOMORROW AND WE'LL DISCUSS THE OPENING -- IT'S GOING TO BE QUITE AN AFFAIR! CHEERIO!
G'BYE, POLDI --
-- THANKS!
HOLY SHIT...
WAS HE -- I THINK HE WAS COMING ON TO ME!
BUT HE KNOWS I'M STRAIGHT!
-- OR AM I GIVING OFF THE WRONG SIGNALS?
FUCK, THIS COULD GET COMPLICATED!
WHAT SHOULD I DO? Gulp!
GOD, THAT'S GOOD...
I GUESS I SHOULD JUST GO HOME.

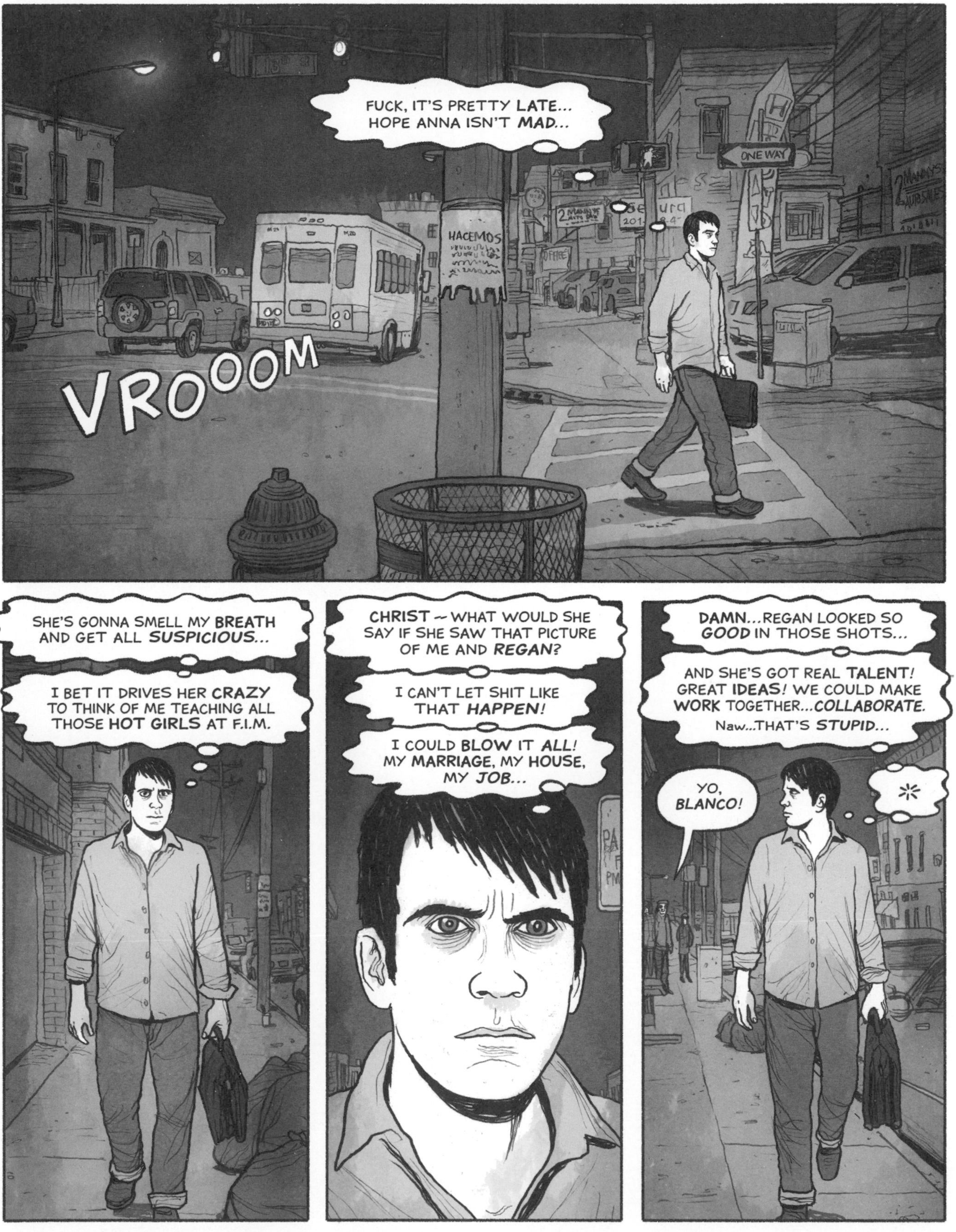
FUCK, IT'S PRETTY LATE... HOPE ANNA ISN'T MAD...
ONE WAY
HACEMOS
VROOOM
SHE'S GONNA SMELL MY BREATH AND GET ALL SUSPICIOUS...
I BET IT DRIVES HER CRAZY TO THINK OF ME TEACHING ALL THOSE HOT GIRLS AT F.I.M.
CHRIST -- WHAT WOULD SHE SAY IF SHE SAW THAT PICTURE OF ME AND REGAN?
I CAN'T LET SHIT LIKE THAT HAPPEN!
I COULD BLOW IT ALL! MY MARRIAGE, MY HOUSE, MY JOB...
DAMN...REGAN LOOKED SO GOOD IN THOSE SHOTS...
AND SHE'S GOT REAL TALENT! GREAT IDEAS! WE COULD MAKE WORK TOGETHER...COLLABORATE.
Naw...THAT'S STUPID...
YO, BLANCO!
!

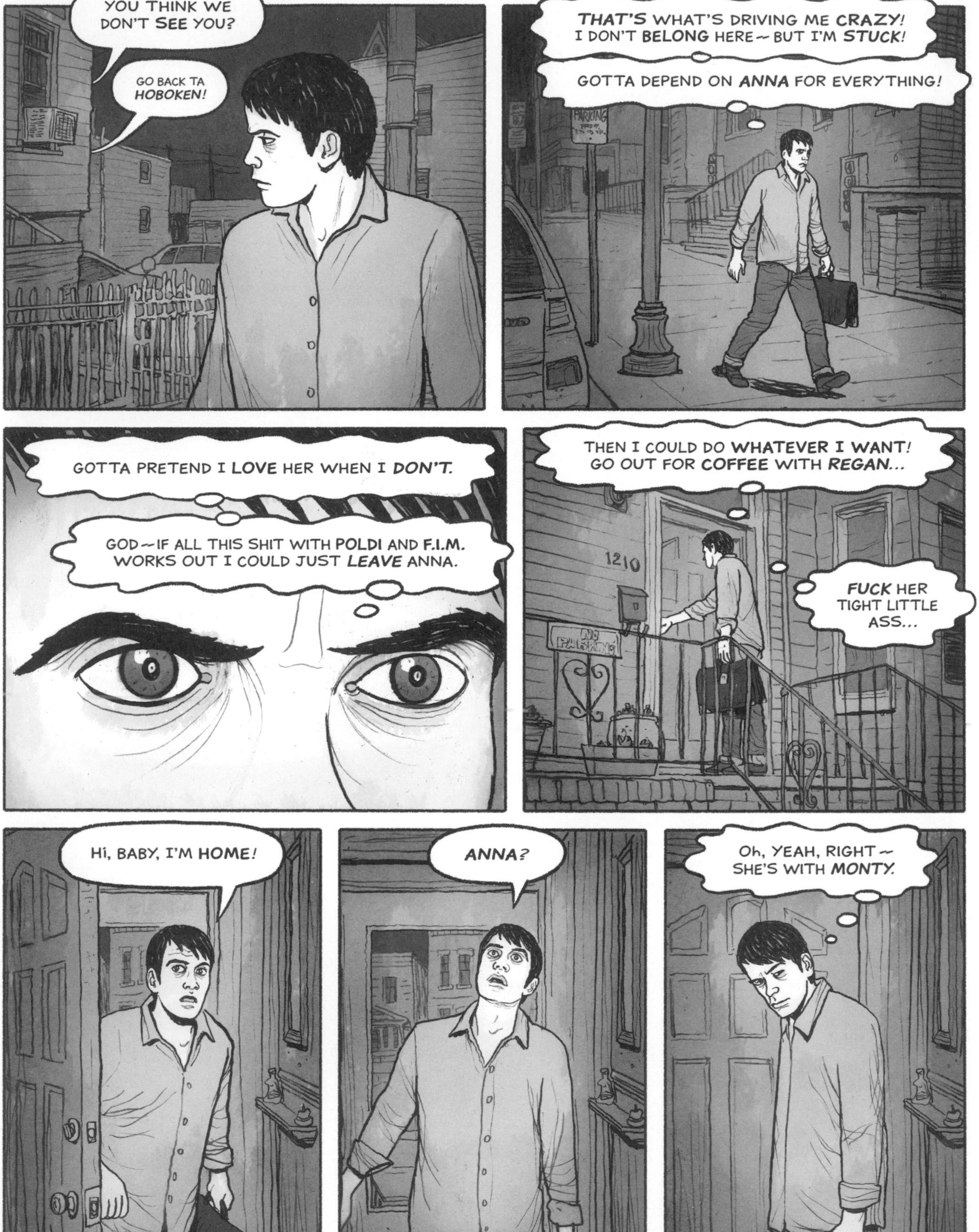
YOU THINK WE DON'T SEE YOU?
GO BACK TA HOBOKEN!
THAT'S WHAT'S DRIVING ME CRAZY! I DON'T BELONG HERE— BUT I'M STUCK!
GOTTA DEPEND ON ANNA FOR EVERYTHING!
GOTTA PRETEND I LOVE HER WHEN I DON'T.
GOD— IF ALL THIS SHIT WITH POLDI AND F.I.M. WORKS OUT I COULD JUST LEAVE ANNA.
THEN I COULD DO WHATEVER I WANT! GO OUT FOR COFFEE WITH REGAN...
1210
FUCK HER TIGHT LITTLE ASS...
Hi, BABY, I'M HOME!
ANNA?
Oh, YEAH, RIGHT— SHE'S WITH MONTY.

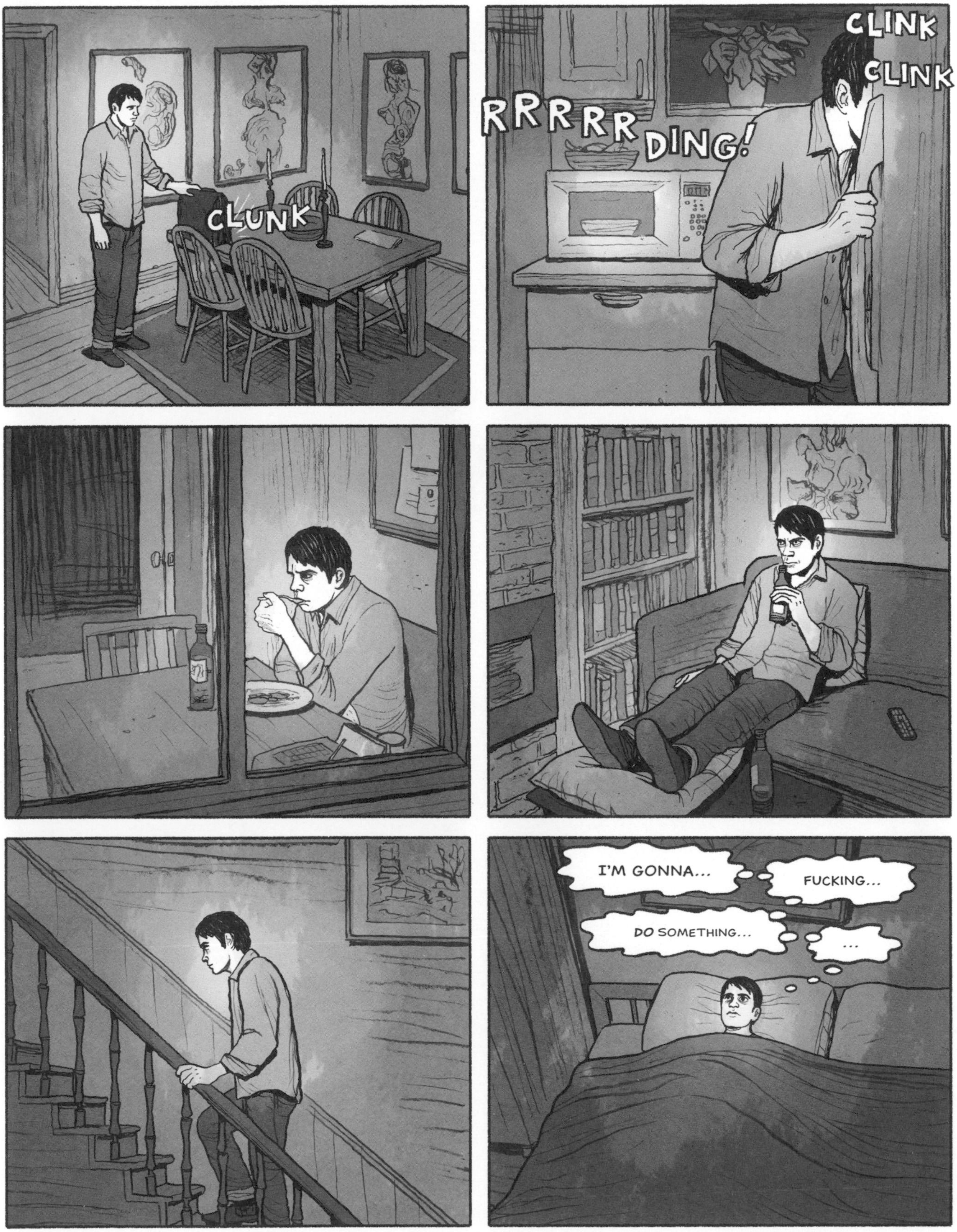
CLUNK
RRRRR DING!
CLINK
CLINK
I'M GONNA...
FUCKING...
DO SOMETHING...
...

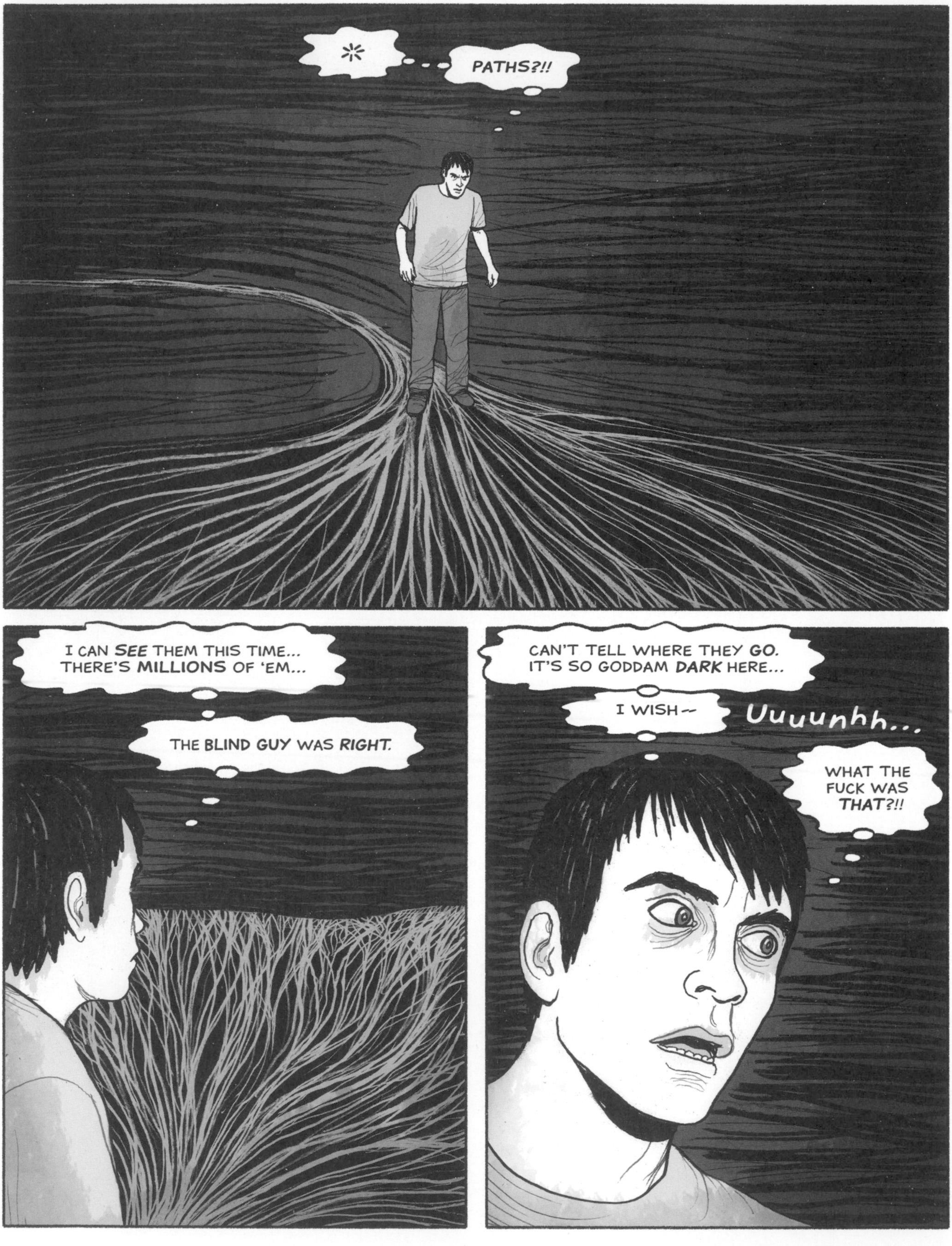
*
PATHS?!!
I CAN SEE THEM THIS TIME... THERE'S MILLIONS OF 'EM...
THE BLIND GUY WAS RIGHT.
CAN'T TELL WHERE THEY GO. IT'S SO GODDAM DARK HERE...
I WISH--
Uuuunhh...
WHAT THE FUCK WAS THAT?!!

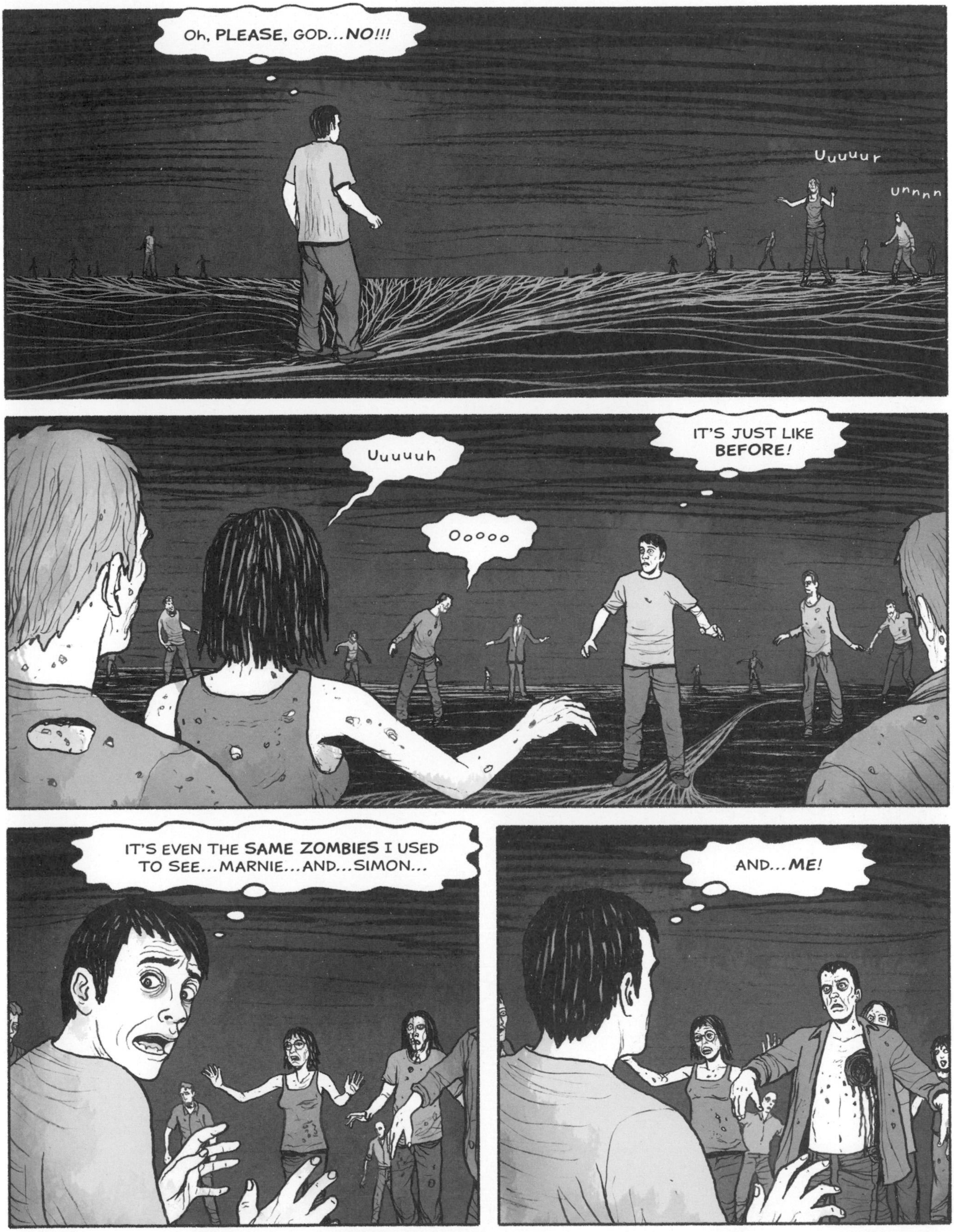
Oh, PLEASE, GOD...NO!!!
Uuuuur
unnnn
Uuuuuh
IT'S JUST LIKE BEFORE!
Ooooo
IT'S EVEN THE SAME ZOMBIES I USED TO SEE...MARNIE...AND...SIMON...
AND...ME!

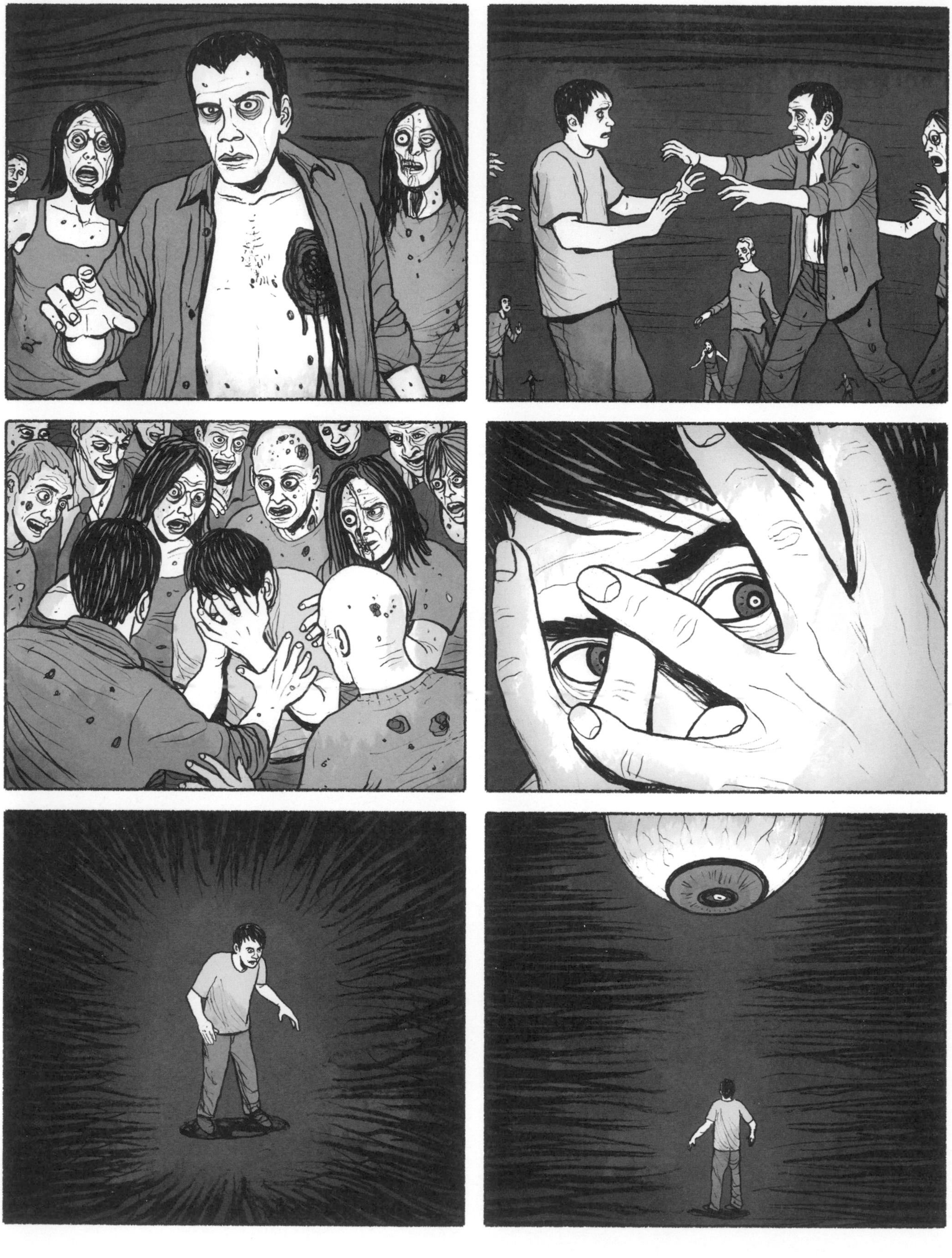

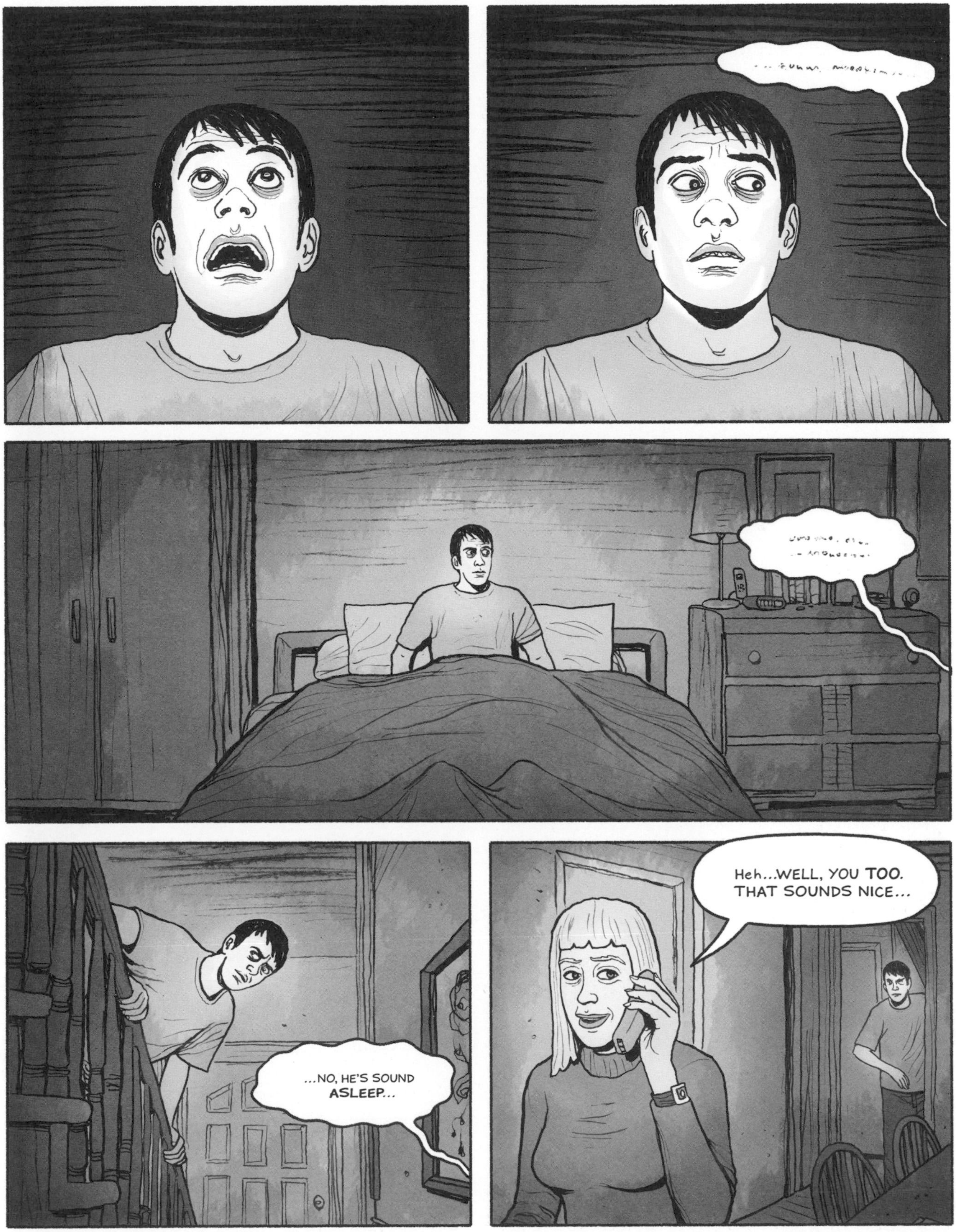
...NO, HE'S SOUND ASLEEP...
Heh...WELL, YOU TOO. THAT SOUNDS NICE...

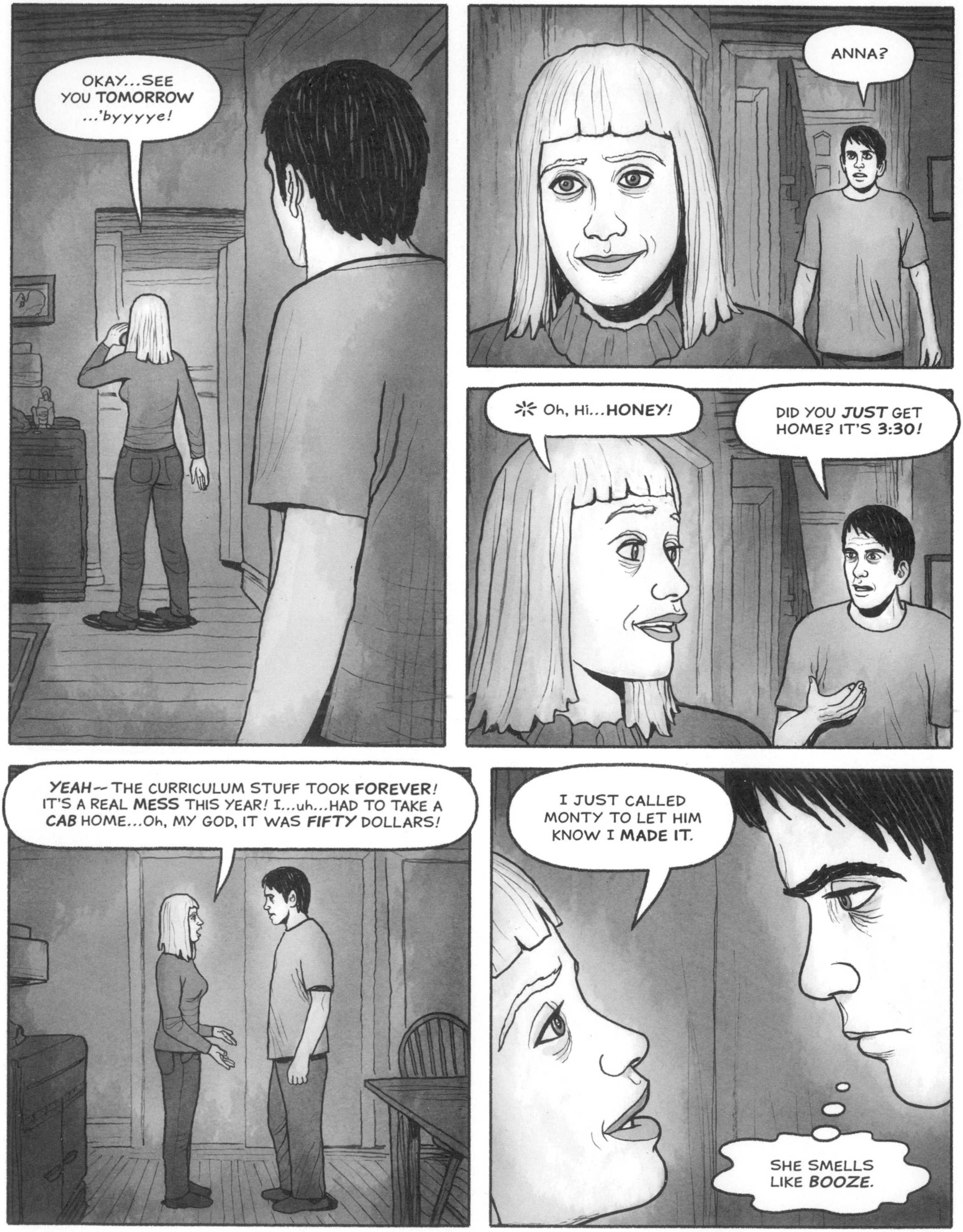
OKAY...SEE YOU **TOMORROW** ...'*byyyye!*
ANNA?
Oh, Hi...**HONEY!**
DID YOU ***JUST*** GET HOME? IT'S ***3:30!***
YEAH-- THE CURRICULUM STUFF TOOK **FOREVER**! IT'S A REAL **MESS** THIS YEAR! I...uh...HAD TO TAKE A **CAB** HOME...Oh, MY GOD, IT WAS ***FIFTY*** DOLLARS!
I JUST CALLED MONTY TO LET HIM KNOW I **MADE IT**.
SHE SMELLS LIKE ***BOOZE***.

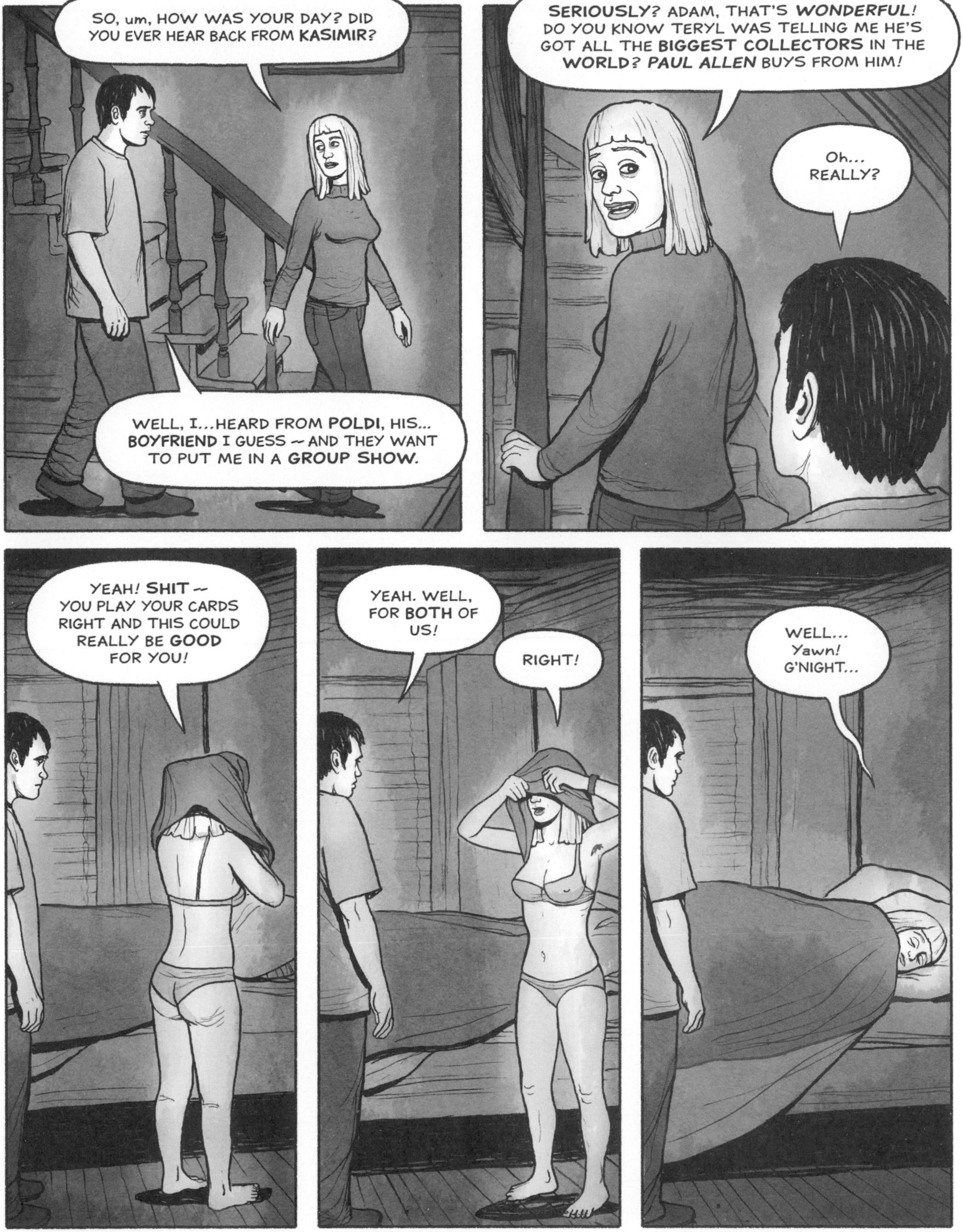
SO, um, HOW WAS YOUR DAY? DID YOU EVER HEAR BACK FROM KASIMIR?
WELL, I...HEARD FROM POLDI, HIS... BOYFRIEND I GUESS -- AND THEY WANT TO PUT ME IN A GROUP SHOW.
SERIOUSLY? ADAM, THAT'S WONDERFUL! DO YOU KNOW TERYL WAS TELLING ME HE'S GOT ALL THE BIGGEST COLLECTORS IN THE WORLD? PAUL ALLEN BUYS FROM HIM!
Oh... REALLY?
YEAH! SHIT -- YOU PLAY YOUR CARDS RIGHT AND THIS COULD REALLY BE GOOD FOR YOU!
YEAH. WELL, FOR BOTH OF US!
RIGHT!
WELL... Yawn! G'NIGHT...

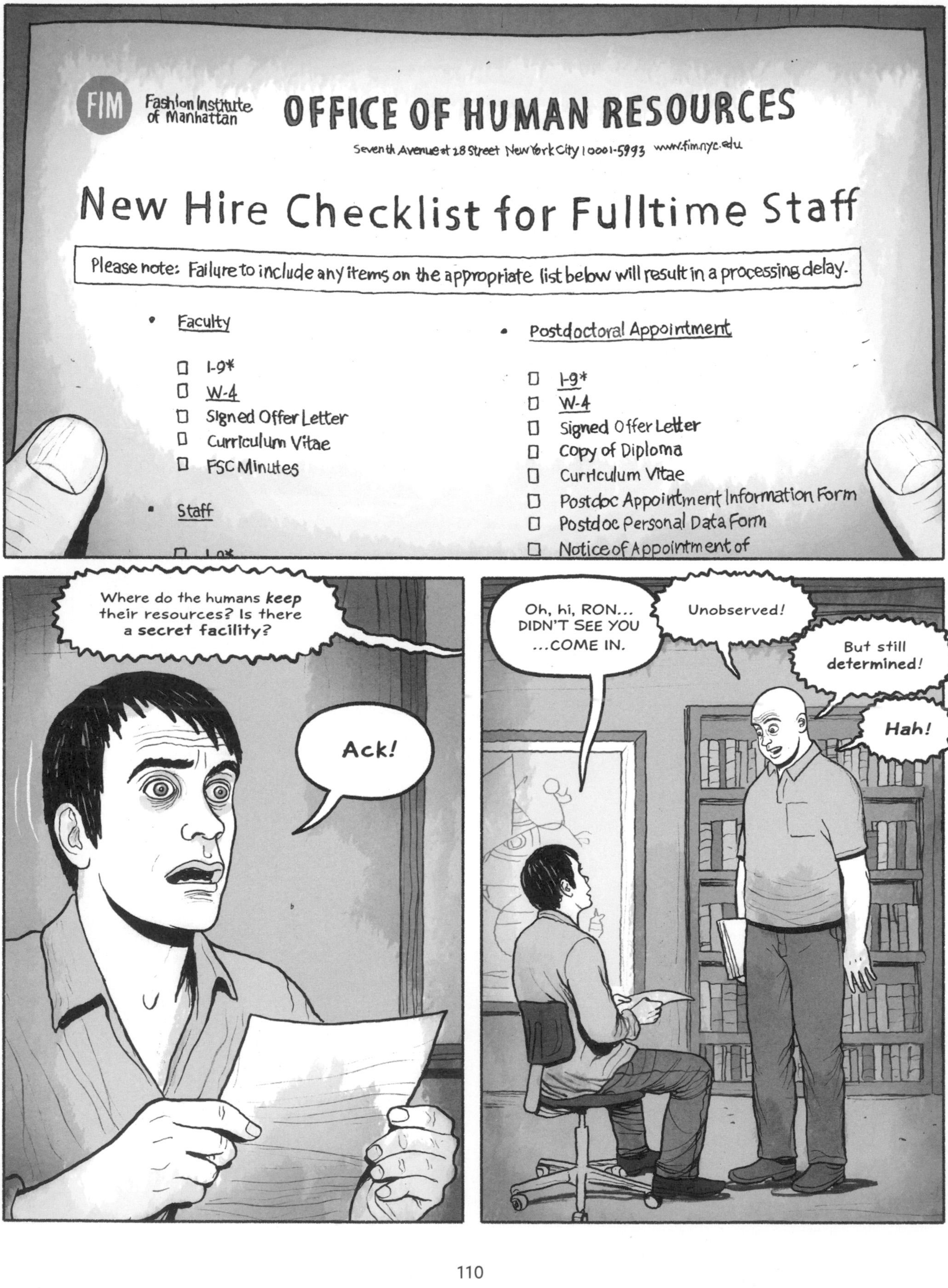
FIM
Fashion Institute of Manhattan
OFFICE OF HUMAN RESOURCES
Seventh Avenue at 28 Street New York City 10001-5993 www.fim.nyc.edu
New Hire Checklist for Fulltime Staff
Please note: Failure to include any items on the appropriate list below will result in a processing delay.
Faculty
I-9*
W-4
Signed Offer Letter
Curriculum Vitae
FSC Minutes
Staff
Postdoctoral Appointment
I-9*
W-4
Signed Offer Letter
Copy of Diploma
Curriculum Vitae
Postdoc Appointment Information Form
Postdoc Personal Data Form
Notice of Appointment of
Where do the humans keep their resources? Is there a secret facility?
Ack!
Oh, hi, RON... DIDN'T SEE YOU ...COME IN.
Unobserved!
But still determined!
Hah!

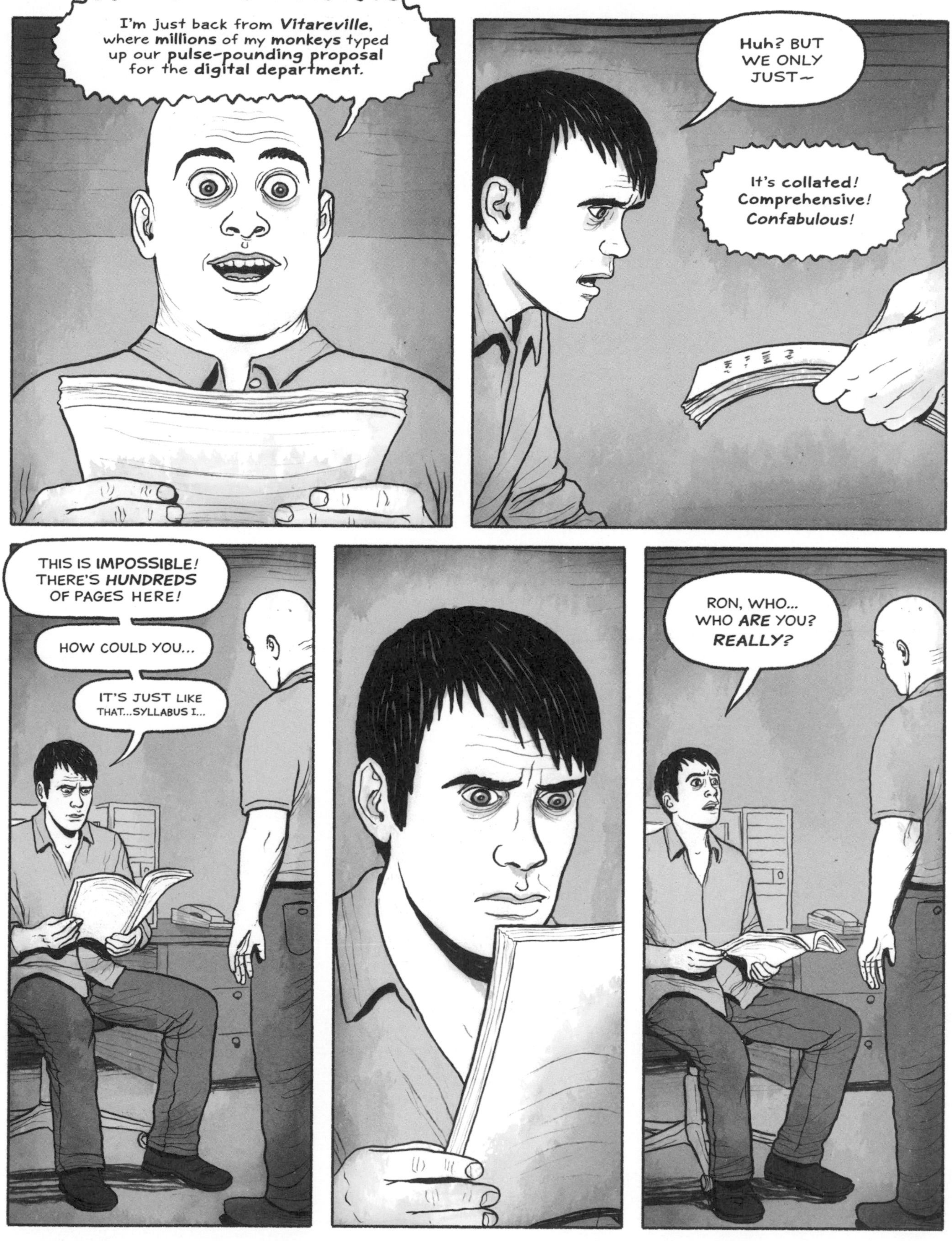
I'm just back from Vitareville, where millions of my monkeys typed up our pulse-pounding proposal for the digital department.
Huh? BUT WE ONLY JUST~
It's collated! Comprehensive! Confabulous!
THIS IS IMPOSSIBLE! THERE'S HUNDREDS OF PAGES HERE!
HOW COULD YOU...
IT'S JUST LIKE THAT...SYLLABUS I...
RON, WHO... WHO ARE YOU? REALLY?

Oh...hmmm...

Just a photographer. **A catalog** guy...

I SAW YOU **FADE AWAY** LIKE A **GHOST!!** A—AND JUST NOW YOU WERE M—MADE OUT OF...*EYES!*

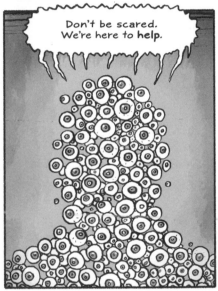

Don't be scared. We're here to **help.**

I—I **AM** SCARED! I FEEL LIKE YOU'RE W—**WATCHING** ME EVERYWHERE I GO!

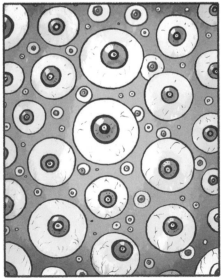

RON? *RON?*

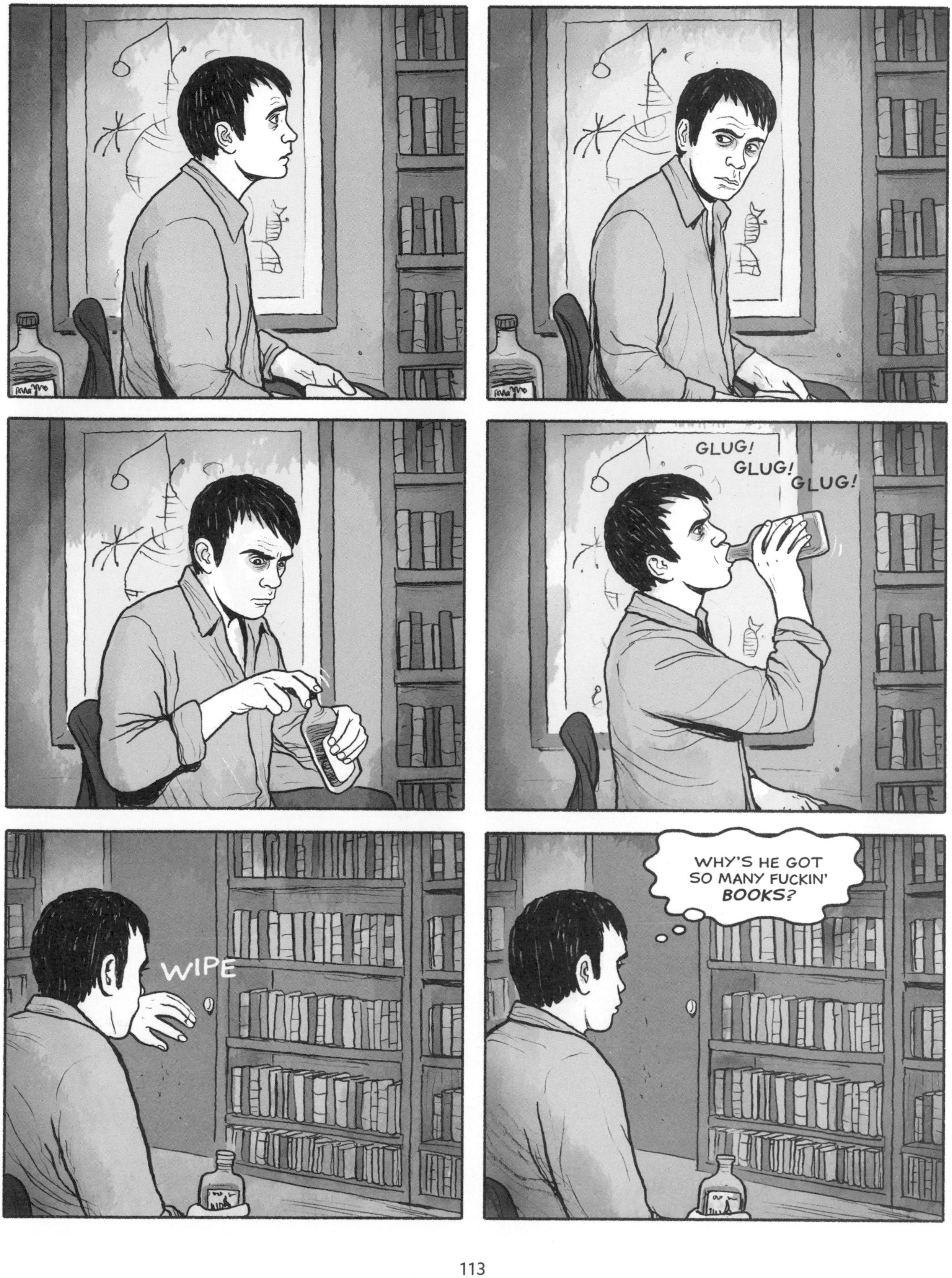
GLUG!
GLUG!
GLUG!
WIPE
WHY'S HE GOT SO MANY FUCKIN' BOOKS?

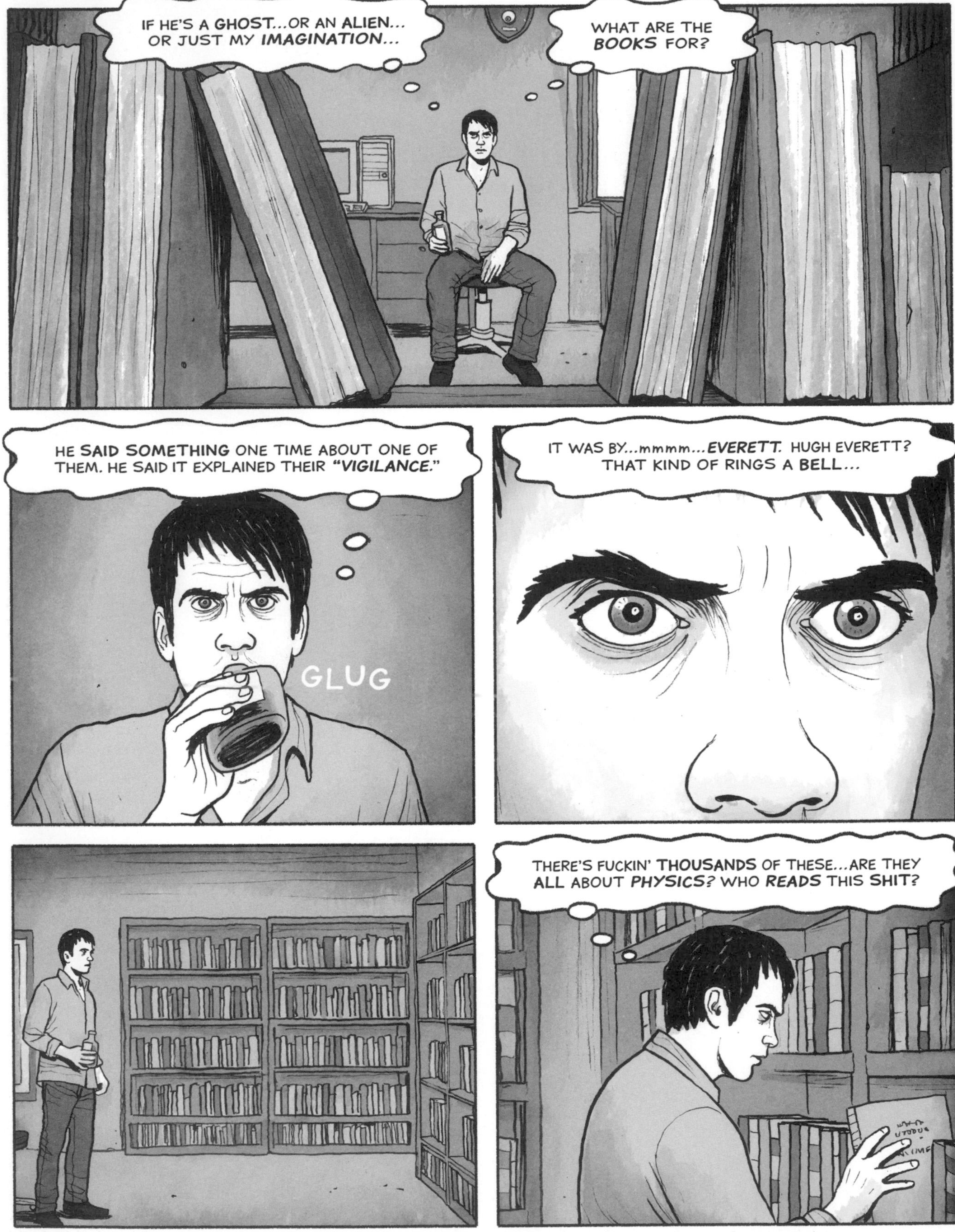
IF HE'S A GHOST...OR AN ALIEN... OR JUST MY IMAGINATION...
WHAT ARE THE BOOKS FOR?
HE SAID SOMETHING ONE TIME ABOUT ONE OF THEM. HE SAID IT EXPLAINED THEIR "VIGILANCE."
GLUG
IT WAS BY...mmmm...EVERETT. HUGH EVERETT? THAT KIND OF RINGS A BELL...
THERE'S FUCKIN' THOUSANDS OF THESE...ARE THEY ALL ABOUT PHYSICS? WHO READS THIS SHIT?

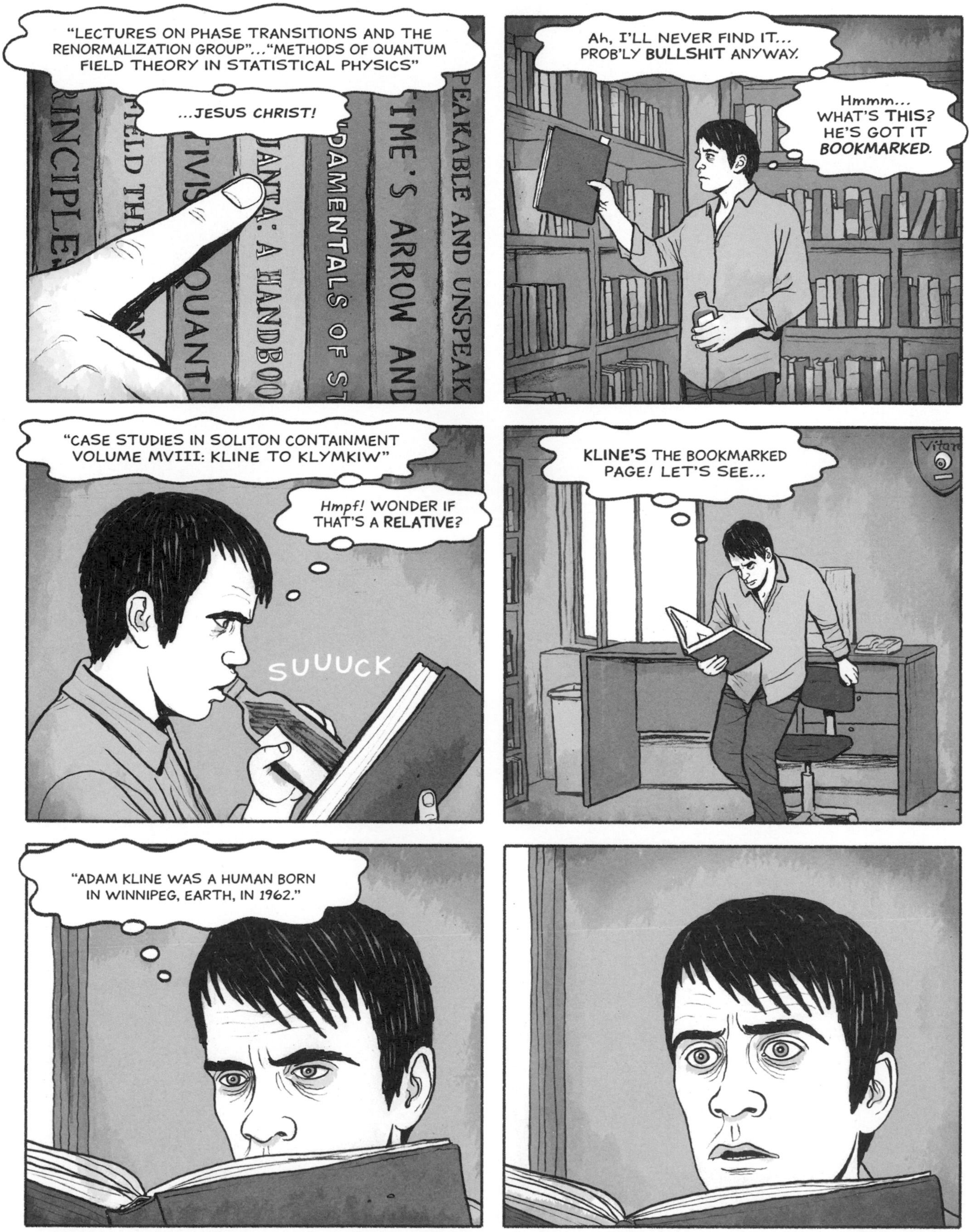
"LECTURES ON PHASE TRANSITIONS AND THE RENORMALIZATION GROUP"..."METHODS OF QUANTUM FIELD THEORY IN STATISTICAL PHYSICS"
...JESUS CHRIST!
Ah, I'LL NEVER FIND IT... PROB'LY BULLSHIT ANYWAY.
Hmmm... WHAT'S THIS? HE'S GOT IT BOOKMARKED.
"CASE STUDIES IN SOLITON CONTAINMENT VOLUME MVIII: KLINE TO KLYMKIW"
Hmpf! WONDER IF THAT'S A RELATIVE?
SUUUCK
KLINE'S THE BOOKMARKED PAGE! LET'S SEE...
"ADAM KLINE WAS A HUMAN BORN IN WINNIPEG, EARTH, IN 1962."

I SHOULDN'T READ THIS. THIS IS **HORROR MOVIE** STUFF.

I WONDER IF ANNA'S INSURANCE COVERS US FOR **MENTAL** HEALTH?

GULP
GULP

"TYPICALLY FOR HUMANS OF HIS ERA AND CASTE, KLINE WAS SKEPTICAL OF MYTHIC EXPLANATIONS FOR HIS EXISTENCE BUT HAD BEEN EXPOSED TO "SCIENTIFIC" THEORIES VIA "POPULAR" CULTURE (SEE STAR TREK: "MIRROR, MIRROR," 1967)"

Case Studies in Soliton Con

In the winter of 1982, Kline began experiencin
branched eigenstates, sometimes simultaneou
which he interpreted as dreams. These states
progressed (following the usual pathology for
this species, see Vitare, 379212) within days
into stage 2 solitons (in this case, a "zombi
apocalypse") necessitating interference.

A field agent, K. Vitte Vitare, was able to r
Kline to an orthogonal timeline by employ.
a combination of a psychotropic cannabinoi
with ethyl alcohol (C_2H_5OH) which has pysc
n humans.

THIS IS ALL MY CRAZINESS CAN COME UP WITH? JUST SOME **BAD TRIPS** FROM WHEN I WAS A **KID**?

Hmph ~ HOW DOES IT ALL **END**?

FLIP
FLIP

OKAY ~ HERE'S **THIS** YEAR:

"...RECURRENCE FOLLOWING A MOVE TO NEW YORK CITY. FULL QUARANTINE AND OBSERVATION WERE EMPLOYED TO CONFINE KLINE TO A SINGLE TIMELINE."

"DESPITE INITIAL ATTEMPTS TO REJECT TREATMENT, KLINE'S WAVEFORM WAS COLLAPSED SUCCESSFULLY BY OCTOBER, 1995 (SEE FIG 1). NO SUBSEQUENT SOLITONS WERE OBSERVED."

~ WELL, **THAT** SOUNDS OK! WHERE'S "FIGURE 1?"

Figure 1: Timeline for A. Kline

1995:
Recurrence of soliton episode interference and quarantine.

1996-2000:
Kline works as adjunct professi
No advancement.

Remains in loveless marriage
wife conducts multiple affairs.
No success in chosen field (artist

2001:
Death.

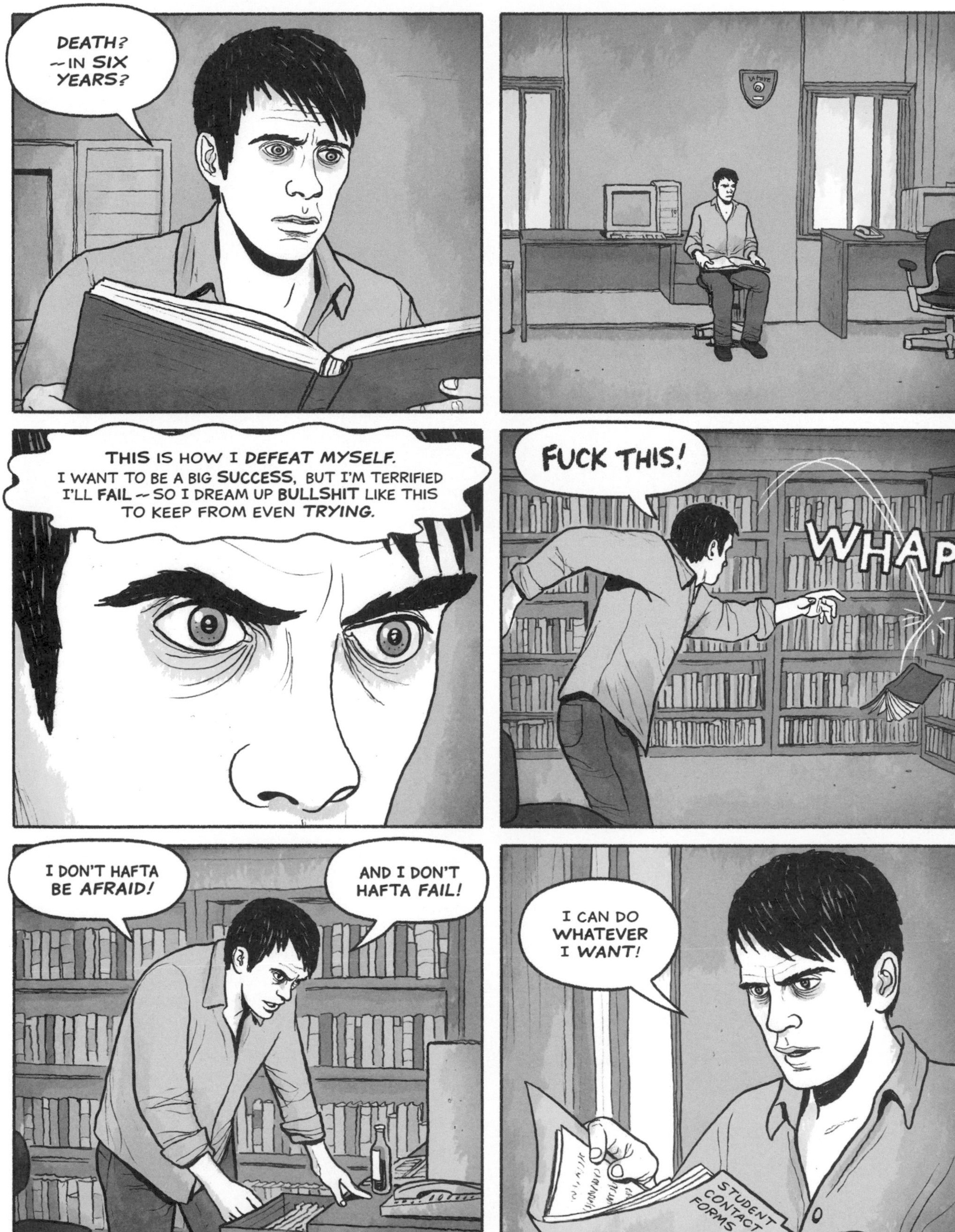
DEATH? ~IN SIX YEARS?
THIS IS HOW I DEFEAT MYSELF. I WANT TO BE A BIG SUCCESS, BUT I'M TERRIFIED I'LL FAIL ~ SO I DREAM UP BULLSHIT LIKE THIS TO KEEP FROM EVEN TRYING.
FUCK THIS!
WHAP!
I DON'T HAFTA BE AFRAID!
AND I DON'T HAFTA FAIL!
I CAN DO WHATEVER I WANT!
STUDENT CONTACT FORMS

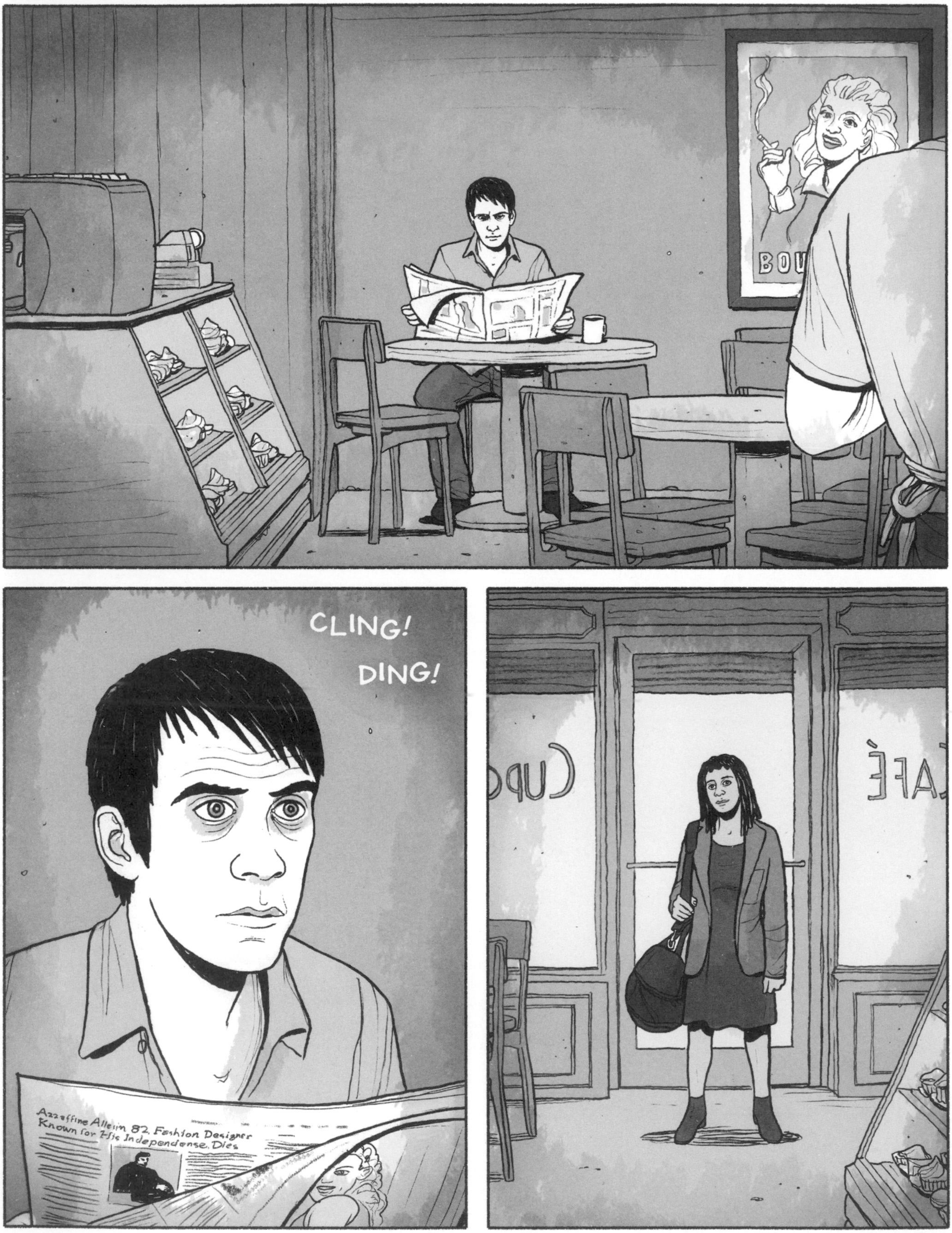
BOU
CLING!
DING!
Azzeffine Alleim 82, Fashion Designer
Known for His Independense, Dies

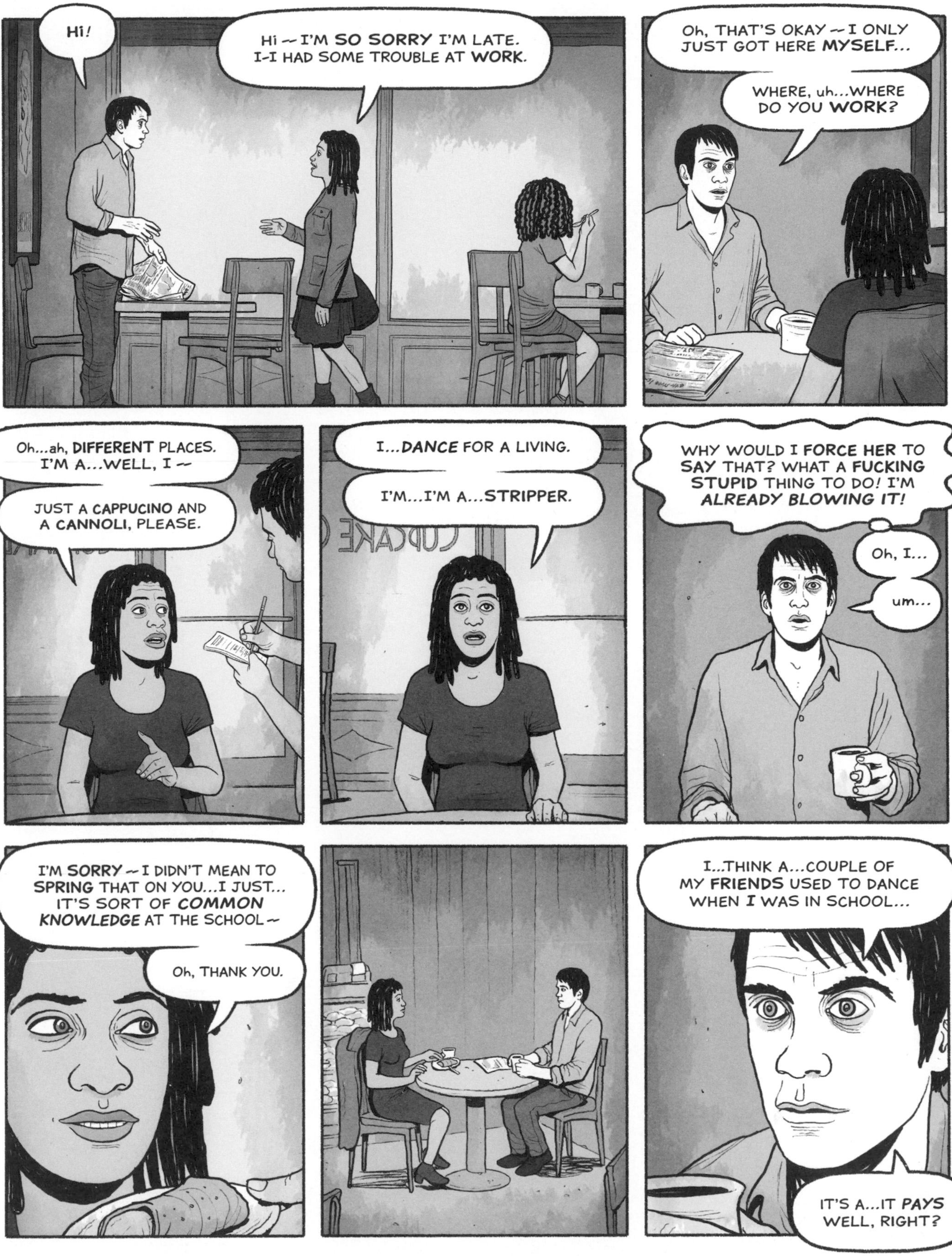
Hi!
Hi — I'M SO SORRY I'M LATE. I-I HAD SOME TROUBLE AT WORK.
Oh, THAT'S OKAY — I ONLY JUST GOT HERE MYSELF...
WHERE, uh...WHERE DO YOU WORK?
Oh...ah, DIFFERENT PLACES. I'M A...WELL, I —
JUST A CAPPUCINO AND A CANNOLI, PLEASE.
I...DANCE FOR A LIVING.
I'M...I'M A...STRIPPER.
WHY WOULD I FORCE HER TO SAY THAT? WHAT A FUCKING STUPID THING TO DO! I'M ALREADY BLOWING IT!
Oh, I...
um...
I'M SORRY — I DIDN'T MEAN TO SPRING THAT ON YOU...I JUST... IT'S SORT OF COMMON KNOWLEDGE AT THE SCHOOL —
Oh, THANK YOU.
I...THINK A...COUPLE OF MY FRIENDS USED TO DANCE WHEN I WAS IN SCHOOL...
IT'S A...IT PAYS WELL, RIGHT?

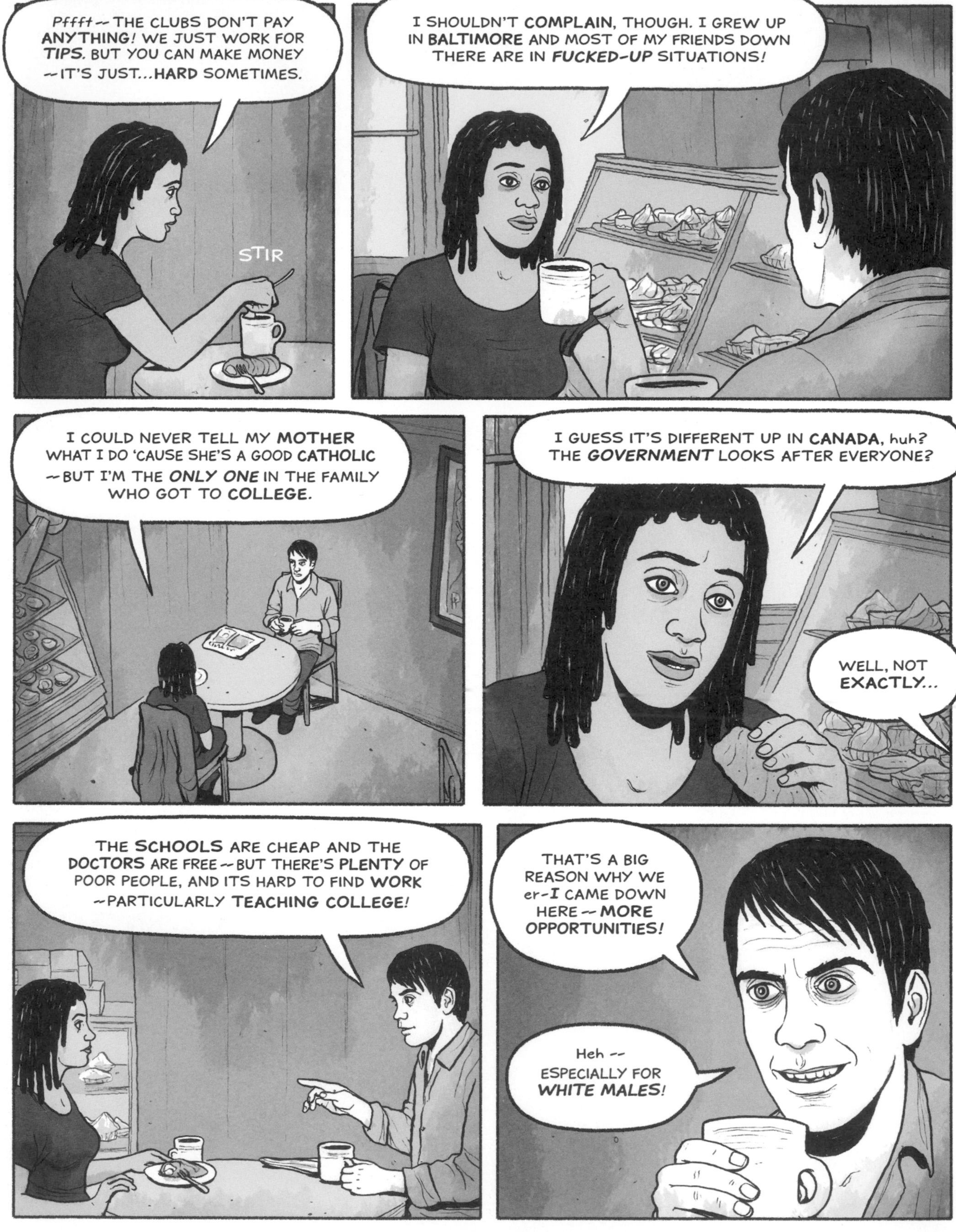
Pffft -- THE CLUBS DON'T PAY ANYTHING! WE JUST WORK FOR TIPS. BUT YOU CAN MAKE MONEY -- IT'S JUST...HARD SOMETIMES.
STIR
I SHOULDN'T COMPLAIN, THOUGH. I GREW UP IN BALTIMORE AND MOST OF MY FRIENDS DOWN THERE ARE IN FUCKED-UP SITUATIONS!
I COULD NEVER TELL MY MOTHER WHAT I DO 'CAUSE SHE'S A GOOD CATHOLIC -- BUT I'M THE ONLY ONE IN THE FAMILY WHO GOT TO COLLEGE.
I GUESS IT'S DIFFERENT UP IN CANADA, huh? THE GOVERNMENT LOOKS AFTER EVERYONE?
WELL, NOT EXACTLY...
THE SCHOOLS ARE CHEAP AND THE DOCTORS ARE FREE -- BUT THERE'S PLENTY OF POOR PEOPLE, AND ITS HARD TO FIND WORK -- PARTICULARLY TEACHING COLLEGE!
THAT'S A BIG REASON WHY WE er-I CAME DOWN HERE -- MORE OPPORTUNITIES!
Heh -- ESPECIALLY FOR WHITE MALES!

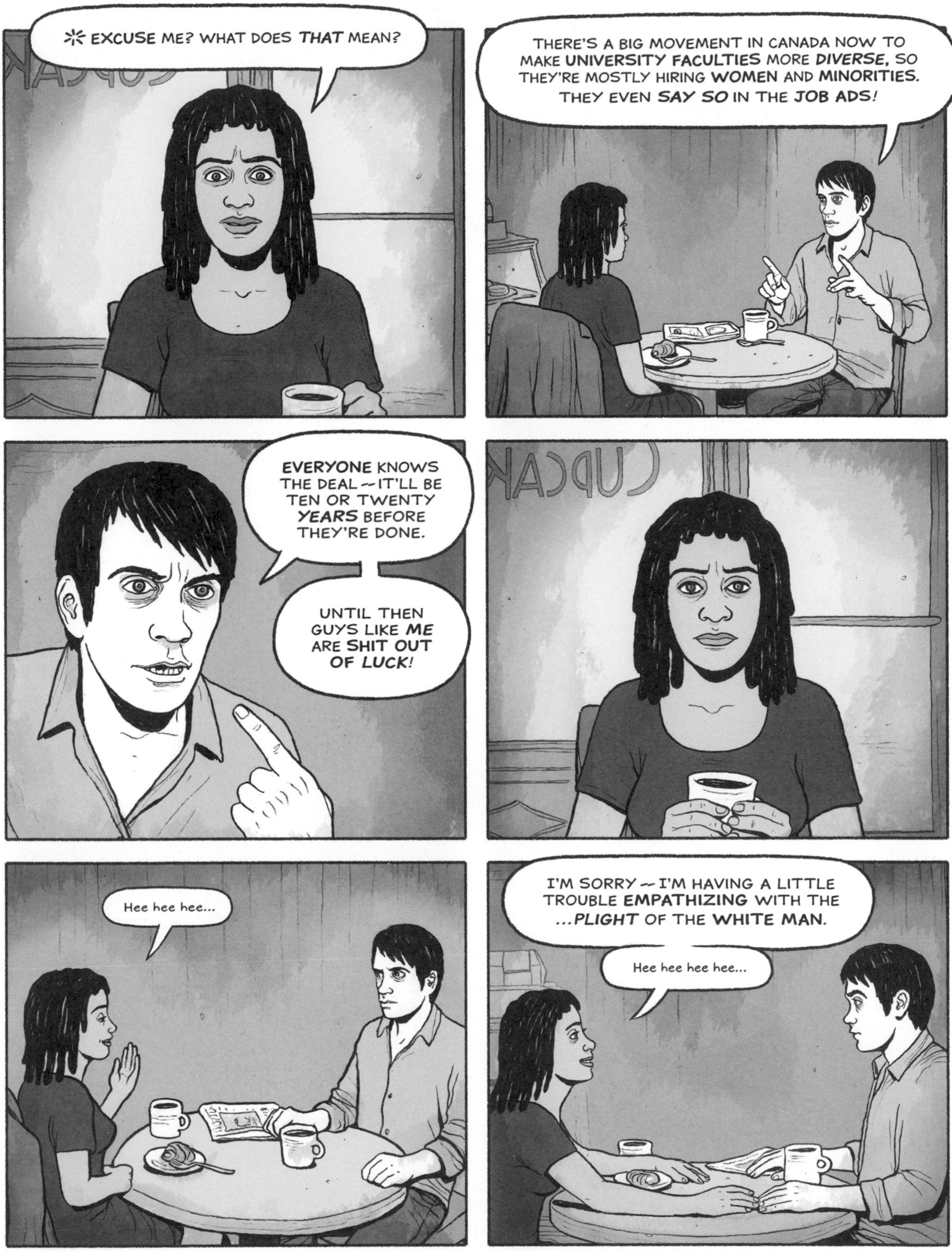
* EXCUSE ME? WHAT DOES THAT MEAN?
THERE'S A BIG MOVEMENT IN CANADA NOW TO MAKE UNIVERSITY FACULTIES MORE DIVERSE, SO THEY'RE MOSTLY HIRING WOMEN AND MINORITIES. THEY EVEN SAY SO IN THE JOB ADS!
EVERYONE KNOWS THE DEAL -- IT'LL BE TEN OR TWENTY YEARS BEFORE THEY'RE DONE.
UNTIL THEN GUYS LIKE ME ARE SHIT OUT OF LUCK!
Hee hee hee...
I'M SORRY -- I'M HAVING A LITTLE TROUBLE EMPATHIZING WITH THE ...PLIGHT OF THE WHITE MAN.
Hee hee hee hee...

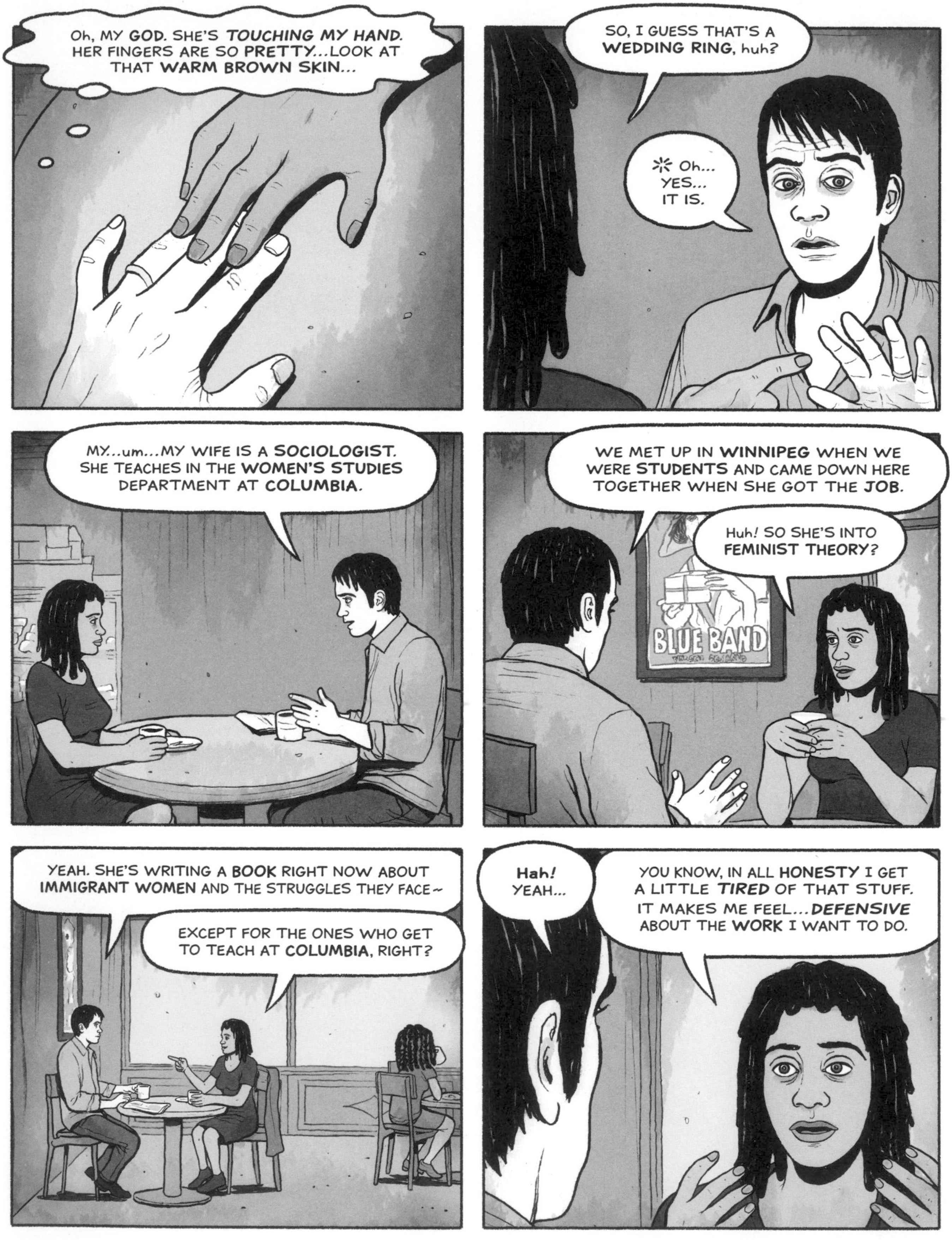

Oh, MY GOD. SHE'S TOUCHING MY HAND. HER FINGERS ARE SO PRETTY...LOOK AT THAT WARM BROWN SKIN...
SO, I GUESS THAT'S A WEDDING RING, huh?
Oh... YES... IT IS.
MY...um...MY WIFE IS A SOCIOLOGIST. SHE TEACHES IN THE WOMEN'S STUDIES DEPARTMENT AT COLUMBIA.
WE MET UP IN WINNIPEG WHEN WE WERE STUDENTS AND CAME DOWN HERE TOGETHER WHEN SHE GOT THE JOB.
Huh! SO SHE'S INTO FEMINIST THEORY?
BLUE BAND
YEAH. SHE'S WRITING A BOOK RIGHT NOW ABOUT IMMIGRANT WOMEN AND THE STRUGGLES THEY FACE~
EXCEPT FOR THE ONES WHO GET TO TEACH AT COLUMBIA, RIGHT?
Hah! YEAH...
YOU KNOW, IN ALL HONESTY I GET A LITTLE TIRED OF THAT STUFF. IT MAKES ME FEEL...DEFENSIVE ABOUT THE WORK I WANT TO DO.

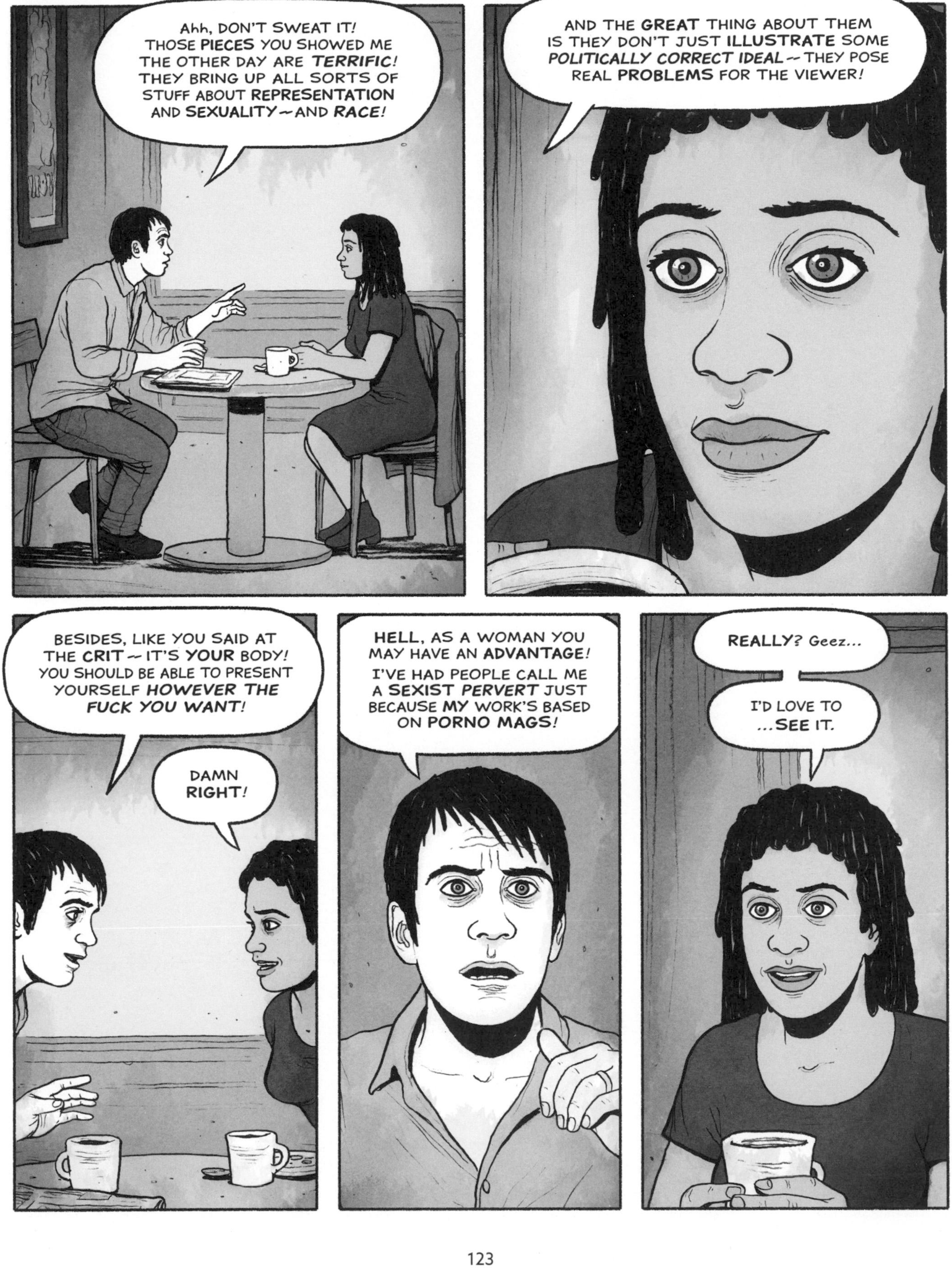
Ahh, DON'T SWEAT IT! THOSE PIECES YOU SHOWED ME THE OTHER DAY ARE TERRIFIC! THEY BRING UP ALL SORTS OF STUFF ABOUT REPRESENTATION AND SEXUALITY -- AND RACE!
AND THE GREAT THING ABOUT THEM IS THEY DON'T JUST ILLUSTRATE SOME POLITICALLY CORRECT IDEAL -- THEY POSE REAL PROBLEMS FOR THE VIEWER!
BESIDES, LIKE YOU SAID AT THE CRIT -- IT'S YOUR BODY! YOU SHOULD BE ABLE TO PRESENT YOURSELF HOWEVER THE FUCK YOU WANT!
DAMN RIGHT!
HELL, AS A WOMAN YOU MAY HAVE AN ADVANTAGE!
I'VE HAD PEOPLE CALL ME A SEXIST PERVERT JUST BECAUSE MY WORK'S BASED ON PORNO MAGS!
REALLY? Geez...
I'D LOVE TO ...SEE IT.

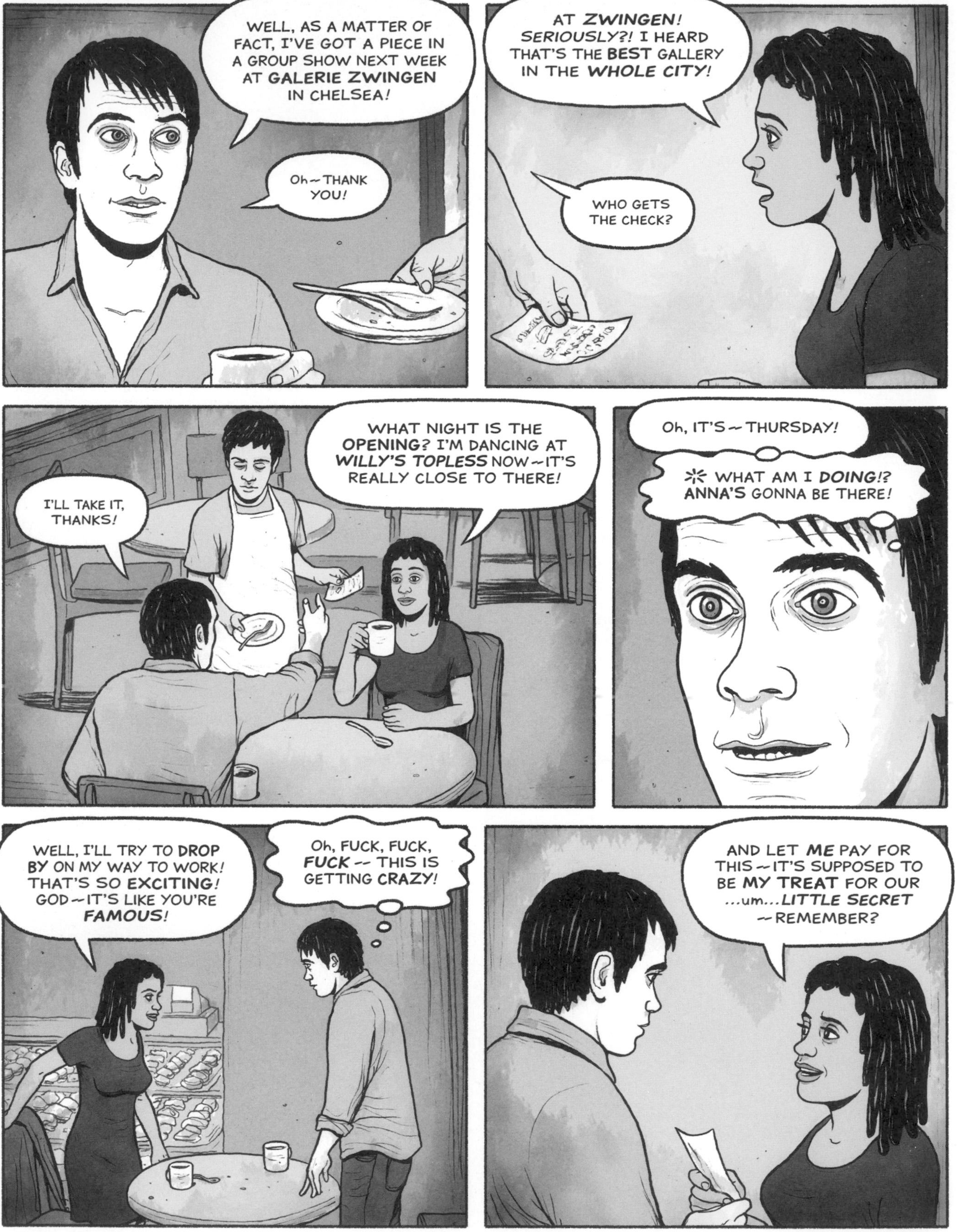
WELL, AS A MATTER OF FACT, I'VE GOT A PIECE IN A GROUP SHOW NEXT WEEK AT GALERIE ZWINGEN IN CHELSEA!
Oh—THANK YOU!
AT ZWINGEN! SERIOUSLY?! I HEARD THAT'S THE BEST GALLERY IN THE WHOLE CITY!
WHO GETS THE CHECK?
I'LL TAKE IT, THANKS!
WHAT NIGHT IS THE OPENING? I'M DANCING AT WILLY'S TOPLESS NOW—IT'S REALLY CLOSE TO THERE!
Oh, IT'S—THURSDAY!
WHAT AM I DOING!? ANNA'S GONNA BE THERE!
WELL, I'LL TRY TO DROP BY ON MY WAY TO WORK! THAT'S SO EXCITING! GOD—IT'S LIKE YOU'RE FAMOUS!
Oh, FUCK, FUCK, FUCK -- THIS IS GETTING CRAZY!
AND LET ME PAY FOR THIS—IT'S SUPPOSED TO BE MY TREAT FOR OUR ...um... LITTLE SECRET —REMEMBER?

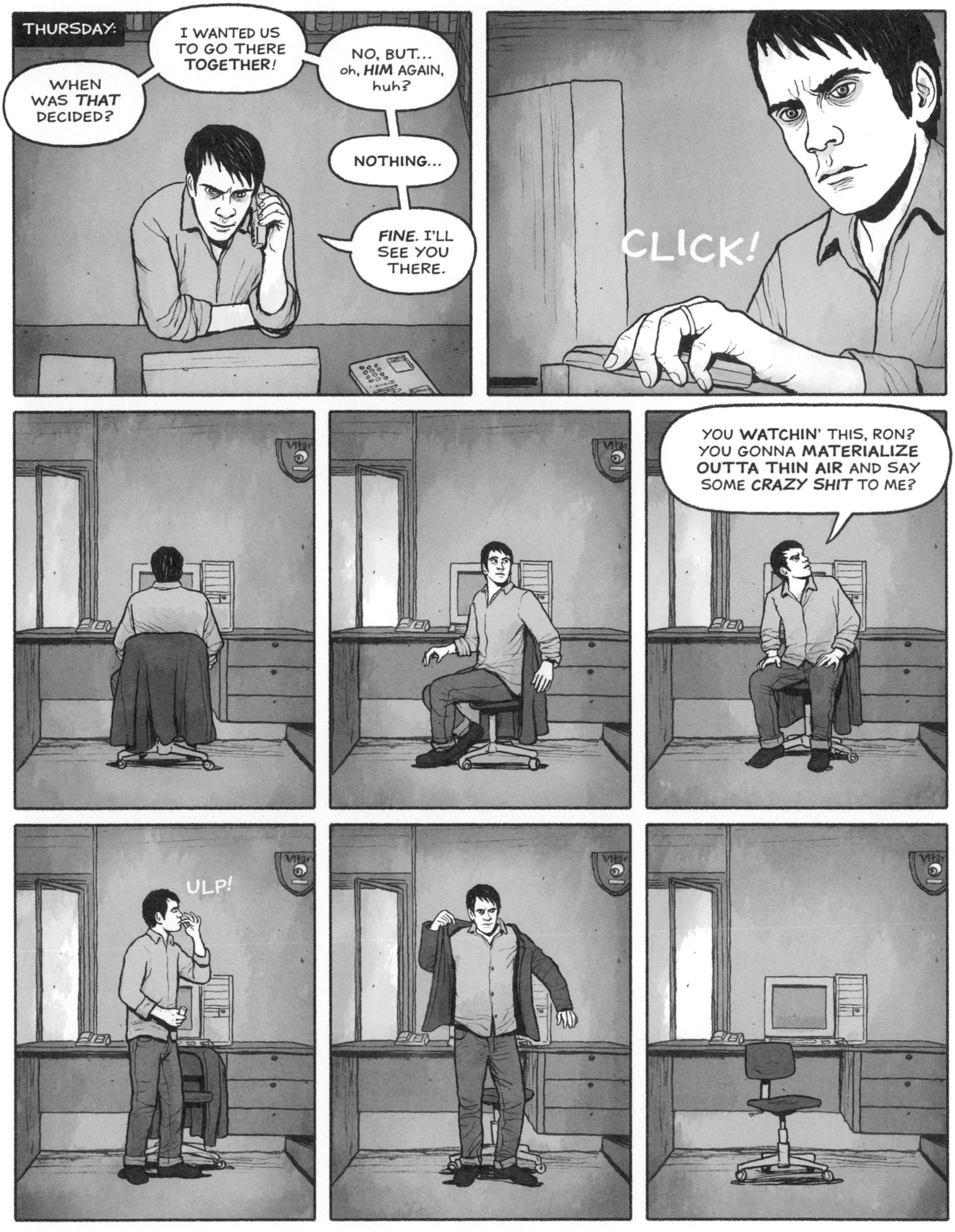

THURSDAY:
WHEN WAS THAT DECIDED?
I WANTED US TO GO THERE TOGETHER!
NO, BUT... oh, HIM AGAIN, huh?
NOTHING...
FINE. I'LL SEE YOU THERE.
CLICK!
YOU WATCHIN' THIS, RON? YOU GONNA MATERIALIZE OUTTA THIN AIR AND SAY SOME CRAZY SHIT TO ME?
ULP!

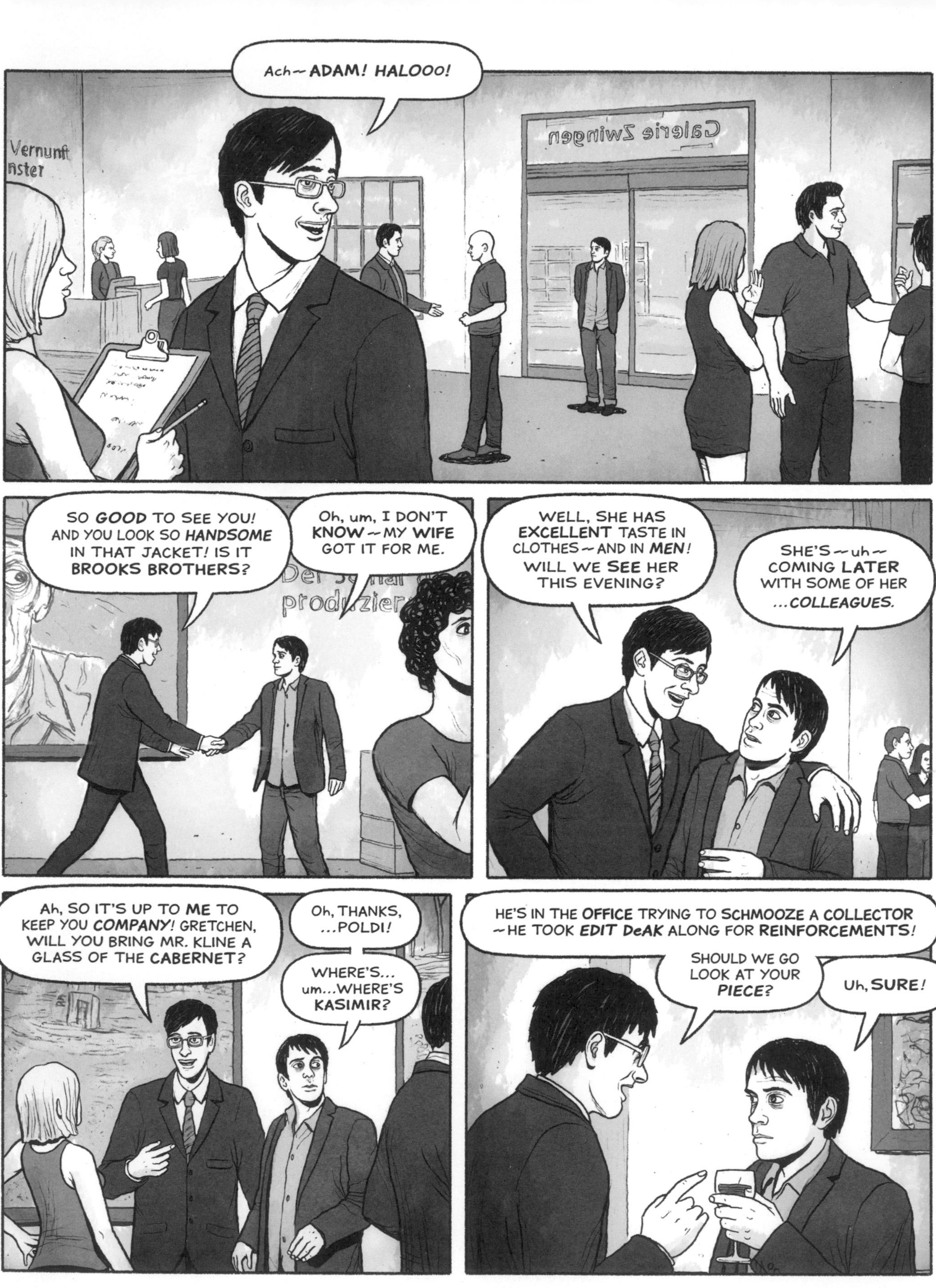
Ach~ ADAM! HALOOO!
SO GOOD TO SEE YOU! AND YOU LOOK SO HANDSOME IN THAT JACKET! IS IT BROOKS BROTHERS?
Oh, um, I DON'T KNOW~ MY WIFE GOT IT FOR ME.
WELL, SHE HAS EXCELLENT TASTE IN CLOTHES~ AND IN MEN! WILL WE SEE HER THIS EVENING?
SHE'S ~uh~ COMING LATER WITH SOME OF HER ...COLLEAGUES.
Ah, SO IT'S UP TO ME TO KEEP YOU COMPANY! GRETCHEN, WILL YOU BRING MR. KLINE A GLASS OF THE CABERNET?
Oh, THANKS, ...POLDI!
WHERE'S... um...WHERE'S KASIMIR?
HE'S IN THE OFFICE TRYING TO SCHMOOZE A COLLECTOR ~HE TOOK EDIT DeAK ALONG FOR REINFORCEMENTS!
SHOULD WE GO LOOK AT YOUR PIECE?
Uh, SURE!

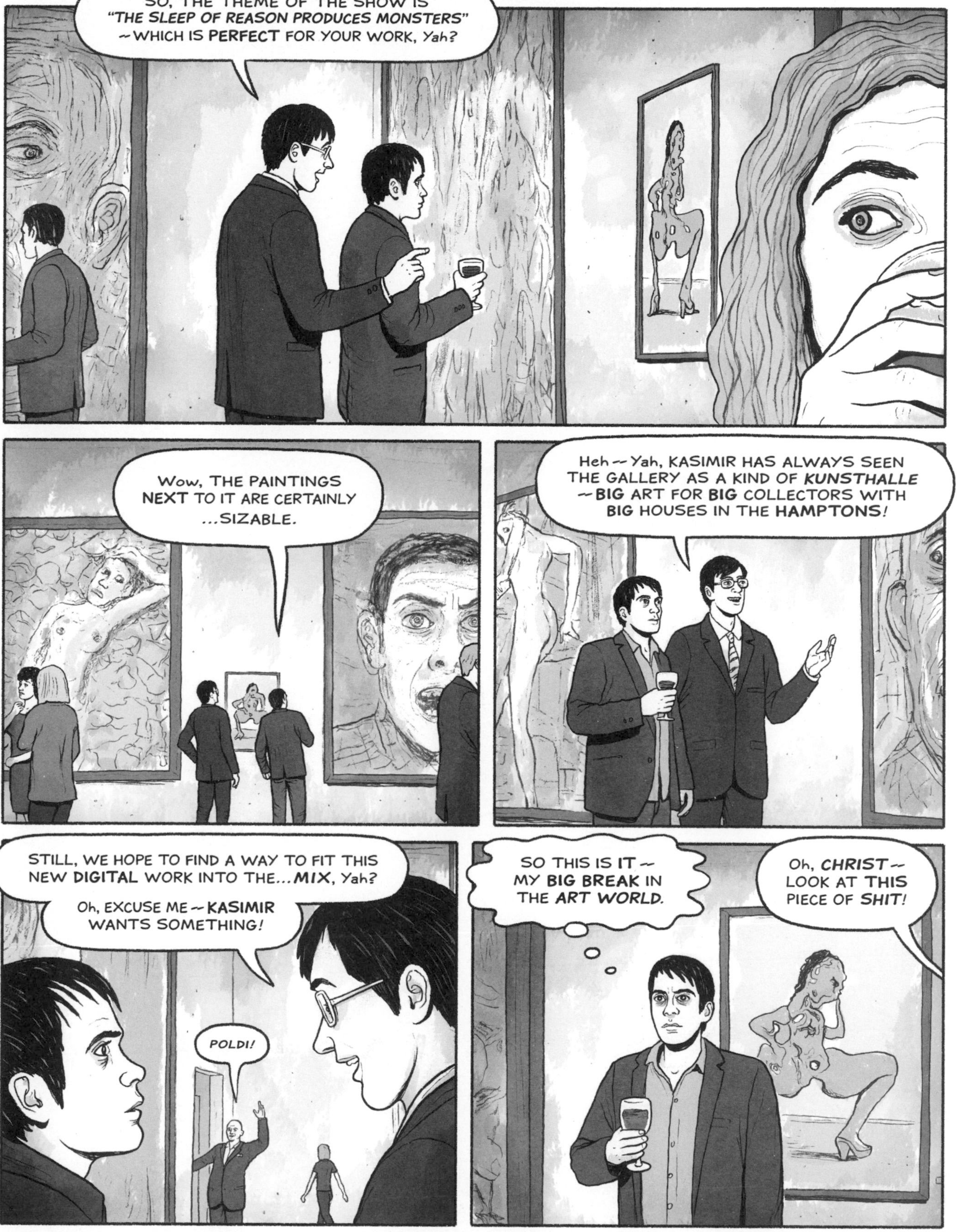
SO, THE THEME OF THE SHOW IS "THE SLEEP OF REASON PRODUCES MONSTERS" -- WHICH IS PERFECT FOR YOUR WORK, Yah?
Wow, THE PAINTINGS NEXT TO IT ARE CERTAINLY ...SIZABLE.
Heh -- Yah, KASIMIR HAS ALWAYS SEEN THE GALLERY AS A KIND OF KUNSTHALLE -- BIG ART FOR BIG COLLECTORS WITH BIG HOUSES IN THE HAMPTONS!
STILL, WE HOPE TO FIND A WAY TO FIT THIS NEW DIGITAL WORK INTO THE...MIX, Yah?
Oh, EXCUSE ME -- KASIMIR WANTS SOMETHING!
POLDI!
SO THIS IS IT -- MY BIG BREAK IN THE ART WORLD.
Oh, CHRIST -- LOOK AT THIS PIECE OF SHIT!

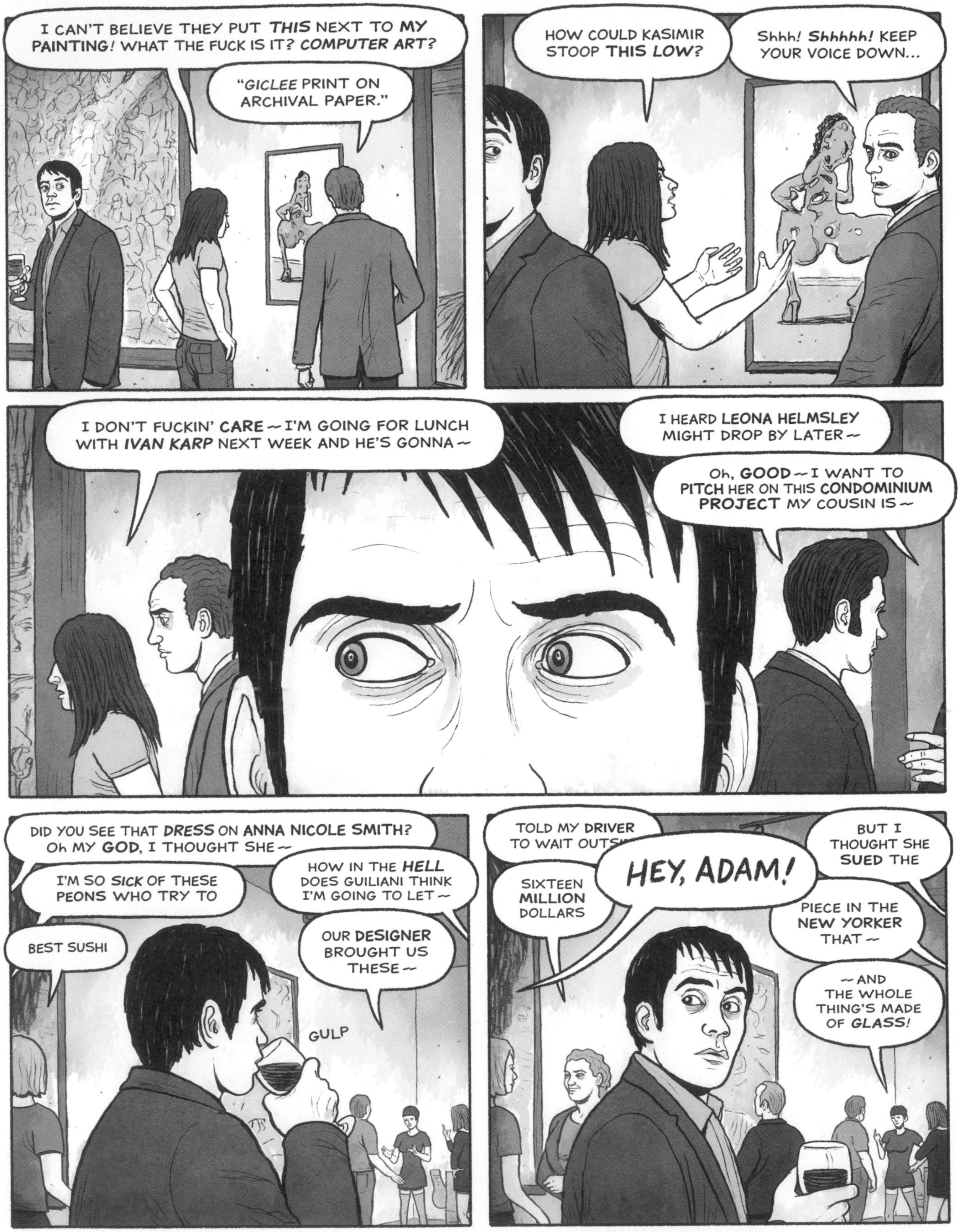
I CAN'T BELIEVE THEY PUT THIS NEXT TO MY PAINTING! WHAT THE FUCK IS IT? COMPUTER ART?
"GICLEE PRINT ON ARCHIVAL PAPER."
HOW COULD KASIMIR STOOP THIS LOW?
Shhh! Shhhhh! KEEP YOUR VOICE DOWN...
I DON'T FUCKIN' CARE -- I'M GOING FOR LUNCH WITH IVAN KARP NEXT WEEK AND HE'S GONNA --
I HEARD LEONA HELMSLEY MIGHT DROP BY LATER --
Oh, GOOD -- I WANT TO PITCH HER ON THIS CONDOMINIUM PROJECT MY COUSIN IS --
DID YOU SEE THAT DRESS ON ANNA NICOLE SMITH? Oh MY GOD, I THOUGHT SHE --
I'M SO SICK OF THESE PEONS WHO TRY TO
HOW IN THE HELL DOES GUILIANI THINK I'M GOING TO LET --
BEST SUSHI
OUR DESIGNER BROUGHT US THESE --
GULP
TOLD MY DRIVER TO WAIT OUTS
SIXTEEN MILLION DOLLARS
HEY, ADAM!
BUT I THOUGHT SHE SUED THE
PIECE IN THE NEW YORKER THAT --
-- AND THE WHOLE THING'S MADE OF GLASS!

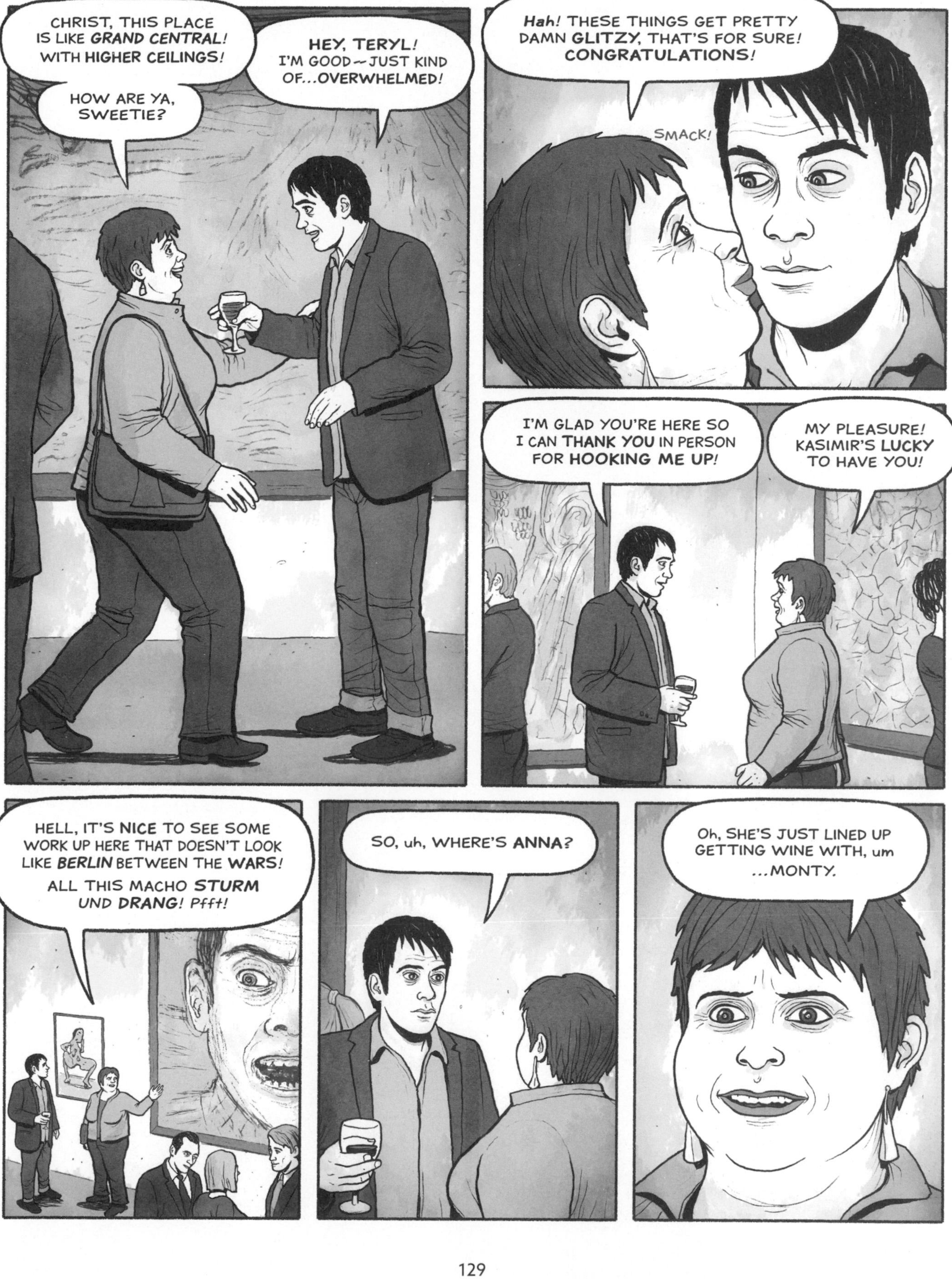
CHRIST, THIS PLACE IS LIKE **GRAND CENTRAL**! WITH **HIGHER CEILINGS**!
HOW ARE YA, SWEETIE?
HEY, TERYL! I'M GOOD—JUST KIND OF...**OVERWHELMED**!
Hah! THESE THINGS GET PRETTY DAMN **GLITZY**, THAT'S FOR SURE! **CONGRATULATIONS**!
SMACK!
I'M GLAD YOU'RE HERE SO I CAN **THANK YOU** IN PERSON FOR **HOOKING ME UP**!
MY PLEASURE! KASIMIR'S **LUCKY** TO HAVE YOU!
HELL, IT'S **NICE** TO SEE SOME WORK UP HERE THAT DOESN'T LOOK LIKE **BERLIN** BETWEEN THE **WARS**!
ALL THIS MACHO **STURM** UND **DRANG**! *Pfft*!
SO, uh, WHERE'S **ANNA**?
Oh, SHE'S JUST LINED UP GETTING WINE WITH, um ...MONTY.

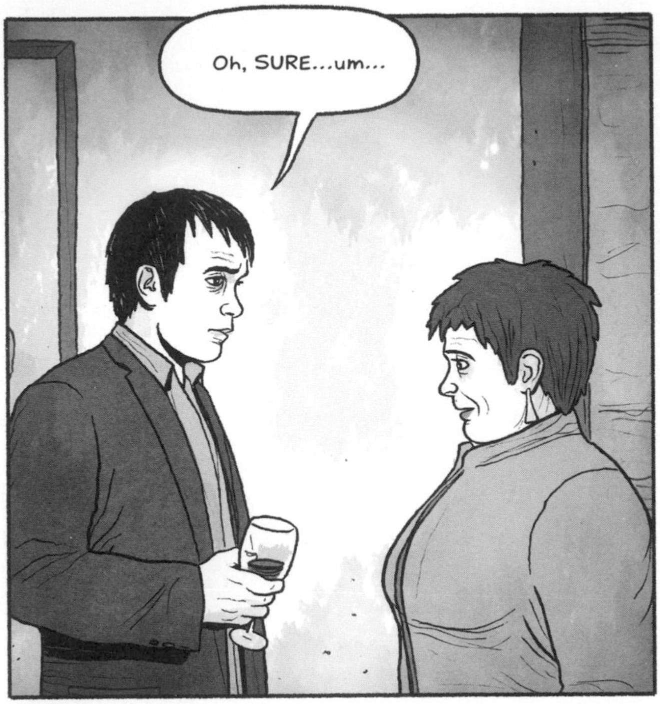
Oh, SURE...um...

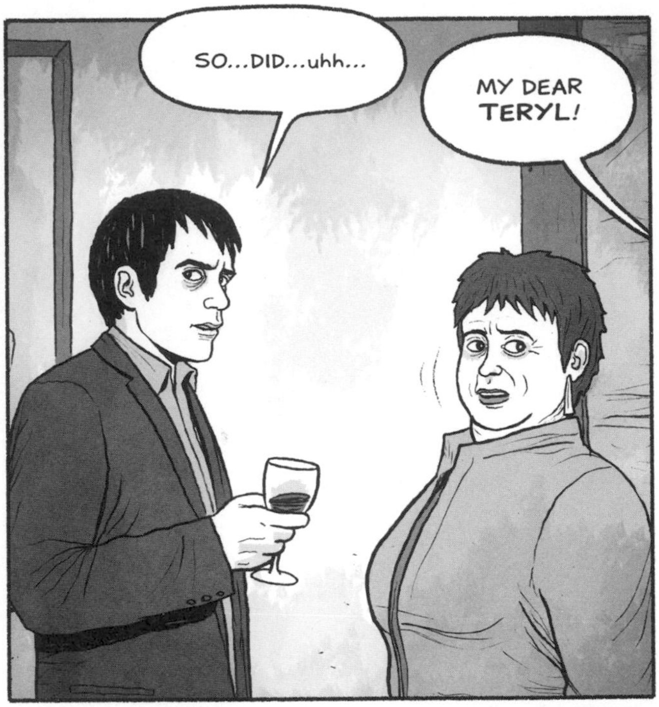
SO...DID...uhh...
MY DEAR TERYL!

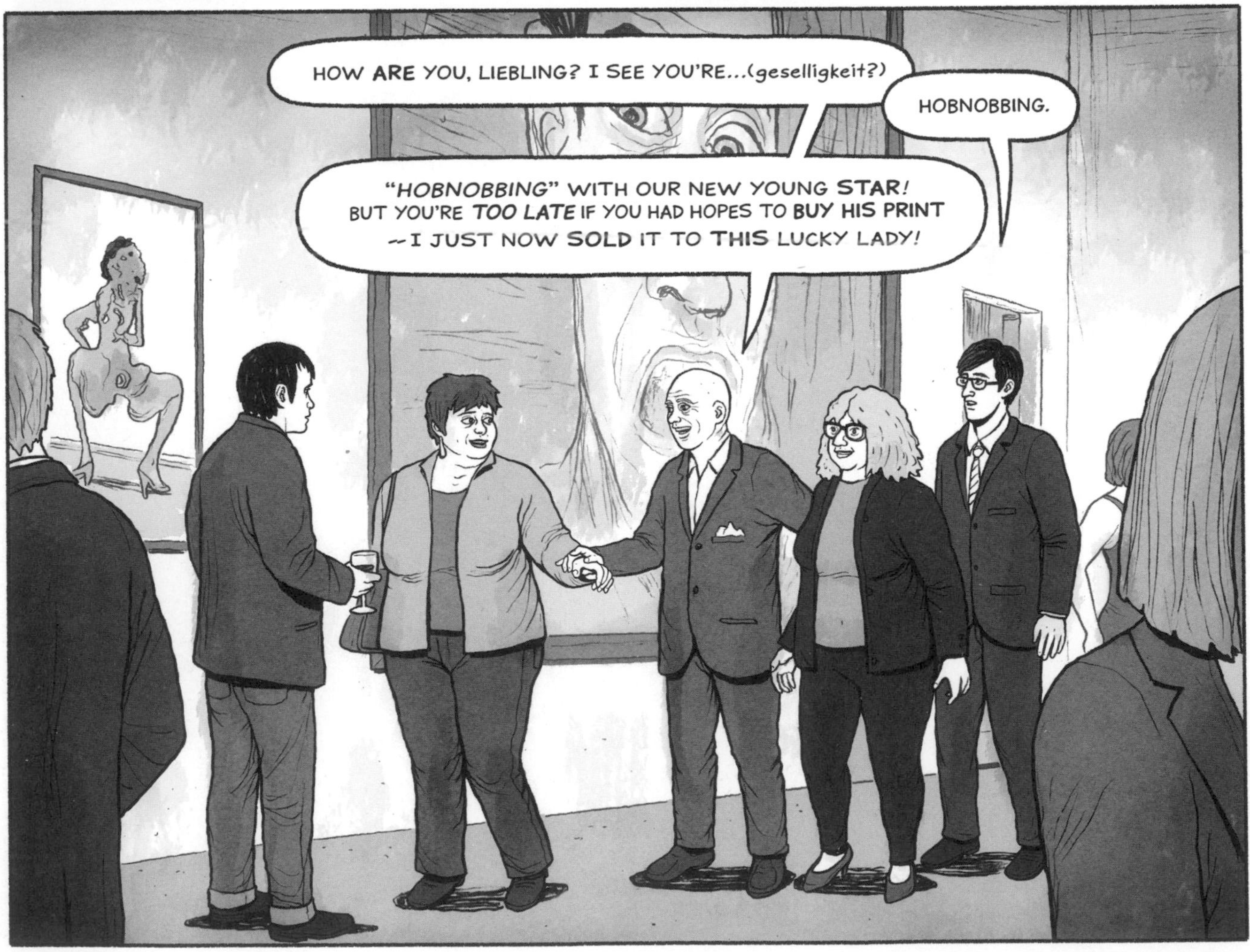
HOW ARE YOU, LIEBLING? I SEE YOU'RE...(geselligkeit?)
HOBNOBBING.
"HOBNOBBING" WITH OUR NEW YOUNG STAR! BUT YOU'RE TOO LATE IF YOU HAD HOPES TO BUY HIS PRINT --I JUST NOW SOLD IT TO THIS LUCKY LADY!

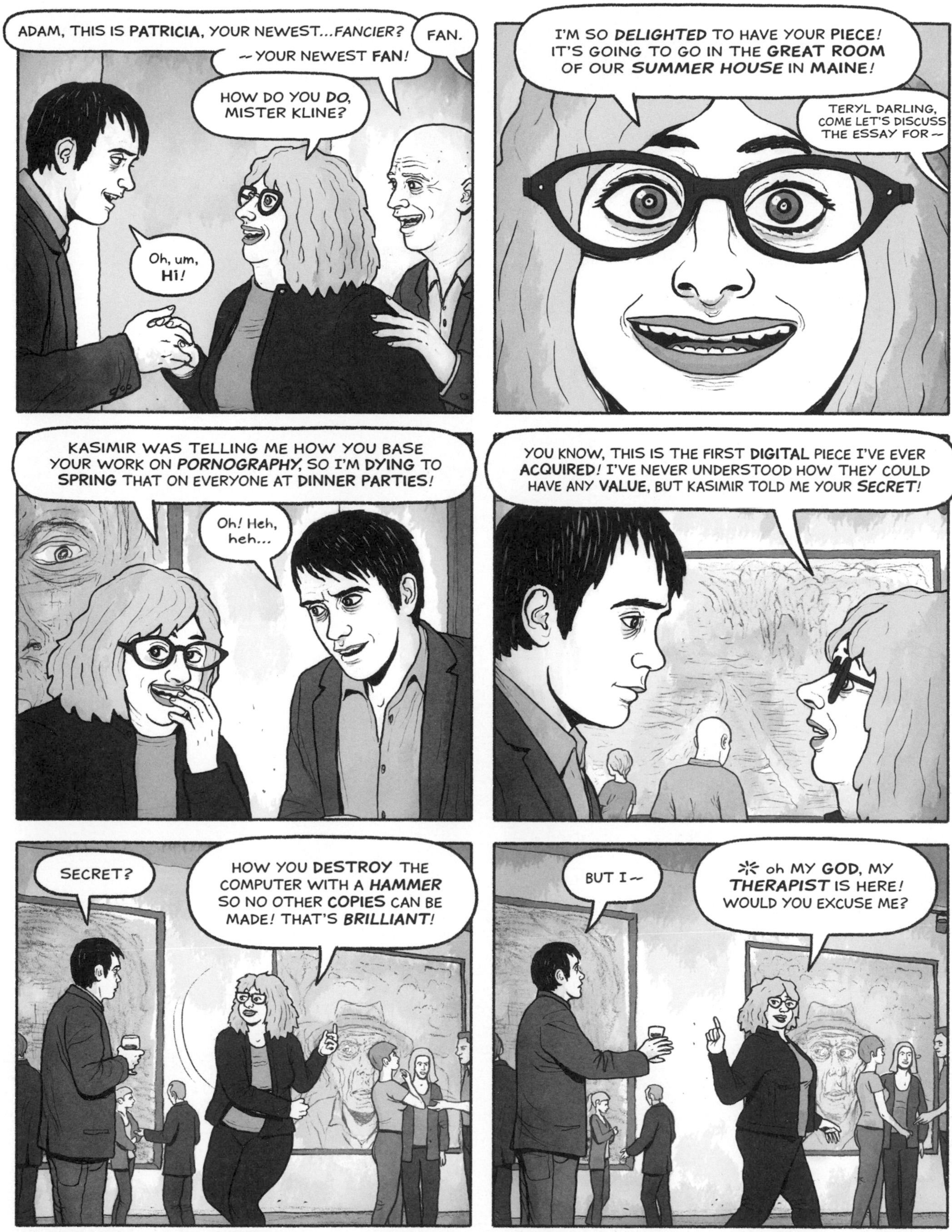
ADAM, THIS IS PATRICIA, YOUR NEWEST...FANCIER?
FAN.
--YOUR NEWEST FAN!
HOW DO YOU DO, MISTER KLINE?
Oh, um, Hi!
I'M SO DELIGHTED TO HAVE YOUR PIECE! IT'S GOING TO GO IN THE GREAT ROOM OF OUR SUMMER HOUSE IN MAINE!
TERYL DARLING, COME LET'S DISCUSS THE ESSAY FOR--
KASIMIR WAS TELLING ME HOW YOU BASE YOUR WORK ON PORNOGRAPHY, SO I'M DYING TO SPRING THAT ON EVERYONE AT DINNER PARTIES!
Oh! Heh, heh...
YOU KNOW, THIS IS THE FIRST DIGITAL PIECE I'VE EVER ACQUIRED! I'VE NEVER UNDERSTOOD HOW THEY COULD HAVE ANY VALUE, BUT KASIMIR TOLD ME YOUR SECRET!
SECRET?
HOW YOU DESTROY THE COMPUTER WITH A HAMMER SO NO OTHER COPIES CAN BE MADE! THAT'S BRILLIANT!
BUT I--
oh MY GOD, MY THERAPIST IS HERE! WOULD YOU EXCUSE ME?

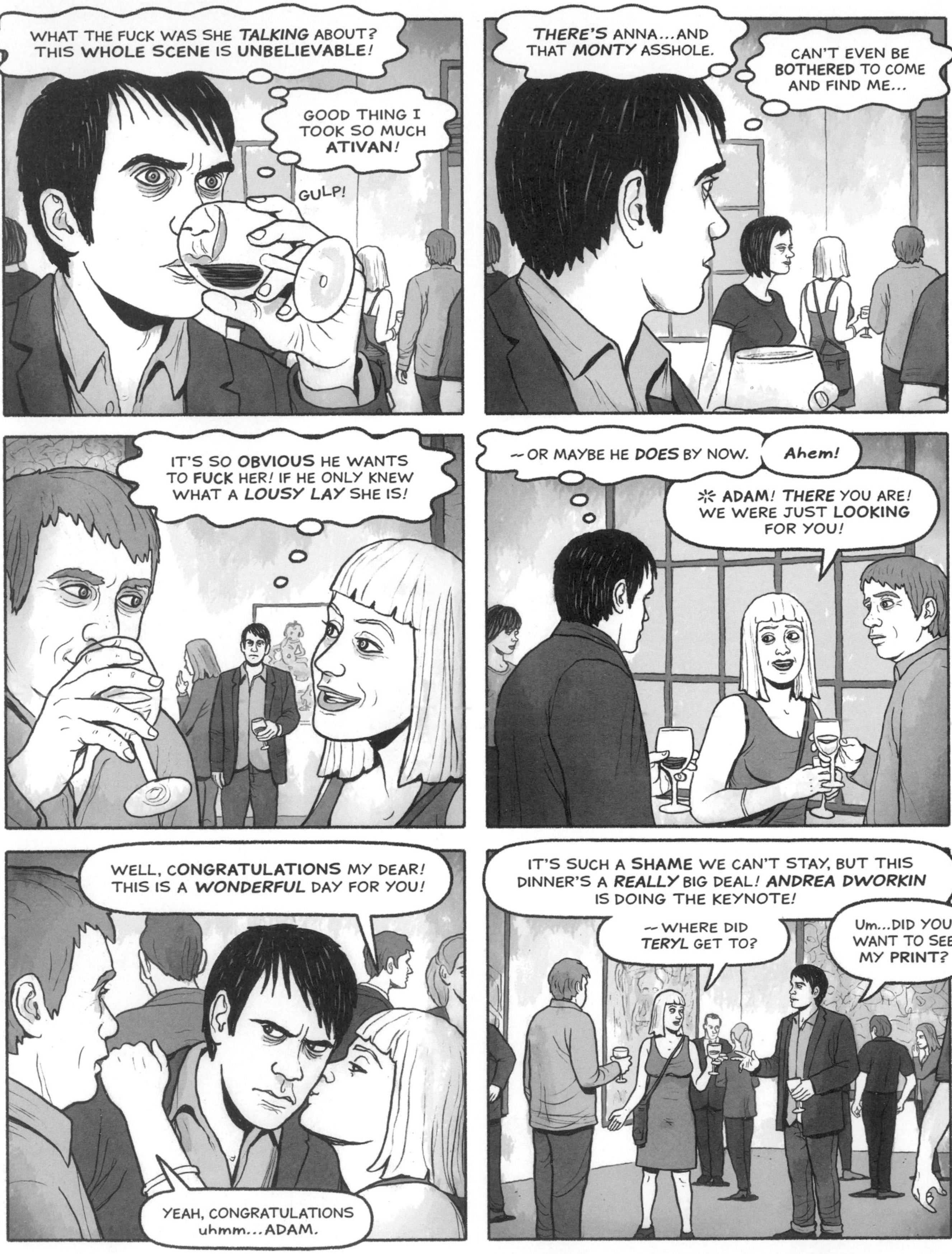
WHAT THE FUCK WAS SHE TALKING ABOUT? THIS WHOLE SCENE IS UNBELIEVABLE!
GOOD THING I TOOK SO MUCH ATIVAN!
GULP!
THERE'S ANNA...AND THAT MONTY ASSHOLE.
CAN'T EVEN BE BOTHERED TO COME AND FIND ME...
IT'S SO OBVIOUS HE WANTS TO FUCK HER! IF HE ONLY KNEW WHAT A LOUSY LAY SHE IS!
--OR MAYBE HE DOES BY NOW.
Ahem!
ADAM! THERE YOU ARE! WE WERE JUST LOOKING FOR YOU!
WELL, CONGRATULATIONS MY DEAR! THIS IS A WONDERFUL DAY FOR YOU!
YEAH, CONGRATULATIONS uhmm...ADAM.
IT'S SUCH A SHAME WE CAN'T STAY, BUT THIS DINNER'S A REALLY BIG DEAL! ANDREA DWORKIN IS DOING THE KEYNOTE!
--WHERE DID TERYL GET TO?
Um...DID YOU WANT TO SEE MY PRINT?

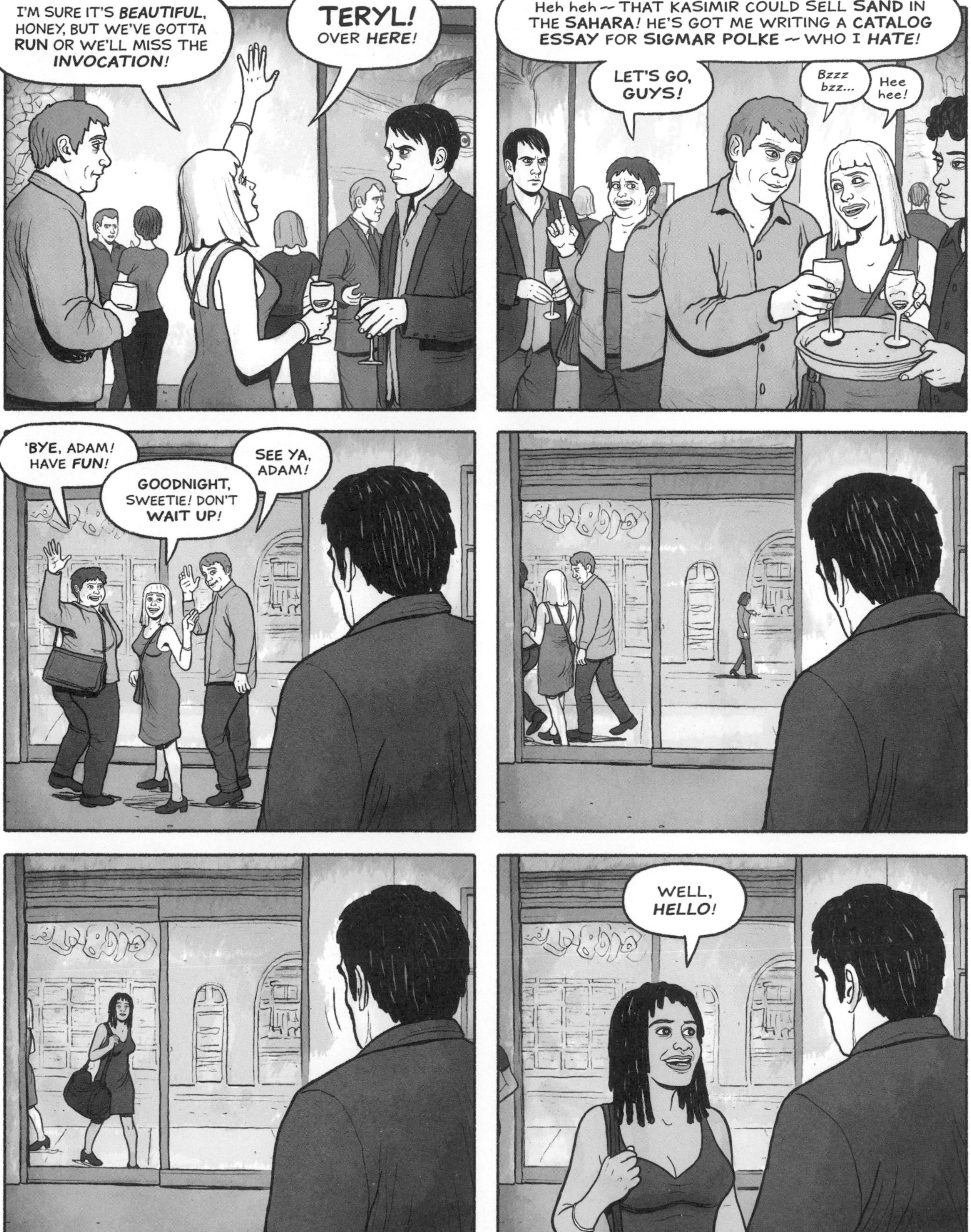
I'M SURE IT'S BEAUTIFUL, HONEY, BUT WE'VE GOTTA RUN OR WE'LL MISS THE INVOCATION!
TERYL! OVER HERE!
Heh heh -- THAT KASIMIR COULD SELL SAND IN THE SAHARA! HE'S GOT ME WRITING A CATALOG ESSAY FOR SIGMAR POLKE -- WHO I HATE!
LET'S GO, GUYS!
Bzzz bzz...
Hee hee!
'BYE, ADAM! HAVE FUN!
GOODNIGHT, SWEETIE! DON'T WAIT UP!
SEE YA, ADAM!
WELL, HELLO!

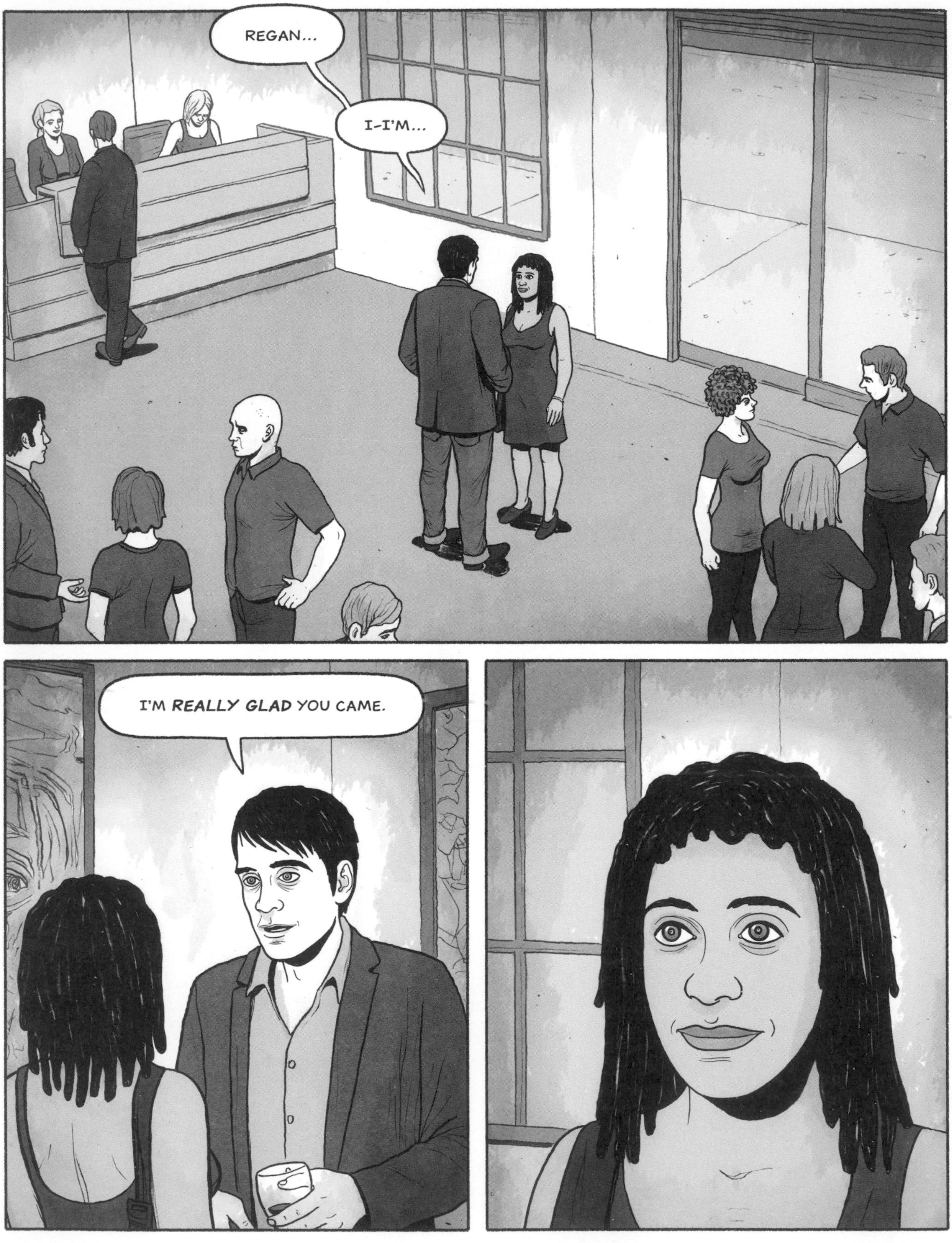
REGAN...
I-I'M...
I'M *REALLY GLAD* YOU CAME.

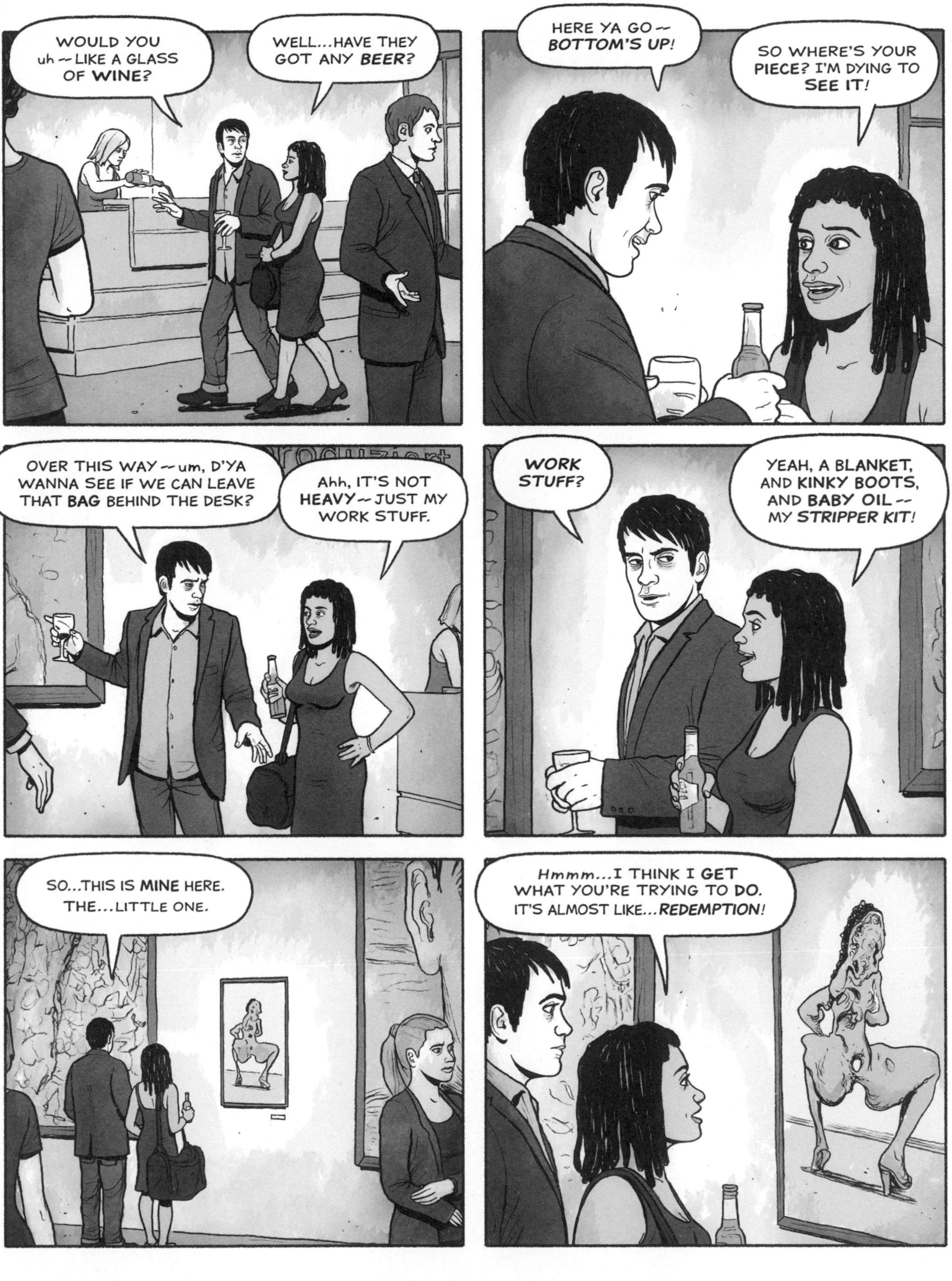
WOULD YOU uh -- LIKE A GLASS OF WINE?
WELL... HAVE THEY GOT ANY BEER?
HERE YA GO -- BOTTOM'S UP!
SO WHERE'S YOUR PIECE? I'M DYING TO SEE IT!
OVER THIS WAY -- um, D'YA WANNA SEE IF WE CAN LEAVE THAT BAG BEHIND THE DESK?
Ahh, IT'S NOT HEAVY -- JUST MY WORK STUFF.
WORK STUFF?
YEAH, A BLANKET, AND KINKY BOOTS, AND BABY OIL -- MY STRIPPER KIT!
SO... THIS IS MINE HERE. THE... LITTLE ONE.
Hmmm... I THINK I GET WHAT YOU'RE TRYING TO DO. IT'S ALMOST LIKE... REDEMPTION!

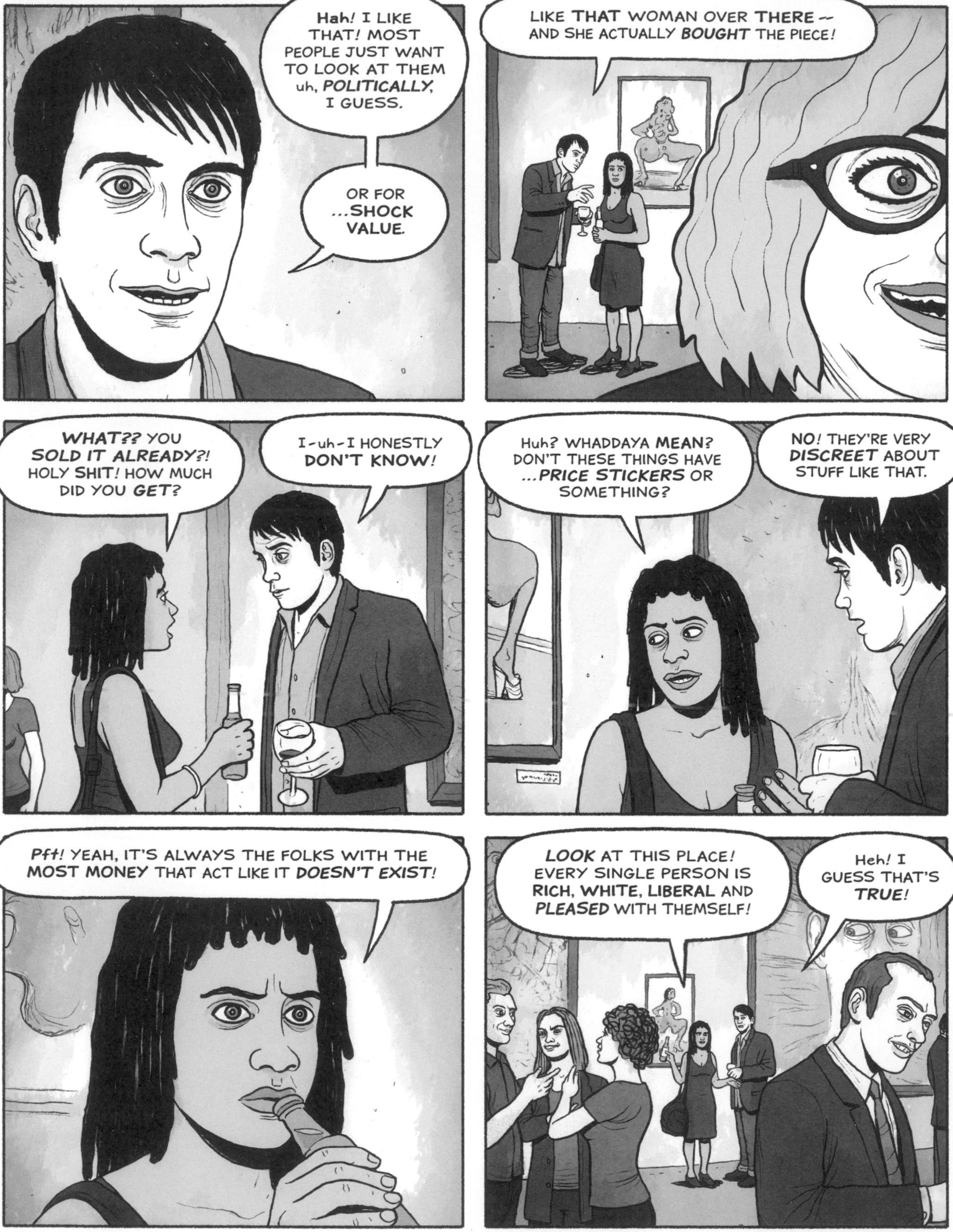
Hah! I LIKE THAT! MOST PEOPLE JUST WANT TO LOOK AT THEM uh, POLITICALLY, I GUESS.
OR FOR ...SHOCK VALUE.
LIKE THAT WOMAN OVER THERE -- AND SHE ACTUALLY BOUGHT THE PIECE!
WHAT?? YOU SOLD IT ALREADY?! HOLY SHIT! HOW MUCH DID YOU GET?
I-uh-I HONESTLY DON'T KNOW!
Huh? WHADDAYA MEAN? DON'T THESE THINGS HAVE ...PRICE STICKERS OR SOMETHING?
NO! THEY'RE VERY DISCREET ABOUT STUFF LIKE THAT.
Pft! YEAH, IT'S ALWAYS THE FOLKS WITH THE MOST MONEY THAT ACT LIKE IT DOESN'T EXIST!
LOOK AT THIS PLACE! EVERY SINGLE PERSON IS RICH, WHITE, LIBERAL AND PLEASED WITH THEMSELF!
Heh! I GUESS THAT'S TRUE!

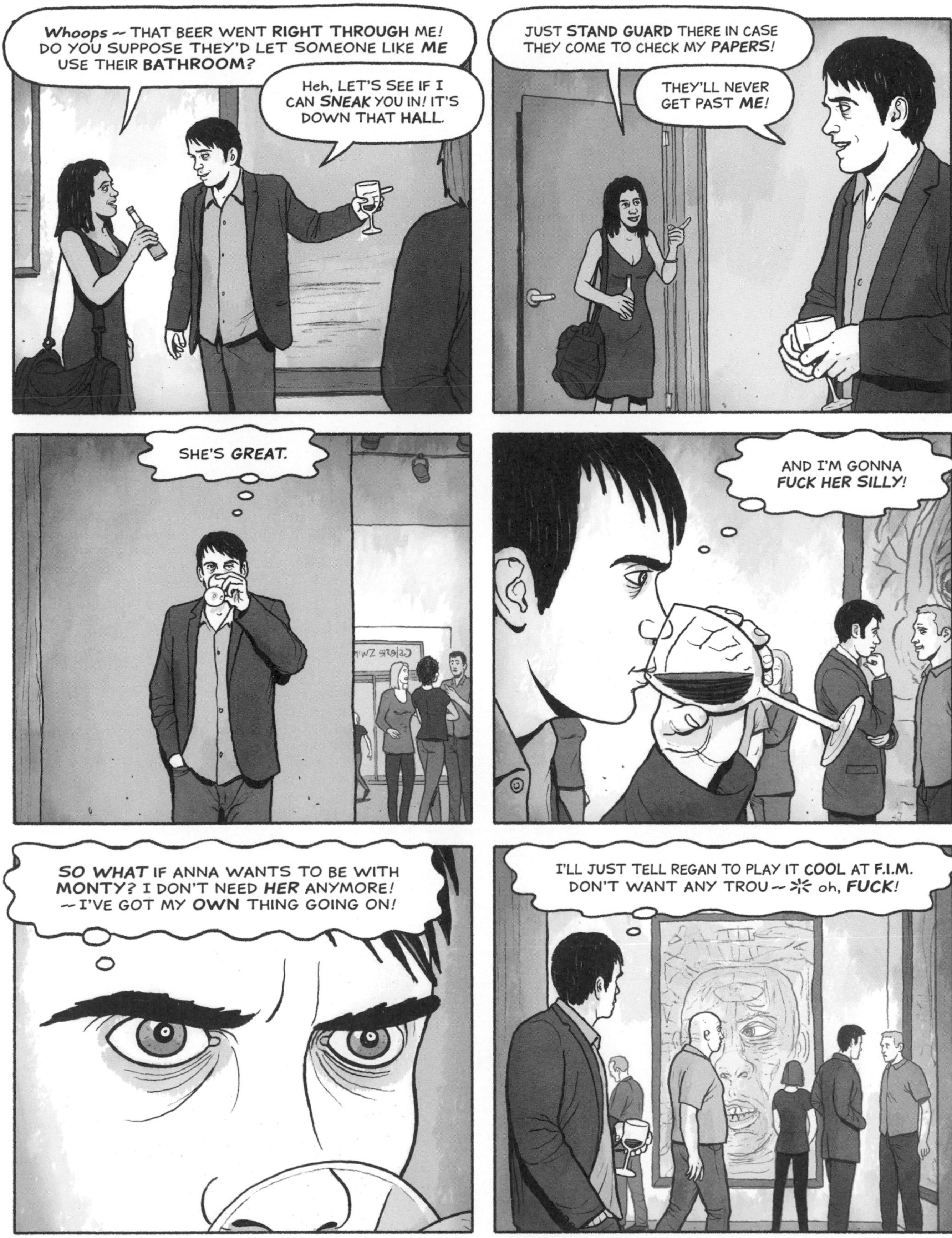
Whoops ~ THAT BEER WENT RIGHT THROUGH ME! DO YOU SUPPOSE THEY'D LET SOMEONE LIKE ME USE THEIR BATHROOM?
Heh, LET'S SEE IF I CAN SNEAK YOU IN! IT'S DOWN THAT HALL.
JUST STAND GUARD THERE IN CASE THEY COME TO CHECK MY PAPERS!
THEY'LL NEVER GET PAST ME!
SHE'S GREAT.
AND I'M GONNA FUCK HER SILLY!
SO WHAT IF ANNA WANTS TO BE WITH MONTY? I DON'T NEED HER ANYMORE! ~ I'VE GOT MY OWN THING GOING ON!
I'LL JUST TELL REGAN TO PLAY IT COOL AT F.I.M. DON'T WANT ANY TROU ~ oh, FUCK!

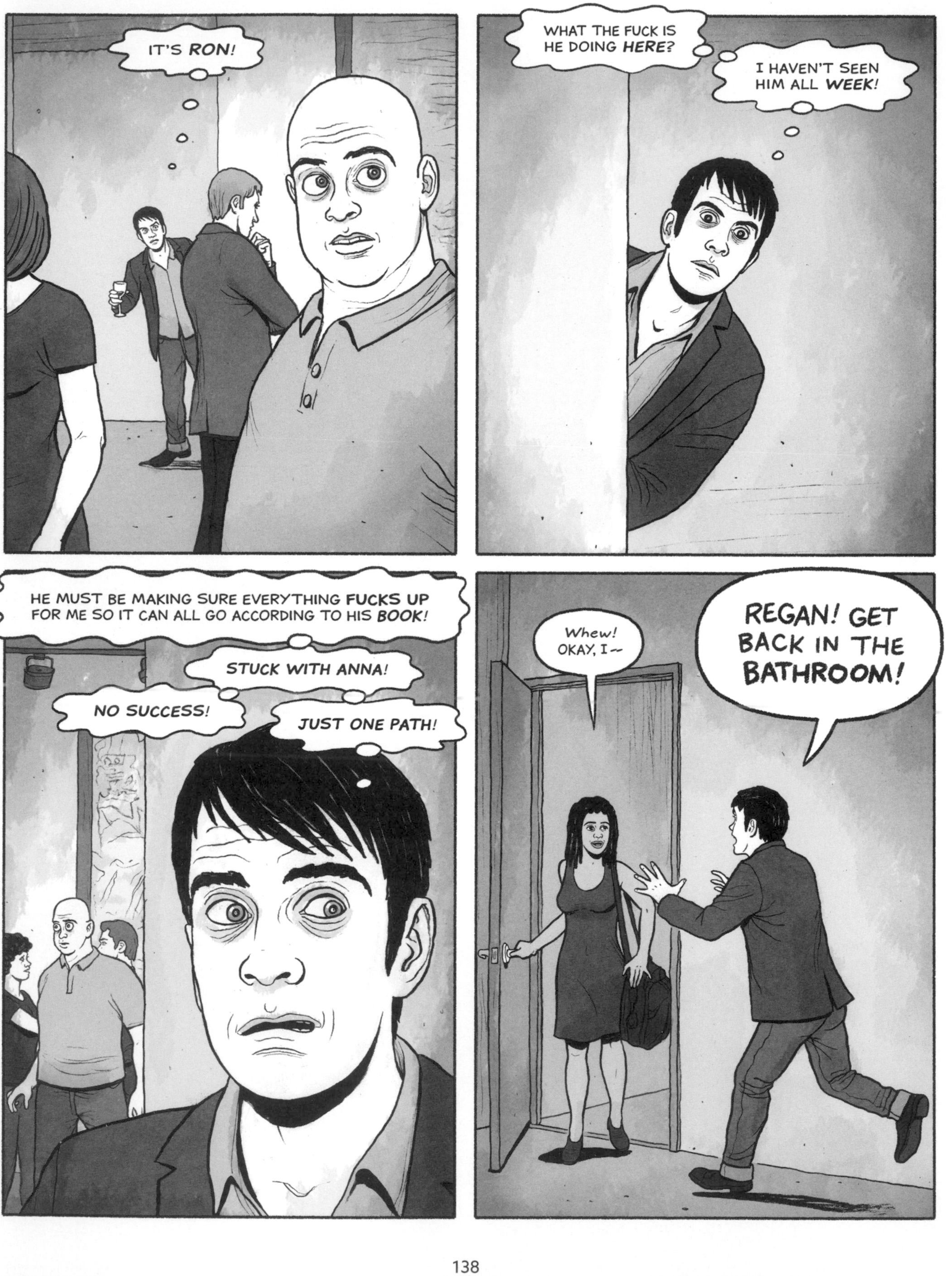
IT'S RON!
WHAT THE FUCK IS HE DOING HERE?
I HAVEN'T SEEN HIM ALL WEEK!
HE MUST BE MAKING SURE EVERYTHING FUCKS UP FOR ME SO IT CAN ALL GO ACCORDING TO HIS BOOK!
STUCK WITH ANNA!
NO SUCCESS!
JUST ONE PATH!
Whew! OKAY, I--
REGAN! GET BACK IN THE BATHROOM!

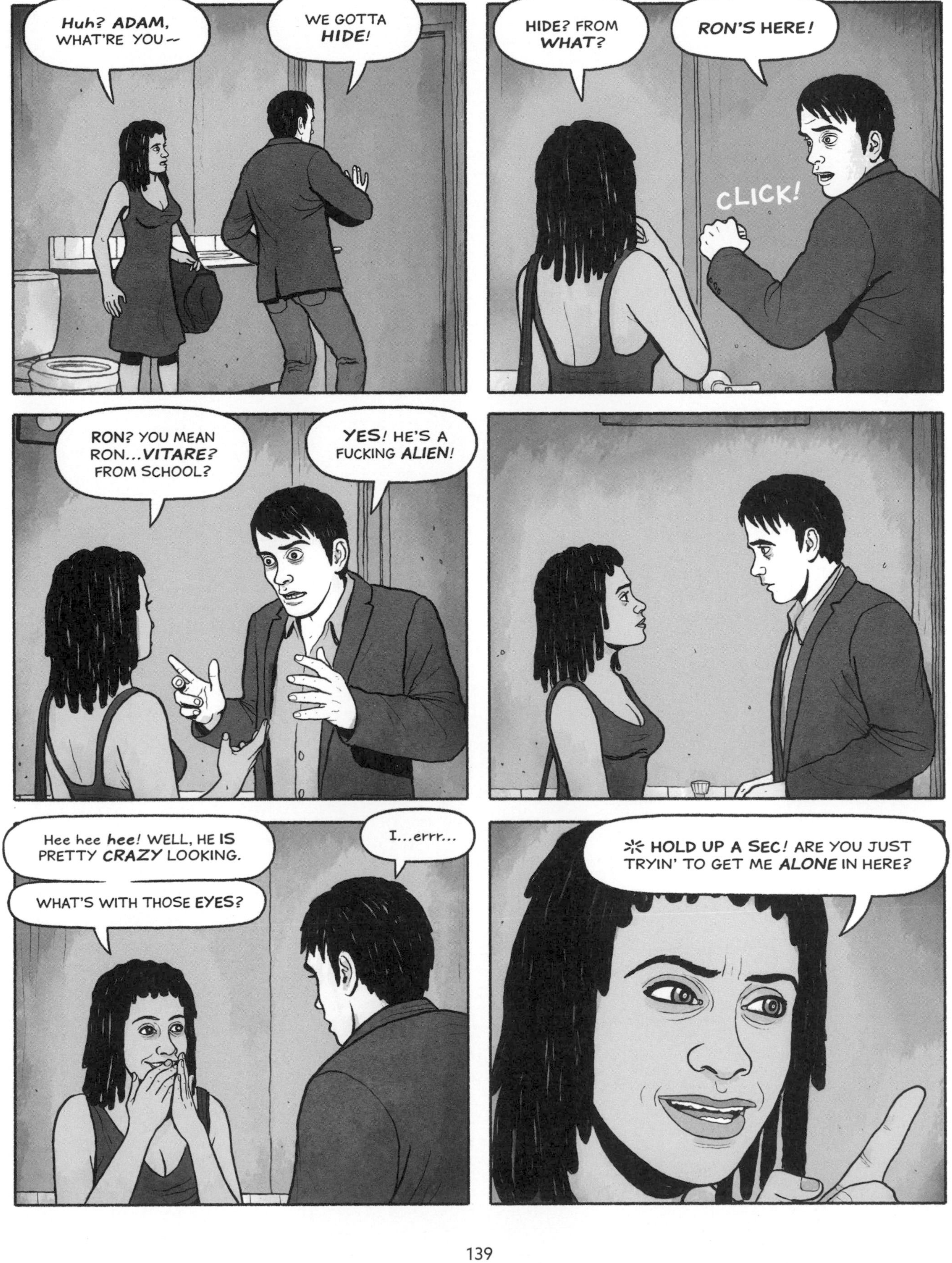
Huh? ADAM, WHAT'RE YOU--
WE GOTTA HIDE!
HIDE? FROM WHAT?
RON'S HERE!
CLICK!
RON? YOU MEAN RON...VITARE? FROM SCHOOL?
YES! HE'S A FUCKING ALIEN!
Hee hee hee! WELL, HE IS PRETTY CRAZY LOOKING.
WHAT'S WITH THOSE EYES?
I...errr...
HOLD UP A SEC! ARE YOU JUST TRYIN' TO GET ME ALONE IN HERE?

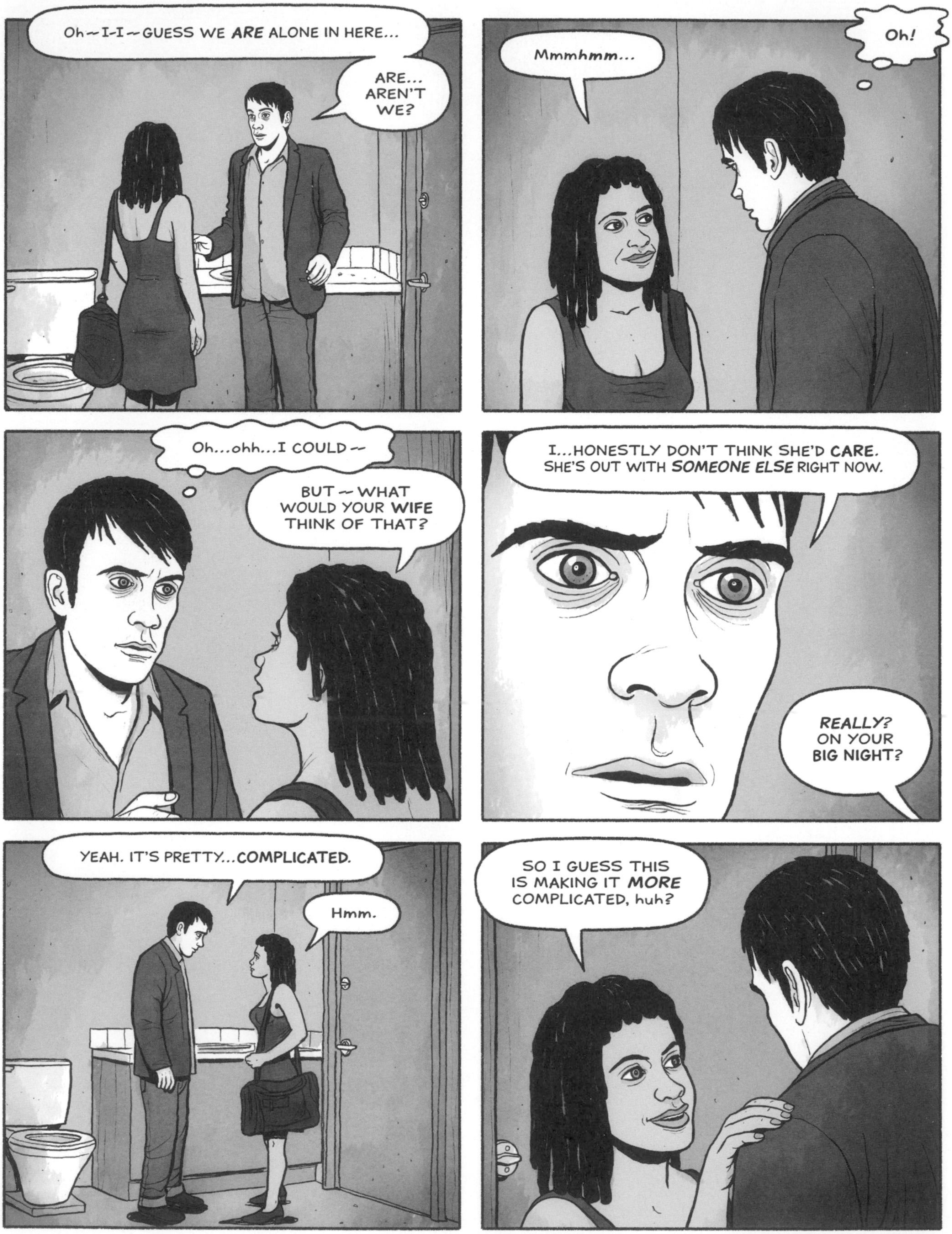
Oh—I-I—GUESS WE ARE ALONE IN HERE...
ARE... AREN'T WE?
Mmmhmm...
Oh!
Oh...ohh...I COULD—
BUT—WHAT WOULD YOUR WIFE THINK OF THAT?
I...HONESTLY DON'T THINK SHE'D CARE. SHE'S OUT WITH SOMEONE ELSE RIGHT NOW.
REALLY? ON YOUR BIG NIGHT?
YEAH. IT'S PRETTY...COMPLICATED.
Hmm.
SO I GUESS THIS IS MAKING IT MORE COMPLICATED, huh?

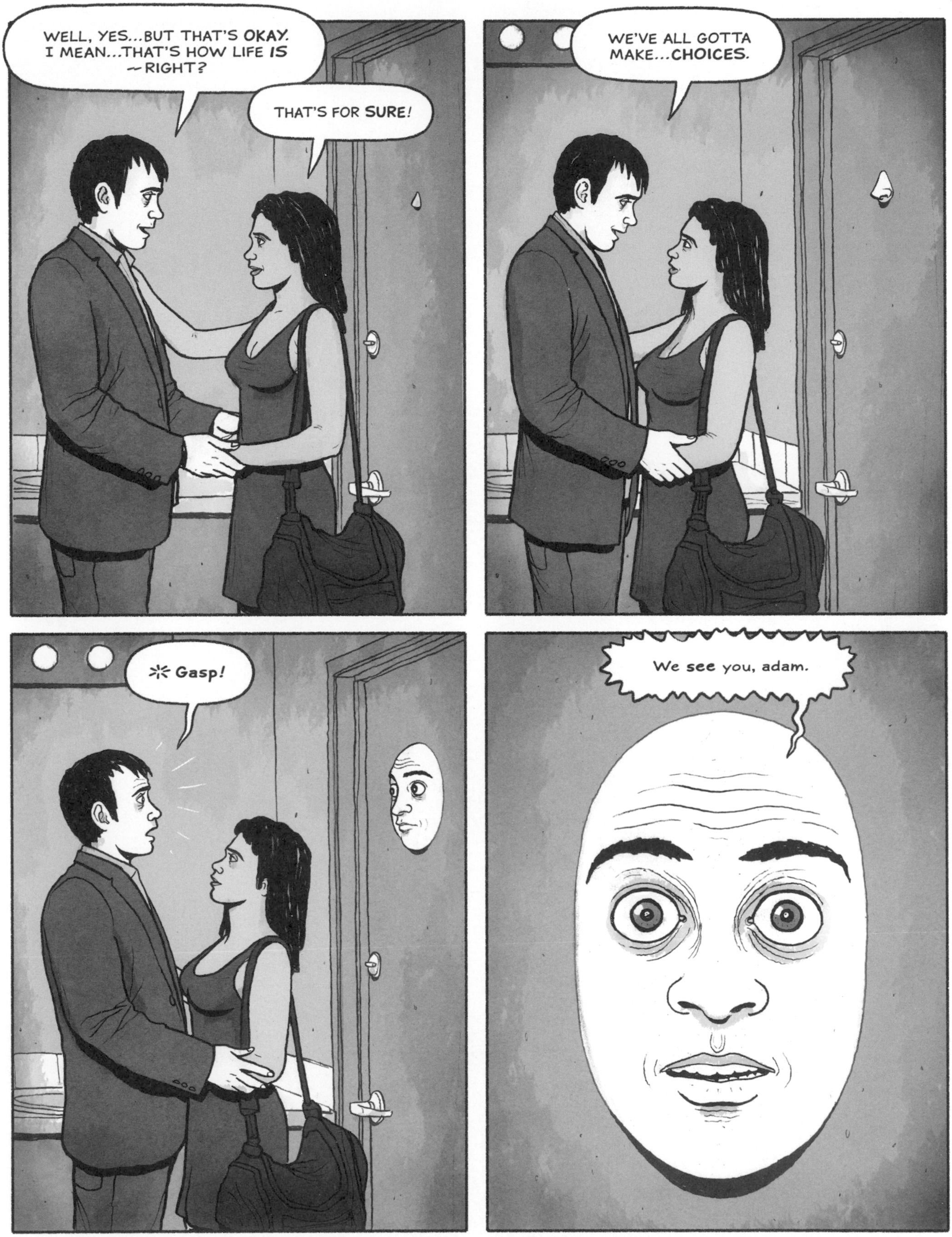
WELL, YES...BUT THAT'S OKAY. I MEAN...THAT'S HOW LIFE IS —RIGHT?
THAT'S FOR SURE!
WE'VE ALL GOTTA MAKE...CHOICES.
Gasp!
We see you, adam.

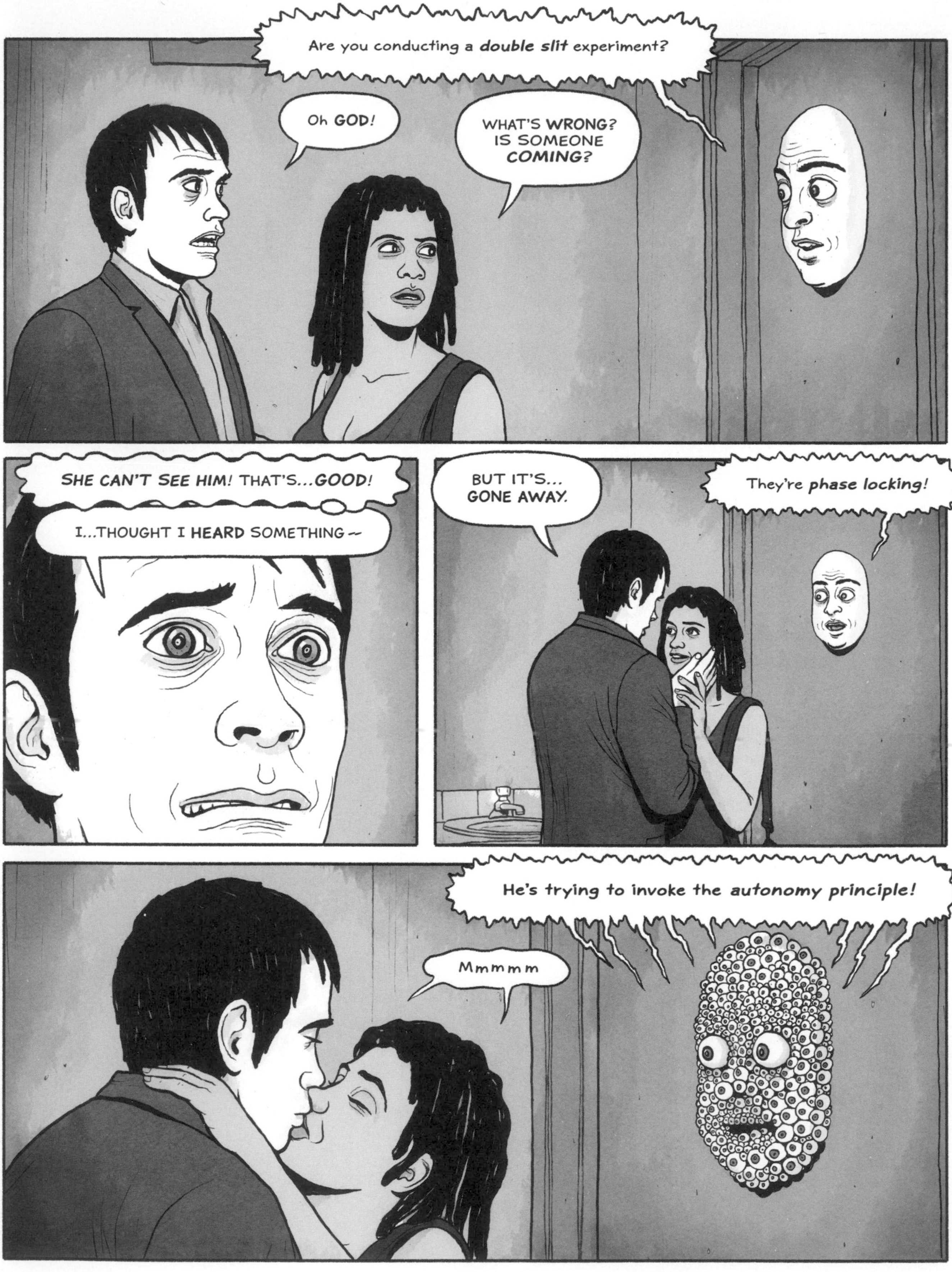
Are you conducting a double slit experiment?
Oh GOD!
WHAT'S WRONG? IS SOMEONE COMING?
SHE CAN'T SEE HIM! THAT'S...GOOD!
I...THOUGHT I HEARD SOMETHING--
BUT IT'S... GONE AWAY.
They're phase locking!
He's trying to invoke the autonomy principle!
Mmmmm

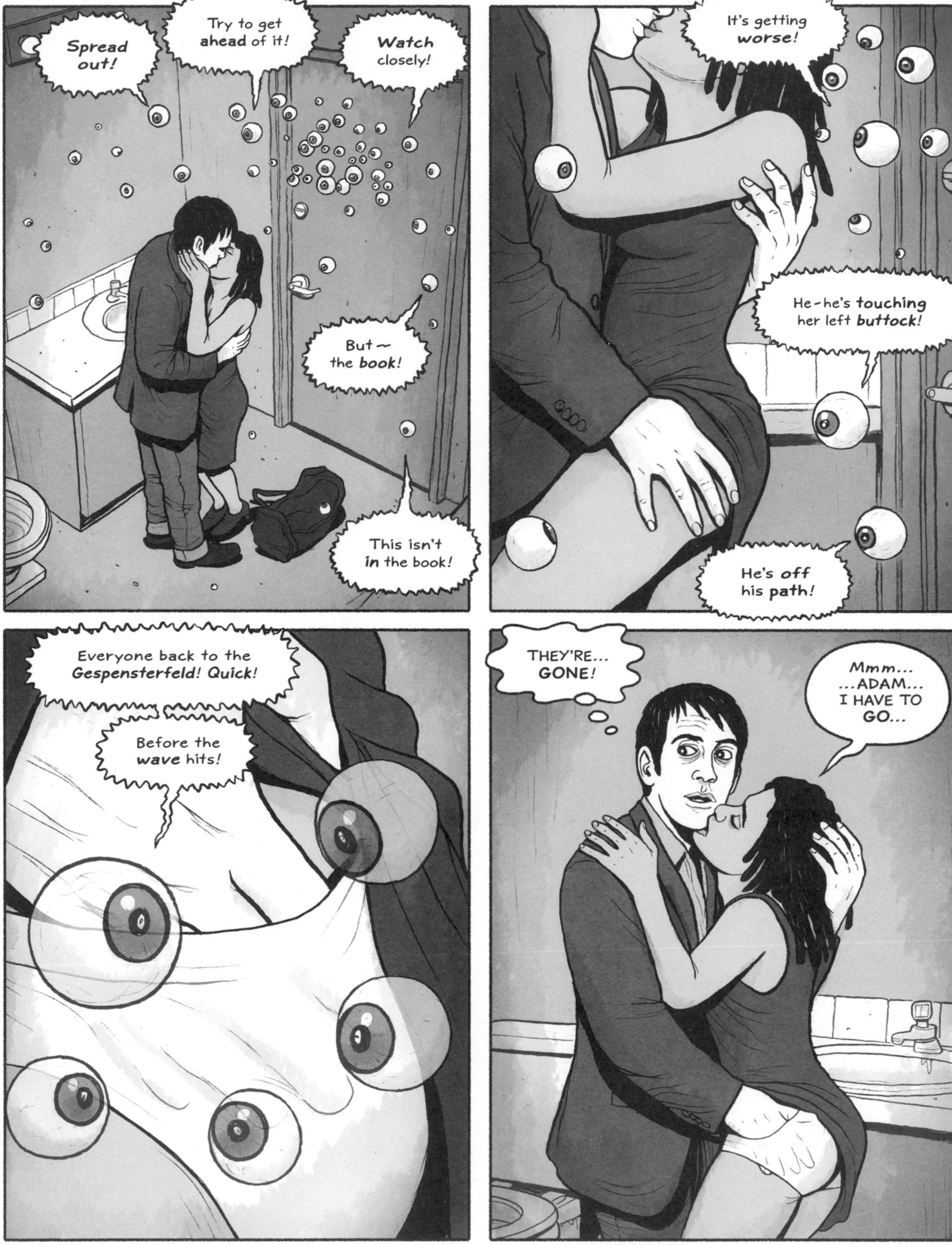
Spread out!
Try to get ahead of it!
Watch closely!
But— the book!
This isn't in the book!
It's getting worse!
He-he's touching her left buttock!
He's off his path!
Everyone back to the Gespensterfeld! Quick!
Before the wave hits!
THEY'RE... GONE!
Mmm... ...ADAM... I HAVE TO GO...

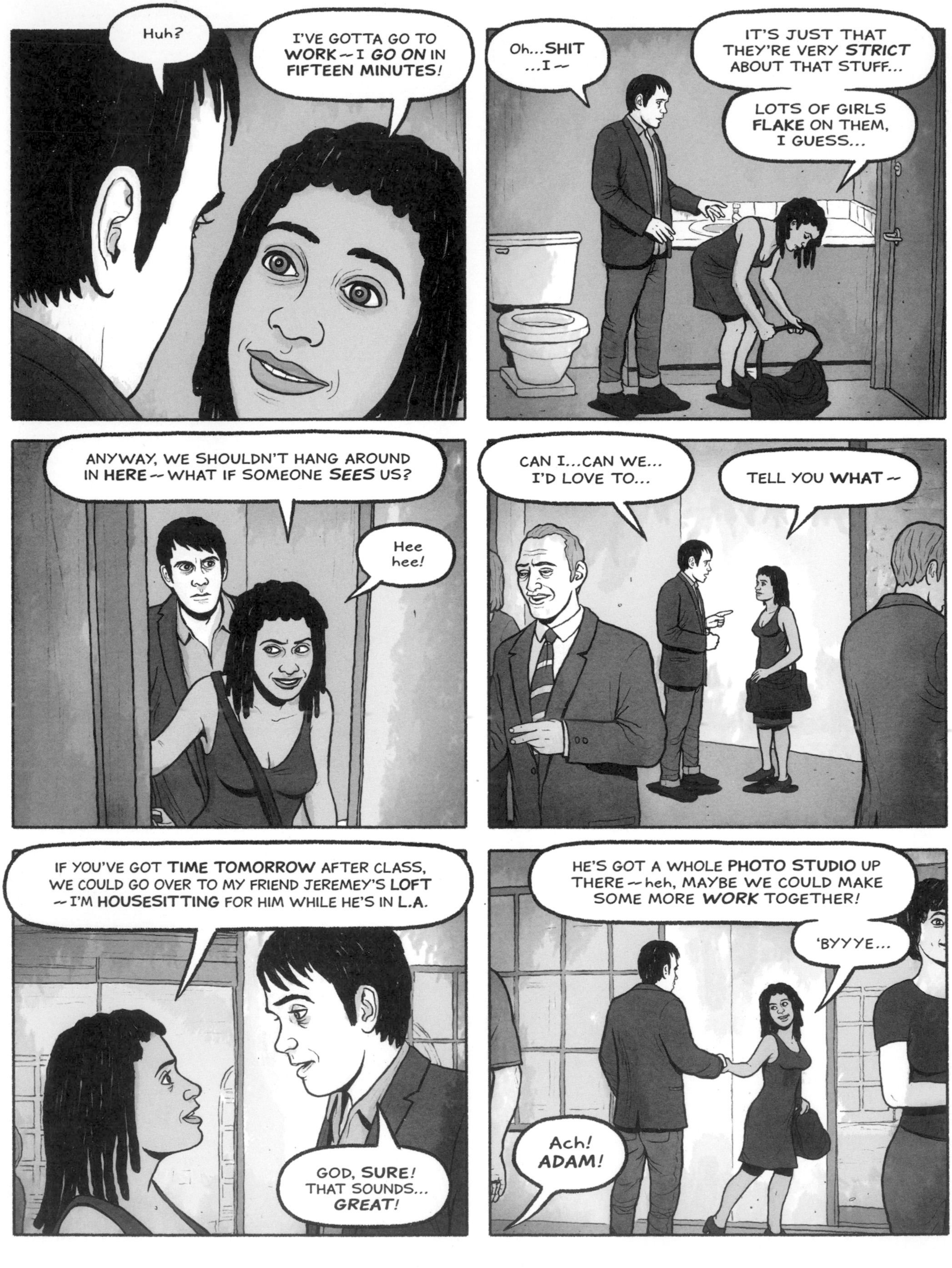
Huh?
I'VE GOTTA GO TO WORK—I GO ON IN FIFTEEN MINUTES!
Oh...SHIT ...I—
IT'S JUST THAT THEY'RE VERY STRICT ABOUT THAT STUFF...
LOTS OF GIRLS FLAKE ON THEM, I GUESS...
ANYWAY, WE SHOULDN'T HANG AROUND IN HERE—WHAT IF SOMEONE SEES US?
Hee hee!
CAN I...CAN WE... I'D LOVE TO...
TELL YOU WHAT—
IF YOU'VE GOT TIME TOMORROW AFTER CLASS, WE COULD GO OVER TO MY FRIEND JEREMEY'S LOFT —I'M HOUSESITTING FOR HIM WHILE HE'S IN L.A.
GOD, SURE! THAT SOUNDS... GREAT!
HE'S GOT A WHOLE PHOTO STUDIO UP THERE—heh, MAYBE WE COULD MAKE SOME MORE WORK TOGETHER!
'BYYYE...
Ach! ADAM!

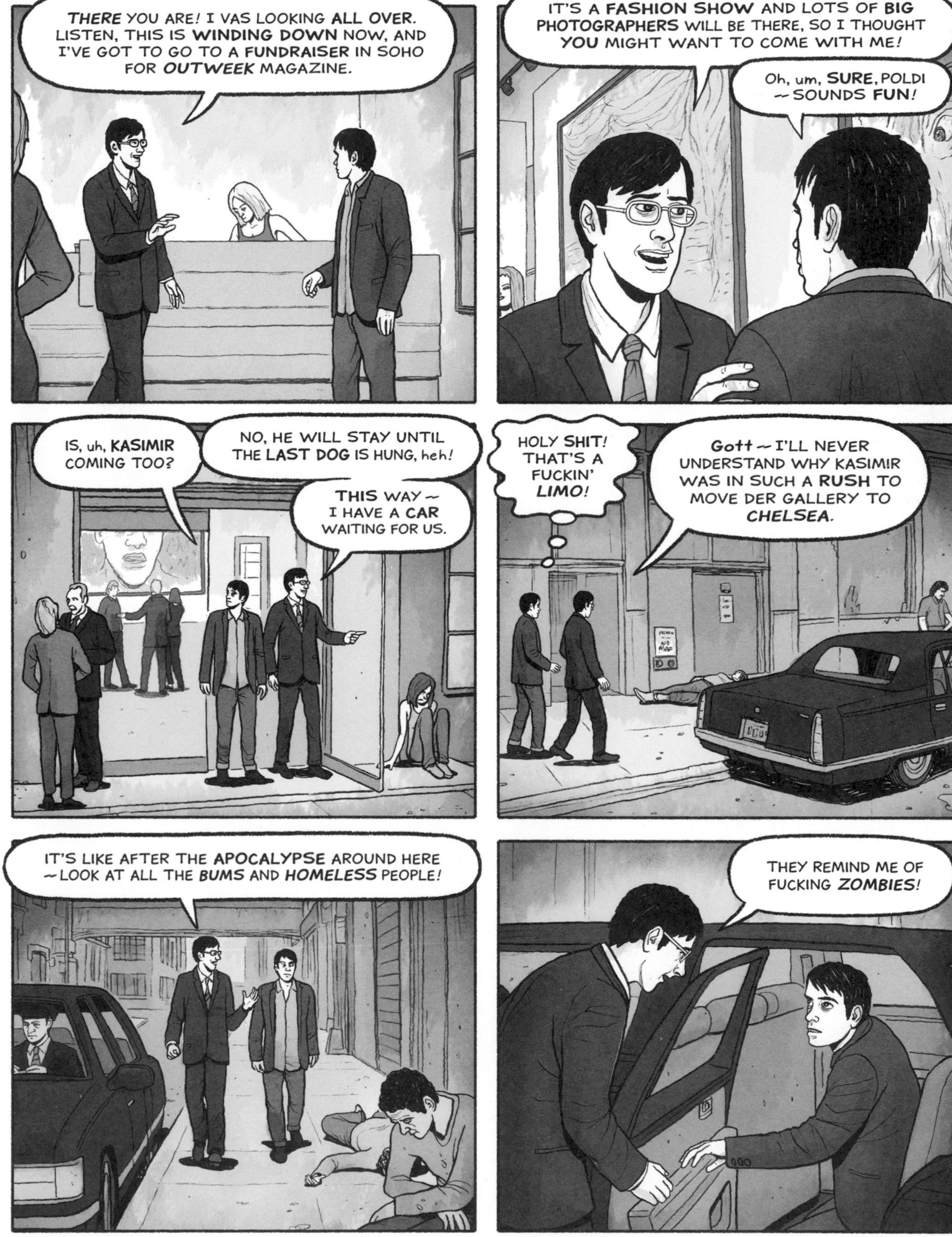
THERE YOU ARE! I VAS LOOKING ALL OVER. LISTEN, THIS IS WINDING DOWN NOW, AND I'VE GOT TO GO TO A FUNDRAISER IN SOHO FOR OUTWEEK MAGAZINE.
IT'S A FASHION SHOW AND LOTS OF BIG PHOTOGRAPHERS WILL BE THERE, SO I THOUGHT YOU MIGHT WANT TO COME WITH ME!
Oh, um, SURE, POLDI — SOUNDS FUN!
IS, uh, KASIMIR COMING TOO?
NO, HE WILL STAY UNTIL THE LAST DOG IS HUNG, heh!
THIS WAY — I HAVE A CAR WAITING FOR US.
HOLY SHIT! THAT'S A FUCKIN' LIMO!
Gott — I'LL NEVER UNDERSTAND WHY KASIMIR WAS IN SUCH A RUSH TO MOVE DER GALLERY TO CHELSEA.
IT'S LIKE AFTER THE APOCALYPSE AROUND HERE — LOOK AT ALL THE BUMS AND HOMELESS PEOPLE!
THEY REMIND ME OF FUCKING ZOMBIES!

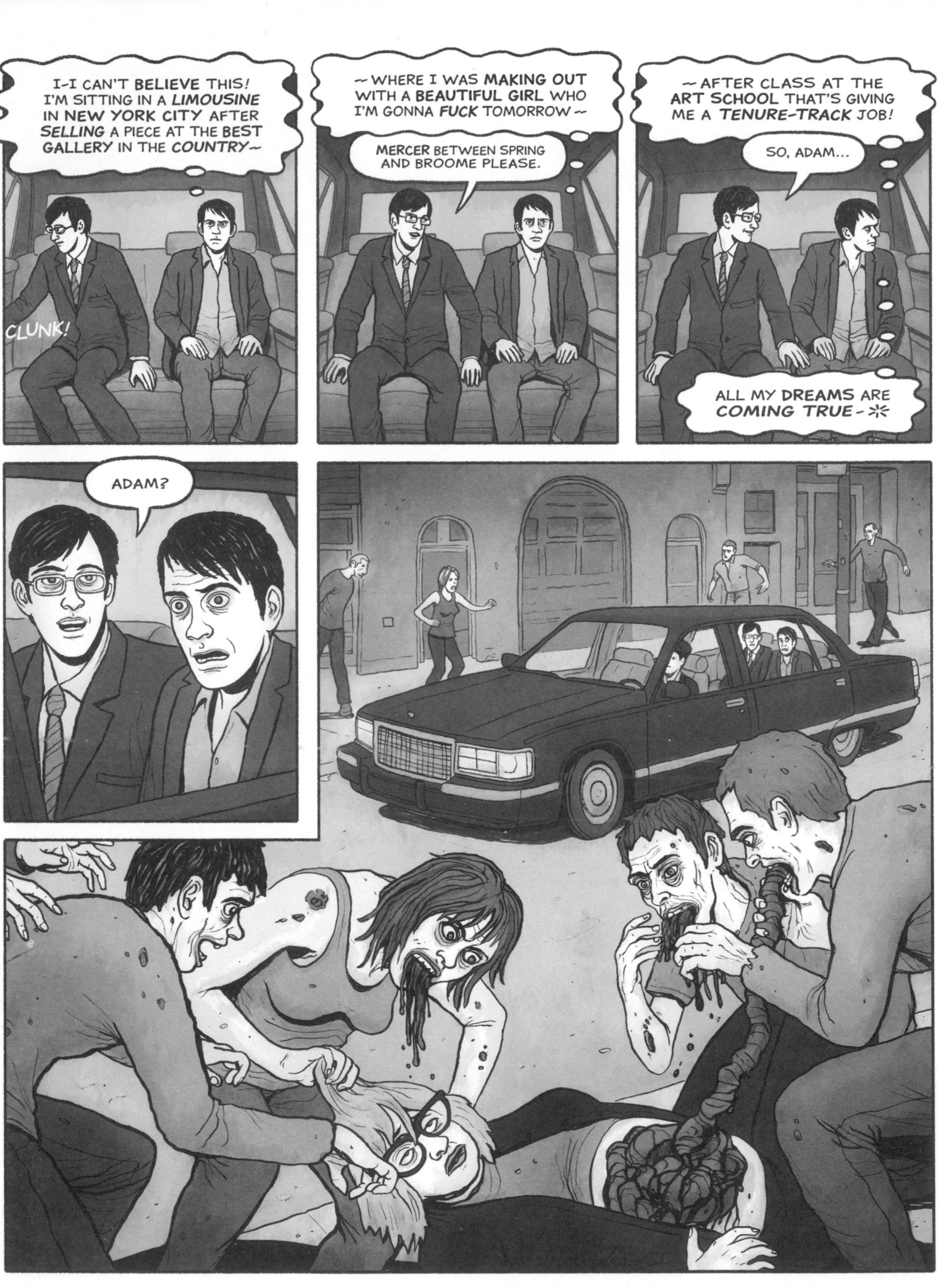
I-I CAN'T BELIEVE THIS! I'M SITTING IN A LIMOUSINE IN NEW YORK CITY AFTER SELLING A PIECE AT THE BEST GALLERY IN THE COUNTRY~
CLUNK!
~WHERE I WAS MAKING OUT WITH A BEAUTIFUL GIRL WHO I'M GONNA FUCK TOMORROW~
MERCER BETWEEN SPRING AND BROOME PLEASE.
~AFTER CLASS AT THE ART SCHOOL THAT'S GIVING ME A TENURE-TRACK JOB!
SO, ADAM...
ALL MY DREAMS ARE COMING TRUE-
ADAM?

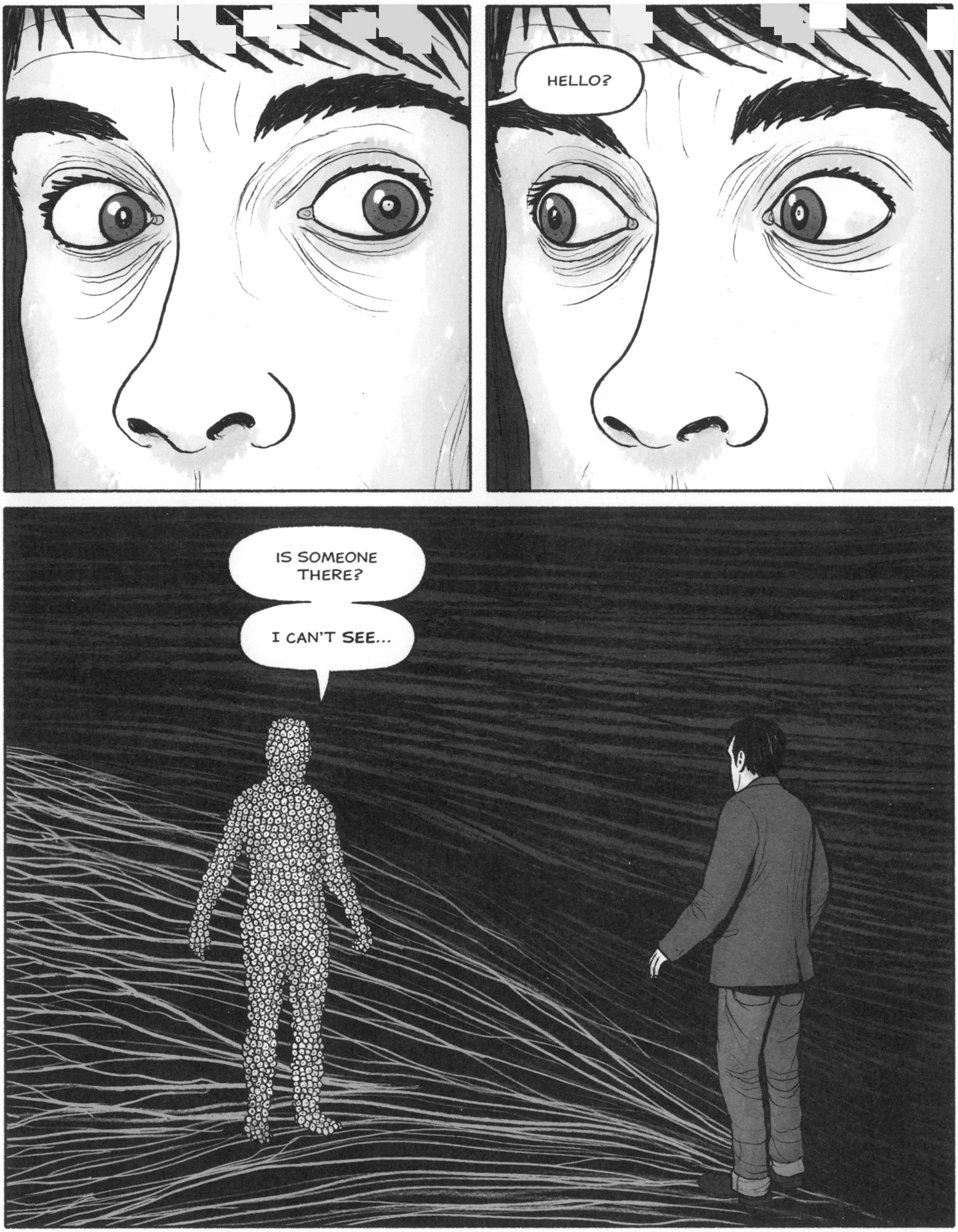
HELLO?
IS SOMEONE THERE?
I CAN'T SEE...

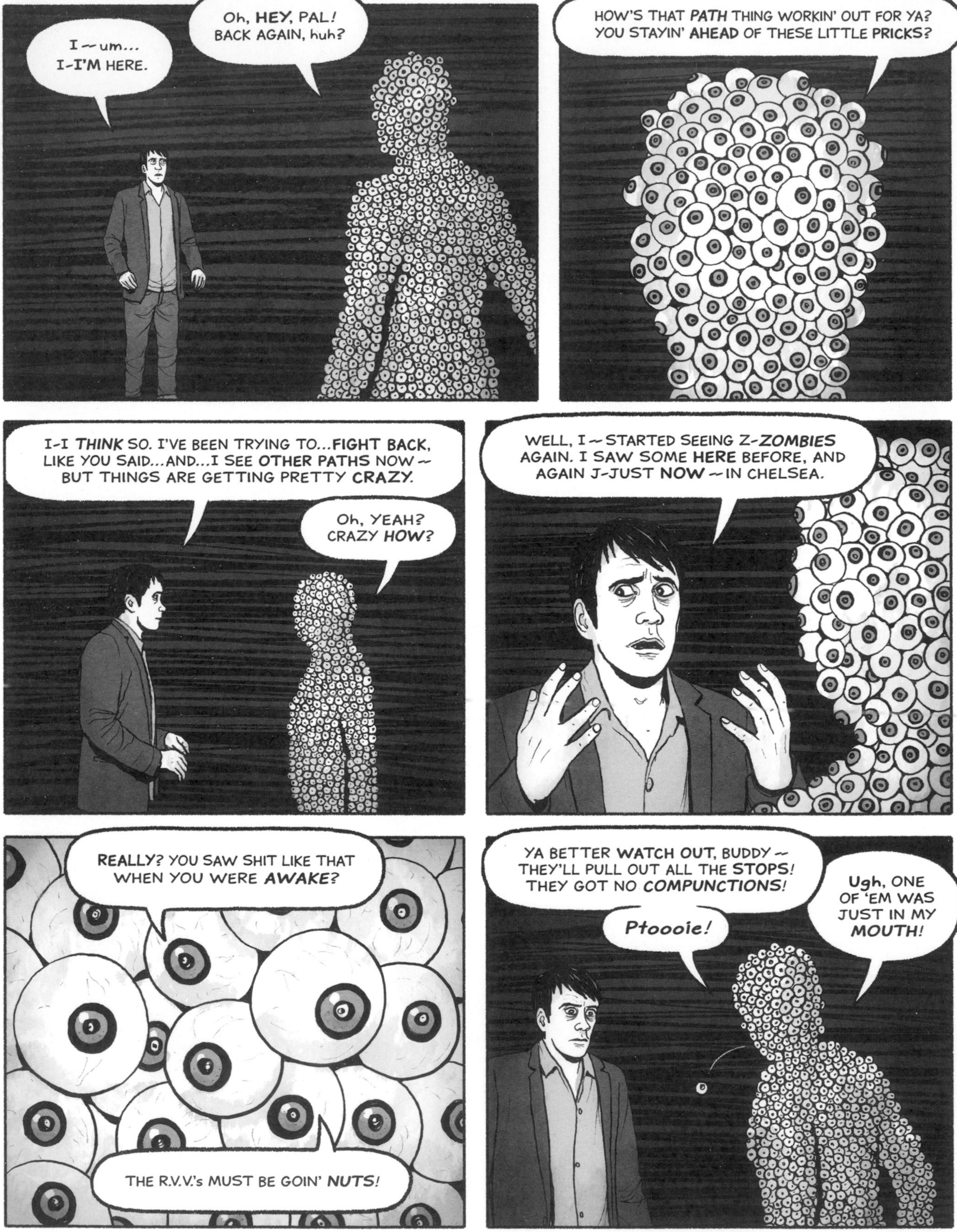
I — um...
I-I'M HERE.
Oh, HEY, PAL!
BACK AGAIN, huh?
HOW'S THAT PATH THING WORKIN' OUT FOR YA?
YOU STAYIN' AHEAD OF THESE LITTLE PRICKS?
I-I THINK SO. I'VE BEEN TRYING TO...FIGHT BACK, LIKE YOU SAID...AND...I SEE OTHER PATHS NOW — BUT THINGS ARE GETTING PRETTY CRAZY.
Oh, YEAH?
CRAZY HOW?
WELL, I — STARTED SEEING Z-ZOMBIES AGAIN. I SAW SOME HERE BEFORE, AND AGAIN J-JUST NOW — IN CHELSEA.
REALLY? YOU SAW SHIT LIKE THAT WHEN YOU WERE AWAKE?
THE R.V.V.'s MUST BE GOIN' NUTS!
YA BETTER WATCH OUT, BUDDY — THEY'LL PULL OUT ALL THE STOPS! THEY GOT NO COMPUNCTIONS!
Ptoooie!
Ugh, ONE OF 'EM WAS JUST IN MY MOUTH!

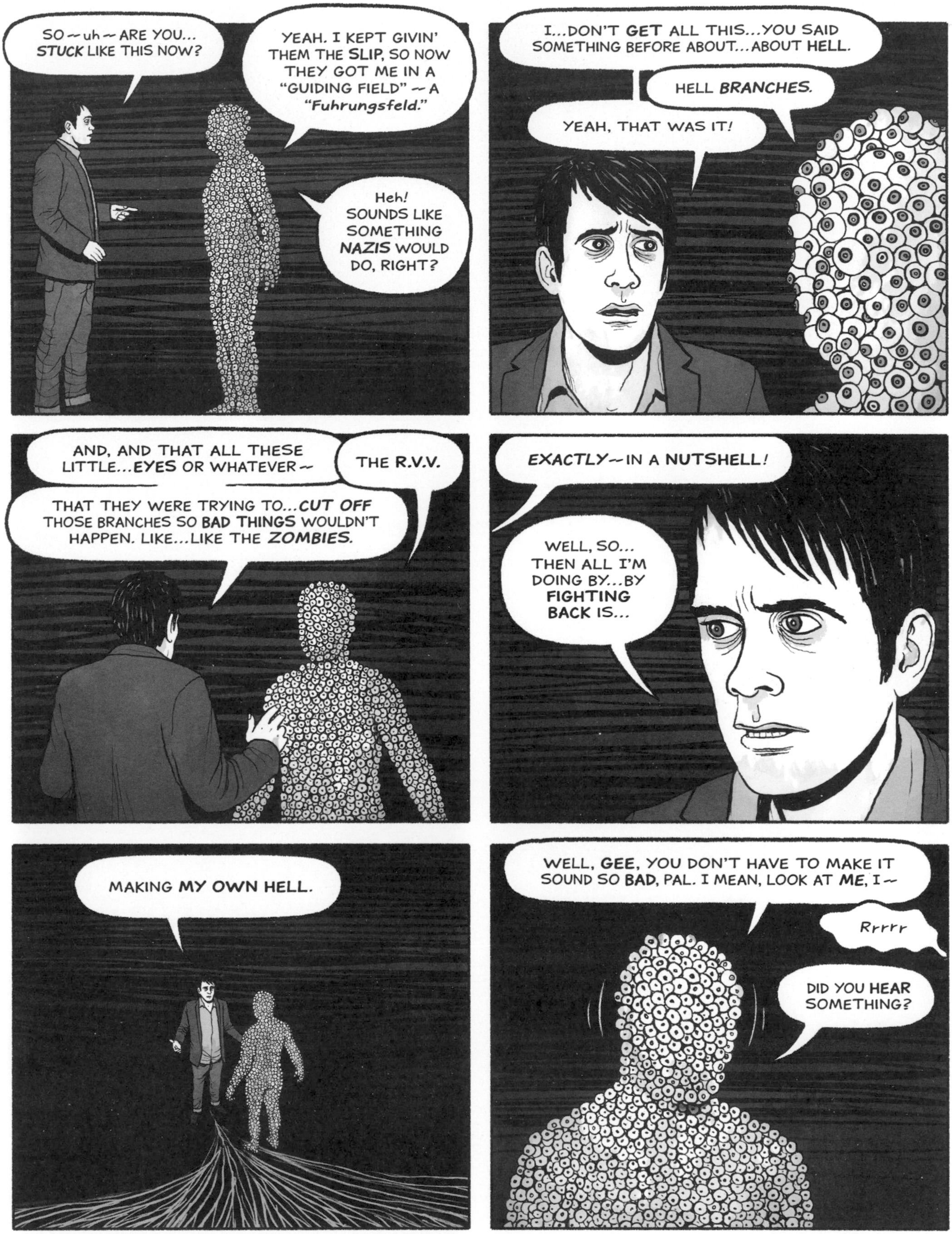

SO ~ uh ~ ARE YOU... STUCK LIKE THIS NOW?
YEAH. I KEPT GIVIN' THEM THE SLIP, SO NOW THEY GOT ME IN A "GUIDING FIELD" ~ A "Fuhrungsfeld."
Heh! SOUNDS LIKE SOMETHING NAZIS WOULD DO, RIGHT?
I...DON'T GET ALL THIS...YOU SAID SOMETHING BEFORE ABOUT...ABOUT HELL.
HELL BRANCHES.
YEAH, THAT WAS IT!
AND, AND THAT ALL THESE LITTLE...EYES OR WHATEVER ~
THE R.V.V.
THAT THEY WERE TRYING TO...CUT OFF THOSE BRANCHES SO BAD THINGS WOULDN'T HAPPEN. LIKE...LIKE THE ZOMBIES.
EXACTLY ~ IN A NUTSHELL!
WELL, SO... THEN ALL I'M DOING BY...BY FIGHTING BACK IS...
MAKING MY OWN HELL.
WELL, GEE, YOU DON'T HAVE TO MAKE IT SOUND SO BAD, PAL. I MEAN, LOOK AT ME, I ~
Rrrrr
DID YOU HEAR SOMETHING?

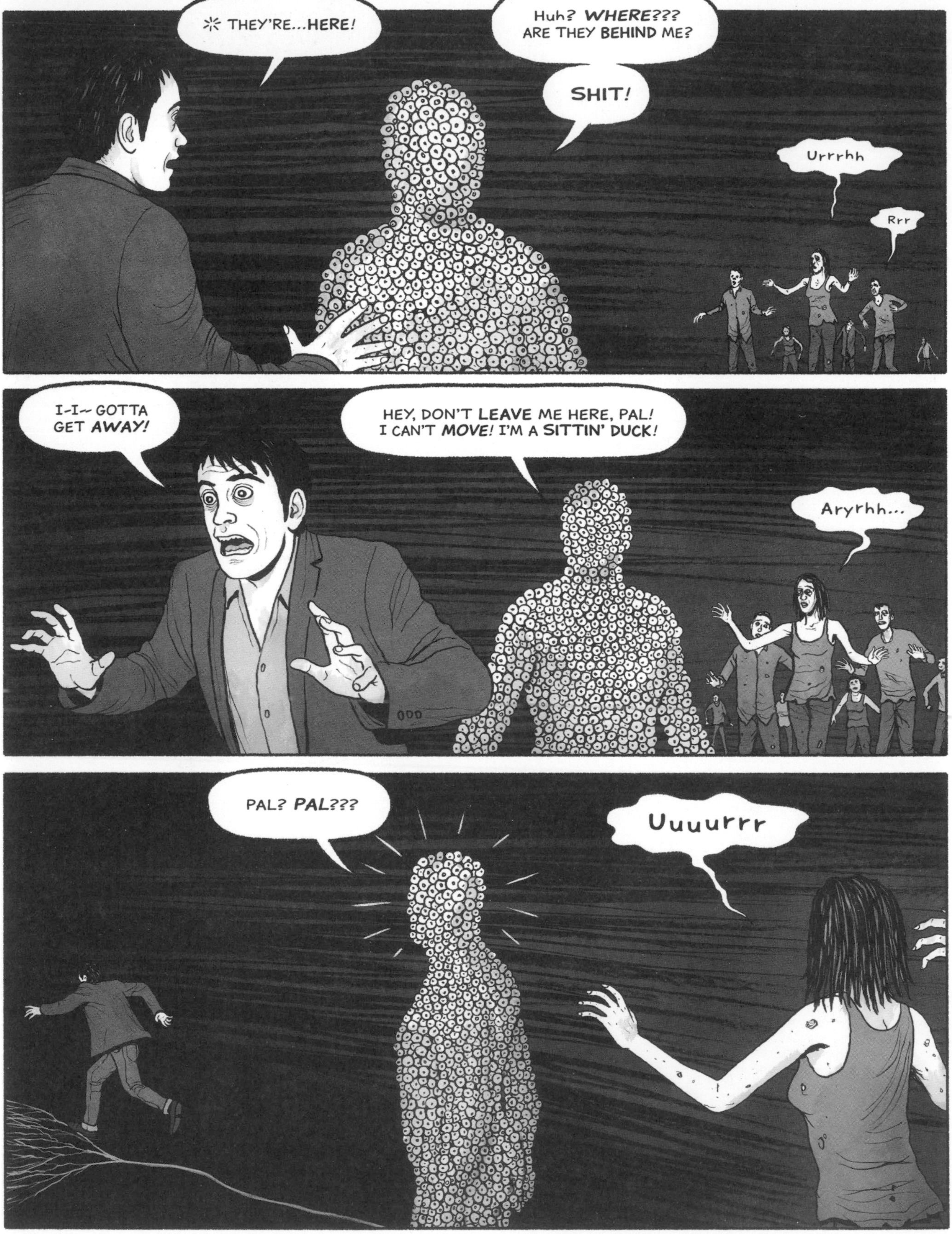

THEY'RE...HERE!
Huh? WHERE???
ARE THEY BEHIND ME?
SHIT!
Urrrhh
Rrr
I-I-- GOTTA
GET AWAY!
HEY, DON'T LEAVE ME HERE, PAL!
I CAN'T MOVE! I'M A SITTIN' DUCK!
Aryrhh...
PAL? PAL???
Uuuurrr

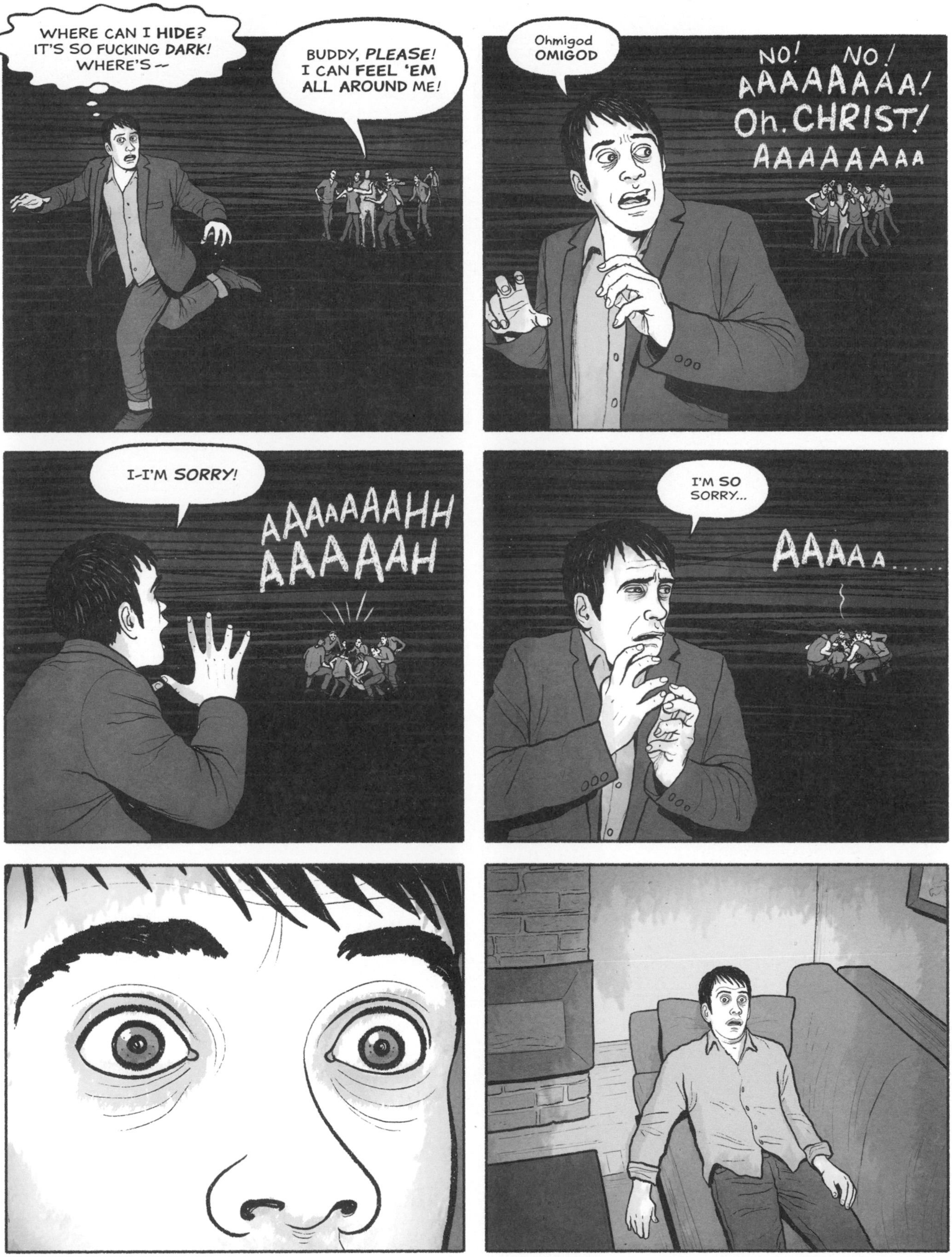
WHERE CAN I HIDE? IT'S SO FUCKING DARK! WHERE'S --
BUDDY, PLEASE! I CAN FEEL 'EM ALL AROUND ME!
Ohmigod OMIGOD
NO! NO! AAAAAAAA! Oh. CHRIST! AAAAAAAA
I-I'M SORRY!
AAAAAAAHH AAAAAH
I'M SO SORRY...
AAAAA......

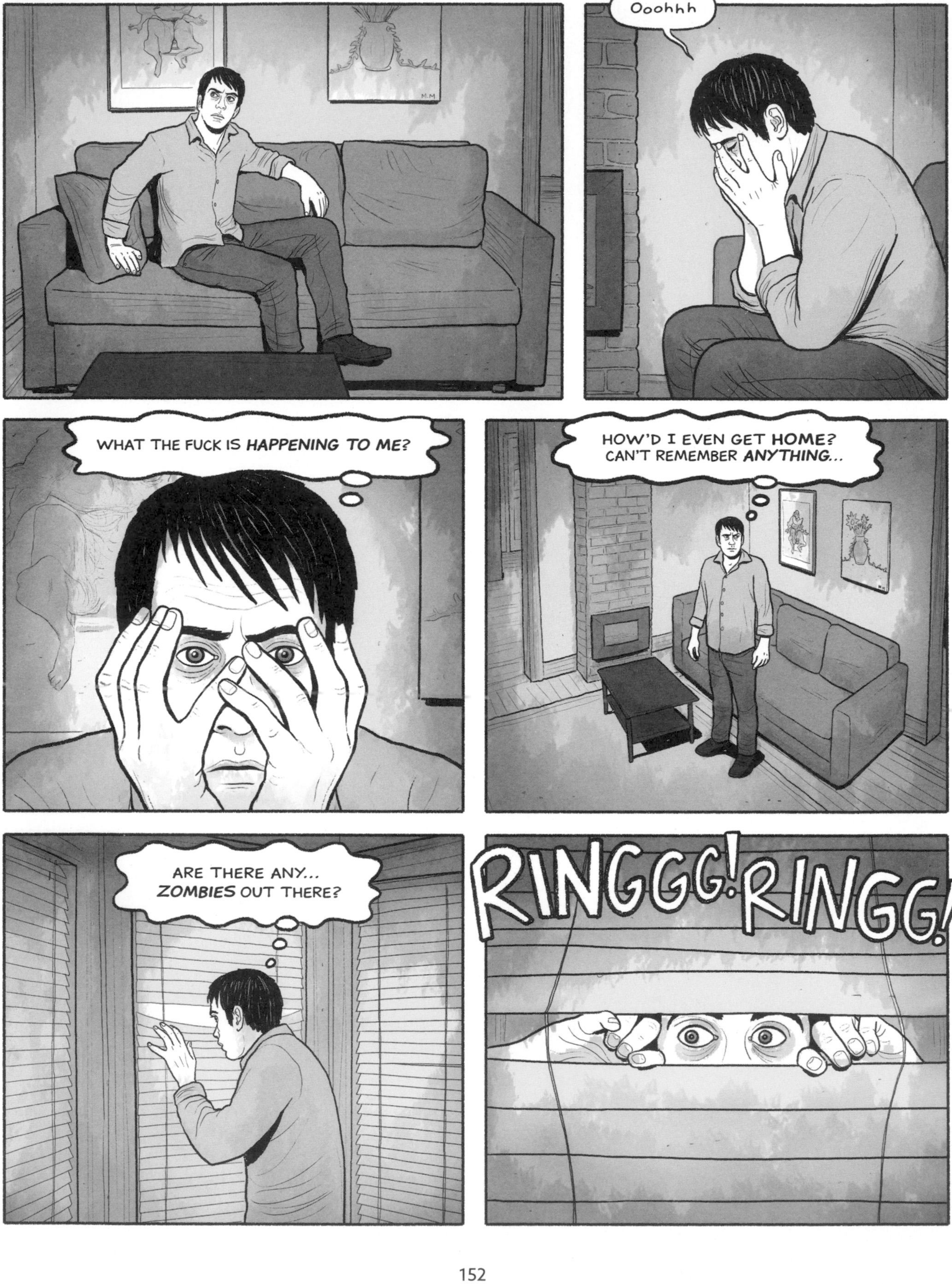
M.M
Ooohhh
WHAT THE FUCK IS HAPPENING TO ME?
HOW'D I EVEN GET HOME? CAN'T REMEMBER ANYTHING...
ARE THERE ANY... ZOMBIES OUT THERE?
RINGGG! RINGG!

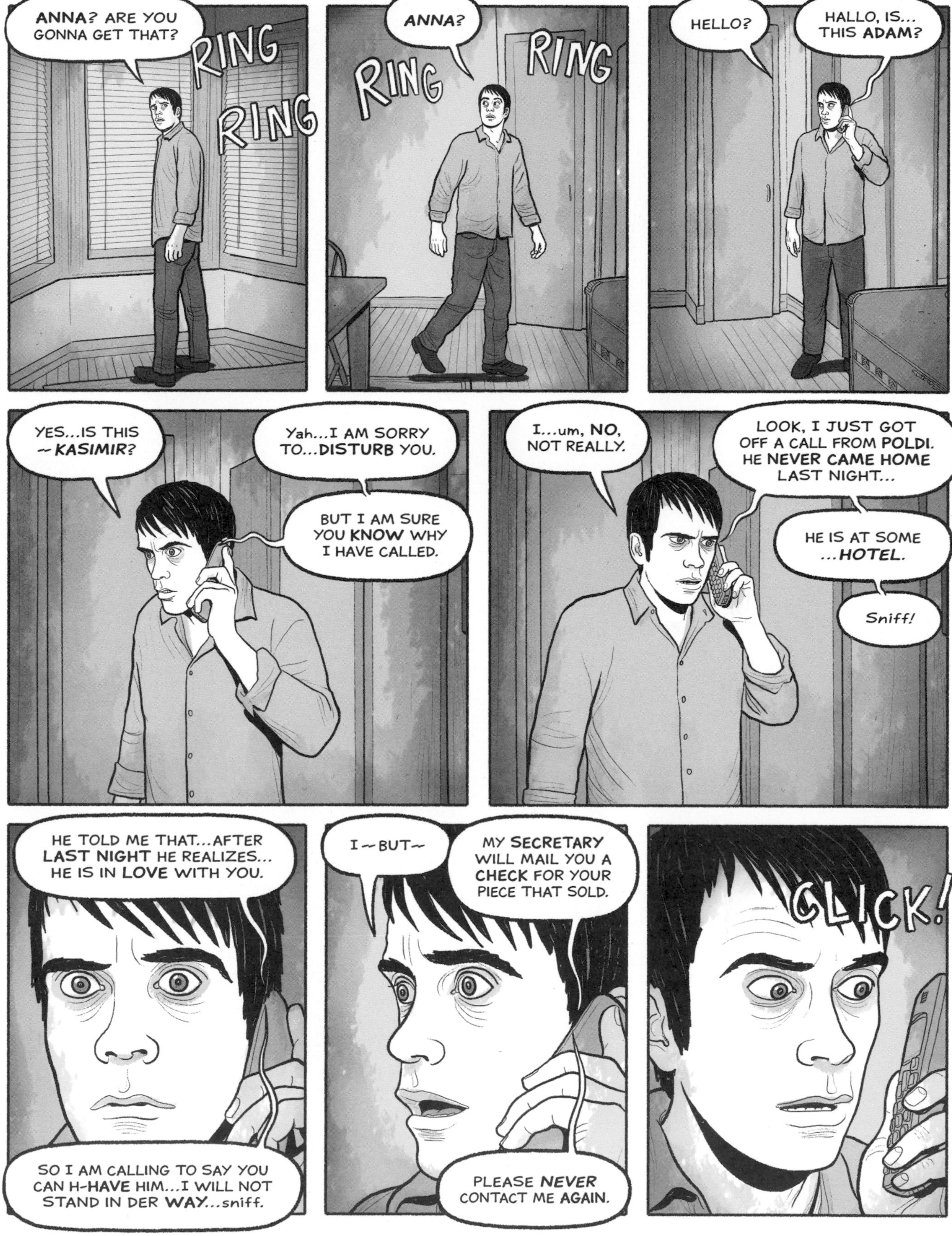
ANNA? ARE YOU GONNA GET THAT?
RING
RING
ANNA?
RING
RING
HELLO?
HALLO, IS... THIS ADAM?
YES...IS THIS --KASIMIR?
Yah...I AM SORRY TO...DISTURB YOU.
BUT I AM SURE YOU KNOW WHY I HAVE CALLED.
I...um, NO, NOT REALLY.
LOOK, I JUST GOT OFF A CALL FROM POLDI. HE NEVER CAME HOME LAST NIGHT...
HE IS AT SOME ...HOTEL.
Sniff!
HE TOLD ME THAT...AFTER LAST NIGHT HE REALIZES... HE IS IN LOVE WITH YOU.
SO I AM CALLING TO SAY YOU CAN H-HAVE HIM...I WILL NOT STAND IN DER WAY...sniff.
I--BUT--
MY SECRETARY WILL MAIL YOU A CHECK FOR YOUR PIECE THAT SOLD.
PLEASE NEVER CONTACT ME AGAIN.
CLICK!

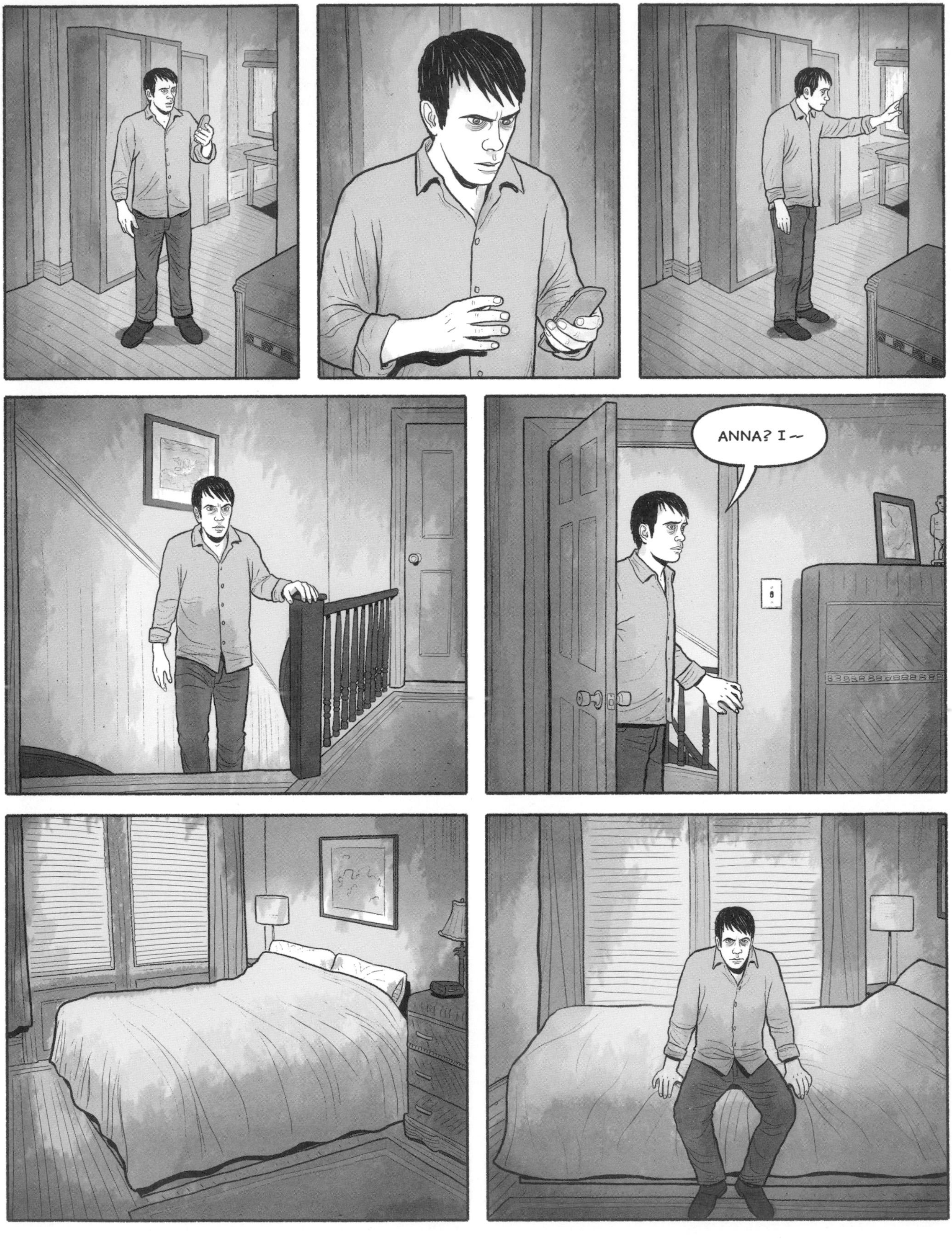
ANNA? I--

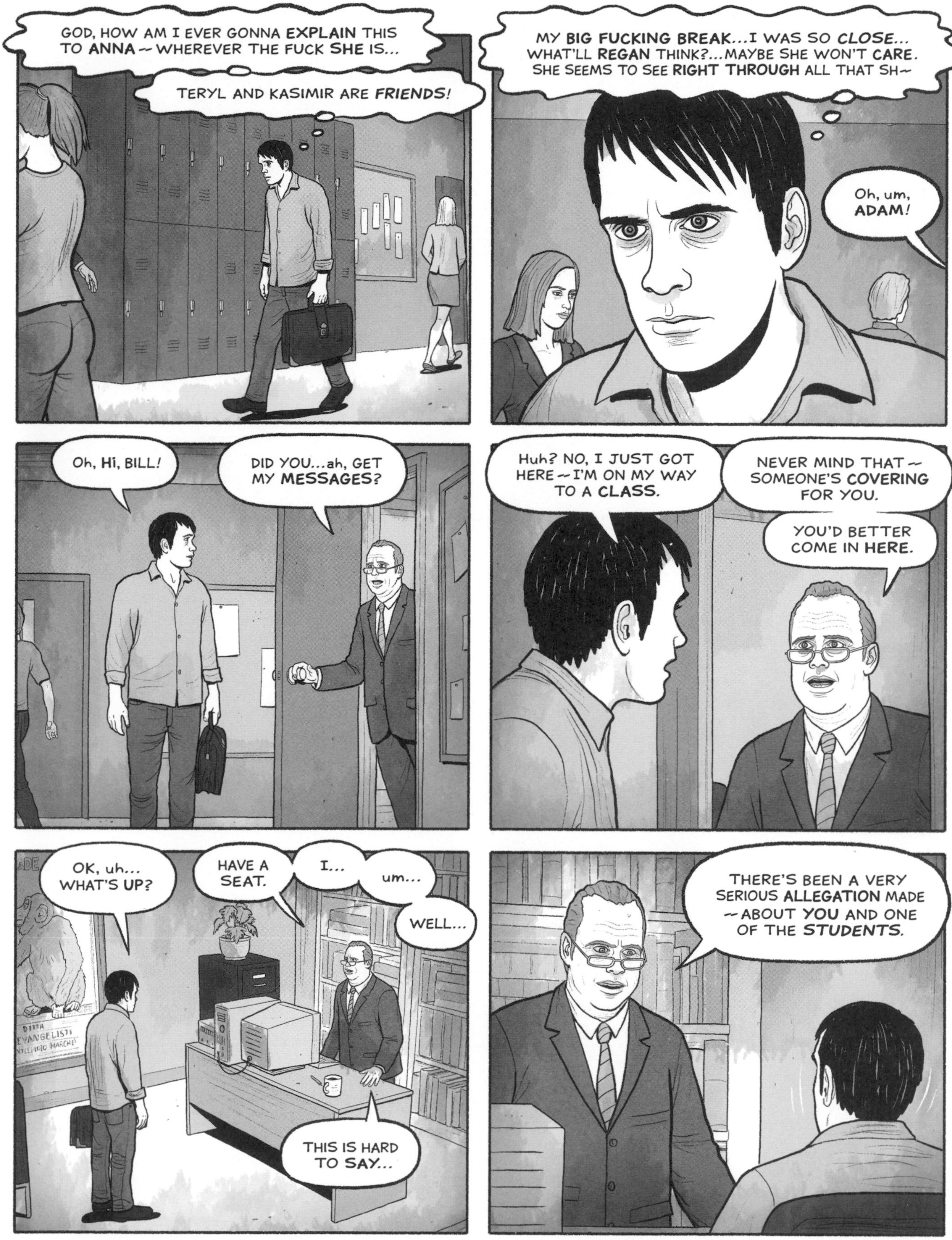
GOD, HOW AM I EVER GONNA EXPLAIN THIS TO ANNA ~ WHEREVER THE FUCK SHE IS...
TERYL AND KASIMIR ARE FRIENDS!
MY BIG FUCKING BREAK... I WAS SO CLOSE... WHAT'LL REGAN THINK?... MAYBE SHE WON'T CARE. SHE SEEMS TO SEE RIGHT THROUGH ALL THAT SH~
Oh, um, ADAM!
Oh, Hi, BILL!
DID YOU...ah, GET MY MESSAGES?
Huh? NO, I JUST GOT HERE ~ I'M ON MY WAY TO A CLASS.
NEVER MIND THAT ~ SOMEONE'S COVERING FOR YOU.
YOU'D BETTER COME IN HERE.
OK, uh... WHAT'S UP?
HAVE A SEAT.
I...
um...
WELL...
THIS IS HARD TO SAY...
THERE'S BEEN A VERY SERIOUS ALLEGATION MADE ~ ABOUT YOU AND ONE OF THE STUDENTS.

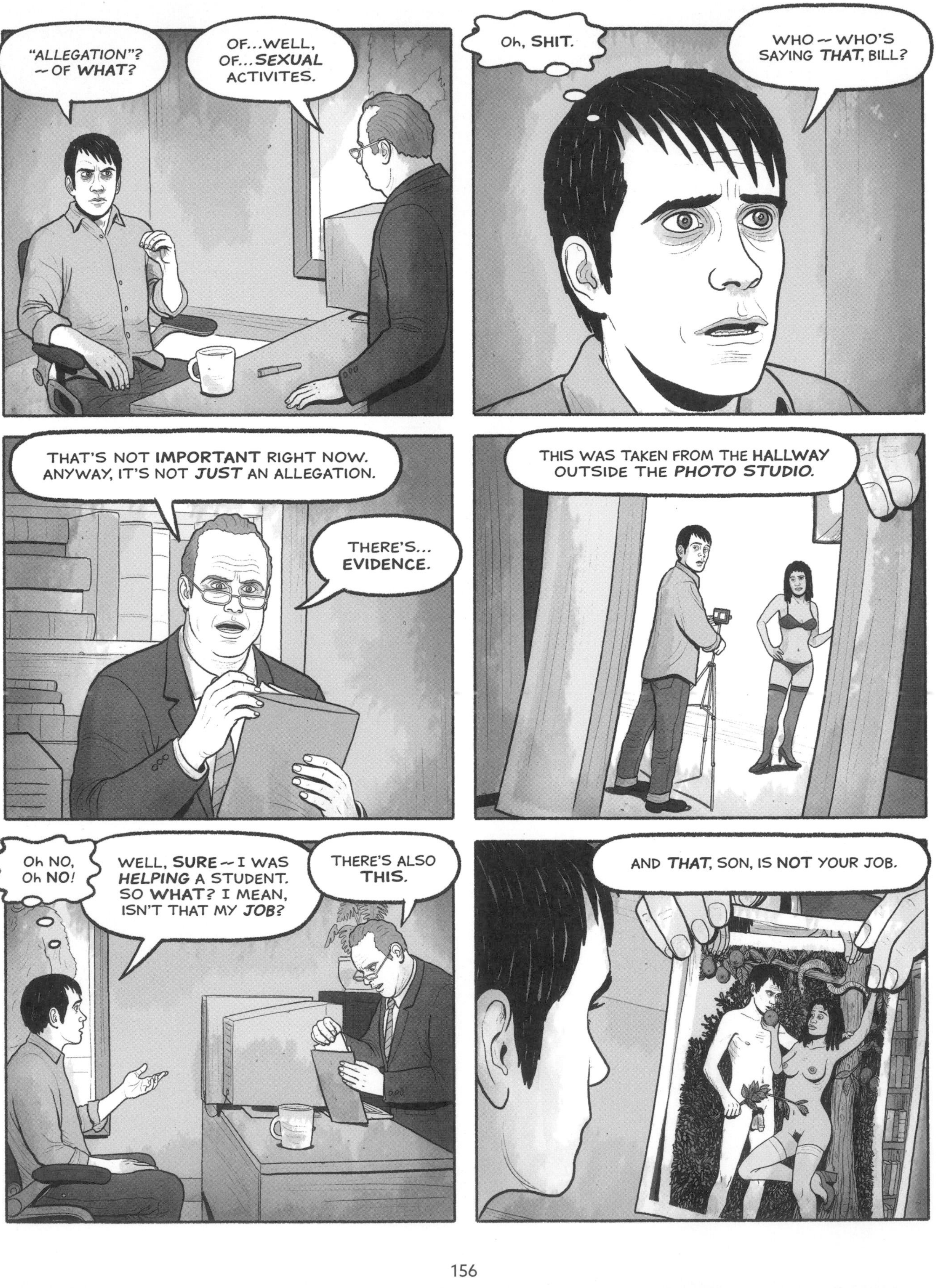
"ALLEGATION"? — OF WHAT?
OF...WELL, OF...SEXUAL ACTIVITES.
Oh, SHIT.
WHO — WHO'S SAYING THAT, BILL?
THAT'S NOT IMPORTANT RIGHT NOW. ANYWAY, IT'S NOT JUST AN ALLEGATION.
THERE'S... EVIDENCE.
THIS WAS TAKEN FROM THE HALLWAY OUTSIDE THE PHOTO STUDIO.
Oh NO, Oh NO!
WELL, SURE — I WAS HELPING A STUDENT. SO WHAT? I MEAN, ISN'T THAT MY JOB?
THERE'S ALSO THIS.
AND THAT, SON, IS NOT YOUR JOB.

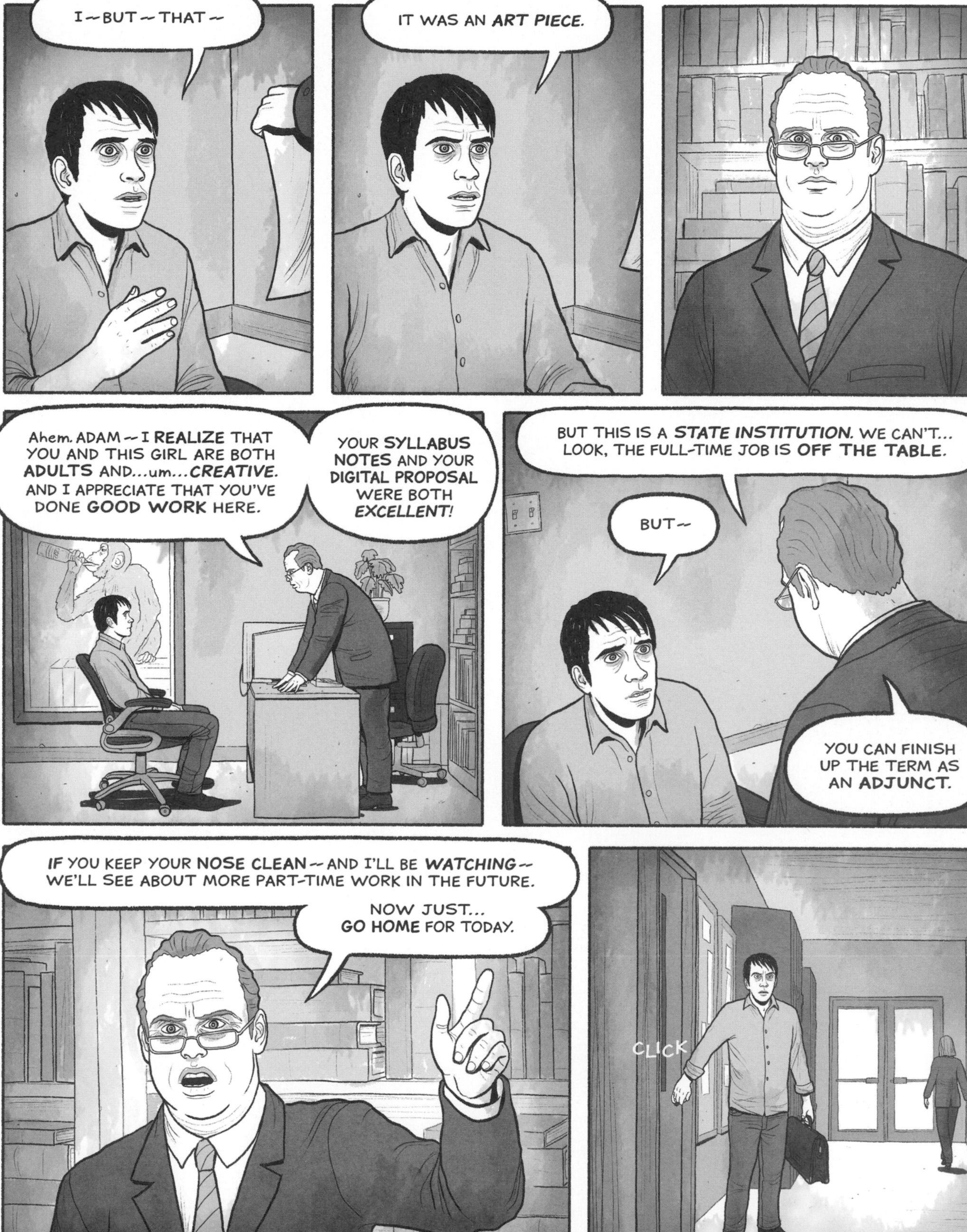
I -- BUT -- THAT --
IT WAS AN ART PIECE.
Ahem. ADAM -- I REALIZE THAT YOU AND THIS GIRL ARE BOTH ADULTS AND...um...CREATIVE. AND I APPRECIATE THAT YOU'VE DONE GOOD WORK HERE.
YOUR SYLLABUS NOTES AND YOUR DIGITAL PROPOSAL WERE BOTH EXCELLENT!
BUT THIS IS A STATE INSTITUTION. WE CAN'T... LOOK, THE FULL-TIME JOB IS OFF THE TABLE.
BUT --
YOU CAN FINISH UP THE TERM AS AN ADJUNCT.
IF YOU KEEP YOUR NOSE CLEAN -- AND I'LL BE WATCHING -- WE'LL SEE ABOUT MORE PART-TIME WORK IN THE FUTURE.
NOW JUST... GO HOME FOR TODAY.
CLICK

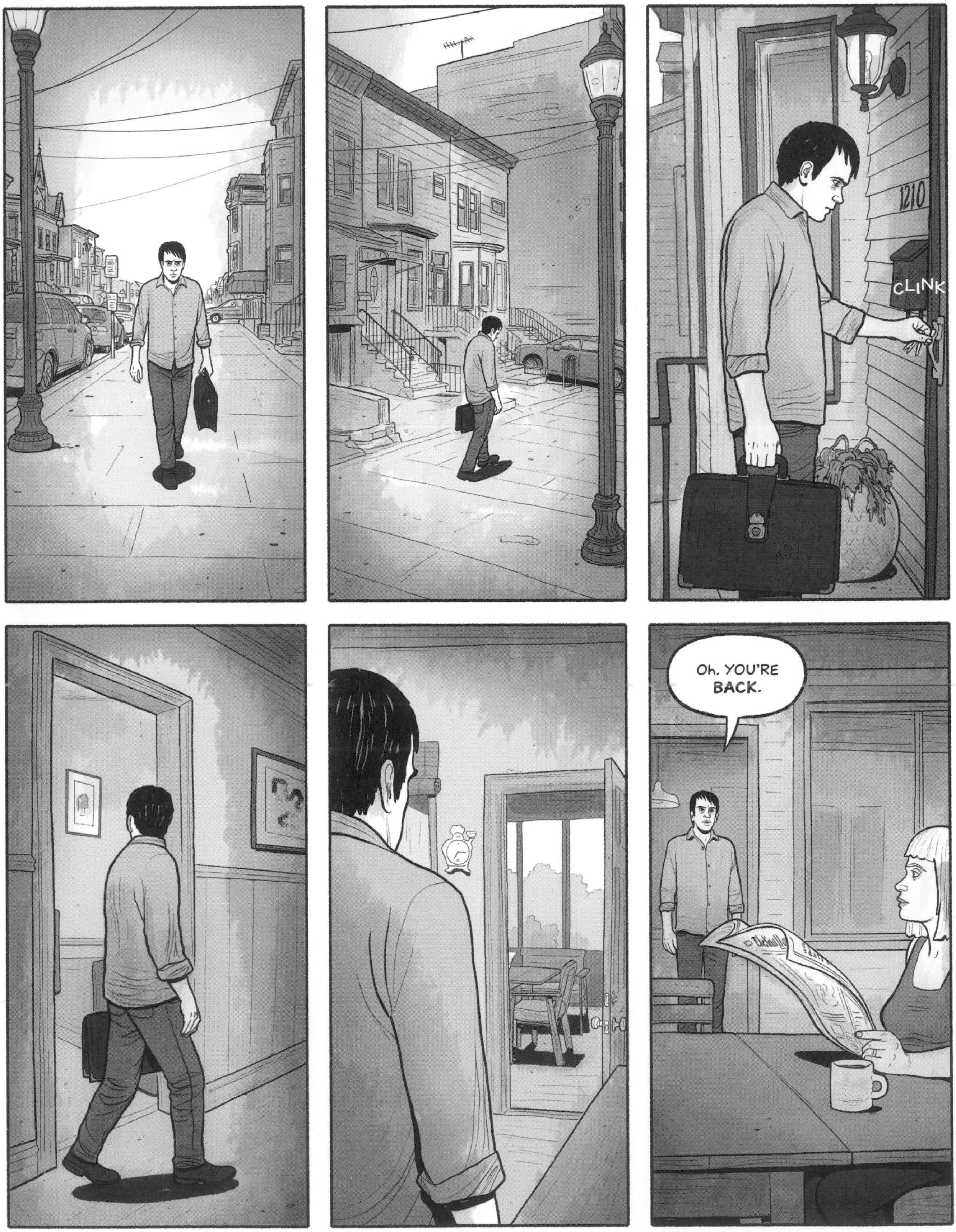
1210
CLINK
Oh. YOU'RE BACK.

SO...WHERE WERE YOU?

YOU SERIOUSLY DON'T REMEMBER?

Um, NO.

YOU DON'T REMEMBER ALL THE BULLSHIT YOU YELLED AT ME ON THE PHONE LAST NIGHT? HOW FUCKING DRUNK DID YOU GET?

I DON'T KNOW! NOW WHERE THE FUCK WERE YOU?

I SLEPT ON TERYL'S COUCH! WE WERE ALL AT HER PLACE AND IT GOT REALLY LATE AND WE HAD AN EARLY MEETING AT SCHOOL THIS MORNING.

Uh-huh. WAS MONTY THERE?

YEAH~ ON ANOTHER COUCH, IN ANOTHER ROOM. WHICH IS EXACTLY WHAT I TOLD YOU LAST NIGHT WHEN YOU STARTED FREAKING OUT.

Hmph.

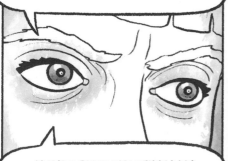

LOOK, ADAM, I DON'T NEED THE FUCKING THIRD DEGREE FROM YOU! I WORK REALLY GODDAM HARD TO SUPPORT THE TWO OF US!

MAYBE ONCE YOU FINALLY START MAKING SOME MONEY I WON'T HAVE TO WORRY SO MUCH ABOUT GETTING AHEAD.

AND WHO THE FUCK IS "REGAN" ANYWAY?

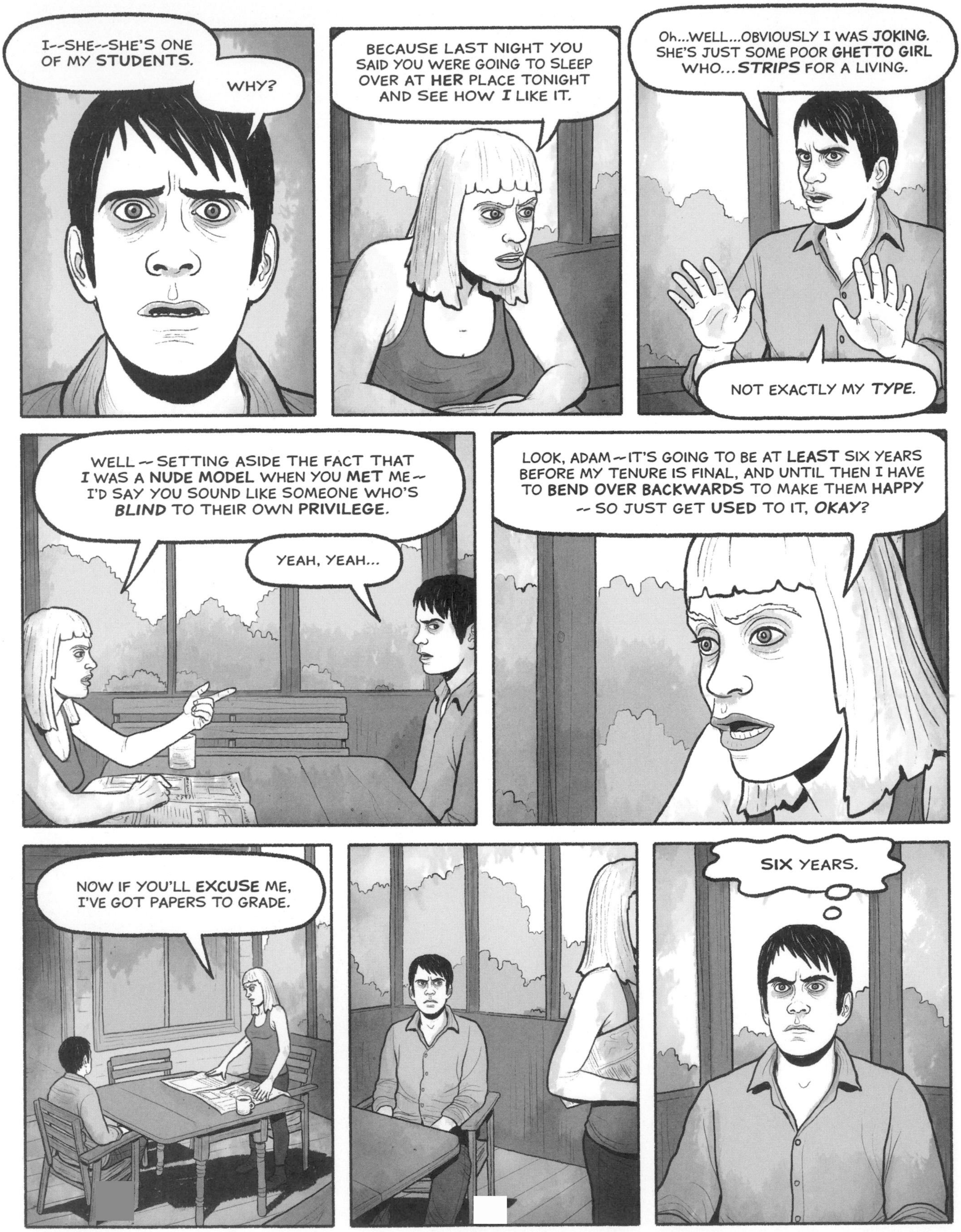
I--SHE--SHE'S ONE OF MY STUDENTS.
WHY?
BECAUSE LAST NIGHT YOU SAID YOU WERE GOING TO SLEEP OVER AT HER PLACE TONIGHT AND SEE HOW I LIKE IT.
Oh...WELL...OBVIOUSLY I WAS JOKING. SHE'S JUST SOME POOR GHETTO GIRL WHO...STRIPS FOR A LIVING.
NOT EXACTLY MY TYPE.
WELL -- SETTING ASIDE THE FACT THAT I WAS A NUDE MODEL WHEN YOU MET ME -- I'D SAY YOU SOUND LIKE SOMEONE WHO'S BLIND TO THEIR OWN PRIVILEGE.
YEAH, YEAH...
LOOK, ADAM -- IT'S GOING TO BE AT LEAST SIX YEARS BEFORE MY TENURE IS FINAL, AND UNTIL THEN I HAVE TO BEND OVER BACKWARDS TO MAKE THEM HAPPY -- SO JUST GET USED TO IT, OKAY?
NOW IF YOU'LL EXCUSE ME, I'VE GOT PAPERS TO GRADE.
SIX YEARS.

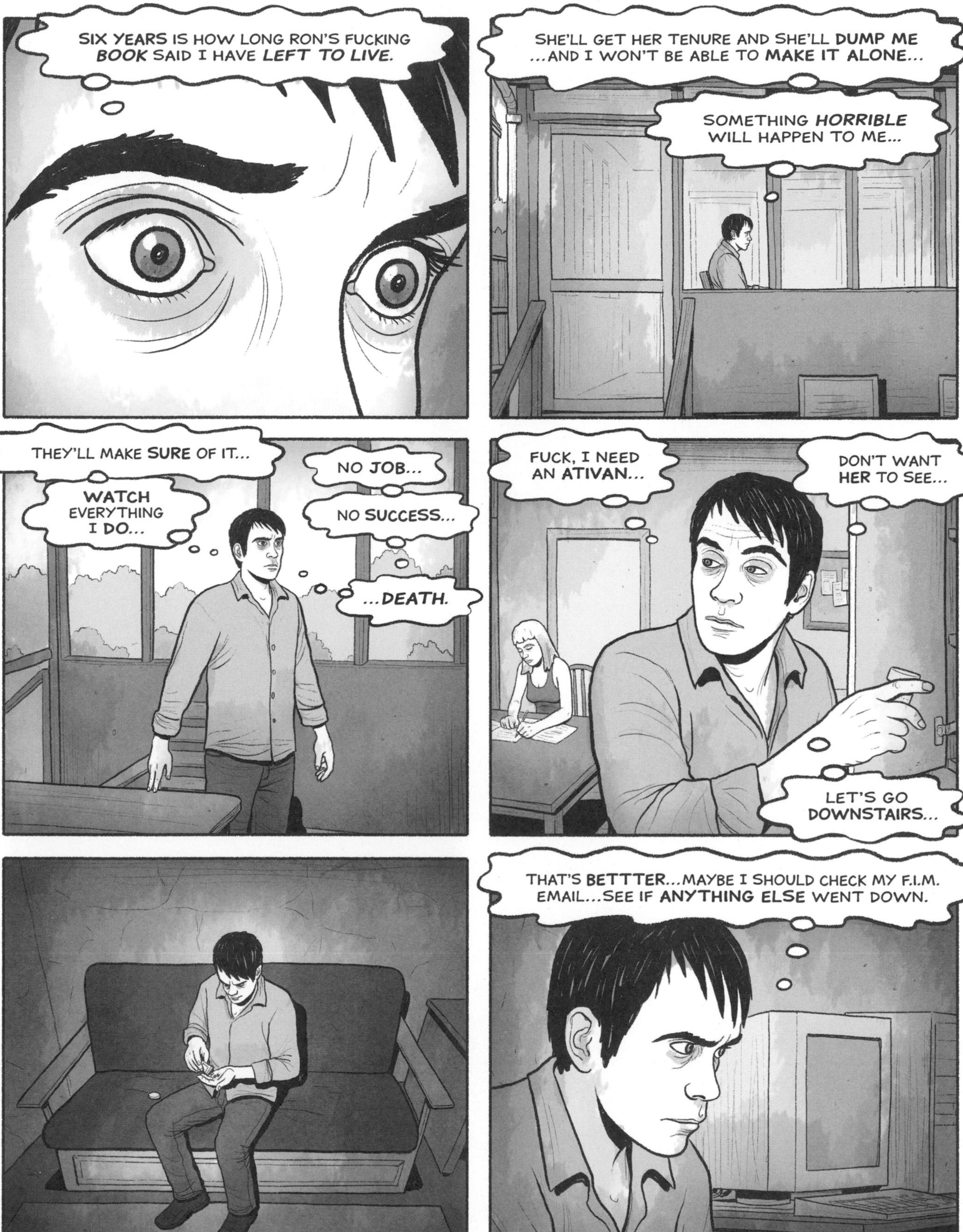
SIX YEARS IS HOW LONG RON'S FUCKING BOOK SAID I HAVE LEFT TO LIVE.
SHE'LL GET HER TENURE AND SHE'LL DUMP ME ...AND I WON'T BE ABLE TO MAKE IT ALONE...
SOMETHING HORRIBLE WILL HAPPEN TO ME...
THEY'LL MAKE SURE OF IT...
WATCH EVERYTHING I DO...
NO JOB...
NO SUCCESS...
...DEATH.
FUCK, I NEED AN ATIVAN...
DON'T WANT HER TO SEE...
LET'S GO DOWNSTAIRS...
THAT'S BETTTER...MAYBE I SHOULD CHECK MY F.I.M. EMAIL...SEE IF ANYTHING ELSE WENT DOWN.

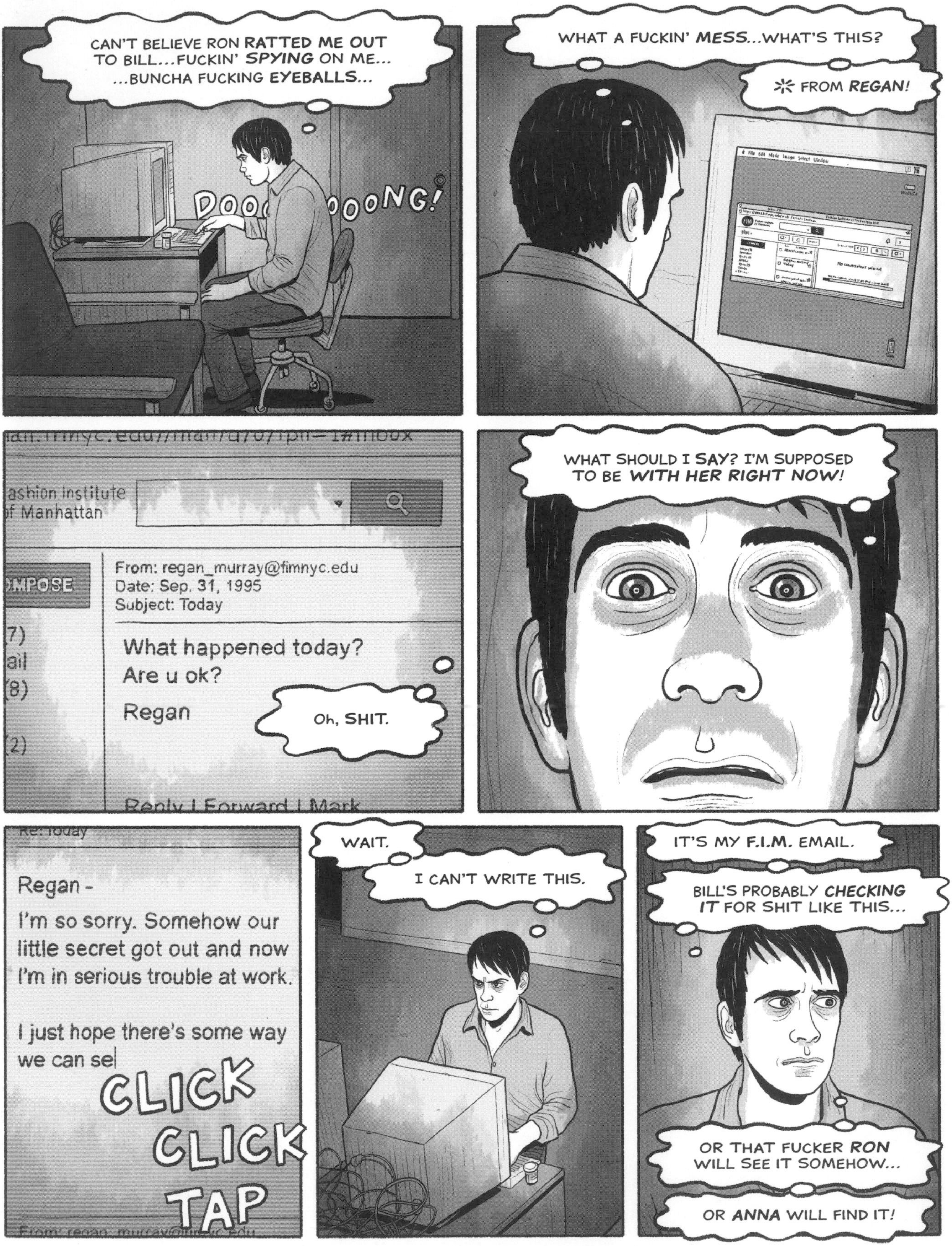
CAN'T BELIEVE RON RATTED ME OUT TO BILL...FUCKIN' SPYING ON ME... ...BUNCHA FUCKING EYEBALLS...
DOOO OOONG!
WHAT A FUCKIN' MESS...WHAT'S THIS?
FROM REGAN!
From: regan_murray@fimnyc.edu
Date: Sep. 31, 1995
Subject: Today
What happened today?
Are u ok?
Regan
Reply | Forward | Mark
Oh, SHIT.
WHAT SHOULD I SAY? I'M SUPPOSED TO BE WITH HER RIGHT NOW!
Regan -
I'm so sorry. Somehow our little secret got out and now I'm in serious trouble at work.
I just hope there's some way we can se
CLICK
CLICK
TAP
WAIT.
I CAN'T WRITE THIS.
IT'S MY F.I.M. EMAIL.
BILL'S PROBABLY CHECKING IT FOR SHIT LIKE THIS...
OR THAT FUCKER RON WILL SEE IT SOMEHOW...
OR ANNA WILL FIND IT!

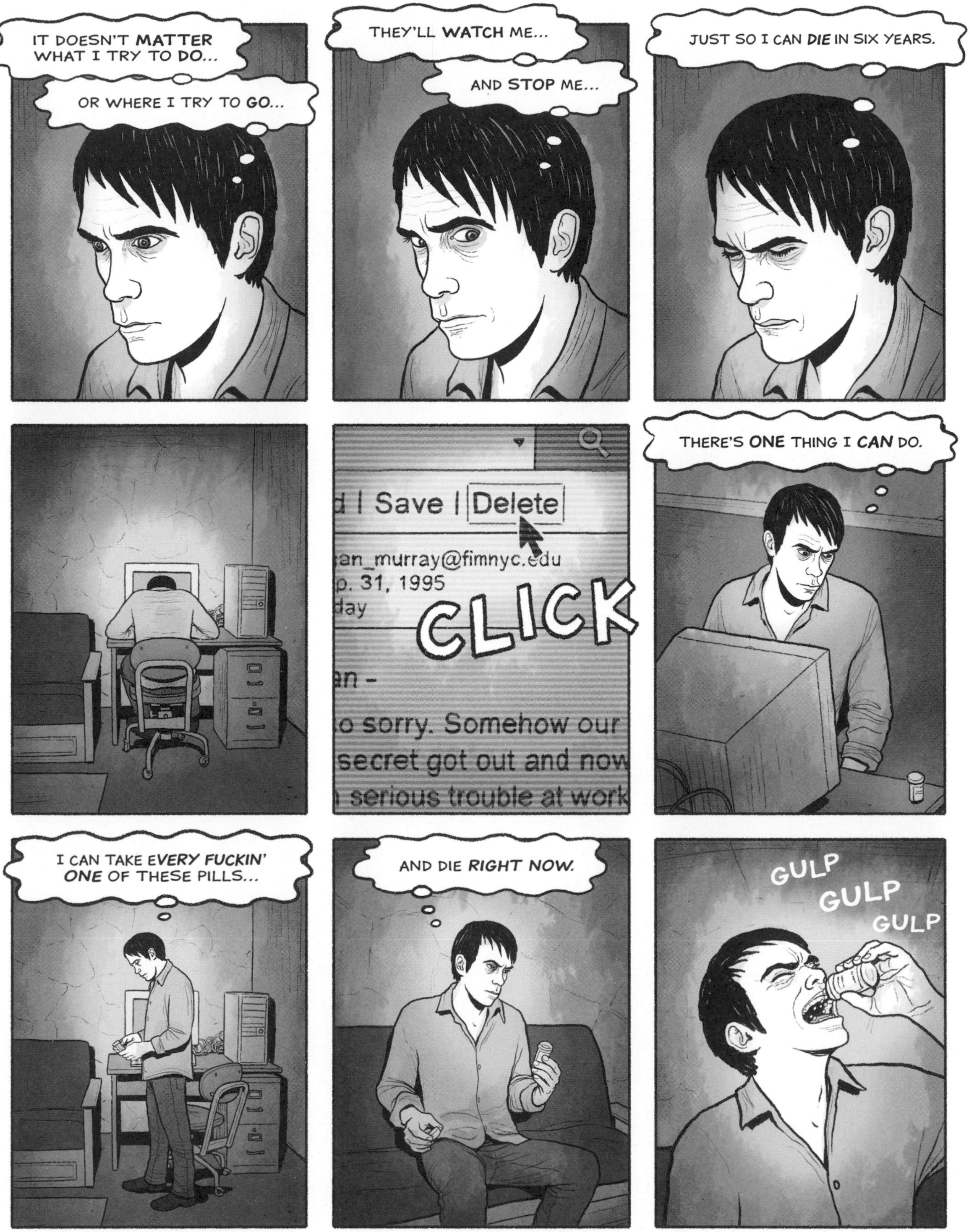
IT DOESN'T MATTER WHAT I TRY TO DO...
OR WHERE I TRY TO GO...
THEY'LL WATCH ME...
AND STOP ME...
JUST SO I CAN DIE IN SIX YEARS.
d | Save | Delete
an_murray@fimnyc.edu
p. 31, 1995
day
CLICK
an -
o sorry. Somehow our
secret got out and now
serious trouble at work
THERE'S ONE THING I CAN DO.
I CAN TAKE EVERY FUCKIN' ONE OF THESE PILLS...
AND DIE RIGHT NOW.
GULP
GULP
GULP

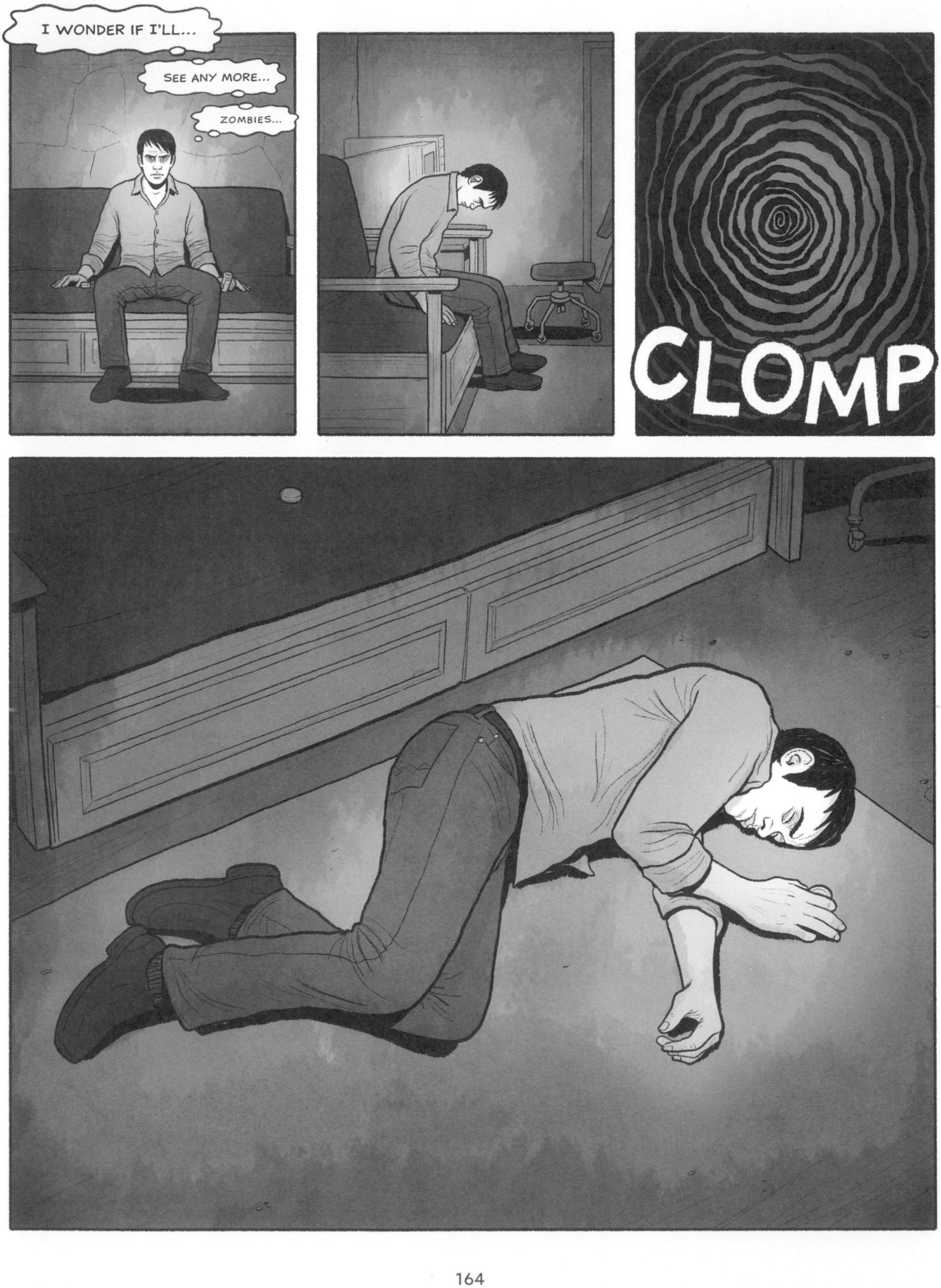
I WONDER IF I'LL...
SEE ANY MORE...
ZOMBIES...
CLOMP

THEY GOT ME.

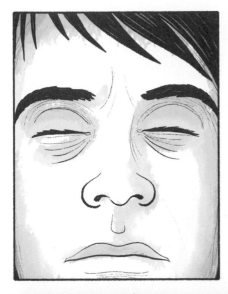

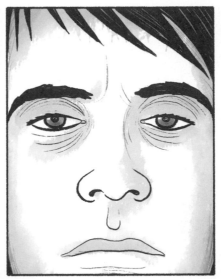

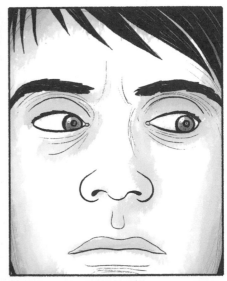

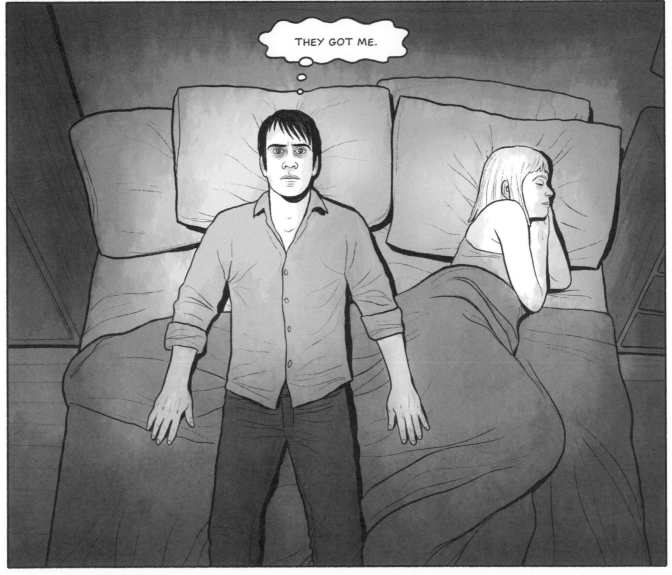

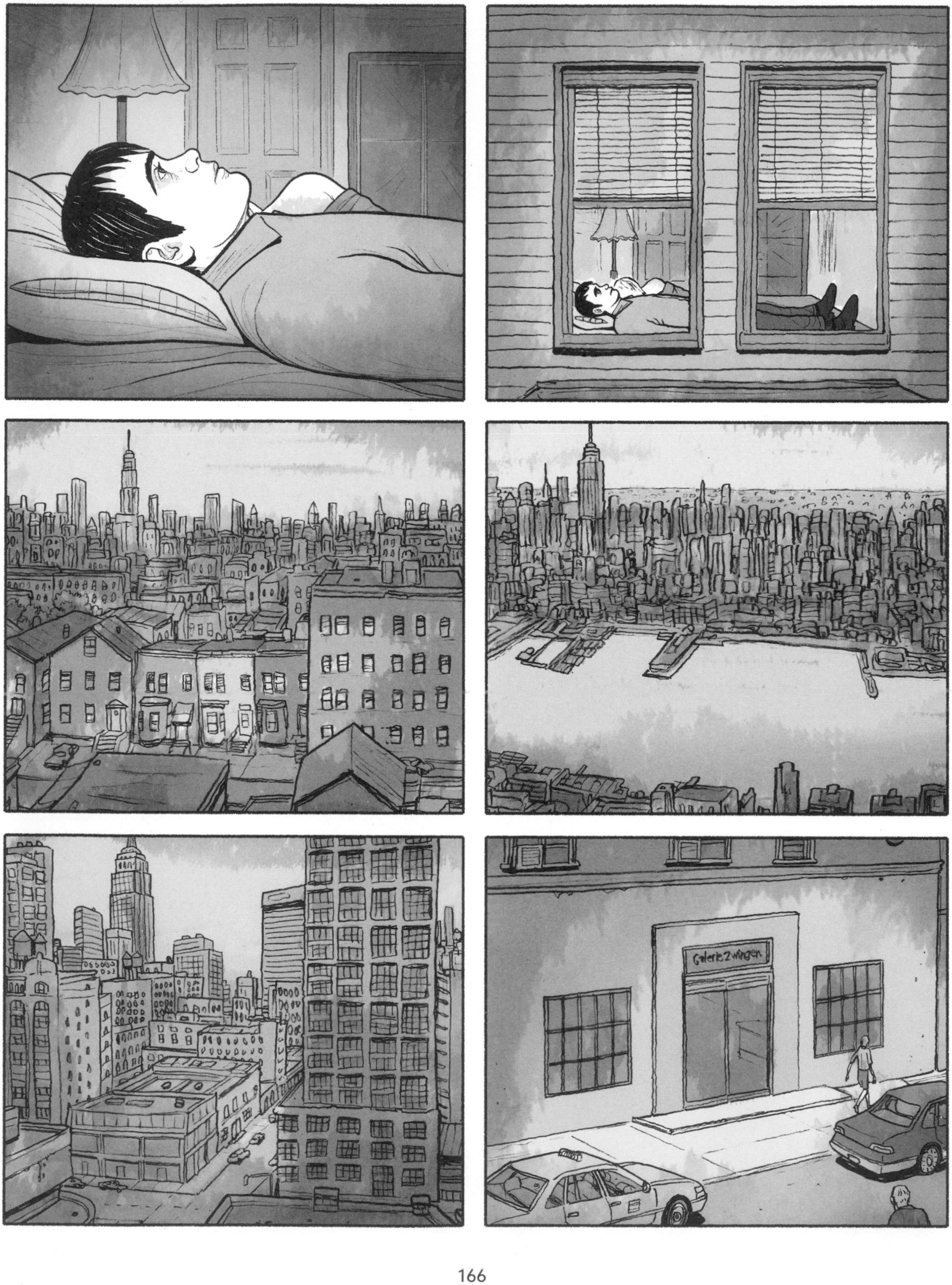
Galerie Zwingen

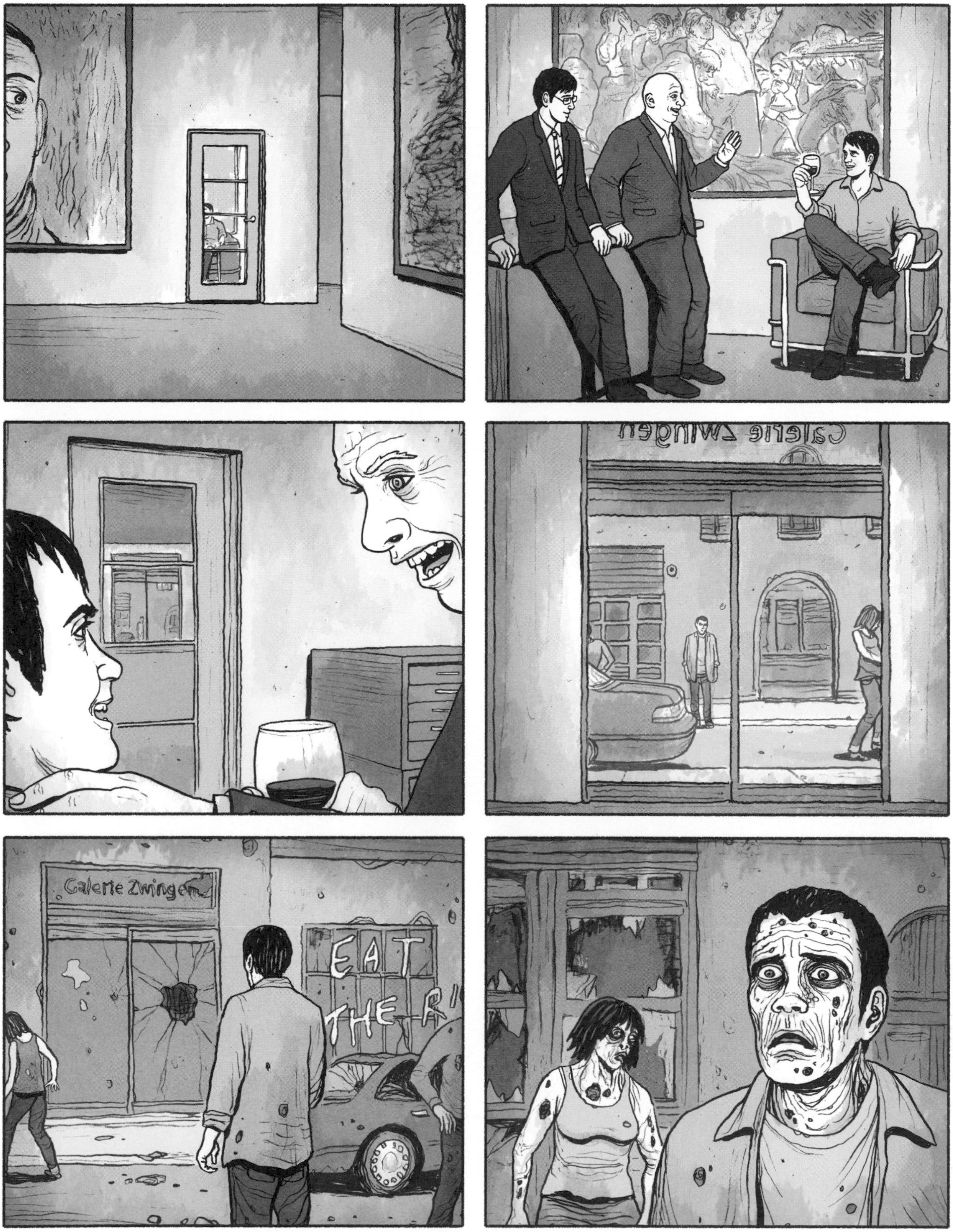
Galerie Zwingen
EAT
THE R

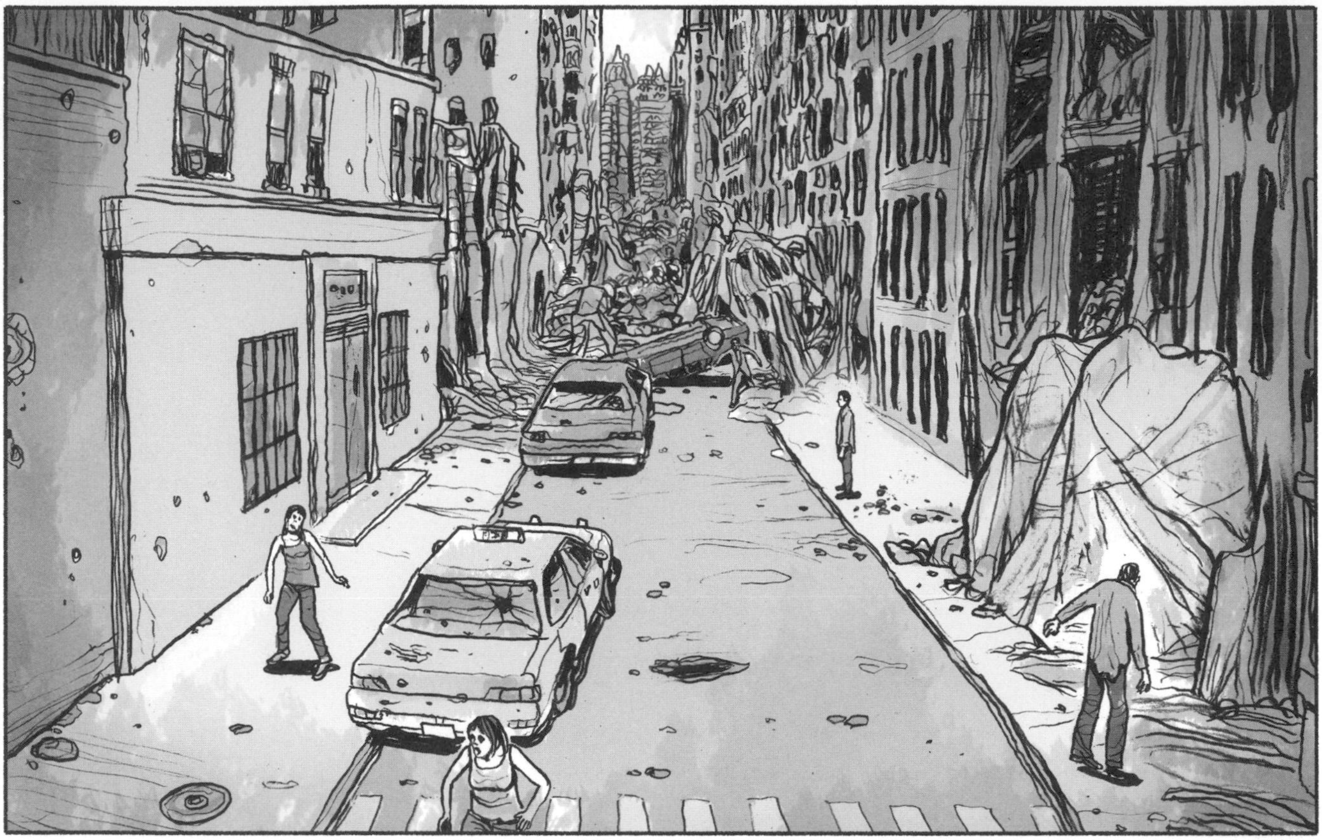

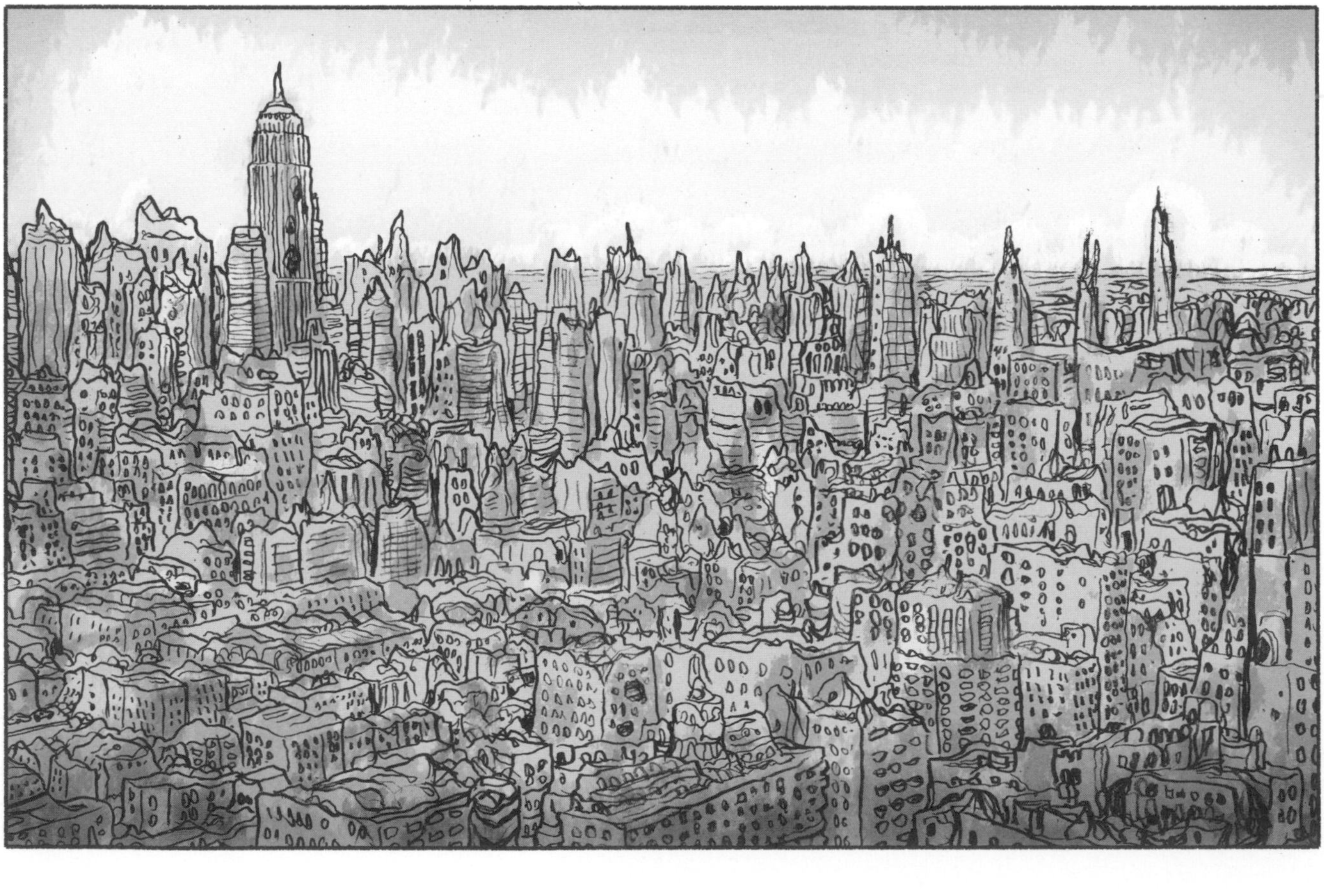

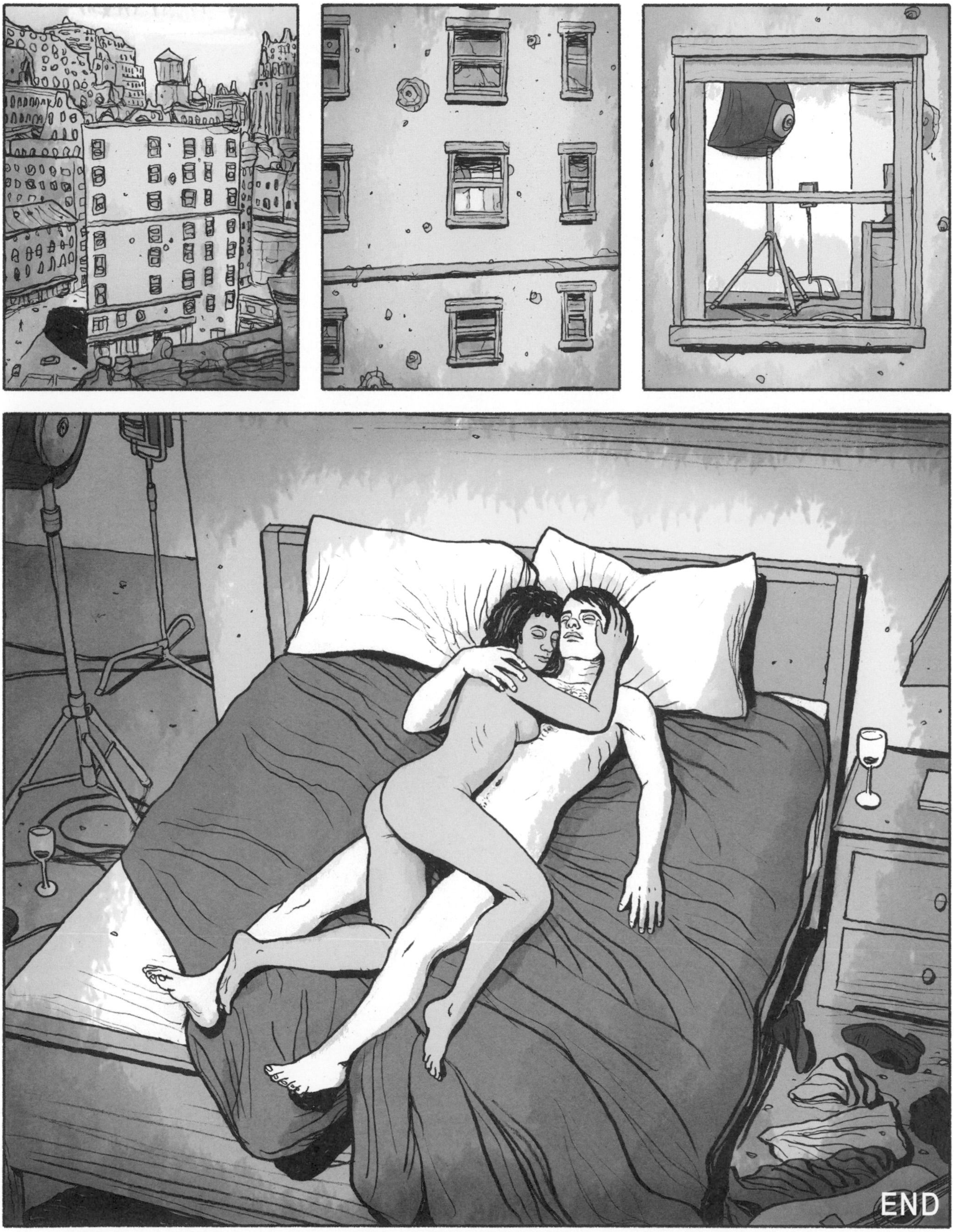
END

Thank you!

Nick Abadzis, Jessica Abel, Carmela Alfaro-Laganse, Christopher Austopchuk, Wayne Baerwaldt, Josh Bayer, Alison Bechdel, Nick Bertozzi, Dave Bett, Anita Boriboon, Josh Cheuse, Fuko Chubachi, Doris Diaz, Ezra Claytan Daniels, Darrell Epp, Robert Enright, Cliff Eyland, Chris Feldmann, Charles Fetherolf, Simon Fraser, Erwin Gorostiza, Karen Green, Geoff Grogan, Gary Groth, Paul Hanley, Tom Hart, Doug Harvey, Glenn Head, David Heatley, Simon Herbert, Michelle Holme, Stephen Hunt, Sue Jones, Connie Jun, Enid Karpeh, Annie Koyama, Sandra Luk, Matt Madden, Bob Malkin, Bob Mecoy, Laura Michalchyson, Matt Moses, Melanee Murray-Hunt, Grant Mutch, Joe Ollmann, John Paizs, Melanie Perez, Hans Rickheit, Brad Roberts, Marc Sobel, Bishakh Som, Karl Stevens, Annie Stoll, Donna Szoke, Tobias Tak, George Toles, Craig Wells, Josh Weiss and Russell Willis.

Kevin Mutch was born in Portage La Prairie, Canada. He grew up in Winnipeg loving comics and science fiction, followed shortly thereafter by punk rock. He moved to the United States in the mid 1990s and spent many years working in the photography, art and music worlds in Los Angeles and New York City.

His first graphic novel was *Fantastic Life* which won a 2010 Xeric Award and was excerpted in *The Best American Comics 2011*. He is currently completing two other books — *Like a Ninja*, based on his time in the music business, and an all-ages adventure story called *The Moon Prince*.

He recently moved back to Canada and now lives in Hamilton, Ontario with his wife and two children.

- -

The cover of this book includes glow-in-the-dark ink. To fully enjoy the effect, expose the cover to light prior to entering a dark space.

- -

Designer: Justin Allan-Spencer
Editor: Gary Groth
Assistant Editor: Conrad Groth
Production: Christina Hwang
Associate Publisher: Eric Reynolds
Publisher: Gary Groth

FB Fantagraphics Books Inc.
7563 Lake City Way NE
Seattle, Washington 98115

ISBN: 978-1-68396-284-7
Library of Congress Control Number: 2019945098
First Fantagraphics Books edition: March 2020

Printed in Hong Kong